A MATTER
OF
CHANCE

A MATTER OF CHANCE

a novel

by

JULIE MALONEY

SHE WRITES PRESS

Published 2018
Printed in the United States of America
ISBN: 978-1-63152-369-4 pbk
ISBN: 978-1-63152-370-0 ebk
Library of Congress Control Number: 2017953864

Book design by Stacey Aaronson

For information, address:
She Writes Press
1563 Solano Ave #546
Berkeley, CA 94707

She Writes Press is a division of SparkPoint Studio, LLC.

For my children

Jenna
David
Kayla

With all my love

With what price we pay for the glory of motherhood.

—Isadora Duncan

When she was born, I named her Lavinia, but I called her Vinni. Her left, sleepy eyelid hung lower than her right, but when she was twenty-two months old, the surgeon took a slight tuck under her brow and made her as perfect as a child could be. By the winter of her third year, signs of the stitches had disappeared. By the summer of her eighth year, her skin was bronzed and beautiful.

YEAR ONE

ONE

THE DAY VINNI AND I LOST EACH OTHER, WE WOKE EARLY to have breakfast on the beach. A giant tote bag stuffed with towels, suntan lotion, and bottles of water rested against the back door. *James and the Giant Peach*, number two on Vinni's reading list, sat in the outside pocket, next to the galleys for my new coffee-table book—*Fashion in the Twentieth Century*—a spin-off from my editorial job at *Hot Style* magazine. A box of pastels—a gift from Evelyn, who lived downstairs—hid in the bottom of the bag; a ratty sketchpad peeked out at the top. Each day I planned on taking the pastels out of the bag, but each day my child wanted me to see something, walk somewhere, or talk more.

She'd start by saying, "I have an idea. . . ."

At the perfect spot, we spread the food out on the matelassé I had rescued from a flea market on Orchard Street on the Lower East Side. After we devoured the waffles and berries, Vinni and I walked along the beach. The early-morning sunlight illuminated the world around us. Even the birds respected the quiet.

In the distance, we saw them—Rudy and Hilda—strolling the way older people do, taking care not to get too close to the water's edge. They waved to us as we walked in their direction. The two fascinated Vinni because they were always together. "I think Rudy is Hilda's best friend. They're like you and me," she declared, as if giving this some thought. Her father and I had separated when she was five. Now, three years later, Steve kept a distant presence in San Francisco.

The couple used to stop and talk to Vinni and me on the beach, but it was Vinni they studied. Sometimes Hilda ran her finger down Vinni's cheek in one smooth stroke, as she complimented her hair or the color of her eyes. I remember how Vinni would just stand there and smile. She never turned away.

What had she seen when I had been studying the color of the ocean?

"Rudy and Hilda don't smile the same way," she said. "Rudy's lips turn up wide, and his eyes look happy, but Hilda's eyes don't smile, even when her mouth does."

"I'm sure Hilda's happy." I smoothed away the dark, wavy hair from Vinni's right cheek as I spoke without thinking.

ℓ

ON OUR WAY back up the beach, I stopped on one of the hilly sand piles common to the Jersey Shore and leaned over to remove a piece of shell wedged between my toes.

That's when I saw Rudy slumped over in the sand. At first I wasn't sure, as he and Hilda were far away, but something made me grab Vinni and run. By the time we reached them, Hilda was leaning in close to Rudy's face. Her arms wrapped around his shoulders as she knelt beside him. He was whispering in German. Hilda nodded, crying softly, kissing his cheeks. She held his right hand against her chest.

The muscles in his face twisted, but he reached for Hilda's shirt collar with knotted fingers and said, "*Geh.*" Twice more he repeated the word. "*Geh. Geh.*"

Go. Go.

I told Vinni to stay with Hilda and Rudy while I raced home to call 911. Usually a cell phone addict, I had tried all summer long to wean myself off this seductive attachment. I have gone over and over why I made this choice—why I made Vinni stay on the beach.

~

AS I REACHED the front porch of the summer cottage, I turned back and the breeze from the ocean swept sand across my face. I blinked away the grainy flecks and as my eyes focused, in the distance, by the water's edge, I saw Vinni's hand on Hilda's shoulder. Hilda was sitting in the sand, with Rudy's head on her lap. I don't know if I imagined it or not, but later I thought I had heard Hilda singing to Rudy.

After making the 911 call at the house, I turned around too fast and tripped over a pile of books stacked on the floor by the couch near the front door. I stumbled and grabbed the air. My arm landed on the lampshade Vinni said reminded her of an old lady's hat. I regained my balance and kept moving. As I slammed the door behind me, I heard a loud crash and knew the table lamp had fallen.

I hurried to the spot where I had left Vinni. She and Hilda were gone. The faded color of Rudy's lips stopped me from touching him. I knelt down and put my ear to his chest.

Rudy was dead.

I looked up and saw two men dressed in shore-police attire—white shirts, navy Bermuda shorts, and skinny navy ties—running in my direction. Two people from the rescue squad, one woman and one man, carried a stretcher behind them.

The tide stilled. The earth stopped its rotation.

"Where's my daughter?" I said to the cop who reached me first. "Where did they go?" I closed my arms around my chest. The August sun was hot for so early in the morning. I shaded my eyes with the side of my hand. Both policemen were on their knees in the sand, bent over Rudy.

"Who?" the woman from the rescue squad asked, as she looked around.

"My daughter. My daughter was here with Hilda. I don't know—"

"Do you know this man?" the policeman interrupted, looking up at me with a baby face full of summer freckles.

"His name is Rudy Haydn. He lives in the yellow clapboard house on Morris Avenue, two blocks down, at number twenty-three. My daughter . . ." I slowed a bit and looked around. *Why did Hilda leave Rudy? Didn't Vinni just say last night that they were best friends?*

"My daughter must be with Hilda." And then I added, "She's eight." I said it again. "She's only eight." My throat closed a little, the way it used to when my father would tell me that my mother had to return to the hospital.

"Who's Hilda?" the policeman asked, as he bent over Rudy. No one was there but Rudy and me.

"Hilda is his wife. She . . ." I looked around. "She must have taken Vinni back to the house," I said, wondering aloud to no one. Panic waited in the pit of my stomach.

A few early risers stopped and stared at Rudy. Two women in their midthirties, both with sun-streaked hair pulled back in a ponytail, had been jogging. They looked like typical Spring Haven mothers: good skin, trim bodies. They wore the latest running shoes, tied in double knots. Women like this learned all about life from their own mothers. They combed their children's hair before they went to school, scrambled eggs, and watered their plants so they wouldn't die.

"Do you need help here?" the taller one asked. I shook my head.

The younger of the two policemen questioned an older couple and a single man in his forties walking a golden retriever. Dogs were allowed on the beach until 8:00 a.m. If Vinni had been here, I know she would have stopped to pet the dog.

More heads shook. No one had seen Rudy fall. More time passed. No one had seen a little girl with an older woman leave the beach.

I continued, "My daughter was here with Rudy and Hilda. I left her here to make the call."

"We'll send someone over to the house," the young policeman said. His voice was deep with confidence. Salt and sun had bleached away some of the letters on the officer's nameplate.

"What's your daughter's name?"

"Vinni. Lavinia. Everyone calls her Vinni."

Should I have fled and run to Hilda's, instead of staying with Rudy?

I must have been with the officers on the beach for at least twenty minutes. No one moved fast. Maybe it was the heat, or the summer laziness that affects small-town police departments.

"We'll need your numericals," the older police officer said, as he stepped to my side.

"Numericals?" I asked.

"Full ID, Social Security, how long you've been down here. You'll have to come to the station and answer some questions."

"Yes, yes, but I've got to find Hilda. My daughter . . . I'm sure my daughter's with her."

I ran toward the yellow house. Rudy and Hilda had always kept their front door unlocked. As a New Yorker accustomed to locked doors, I found this strange. Now, when I turned the handle, the door didn't budge. I called out for Hilda as the sun beat down hard on my head. To the right of the top step, where I stood, I saw Hilda's beach shoes—old brown sandals with ankle straps—thrown to the side in the garden, sitting among the purple and white pansies. It had been at least fifty minutes since I had last seen Vinni. Hilda's shoes tossed in with fresh mulch sent a wave of illness over my body.

"Vinni!" I screamed, as I banged on the door.

I ran around to the back door and pushed it open. The silence in the house lashed across my face. I raced from room to room. *Why did I take so long?*

I heard someone come up the steps and turned to see the young officer from the beach.

"I checked all the rooms. They're not here," I said. "What's happening? Where are they?" My voice rose as I moved my face close to his, and he took a soft step back. "Something . . . something's not right. Where are they?" Repeating the words offered no comfort.

Another officer, who had been dispatched to check the house before I got there, had been poking around the garage.

"The car's gone," he said, as he stepped inside the kitchen. "Looks like someone had an oil leak. There's fresh drops of oil on the concrete floor."

Sixty minutes had passed since I had last seen Vinni.

TWO

THE MISTAKE I MADE WAS NOT MOVING FAST ENOUGH.

"Time counts." The Spring Haven detective spoke as if he were measuring each word before it dropped from his mouth. He was of average height—maybe five foot ten—and had a solid build for a guy who looked like he had been sitting behind a desk for at least a decade. He was probably in his late thirties, and still had lots of thick, dark hair that looked hard to comb. My mother would have called it Italian hair.

It was the detective's idea that we go back to the house in case Vinni returned home. He and I sat across from each other at the kitchen table that only the day before had been an innocent dining set with four chairs, four blue plaid seat cushions, and one rectangular table. Now, I popped up and down from the seat, unable to be still one minute and frozen with fear the next. I loathed the blue plaid. When I dropped my head, the tiny squares made me dizzy.

"Time counts." Detective D'Orfini said it twice the day Vinni disappeared. "The idea that Hilda and your daughter, Vinni, are together is a working assumption. It's just one of them. There may be a third party involved in all of this. Or Vinni may be with a friend. We can't rule out anything. The important thing is for you to stay calm. Calmness is key."

"She's my only child," I said. My voice weakened behind my teeth in the back of my throat. I jumped up and walked into the living room and saw traces of Vinni from the morning. A pair of hot-pink socks was on the floor, next to the waist-high bookcase filled with decades-old issues of *Ladies' Home Journal*. She had two backpacks. She had taken one to the beach with her. The other one was at my feet. Unzipped, it held a bag of half-eaten popcorn, two Hershey's Kisses, a mini-container of Altoids mints (a symbol of status among eight-year-olds at her school), and a short-sleeved, eco-friendly green T-shirt that read STAND UP FOR PEACE.

One hour turned into two.

"I'll need a list of Vinni's friends from school," D'Orfini said. "Maybe she saw one of them down here at the beach. Her teachers, too. And friends here in Spring Haven."

I had already called the little girl whom Vinni had met less than two weeks ago on the beach. It was 8:00 a.m. when her mother picked up the phone. I apologized for disturbing her, then hung up quickly when I learned Vinni wasn't there. I imagined the other mother hanging up and climbing into bed with her safe child. Promising her pancakes with warm syrup. Curling her fingers around her daughter's small hand.

That is what I would have done.

Looked after my own.

చ

"DO YOU HAVE a child identification box?" D'Orfini asked.

"A what?" I said.

"It's a good idea for every parent to have a box that holds a current photo of her child, dental records, medical records, even a list of friends and teachers, updated each year."

I stumbled into the bedroom, grabbed my black leather tote bag, and returned to the living room. Vinni's third-grade school picture was in my wallet. I reached in and handed it to him. He looked at me for a moment and then said, "We'll make copies."

I opened up my laptop and went straight to my photo library.

"These are good. I'll need these forwarded to the station," D'Orfini said.

$\backsim$

FIVE HOURS LATER, I called Vinni's father from the police station in Spring Haven. The cheap plaque on the edge of Detective D'Orfini's desk said his first name was John. Johnny D'Orfini. Sounded like a kid who hung out with pizza delivery boys when he was in high school. Slid into criminal justice when he decided firehouse cooking wasn't going to be what he expected on a dinner plate. Graduated from college and then moved back home to run his small-town police department. Each time he spoke, I found myself hopeful that he'd tell me where to go to grab my child's hand and take her home. His green eyes caught me from the beginning.

"Steve? Vinni's gone."

I made the call because he was her father, even if he hadn't talked to her all summer. Vinni loved her dad, but she had learned to expect little from him.

"Maddy, I just got into the office. I'm getting ready to fly to Hong Kong this afternoon. What do you mean, Vinni's gone? What the hell are you talking about?"

Steve had never been my go-to guy in a crisis. He didn't like to be interrupted.

"I don't know. We went to the beach early this morning . . . and then Hilda and Rudy . . . Hilda was crying and Vinni stayed . . . and . . . oh my God, Steve, she's gone."

Seconds piled up. No words came from either of us. I could hear Steve breathing in that racing way he had when he was trying to keep control, before he spoke. "Who are Hilda and Rudy? Where the hell are you?"

My voice quivered. "I'm at the police station in Spring Haven. You *know* that Vinni and I rented a house down here for July and August. You *do* remember that, don't you, Steve?"

"What are you doing at the police station? And who is Hilda?"

I was crying. For a minute, I wished Steve had been there with me; I thought he would have been better than no one. Then I caught myself.

"Put somebody else on the phone." I recognized the steel in Steve's voice. It was better that he was across the country in San Francisco. I could already hear the lecture he'd give me on responsibility, on not paying attention, and a general berating about any parental belief in myself that I had built up in the three years I had been raising Vinni alone.

I passed the phone to D'Orfini.

ഄ

EVEN AS A young child, Vinni had different perceptions of her dad and me. When he called in June, two weeks before the end of school, and explained that he was not returning from Sydney as planned, she didn't cry or throw a tantrum. It was another one of those times when I looked at her with a stranger's eyes, examining her young face, searching for a hint of maturity. But there were no outward signs. It was all about her brain and her heart and how they grew entwined within a silk mesh of compassion. She snatched questions out of the air.

"Does everyone have a heart?" she asked.

"Well, of course, honey," I answered.

"Everyone?" she asked again, doubting that I had understood the question in the first place. I began to explain, but I think I lost her after the first sentence. I know she got what I meant. When she understood something, her forehead did this little funny lift and receded like a drawn-out sigh.

Except for a slight dip in her chin, Vinni's face made an almost perfect circle. The dip added a sense of seriousness. Her dark hair and deep brown eyes were my father's. Vinni's lips were so full, I never doubted men would kiss them when she was older. She looked nothing like me, except for the hair, although Vinni's had a strong hint of gold folded in among its thickness. When she was a baby, I shampooed her hair in the kitchen sink while cupping her head in my palm. As I gently massaged her scalp, I studied her features as if I were seeing them for the first time.

From the beginning, I knew Vinni was a different child. She had a strong presence that made me aware when she was near, even before I could see her.

"Mommy, watch me," Vinni used to say.

When I looked up from stirring a pot of chicken soup that I made one winter Saturday, Vinni was staring up at me with a napkin floating on her head. "Doesn't this make me look like a fairy?" Vinni danced around me in a circle, her eyes looking upward like safety nets ready to catch the floating napkin should it dare to slip. Once, she told me she was practicing being "invisible."

"How do you do that?" I asked.

"I tiptoe." With a scholar's concentration, Vinni stepped one foot in front of the other. She kept her gaze locked on the tile floor beneath her and held her arms crossed over her chest.

"Can you still see me?"

"Yes," I answered. "But you look smaller."

Vinni smiled up at me. "That's how it starts," she said. "I get smaller until I'm invisible."

STEVE FLEW IN and stayed with me in the rental in the guest bedroom. We walked around like zombies, not touching each other. We ate standing up, each of us looking out an open window, as if Vinni might run by and we would reach out and grab her. I avoided Steve's stares as much as I could. At first, he bombarded me with questions: Why had I left Vinni alone? How long had I been gone? What did I know about Hilda and Rudy?

ONE EVENING, THEY had invited us to a dinner served on blue plates at their home. Over sauerbraten and potato dumplings, Rudy reminisced about his days as a student and then as a professor at Heidelberg University in Germany.

"This is where I met my sweet Hilda," he said. He closed his eyes for a moment—long enough for Vinni to ask, "What was she doing there?"

"Vinni, honey," I interrupted.

"Ah, it is all right." Rudy sat up a little taller in the chair and twisted his body in Vinni's direction. She sat on the floor, with her arms wrapped around the tops of her knees.

"I was a professor in the philosophy department. I like ideas. I like to make people think about what they believe." Rudy leaned in closer to Vinni. Hilda's eyes fixed on her husband. She listened to him speak and nodded in agreement.

"Hilda was just a girl," he said.

"I was twenty-one!" she exclaimed.

"Just a girl."

Hilda clasped her hands with excitement, fingers tip to tip in what resembled a jubilant prayer.

"I was at the Hackteufel café with my colleagues when I saw Hilda with her friends across the room. We used to go there, the young professors, and talk philosophy. We smoked and drank coffee and beer."

Vinni was insistent. "And did you like her?"

Rudy laughed. "Ah, yes, my little girl—I liked her from the start."

"Why did you leave Germany?" I asked.

Hilda set down on the table a pedestal cake dish filled with vanilla iced strudel. "Come and taste," she said. "I had a doctor's appointment today in New York and stopped off at my favorite bakery." Hilda looked over at Rudy. Their eyes locked as she smiled without parting her lips. Hilda tilted her head.

So this is what it could be like, I thought. *A man and a woman loving each other after all this time. Sending messages without words.*

Rudy continued. "The opportunity to come to the United States to head the philosophy department at Columbia University . . . well, this, I couldn't pass up. Twenty-three years ago." Rudy sighed as he placed the coffeepot on an iron trivet on the table. Hilda touched his wrist with the tips of her fingers but then withdrew them onto her lap.

"And you stayed all these years? Didn't you miss Heidelberg?" I asked.

Hilda surprised me by answering before Rudy.

"I miss Rodenbach more than Heidelberg. I grew up on a farm with lots of pigs." Hilda leaned forward and fixed her eyes on my only child.

"And, oh, the smell in the summer was so strong—those

pigs! But most of all I miss the smell of the land," she said. Her long hair, twisted into a graying bun, sat on the top of her head like a cupcake. Curly wisps framed her face. She touched her temple as she remembered.

After dinner, Hilda asked Vinni direct questions.

"Tell us, what is your favorite thing to do?"

"Be with Mommy," Vinni said.

I knew Vinni liked to be with me. It's natural. Children are supposed to like their mothers, aren't they? Mothers are supposed to hold their hands when they're afraid.

I'm the one who grew up *unnatural*. Vinni knew nothing about this. There was nothing for me to hold on to when I was afraid. Instead, I stood still. My arms hung.

"Mommy works a lot, and so this is our special summer."

"Special?" Hilda asked.

"We have breakfast on the beach. Early. Mommy reads and writes."

"And tries to paint," I added, with a nervous laugh. I picked at the overgrown cuticle on my left index finger. The summer sky began to darken, making way for an early-evening shower.

"When she's busy, I read. Mostly books for school. I like to find out about people."

"What kind of people, dear?" Hilda asked.

Vinni's face creased into a bright smile. No wonder she was the center of attention.

"The kind of people who get into trouble and then have to find a way out."

"I believe we have a budding philosopher in our midst!" Rudy said.

Hilda turned toward me. "Your work . . . it keeps you away from your child?"

Her voice had a sternness I hadn't noticed before. I continued to pick at my finger without looking at it. For a moment, I wanted to be gone from there. I needed air.

I wasn't sure how to answer without stuttering. My neighbor Evelyn was always inviting me to come down to the studio to paint with her. It simply wasn't possible to do what I had done before Vinni was born. I was uncomfortable with any answer I could think to give. I hesitated, realizing I had dug too hard on the crusty cuticle, until it bled.

Hilda's gaze hardened, but then she said, "Listen to me. I sound like an old woman. Let's have dessert."

Tenderness returned to her round face as quickly as it had disappeared.

THREE

THE FIRST NIGHT IS NOT THE WORST WHEN SOMETHING bad happens. Every night that follows is the worst.

The FBI took over the police station in Spring Haven. I could see from the beginning how John D'Orfini searched for solid footing as the men in suits claimed his space. Two from the team had been assigned to stay at the rental house with Steve and me. In the beginning, they stayed there for hours and hours. But that was in the beginning, when I wondered if I was supposed to prepare and serve coffee in ceramic mugs or Styrofoam cups for the investigating agents. Were there rules written for mothers of missing daughters?

Everything they asked, I did. I asked questions. I gave answers. I appeared on the local television news. I helped at the checkpoints with the rest of the fourteen full-time police officers called in to search for a missing child. We held up Vinni's photo to drivers, passengers, and curious children in seat belts who strained their necks forward to see the picture.

I did what I was told to do.

You would not have done more than I.

In the beginning, things appeared to happen. Steve set up two websites and hired a young student from Rutgers University Law School who was on summer break to manage them. I let him take the lead. I knew the rhythm. John D'Orfini instigated the reverse 911, something I had never heard of, that moved the investigation forward. Officers on duty and those called in on their vacation day made calls alerting the community to a missing child. "Vinni. Full name Lavinia Stewart. Eight-year-old female. Dark hair. Last seen wearing a yellow two-piece bathing suit with blue hooded sweatshirt. Could be traveling with an older woman." Snippets of conversation drifted in and out, as I was part of the call team. When the detective pulled up a seat for me next to him, I was aware of my own sound and how it sat inside my chest. Flat, uncurled, like broken sticks.

~

SIX DAYS AFTER Vinni disappeared, Steve and I listened to John D'Orfini explain why he rejected an immediate AMBER Alert, a cooperative program between the law enforcement community and the media that sends a warning when a child under eighteen has been taken. On highways, electronic signs beam information about the missing child. In theory, an observant driver who calls the police after seeing a child fitting the description has the ability to stop an out-of-state kidnapping. Maybe a murder.

John D'Orfini lifted his green gaze above mine so he wouldn't see me when he spoke.

"All the pieces have to fit together before we sound the AMBER Alert. If we overutilize it without due and prudent fact finding, we can abuse it. Prudence is key.

We don't know if it would have helped. We had to piece together that the suspect was headed out of state," he said. "We didn't have the answer. First, we had to check the hospitals to see if someone matching Hilda's description had been admitted. We contacted other law enforcement agencies to see if she had shown up—alone or with a child."

"I need you to be more specific, Detective!" I said. "What agencies?" My voice cracked.

John D'Orfini hesitated and looked down, but only for a second. Then he focused on me and me alone when he spoke. "To the south, we've hit every police department from Sea Girt through to Philadelphia. To the north, we've spoken to departments from Belmar through to Bergen County and upstate New York. These are the quickest routes out of the state, and since the car has been missing, we're assuming that the suspect drove out of here. Public transportation would have tracked her and the child by now. An APB—uh, sorry, all points bulletin—went out after twenty-four hours to points of nearby public transportation."

"Twenty-four hours?" I jumped up. How do you sit still and talk about a missing child when it's not somebody else's? "That was too damn long to wait to do this!" I pushed my fingertips into the middle of my forehead, sliding my thumb back against my left temple. I pressed hard, as if I could jam everything back into my head, away from spilling into the room. Steve sat next to me. At any moment, I suspected, he would reach for my arm and tell me to sit the hell down. He was used to men sitting around a conference table and talking in turns.

Three FBI agents sat stiffly in their seats, their suit jackets thrown over the backs of their chairs. One leaned forward and said, "We narrowed the investigation, but only after we confirmed that Hilda wasn't on the outer perimeter."

I mumbled the words *outer perimeter* and shook my head. I pressed my top teeth onto my tongue. I said the words again, but more loudly. "Is that an FBI term? Because I don't get it." My voice was high, shrill, like it had sprung out of the top of my head. *Whose voice is this?*

It wasn't an actual question, but John D'Orfini answered,

"We still don't know for sure—that is, we don't know if Hilda has left the immediate vicinity—but we're proceeding." He stopped and cleared his throat, as if the words he had uttered were about to grow thorns.

I stared back at him, and for the first time I noticed he had a small mole to the left of his chin, on the lower half of his cheek.

I was still standing when I raised my voice. "But an AMBER Alert might have slowed Hilda from wherever she was headed. We could have tracked her car," I said. I could feel the heat on my face. Accusation rose up through my throat. I leaned farther over the table, with my knuckles folded tight underneath my palms.

John D'Orfini listened but then shook his head. "There aren't any rules on how much time needs to pass before we instigate the alert. I thought it was the right call." He hesitated but then plunged forward. "I take full responsibility." He swallowed and waited, as if I might like the idea of "no rules." There was no manual detailing protocol. It was all about judgment and John D'Orfini and how I had to trust this man to help me.

"One more thing." John D'Orfini spoke slowly. "We found out that Rudy and Hilda put their house in a trust."

"Which means?"

"They hired a lawyer to take care of everything: taxes, all the bills, including selling the house. I checked with our tax office, and they sent the tax bills to the trust in care of a lawyer in New York City."

"What's his name?"

"I've already tried to talk to him, but he won't speak to me; he cited attorney-client privilege. What I can tell you is that Rudy and Hilda planned on leaving Spring Haven."

"Is the house for sale?" I asked.

"Not officially, but we've learned it's going on the market in a few weeks."

I looked down and fought back tears. Would all traces of Hilda and Rudy disappear, like Vinni? Darkness filled me so completely that I almost missed hearing John D'Orfini. If I could have gone back and begun Vinni's life again, I'd have stayed closer.

"Our agents have already visited the philosophy department at Columbia University, where Rudy was a professor and head of the department before he retired."

"Why wasn't I told about this?"

"Maddy, for God's sake," Steve said, "let him finish."

I glared across the table at my former husband.

"We hoped we'd get something from Rudy's former colleagues. About either Rudy or his wife."

Was it compassion or pity that I detected in John D'Orfini's voice? I couldn't tell.

"Rudy was there for over twenty years. He was highly respected as a scholar. 'Brilliant' is what they said. Clear-minded and brilliant. Devoted to his students. Of course, we'll want to talk to everyone who worked with Rudy. It'll take time."

I remembered what he had said earlier. *Time counts.* I wouldn't forget this.

ꝰ

WHILE RUDY'S BODY lay cold and unclaimed at Monmouth Medical Center, Hilda and Vinni disappeared under the closed eye of the amber light. Along with the police department, I canvassed the neighborhood. We went door-to-door. People looked at me with pity and horror. I spun in and out of that first week. Steve grew quieter in the second. Time passed. When he returned to San Francisco, I cried on a bench on the Spring Haven boardwalk. The night's summer breeze felt warm, until I realized I couldn't stop shaking. While the moon's face lit up the world, I sat in the dark and cried. Hilda and Rudy hadn't seemed like bad people. Now that Rudy was dead and Hilda and Vinni were missing, I traveled to a place where evil prescribed the itinerary.

By the time I returned to my apartment in New York City, Vinni had been gone for thirty-one days. It is impossible to understand how time does not stand still even when we beg it to stop. Day becomes night and repeats itself.

Steve was back at work in San Francisco. I stopped in at the editorial offices for *Hot Style* magazine in the evenings, after I was sure everyone had left for the day. When I walked into my office, I let out a deep sigh. I wasn't even sure that I belonged there anymore. I picked up a framed photo of Vinni sitting on a gold-colored horse at the carousel at Bryant Park in the middle of Manhattan.

"Where are you, love? Where the hell are you?" I said out loud.

I left notes for the young intern I had hired for the summer. I talked on the phone to the editor in chief, who told me to take as long as I needed . . . but this was all in the beginning, when everyone clung to the hope that the police would find my daughter and together our lives would go on and bad things would happen to *other* people.

During the second month that Vinni was gone, life had no timetable. John D'Orfini called me daily, but with nothing to report. I dreaded his "hello." My day-to-day living consisted of going for long walks or staying in bed and waiting. I ate in spurts, collapsing on the couch with a bowl of cereal or crawling into bed when I could no longer bear the silence in my life.

Then John D'Orfini stopped calling.

Had he sensed my despair?

࿇

ON A COLD afternoon in November, I drove down to Spring Haven. Detective D'Orfini offered me coffee. I refused twice. After that, he fixed me a cup and put it on the desk, with a pack each of Equal and sugar next to it, two mini-creamers, and a wooden stirrer on a napkin.

"Madeline? Or is it Maddy?"

For more than two months, John D'Orfini had been calling me Ms. Stewart. I hadn't cared until he said my first name and it sounded . . . sweet.

"Maddy's fine," I said.

John D'Orfini began, "I thought . . ." His eyes changed from green to blue, depending on what tie he wore.

I hesitated, moving my chin forward, as I did when I was about to say something I'd rather not. I liked him, but I wish I hadn't met him.

"Detective D'Orfini, I'm not interested in your thinking process." I moved my hips to one side of the folding chair, letting my cashmere skirt ride up where it wanted. I continued talking, sensing that at any moment John D'Orfini was going to interrupt, like a parent unwilling to wait for a child's explanation.

"I'm tired," I said. "My daughter's been missing for almost three months. I don't sleep. I'm living on yogurt and Grape-Nuts and lots of coffee. I hang out at Barnes and Noble to lose myself in a book, but instead I just lose my *self* a little more. I'm scared that if we don't find her . . ." I dropped my head back and closed my eyes.

Since that day in August, John D'Orfini's skin had lost its

shade of summer. His cheeks had thinned, making his eyes look wider and deeper set. His impenetrable stare made it impossible for me to read what he was thinking. Why did I care? I turned my head and looked out the window to the right of the detective's desk. It faced a quiet seaside town where disappearing children were unheard of.

Until Vinni and me.

"I keep asking myself what I did wrong." I moved closer to the edge of my seat, gripping D'Orfini's desk. He leaned back in his chair without taking his eyes off me. I could feel their presence on my face, watching for what? For me to confess that I had hired a private investigator after trolling the Internet for someone with credentials who looked like he was hungry?

I kept talking.

"I hired someone," I squeaked out in a voice I didn't recognize. A bird's, perhaps. "A private investigator. I had to do something."

John D'Orfini knew how to wait before he spoke.

"He scares me," I said.

"I know."

"You know that he scares me?"

"I know that you hired someone. It's my job to know."

"I thought your job was to find my daughter." I turned my head away. I didn't like how I sounded, but I couldn't stop myself. Heat hit me from head to toe. Strange. John D'Orfini's office was always cold—even the edge of his desk.

"Why didn't you say something?" I asked, in a tone of irritation combined with something sounding like defeat.

John D'Orfini had a way of letting a question float around the room until it landed in the most preposterous position.

"I don't know how you found him, but you're wasting your money."

There it was. Blunt and heavy.

I lowered my eyes and rubbed my forehead back and forth with my second, third, and fourth fingers, drawing a steady line across the middle of my skin.

"He smells, you know. When I walked into his office, it smelled like a boys' locker room. I think it was the sweatshirt he was wearing."

"TEXAS in big white letters, with orange sleeves pushed up above his elbows?"

I dropped my hand in my lap and looked up.

"I wrote him a check for twenty-five hundred dollars before he told me the dismal statistics on a missing child being found alive after forty-eight hours."

John D'Orfini ran his hands through his hair and leaned back so far in his chair that I thought it might tip over. He exhaled deeply, pushing an involuntary sigh from his throat.

"Do yourself a favor and don't see him anymore. He'll rip your heart out while he's taking your money." His voice deepened on the word *heart*.

Without a sound, John D'Orfini released the backbend of his chair and leaned over his desk, his forearms resting on the cold wood. In a husky voice, he said, "I don't want to see that happen."

"Which part?"

"What?"

"Which part? The heart part or the money part?" My eyes filled. His tone softened.

"I know this guy. He could mess up the investigation, scare away potential witnesses. He's only going to be following our tracks anyway. And besides, it's too soon to quote statistics."

I believed him because the alternative was unbearable. I looked at the serious detective who sat across from me. I opened my mouth and spoke, leaving space in between my words.

"Over and over, I ask myself, *What should I have done to keep my child safe?*" One beat. Two beats. Three beats passed. John D'Orfini said nothing in response. Instead, he stood up. His lips parted, then closed. One more beat of silence lingered, before he said, "Let me get you another coffee."

His tone changed to one that men use when they think the women around them have gone mad. If I was mad, then I had reason. When I was questioned, I felt the weight of everyone's judgment. I saw how John D'Orfini, the media, Steve, and strangers looked at me on the street.

When I was able to fall asleep, I slept for three-hour stretches during the night. Sometimes two. Often when I awoke, I had a fleeting moment of expecting to see Vinni standing by my bed. For a few seconds, I'd forget she was gone. I loved being in the dark when this happened. I loved not moving. I thought if I stayed still, I could reel in the nightmare and turn back the clock. I stared at the ceiling, knowing I had to pee but afraid to leave the bed and step into reality. All it took was the slightest movement, and then I remembered that Vinni was gone. My chest ached and ballooned with each breath. Inhale. Exhale. The ache swelled and settled. Swelled and settled.

"Beating yourself up isn't going to help us find your daughter. What I suggest is you let us do our job." I think John D'Orfini aligned himself with the FBI for my sake. The detective had stepped back inside the protection of his somber sports jacket, hiding a pair of broad shoulders.

"Stop telling me what to do! 'Suggest'? Did you say 'suggest'? Is this what it comes down to? Suggestions?" My speech turned sloppy. My voice dropped down into my throat, where it waited for moments like these to rise and lash out. The birdsong from my earlier tone flew away.

I jumped up. "I have to find my daughter. I can't sit around here and do nothing. I know she's out there. It's just . . ." I stumbled for words. "Vinni is different from other children. She senses things before they happen. There's something I haven't told you."

John D'Orfini stayed silent. I sucked the inside of the bottom of my mouth with little bites. "That morning as we walked on the beach . . . she said she knew I loved her differently than her father did. 'Daddy is different than you, Mommy,' she said. 'If I lose you, I know you'll never give up looking for me.'

"'I'll never lose you, honey,' I said. 'Never, never, never.'"

"Your daughter's a pretty special child, isn't she?" The words fell out of John D'Orfini's mouth, but he leaped over them and added, "We'll find her."

I grabbed my black leather tote bag, catching the long handles on the back of my chair. As I pulled harder, the straps tangled more and dragged the chair with me as I tried to move away from John D'Orfini and his stare. The chair squealed as it followed behind me like a wounded puppy. I didn't look back. I ran. I wanted to get the hell out of there and get out of the hell I was living. I started the car and drove up the Garden State Parkway. What had begun as a drizzle picked up until I could barely see beyond the windshield.

I skidded to a stop on the side of the highway and grabbed my cell phone from the pocket inside my tote. I hit the key for John D'Orfini. He had given me his direct extension and told me to call him anytime. I knew he'd pick up on the third ring. This was his style. Keep them waiting.

He hardly finished answering, "John D'Orfini" when I cut him off.

"Look. I don't think you get it. This is not just another child missing. This is Vinni. This is my . . ."

I lost it. I started choking on my own words, until spit and tears and phlegm mixed together and paralyzed my speech. Alone, on the shoulder of the highway, I let go of every ounce of fight that had sustained me. I needed help but didn't know whom to ask. I sunk low in my seat behind the wheel and let my heart go.

"Maddy? Where are you?"

"Maddy?" After what seemed like a long time, with John D'Orfini waiting on the line, I spoke in a voice that I squeezed out from the bottom of my heart.

"I'm nowhere." Then I hung up.

I turned off the engine and watched the raindrops hit the windshield. Dozens fell at a time, splashing the glass. I closed my eyes and unraveled. Slowly at first, and then like a train picking up speed down a long stretch of open track, I began to tremble. My shoulders fell over the steering wheel. My head hung and bobbed like one of those dangling toys people hang from their car mirrors.

My pain fell onto the seat and settled in pools around the floor mat beneath my feet. It seeped its way into the back of the car and slipped through the bottom of the closed passenger doors. It hit the gravel on the shoulder of the road.

I vomited out the window. From inside the car, I gagged on the idea that I might never see Vinni again. Maybe it was a good thing I threw it all up. Otherwise, how could I have believed she was alive?

I closed my eyes. The sweat from my head wet the seat's headrest as I stretched my neck back and up. My lower lip turned downward. My jaw released. I wiped my mouth with the sleeve of my jacket. I smelled rotten, like fresh vomit.

"Baby's Feet." Don't ask me why I thought of this now, but I did. I traveled backward, with my eyes closed. Once, I had picked up a pale nude stone—flat and smooth—and showed it to Vinni. "What color would you say this is, honey?" Without hesitation, she replied, "Baby's Feet."

This is my smart child.

ॐ

FOURTEEN WEEKS AFTER Vinni had vanished, I walked up Fifth Avenue in New York City in the direction of St. Patrick's Cathedral. As I crossed Thirty-Sixth Street, I skirted around a construction site directing pedestrians to walk through a narrow pathway into the street.

I was thinner than I used to be and wore my hair pulled tight into a ponytail reminiscent of my preteen years. My hunger went untended as I ignored the croissants in the window of Au Bon Pain on the corner.

Sometimes if I saw a woman holding a child's hand, my heart beat more quickly. My memories slid quickly into chaos, and what was real versus what was not got scrambled. What Vinni wore was still vibrant in my mind. What she said was distinct.

I chose a pew in the middle on the left side of the aisle, knelt down, and prayed. My lower back rested softly on the seat's rounded edge. Ever since I moved to the city, I couldn't resist stepping inside the cathedral when I passed by. It had nothing to do with my parents' Catholicism or with my having been baptized in the church or with feeling full of grace. I liked the peace it gave me when I sat in the pew and soaked in the quiet. I talked to God inside my head, and it made me smile.

This was before I lost Vinni.

The size of St. Patrick's Cathedral did not diminish what was in my heart. Its huge pillars hugged row after row of candles waiting to be lit with requests. *What is everyone praying for?* I wondered. *Money? A career promotion?*

How many women were lighting a candle asking God to return their daughter? The woman across the aisle showed nothing on her face as she knelt upright, keeping her back straight and long. I noticed her hands. Palm to palm, fingers pointing upward, they aligned themselves perfectly, directed toward heaven. The man sitting next to her appeared interested in the architecture. I focused on the woman. She turned toward me and gave me a gentle smile, as if she knew I was in pain. Did I imagine the smile? I looked away and bowed my head. What was the right kind of prayer? How long should I stay on my knees? I looked back across at the woman who had smiled at me, but she was gone. My heart sank. What was happening? Was I fading away or coming back to life?

FOUR

I LEFT THE APARTMENT ON A COLD MORNING IN EARLY December and traveled north uptown, toward Columbia University. Ever since John D'Orfini had mentioned that the FBI had contacted Rudy's former colleagues in the philosophy department, I'd had the idea to go there myself. I googled Rudolf Haydn, and a link appeared, featuring a photo of Rudy presenting a philosophy department prize to a graduate student. In the photo was another professor, the advisor of the prizewinner.

I made an appointment at Philosophy Hall for 10:00 a.m.

Dr. Baretta was a man in his late sixties with a handsome crop of thick white hair. He taught a course called Rational Choice. When I entered his office, he greeted me with a formal handshake and gestured for me to sit. I smelled the scent of papers and books—lots and lots of books.

"Thank you for seeing me," I said.

"Of course, but I'm not sure what I can do for you."

I told my story. He listened. He rested his chin on his fingertips, with both palms touching. His desk had several nicks in it around the edges where once they had been smooth and polished. The winter light from one small window lit the top of a wide bookcase overloaded with books stacked every which way. Piles of varying-size texts sat on the floor, their spines facing the center of the room.

"Was there anything unusual about Dr. Haydn?" I said.

What did I know to ask other than that?

Tell me something I need to know.

"Dr. Haydn was a brilliant philosopher and teacher. Everyone would agree. I was privileged to work with him all these years. He originated the curriculum for the popular course Rational Choice. He asked me to continue teaching it after he retired. I was deeply honored."

Dr. Baretta talked about Rudy's skills, his love of his work, and the way the university had revered him, as his farewell dinner, two years earlier, had demonstrated.

What does any of this have to do with Vinni and me?

"I'm afraid I haven't been able to help you," Dr. Baretta said.

I got up to leave. I shook the professor's hand and moved toward the door. Dr. Baretta had already sat down and began shuffling papers.

"There is one thing," he said in a quiet voice.

I stiffened and turned.

"One Sunday, Dr. Haydn invited my wife and me to his home on Riverside Drive for dinner. It was a rare invitation, a lovely evening with him and his wife, but I left wondering how one could live so well on a professor's salary. His apartment was, shall we say, astonishing!"

"What does that mean?" I took a few steps to the center of the room.

"Art. Music. Books. All of it, in copious amounts. The apartment alone was in one of the city's most exclusive neighborhoods."

Dr. Baretta returned to his work, picked up a pen, and, head bent, said, "I'm afraid it's nothing. My observation is that of a jealous old man. You must excuse me."

On the subway ride home, I wondered about the philosophy

professor's comments. *Art. Music. Books . . . Copious amounts . . . Most exclusive neighborhood.*

Who were Hilda and Rudy Haydn?

Had the FBI knocked on doors in their New York City apartment building and asked the same question?

౿

THE TRAIN WAS stifling, so I got off a stop early. When I reached the corner and saw my building, I ran down the block and up the front steps and fumbled with my keys to get inside. Once there, I leaned against the interior door, out of breath. I closed my eyes. I could feel a thin layer of sweat around my belly. I started up the stairs and heard a door open as I crossed the third-floor landing. A familiar voice called up to me.

"Maddy, would you like to join an old woman for a cup of tea?"

Although Evelyn Daly lived an artist's life in a studio downstairs from Vinni and me, it seemed as if she were only a room away. She was the grandmother Vinni never had. I had called her in a panic that first day Vinni was gone. Since then, we had spoken at least once every twenty-four hours. She tried to comfort me, but she never hushed me up. Soon, she was saying, "Come home. You need to come home."

I fell into her arms. She held me like my own mother never did, as we cried together. She led me over to the couch, and I lay down with my head resting on a purple velvet pillow. She covered me with a cotton blanket. When I awoke, she was painting a few feet away from me. Later that evening, she warmed soup and together we sipped from small bowls as we sat by the window overlooking the street.

"I have nothing to say," I had said.

"I know."

Many nights, I'd go downstairs to Evelyn's and sit and watch her paint. I had no desire to continue my own work at the easel. Somehow, she understood.

"Staring is good for you. Quiets the mind," Evelyn would say, and so I sat and stared—at her, at her paintings, at the couch, and out the window.

She was probably in her late seventies—a guess that I made and she never confirmed. She wore bright red lipstick, slightly missing the natural curvature of her upper lip. Her silver hair was wound around in a twisted knot between two Japanese-style orange combs. For an older woman, she had unusually broad shoulders, as if announcing to the world, *I have ideas.*

"I have lavender tea brewing," Evelyn said. "Come in and choose your cup." I followed her down a linen-white hallway with vignettes of contemporary minimalist art positioned on both walls. Thirteen individual cups with matching saucers sat meticulously balanced equidistant from one another on two wooden shelves.

Evelyn opened the door to the china cabinet. "Pick one, dear."

I reached in and lifted the teacup next to the end on the top shelf.

"Ah . . . the French painted faïence. Your favorite," she said.

Light from the north coated the walls, exposing stacks of paintings on canvas and Masonite. The only feeling close to the warmth I experienced at Evelyn's had been in my Saturday-morning pastel class four years earlier at the Art Students League on Fifty-Seventh. I used to paint from nine o'clock to eleven o'clock and race home to a pouting Steve by eleven-thirty.

"Stop thinking like an artist," Steve said when I brought

home pint-size sample cans of paint one Saturday after class and drew thick stripes of different shades of yellow on the bedroom wall. "Just make a decision. Yellow is yellow." Soon I was skipping class every other Saturday to try to ease the tension between us. I painted with Evelyn late at night when Steve was away and the latest issue of *Hot Style* magazine had been put to bed for the night. I was so tired I could barely lift my arms, but when I painted at Evelyn's, I unearthed a desire I had tamped down. What I felt found its way from my fingers to the painting, but with no support at home, my inner critic grew fat and wide.

"Just explore without expectation," she used to say, as she coaxed me into experimenting.

I was searching for a subject. A series that told a story, a small opening into a scene—anything would have helped. While Evelyn's work screamed freedom through her large strokes, mine whispered, *You're too careful.*

Since Vinni's disappearance, Evelyn had grown quiet. Once, I said, "Say something," and she walked over to me and kissed me on the forehead. I had always assumed that it had everything to do with my child. People didn't know what to say, other than something like, "You're in my prayers."

I wanted to shoot back, "I'd rather be in Vegas."

I had tried prayers. At least a gambler had a chance.

FIVE

"WHO WAS THE FIRST PERSON YOU CALLED AFTER THE police?" Steve asked.

It was 3:00 a.m. East Coast time. I had finally fallen asleep around 2:00 a.m., thankful for Ambien.

"The realtor," I said.

"Why did you call him?"

"I told you: he was the only person I could think of. And besides, he was friendly to us," I answered, becoming more aware with each word.

"Who was this guy?"

"Steve, we had him over for dinner twice. Nothing serious. Can we stop talking about the goddamn realtor?" I asked.

"Not yet," Steve persisted.

I didn't want to talk anymore, although Steve's voice was not as loud as it had once been. He could still become impatient, though, and when I detected it in his tone, my own grew nasty.

"I'm hanging up. I'm done." I went to put the receiver down, but as soon as I did, I woke up fully, furious that Steve had called me in the middle of the night to talk about something we had gone over and over these past five months.

"Steve, it's late." He had forgotten I was not on California time.

"I'm sorry. It's just that I keep thinking about the realtor who rented you the house."

"What about the realtor? What about the damn realtor?" I said. "Are you really going to bring this up again? Haven't I told you about the guy a million times? He's the only person I knew to call down here. I couldn't think of anyone else!" I was losing it—I knew it and Steve knew it. Except, for some reason, he didn't start yelling at me. Since Vinni had been gone, he'd been more patient. However, his attorney self couldn't stop analyzing. He hated it when he couldn't figure things out.

At a dinner party hosted by a colleague in the magazine business—someone looking for an extra couple to sit at the Hawaiian wood dining table—Steve and I sat across from a white-haired novelist and his Tahitian beauty of a young wife. When the discussion turned to Pete Hamill's latest essay collection, Steve interjected, "Wasn't he a high school dropout?" That alone wouldn't have been bad, had he followed it up with what a success the guy had become, but leaving things alone burdened Steve. Everything found its way into the world of pollutants.

"He missed the point on his essay on tar."

"Tar?" our host asked. "I don't think that was Pete Hamill."

"Yup. Hamill wrote it. Positive."

The Tahitian beauty shook her head. The novelist said, "You must be thinking of someone else."

"No, I'm right. I remember because Hamill's usual subject matter revolves around New York and this was completely off his mark."

I kicked Steve under the polished table, but he dug in his heels.

Looks exchanged across the table signaled a polite weariness.

On the way home, I said, "Why did you have to make a scene?"

"Why didn't you defend me?" Steve asked.

A MATTER OF CHANCE | 37

"You were wrong. Everyone could see that. It didn't have to be a big deal, but you made it into one."

"I wasn't wrong," he insisted.

Toxins invaded our household, our language . . . even our silly discussions on what to eat for dinner. "Chicken? I'll skip the pesticides, thank you," he said. Soon, he stopped reaching for me in the bedroom.

The day he moved out, I bought a new set of sheets and a lush quilt covered with blue peonies. I pulled the shades up as high as they would go. I needed the light.

Steve moved across the country and settled in San Francisco. By the time we got around to working things out via the lawyers, Vinni was six years old and I was facing thirty-four. Vinni and I stayed in the apartment. Steve's work as an environmental attorney sent him around the world, but his monthly checks arrived on time.

~

I LAY THERE wide awake until Rodenbach slipped its way into the forefront of my brain and exploded. Rodenbach. Hilda's hometown. For weeks, I'd been questioning why no one flew over there to investigate. I lay there in the dark as more questions banged around in my head. I sat up and called Steve. I charged in as soon as I heard him pick up the phone.

"I want you to go with me to Rodenbach. Germany. I know the FBI communicated with the police in Hilda's hometown, but that's all it was. A fax? An e-mail? No one went over there. We need to go!" I took a breath. "I don't want to argue with you about it."

How can I sound so certain that this is what we need to do?
I'll tell you why. Vinni is my girl.

"Steve?"

"When?" His voice was near sweet.

This was Tuesday. We left on Friday. Five months from when Vinni was taken. I dared not believe it was too late. During this time, I had relied on the FBI, the Spring Haven police department, the justice system . . . and prayer. Prayer? I had no choice. I believed obedience dictated resolution. I believed happiness resulted from doing the right thing. I lived inside a blur, dependent upon rules, doing what I was told by people of authority who didn't begin each day wondering how deep a hole in the heart could go. I let myself be led . . . until I stopped.

Five months is a long time only when the heart stops reading signals from the brain. I convinced myself I was not too late.

All I told John D'Orfini was that I was flying out to see Steve in San Francisco. I didn't want a bureaucratic mess trailing behind me.

I acted on my own.

I broke the first rule: tell all.

I booked my ticket for ten days.

My mother used to say, "Maddy, tell me what you're thinking." But I had learned at an early age that "telling" didn't always work out well. The FBI had not sat at the dinner table with Hilda and Rudy as they described Rodenbach. They had not seen their faces. I am the only one who knew that something passed between Hilda and Rudy when they mentioned their homeland. Something they chose not to speak about.

Steve met me in Frankfurt, the major airport closest to Rodenbach. We rented a car and drove the thirty-one miles to Hilda's birthplace. It might as well have been a million miles past the sun.

I had expected New York City bleakness to follow me to western Germany, but it was a warmer-than-usual January day, with cyclists taking advantage of the remarkable weather. As we drove by farm after farm, I saw thoroughbred horses, calm and well behaved, heads bowed to the ground, in a land where residents' prosperity showed in their equine inventory. I had researched Rodenbach before I'd left and learned it was part of the Rhineland section of the country, known for its vineyard slopes and hospitality to hikers, cyclists, and horse lovers. Tourists gathered to navigate the huge Palatinate Forest Nature Park, most of it under woods.

No category of tourism described why Steve and I had traveled to this idyllic part of the country. Other than an old priest we interrupted amid a hot sauerbraten lunch, no one had seen Hilda since she was a girl in her early twenties. The priest invited us to join him at his dining table, and although Steve hesitated, I accepted for both of us. We learned that just the day before, a younger priest, a deacon, newly assigned to take over for the retiring priest, had arrived to begin preparations to relieve the old priest of his duties. He spoke enough English to interpret for his predecessor.

"Hilda was the daughter of a prosperous farmer who bought parcels of the surrounding land until it grew to be the largest farm estate in Rodenbach. The farm they lived on was known for its watchdogs that guarded the pigs." The old priest had known the family since Hilda was a girl of six.

"As a child, Hilda sang in the choir. Beautiful girl. Beautiful voice. I remember she sang a solo in the Christmas pageant one year."

We stayed for a short time, as I could see the old man's eyelids growing heavy while we sipped our tea.

Steve and I showed Vinni's picture to everyone. People shook their heads and kept walking. Others touched our hands.

Some made the sign of the cross. On the drive back from Rodenbach, I thought about Hilda and Rudy's meeting and falling
in love and leaving Germany. Did they really leave because
Rudy was offered the job at Columbia? Something gnawed at
me, until I begged Steve to stay longer in Germany.

"Where do we begin?" he asked. "We've got nothing."

"Heidelberg is only three hours away. Why don't we see if
that café where they met is still here?"

We changed our flights and checked in to an old but famous
building called the Hotel zum Ritter in Heidelberg, where the
clerk assured us we could park our car at the curb while we
dropped off our bags. The Hackteufel café—the oldest café in
town—was still in business. When I stepped inside, I reached for
Steve's arm as my heartbeat sped up.

"What?" he said.

I hadn't touched any part of Steve in a long time.

"What if we're close but can't see her?"

"Stop." Steve took a breath. "You wanted to come here, and
we did." I knew he was hurting by the way he held his face: set
square like a block, no flexibility in sight.

I couldn't help him. I needed strength to believe that Hilda
was somewhere alive with Vinni. I could smell my child. It was
just that no one else could.

Steve spoke to the manager with poorly aligned bottom
teeth while I showed pictures of Hilda and Vinni to both of the
waitresses and the one lone waiter grabbing a smoke at the door.
At first I wondered if they understood my questions in English,
but each answered with a shake of the head and an uncomfortable look in their eyes as I insisted they look again at the pictures printed on the paper.

From the café, we moved on to the museum and lucked into
spending time with the oldest docent, a volunteer named Max

who spoke perfect English and who met with us upstairs in a wood-paneled assembly room. Although he was sympathetic to our story, he relished the opportunity to tell us about the history of the university, even going so far as to name Jewish professors who'd had to flee the country. Later, he took us downstairs and showed us their pictures, framed on the walls in rows of honor. His kindness prompted me to ask him if he'd help us with our visit to the town hall the next day and serve as interpreter if we needed one. He agreed, and we left with plans to meet in the morning.

At the town hall, we found records of Hilda and Rudy's marriage date and the names of their two witnesses, both of whom were now deceased. We were lost in a town full of history that kept us asking questions for three more days. That's all we had—questions without answers. We said goodbye to Max and thanked him for his compassion. I watched the old man walk away. I waited until I could no longer see him in the distance before I turned in the opposite direction.

SIX

EVERYTHING I KNEW ABOUT PSYCHOLOGY TOLD ME ANGER was part of grieving. Loss involved stages of awareness. Although I never accepted the possibility of Vinni's being gone forever, anger slammed me in the gut. By the end of spring, it had stopped up the natural swallow reflex so I could barely eat. Evelyn urged me to get a physical examination. She made the appointment and insisted on coming with me. "Just to make sure you walk through the door," she said, as we stepped into the cab and she directed the driver to take us to Seventy-Second Street and Amsterdam.

Dr. Stanley Goodman was an older man with a bent back, accustomed to years of listening to heartbeats and sad stories whispered in confidence as he placed his stethoscope over his patients' chests. He greeted Evelyn with a warm hug and looked at me with eyes that took me in in one whole piece.

Evelyn chose a seat in the waiting area. As we were the last appointment of the day, the room was empty. Several issues of *Gourmet* magazine were strewn carelessly on an old coffee table.

"I'll be here, Stanley, if Maddy needs me," Evelyn told the doctor.

He extended his arm for me to walk down the hallway.

"Turn at the first door on the left," he said. We both walked into a sunny room with an examination table set against the inside wall, across from a window that opened onto an inner courtyard. The electric shades worked from a switch by the door. He must have seen my surprised look at what I saw through the window. Young children knelt side by side at beds of dark mulch, planting pink and white impatiens bordering the sun and shade. Three adults were on the ground with the children, helping them dig the earth apart to make larger holes for rosebushes. Small yellow blooms hinted at what was to come in the summer months ahead.

The doctor waited for me to sit down on the examination table. He spoke as he pressed the button on the electric shade.

"Have you always been this thin?"

I looked toward the window at the children gardening. A dark haze covered my eyes. A wave of heat from the pit of my stomach wound its way through the top of my head.

"I think I'm fainting," I said. Then I blacked out.

When I opened my eyes, I saw both of them standing over me. Evelyn's eyes had narrowed into concern. Dr. Goodman held my hand.

"You're pushing back life. Refusing to take it in," he said.

I stole a glance at Evelyn. She nodded her head and smiled gently. I didn't speak. I waited for more.

"I know about your child's disappearance. Evelyn told me when she called for your appointment. But I want you to tell me."

Evelyn kissed me on the forehead and left the room. I was too tired to move. I lay on the exam table and said nothing.

I wanted to die.

Should I have made Vinni more afraid? Was she too trusting?

I thought of Vinni and how she had never cried out for me that day at the beach. Had she thought I wouldn't hear her?

My father used to say, "Your mother is sick. She cannot hear you."

I looked at several children planting flowers, their hopes pinned on blossoms promising to bloom.

"Lovely, isn't it?" Dr. Goodman broke up the fantasy in my head. I slid from the examination table and sat down on the small couch across from his chair. The window facing the court-yard separated our seats.

He pointed to the children, the flowers, the secured haven behind his office. "'Put something pretty back there,' Evelyn said. And you know, when she said it, it made sense. She arranged for a local nursery to partner in an after-school program with the neighborhood elementary school. The children are my gardeners!"

Dr. Goodman's bent spine fit neatly under the window sash as he leaned over the sill and waved to the children.

He turned and said, "You're suffering—I see it—but you'll be of no use to your daughter if you're sick. You have to start eating—"

I interrupted him. "No, no, no." I shook my head back and forth. "I'm not sick. I'm tired, that's all."

"You need nourishment." Dr. Goodman rose and opened the door. He confused me, because he had asked me to tell him about Vinni and now he was gone. As I waited, I looked out at the garden. A few minutes later, he returned with a small bowl of just-washed strawberries and set it down on the table in front of the couch. He moved aside an assortment of cooking maga-zines.

"Do you like to cook?" I asked.

"It's my hobby."

I reached for a fresh strawberry. I knew Dr. Goodman was waiting for me to tell him about Vinni, but I wasn't sure I wanted to. He was a different kind of doctor. *Old-school*, I thought. When he spoke to me, I had the feeling he was paying attention. When he placed the stethoscope on my back and asked me to take a deep breath, I was barely able to inhale.

"How long has Evelyn been a patient of yours?" I popped a strawberry into my mouth. I hadn't eaten anything this good in a long time. The berries reminded me of the breakfast that Vinni and I had had on the beach on the morning of her disappearance.

"Evelyn isn't my patient. She was my wife a long time ago."

I began to cry. He sat there without saying a word. It was nice to have someone not expect a story.

"Vinni will turn nine in May. She's been missing for five months."

Dr. Goodman said nothing. My breathing slowed as I reached for another strawberry and ate it whole, enjoying its juice as it rolled around my tongue. Its perfect sweetness soothed me. Or maybe it was sitting by the open window, or in a room with walls painted pale yellow. "The strawberries are delicious." I avoided talking about Vinni, but Dr. Goodman asked me a question that made me swallow my hesitation.

"You believe she's alive, don't you?"

"Yes."

SEVEN

SPRING BLOOMED, AS IT ALWAYS DID. FIRST CROCUSES, followed by the blooms of tulips and daffodils. I ignored the flowers, but I could not hide my eyes from staring into the black of night. I prayed that wherever Vinni was, she could see the moon and the stars. I fooled myself into thinking maybe we were watching them at the same time.

I continued driving back and forth to Spring Haven, dreading the ride home alone. Sometimes I met with John D'Orfini at his office, but his sad face behind the professional exterior frustrated the hell out of me and I found myself fleeing to the boardwalk. "I wish there was more," he'd start.

When I'd get to the spot on the beach where I'd last seen Vinni, I'd stop and hang my arms over the railing and stare. I'd stare and stare and stare, waiting for my girl to appear out of the sand.

On May 30—I know the date because it was Vinni's birthday—I stood at a sink, staring at the soapy lather, as I washed my hands in a restroom on the Garden State Parkway. Over the outside and around into the palms, I massaged and soaped. I looked up into the mirror over the sink to my left and caught the eye of a woman wearing a veiled hat shaped flat like a pancake. She stared back at me and then pointed to a card by the hot-water faucet that read READINGS BY JACINTA. With her right hand closed into a fist, she began to beat on her heart. I turned quickly and left the card at the sink and walked over to grab a paper towel. From behind me, I heard a voice say, "I can help you."

I turned and came face-to-face with the woman as she placed the card in my hand. She was dressed in red, except for the black hat topped with a thin veil covering her forehead, eyes, and most of her nose. The red of her lips haunted me all the way home as I drove in the fast lane, switching over to the turnpike until I exited for the Holland Tunnel.

Psychics were all over the city. I didn't have to go to New Jersey for a reading by Jacinta, but that is exactly what I did. The back of her card listed aura and tarot-card readings, crystal-ball readings, past-life regressions, and dream interpretation. I used to laugh at those who believed in psychic mediums, but what I used to do had nothing to do with what I did now. Nothing.

What no one knows is that I began to visit my mother's grave in New Jersey. I took flowers and placed them in front of her headstone. I spoke out loud and said, "Give me something to hang on to." Before Vinni disappeared, I pushed thoughts of my mother out of my mind. Why was it now that I needed her, more than I did when I was a child drowning in macaroni and cheese and television?

&

JACINTA WORKED OUT of her house on a busy highway headed in the direction of the Delaware Water Gap. She explained that her great-grandfather had built it years earlier, before strip malls sprang up and took out the trees. A FOR SALE sign leaned against a wire fence enclosing a narrow side yard. The house smelled of old wood. The past lurked in every corner and floorboard.

"You were born surrounded by darkness. You've been fighting negativity your whole life," she said. "We have a lot of work to do."

"All I want to know is where I can find my daughter." I kept my jacket on but unzipped it. I rolled my fingers around my car keys stowed in my right pocket. Years ago, the room had probably been the front parlor, with at least one velvet couch nestled against a wall, but now there was only a small, circular table with two chairs on either side covered in faded green fabric.

"You should wear a blue scarf around your neck. Blue is the color of the throat chakra. You need to clear out space in your lungs so you can breathe. This is the first thing we must do: create positive space."

She opened a drawer and took out a silky blue scarf and draped it around my neck.

"Uh, this isn't why I'm here."

"You must meditate."

"I don't think—"

"You can pay for the scarf in three installments of sixty dollars each."

Why were we talking about money? Hadn't she heard me?

Jacinta lit a candle that smelled of hyacinth.

"My name means *hyacinth*. Did you know that?" She spoke in a thick voice that sounded as if a dollop of mashed potatoes hadn't yet found its way down her throat. "You need to call me each morning for a week, so we can begin the removal of darkness in your life."

"By phone?" I asked. Chakras? I'd try anything, and if that meant I had to wear a blue scarf around my throat, I'd do it.

I lasted a week. On the seventh day, Jacinta's sister answered the phone and said she was at her church at an emergency meeting but that Jacinta wanted me to come to her house, as she had had a dream about me. I had been in a panic earlier that morning when I couldn't find the blue scarf. I tore into everything in my top dresser drawer, although I knew that I hadn't put it there. Jacinta had instructed me to keep it in sight at all times and to drape it over the doorknob in whatever room I was in when I wasn't wearing it. So where was it? I opened the bottom drawer and started throwing things onto my bed. I went from bedroom to bathroom to kitchen and back again. Over and over, I slammed more drawers and flung open the bedroom closet door, until I collapsed in a fit of tears and frustration on the floor. There it was—under the bed. It was a cheap-looking thing made from a synthetic fabric that made my skin hot. I washed my face and left the apartment with the scarf folded end to end and looped once around my neck.

Detective D'Orfini called me as I headed over to Ninth Avenue to the tunnel, to leave the city for my final visit with the psychic.

"Just checking in," he said.

I touched the blue around my neck and said in a small voice, "Does your police department ever call upon psychics?"

"Why?"

"It's just a question. Can you give me an answer?"

"The answer is no." He waited and said, "Are you seeing a psychic medium?"

"Of course not," I said. I thought about the burgundy-black nail polish that Jacinta wore on her fleshy fingers. I thought about the way her nose widened at the tip and how she swirled her tongue around her top teeth before she asked me for more money.

When she showed me a catalog advertising a $5,900 gold chain and pendant claiming to protect a life from negative energy, I said, "I don't have that kind of money."

"Can you borrow it?" she asked coolly.

My heart sank. I'd wear a rat's claw around my neck or a vial of blood if it meant that I'd wake up and discover that this was all a dream—a very bad dream. But I knew that a piece of jewelry wasn't the answer.

"Do you like hyacinths?" I asked John D'Orfini.

"The flower?"

"Yes, hyacinths."

"Uh, I don't know. Do you?"

"Not anymore. Their smell offends me."

If John D'Orfini suspected I'd seen a psychic, he never gave it away. The last time I saw the gypsy, I stood up in the middle of a meditation and walked out. Her eyes were closed. Mine were not.

I drove around before I headed back into the city. Somewhere on Route 46 East, I threw the scarf out the window and watched it fly away through my rearview mirror. Within seconds, I couldn't see a hint of blue anywhere. Like magic, it was gone.

EIGHT

MEMORY DEVOURED THE SUMMER OF THE ONE-YEAR anniversary of Vinni's disappearance. I thought about renting the house—the perfect punishment—in Spring Haven, but I knew that wasn't the answer.

John D'Orfini kept his eye on the calendar. In the weeks leading up to the first anniversary, he called and left a voice mail: "Just checking in. D'Orfini." His voice made me crack a grim smile. I couldn't deny I liked that he called even when we both conceded the FBI was clearly in charge of the case. A grieving mother was supposed to wait. Hearing from John D'Orfini tided me over during the bleak days when nothing— not one damn thing—happened, unless you counted the rhodo- dendrons blooming on schedule.

Birthdays, graduations, anniversaries, and, yes, even dates of death carry markers or celebrations. But what was I supposed to do with the approaching anniversary date of Vinni's disappear- ance? With each passing day, it seemed, the sky dropped a little more and the air around me grew heavier. I walked the streets, but I stopped noticing things. Sounds fell on deaf ears. I could not believe that I had lived one whole year without Vinni. I had been back at work at the magazine full-time since January 2, but I was well aware that my two assistant editors shouldered most of the workload. People covered for me when I found it impos- sible to focus. Some afternoons, I slipped out of the office, went home, and hid with a bottle of chardonnay and a bag of chips. On the weekends, I hardly moved from my bedroom. I drugged myself to sleep.

Evelyn dropped off soups bought from a local artisan market, along with fresh rolls tucked inside a brown bag, outside my apartment door. She continued to encourage me to paint, inviting me to exhibits in the West Village, where she was a bona fide celebrity among the young artists, who must have wondered why this older woman dressed in reds and purples brought a drab woman dressed in browns and grays.

When she gave a demonstration on light and shadow, she insisted she needed me to help her carry a tote bag of materials that I knew she could manage herself. All the way home, she tried to engage me in conversation. "What did you think of the middle-aged man who asked me, 'Where do your ideas come from?'"

I laughed. Finally. I laughed out loud. "And you said, 'From outside my window'! How could you?"

"I couldn't resist, darling." With a dramatic swoop, she flung her sea-green shawl over her shoulder.

For a moment, I had a glimpse into what I couldn't name, but I knew I had broken through to something only Evelyn could give me.

WHEN JOHN D'ORFINI suggested I come to his office on an afternoon in the beginning of August, I believed it would be another routine conversation.

"I know this month is going to be a hard one for you. I thought if we reviewed a few things . . ."

"Is there something new?"

"No. Well, I don't think so, but I like to keep in contact with those hurt on my watch."

"So it's a territorial thing, Detective? Have those guys in suits finally given you back your office?" I knew that the FBI had closed shop in Spring Haven after three months of checking out hundreds of leads to nowhere. What I continued to learn was how seriously John D'Orfini took any crime committed on his "watch." Vinni's disappearance was by far the most heinous crime he had seen in the eight years since he'd been assigned to Spring Haven. Meeting him at his office confirmed my suspicion that his interest bordered on a carefully hidden obsession.

I had no objections, but first I had a stop to make.

♪

WHEN I PULLED up to the house where Rudy and Hilda had lived, I remained behind the wheel, feeling almost calm. Real estate prices in Spring Haven had always been high, but a three-bedroom Cape Cod with a screened-in porch facing east for the morning sun fell into the category of not being fancy enough for the rich but priced too high for the almost-rich. It was a long-standing joke that Spring Haven was called the land of the Irish Mafia. Maybe that was why this German-speaking couple kept quiet, although their neighbors referred to them as "polite" and "sweet." Was Spring Haven the perfect place to look for a child? Or had the idea surfaced when they'd laid eyes on Vinni digging in the sand, running back and forth to the ocean with a bottle to fill with water and pour into the large holes? One comment that popped up over and over during interviews with anyone who had contact with Rudy and Hilda was that they were "intelligent."

Oh, yes, something else stayed with me—something that John D'Orfini said was repeated in several FBI reports.

"The couple was often seen holding hands on the beach as they walked in the early morning."

To leave Rudy's body unclaimed. How did this make sense? I identified the body, but I did not bury him or take responsibility. I had no space to grieve for Rudy until years later, and even then it was small.

I got out of the car near noon, when the sun was at its strongest. I walked around to the back door. I tried the handle, never expecting it to turn with a smooth click. I stepped into the kitchen and stopped. Five steps to my right was a small alcove for the washer and dryer. Beyond this, a bathroom papered in a design of green ferns, whose only source of natural light was a small, hard-to-reach window, smelled stale, like mold. They were close to the beach, and the lack of air meant the smell from the ocean turned the house into an unpleasant walk-through for a prospective buyer. A dining table placed at the window faced the front of the house. I stood to the side so I wouldn't be seen from the street and continued into the living room, decorated with two fat, gray floral love seats. I sat down and looked around at the emptiness.

The house had been "sanitized." That's what the FBI told me: "We've sanitized the house." I took it to mean that anything personal had been bagged and brought to the station for prints. No grocery lists. No photos. No clothes in the closets. No shoes at the door. No remembrances of any life lived in the house. Everything had been swept away, except rows and rows of books shelved along one wall of the bedroom. Books on philosophy by the German philosophers Immanuel Kant and Friedrich Nietzsche. Titles like *Beyond Good and Evil* and *Human, All Too Human* jumped out, but all I allowed myself was a slight touch of their spines. There were books by Ayn Rand—someone I had read in college—and Ralph Waldo Emerson, remembrances from high school. Art books with glossy pages of prints by Max Ernst and Hermann Hesse stood straight and neat on shelves filled with philosophy and art. Other shelves held a large collection of small and large books on seeds and floral creations by designers from Kiev to New York.

Hilda deferred to Rudy in the few conversations we shared, but I do remember how once we spoke about the life expectancy of an orchid.

"With the proper care, an orchid can live longer than I expect to myself."

Vinni and I both spoke about it later. The next day, I surprised her with a white orchid centered with purple.

"I love it! I love it! I love it!" she squealed. Then she threw her arms around me.

~

I KNEW LITTLE more than what I knew one year ago, when I had a daughter who sang with me to "Dancing in the Streets," by Martha and the Vandellas, as we grooved up the Garden State Parkway.

Vinni liked the music I liked. She made no fuss that the music was old. She wasn't that kind of girl. She was special.

This is what I want you to know.

John D'Orfini glanced at the clock on the wall as I walked into the police station on Third Avenue. "Traffic?" he said.

I skirted the lie. "Sorry I'm late."

"Can I get you a coffee?"

"No. Thanks. Why did you want to see me?"

"I want to make sure you know where things stand now that a year has gone by and . . ." He nodded his head as if he wanted me to help him out with the rest of the line.

It wasn't going to happen. Instead, I leaned back into my chair. My shoulders fell to protect my chest, creating a hard shell around my heart from the middle of my back.

"The case stays open, of course, but after a year, the leads get fewer. Right now, there's very little. The FBI has a long list of missing children. This is where Spring Haven is different, because your daughter is the only missing child on *my* list. Do you know what I'm saying?"

John D'Orfini walked around and sat on the edge of his desk. He crossed his arms, but they looked awkward, like they didn't belong there. He held his elbows too far away from his chest, suspended, so they made his shoulders inch toward his ears.

"I'm seeing this case through. I owe it to you and to Spring Haven."

I don't care about your little town, I thought.

YEAR TWO

NINE

ON THE WAY TO ST. PATRICK'S CATHEDRAL, I PASSED children dressed as bumblebees, dinosaurs, and princesses in tutus, stopping in at neighborhood bodegas for Halloween candy. I tried my hardest to ignore them as I slipped down side streets and walked north on Fifth Avenue. My idea was to drop in and light a candle. I had been doing this a lot lately. The flickering of the dozens of votive messages returned me to the image of the sun glistening on the water at the beach. I knelt down and smelled my girl, imagining the salt water was the closest I could come to inhaling her. I closed my eyes and pretended.

I was back on the street an hour later. I walked uptown without having any idea of where I was going. All I knew was that the sun—unusually warm for an afternoon on Halloween—felt good. I walked with my jacket tied around my waist. I kept going until I realized I was close to where Rudy and Hilda used to live on Riverside Drive. I headed left in the direction of the river. Apartments with high price tags in buildings maintained for the rich enjoyed breathtaking views of the George Washington Bridge and the Hudson River. Although John D'Orfini had told me that the FBI had spoken with all the residents of the building, they had come up with nothing useful for the investigation, other than learning Rudy and Hilda were participants in a long-standing monthly book club with two other couples in the building.

I walked up to the doorman and lied. As a magazine editor, I knew how to approach people to get them to talk, so I said I was working on a story about the book club that had been going on in the building for several years. "Could you see if the participants are in?" I asked. I had no names. I carried a medium-size tote. I wore a pair of dark sunglasses. I used the professional tone of voice that had always been so reliable in the past. I smiled. I walked through the door and waited in the lobby. Within minutes, a white-haired woman wearing large, black-rimmed eyeglasses got off the elevator.

"Ms. Stewart?"

"Yes. I'm, uh, doing a story—"

It was she who interrupted before I went further.

"Let's talk upstairs. My husband is home. He began the book club over twenty years ago."

Once inside the apartment, I dropped the charade. "I'm sorry. I didn't know how else to . . . I was afraid . . . I'm hoping you'll talk to me about Rudy and Hilda Haydn."

The man stood. "Who are you?"

"I'm Maddy Stewart. The police believe Hilda kidnapped my daughter."

He sat down next to his wife on the small brocade couch.

"Rudy died a year ago, and Hilda . . . well, she was always the more quiet of the two," he said. "We—my wife and I—are very sorry about what's happened."

The woman removed her glasses. "We've already spoken to the FBI." She touched the top of her husband's hand and let her hand rest there.

My questions didn't seem right. Even as I asked them, I sensed their awkwardness. The other couple in the book club was vacationing on one of those luxury residencies at sea for eight months. The man ended by saying, "What can we tell you other than that Rudy and Hilda were intelligent—highly intelligent—people who were loving toward one another?"

The woman continued with a hint of sadness. "I suspected they missed home. Somehow, going back there didn't seem to be an option. I don't know why."

They offered me a cup of tea, but that wasn't why I had come. When I left, I had more unanswered questions. I walked to the nearest subway stop and rode home. I knew I'd walk more the next day.

⁂

JOHN D'ORFINI HELD a ballpoint pen in a ready-to-write position. Whenever we spoke, I had the feeling he was waiting for a revelation. This time, I had something to tell.

"I walked out on my job last Wednesday," I said.

"What do you mean?"

"I was walking in the rain around lunchtime, and I just kept on walking. I didn't go back to the office. I couldn't. I'm tired of the pity."

"Pity?"

"Everyone looking at me as if I've done something wrong. As if I'm responsible. Mothers are supposed to be better than that. Right?"

John D'Orfini cleared his throat and settled into his chair. His office was cold. I knew if I checked the thermostat, it would probably be in the midsixties.

"I hear you. I'm just not sure I understand. You seem too responsible to—"

"Walk away. Right? That's what you're saying, isn't it?"

"Yes."

"I had a case of responsibility the next day. I returned to work thinking I could handle things."

"And you couldn't?"

"It's been getting harder for me to go back to the office after taking walks in the middle of the day. I've started having panic attacks."

"Are you getting help with this?"

I turned my head toward the window to the right of his desk and ignored the question. I replayed the mess from earlier in the week in the restroom.

As I sat on the toilet, a wave like a monsoon washed over me. I felt trapped inside the stall. Unable to wipe, get up, pull up my slacks, and walk to the sink and wash my hands. The simplest things were all of a sudden out of reach. My heart raced, and I started hyperventilating. Someone from the other side of the toilet asked if I was okay. More voices. Concern. I watched pairs of flats and boots pivot, stand still, turn, and pivot some more. Then I heard the voice on the phone from the previous night.

"Maddy? Can you come out of there?" Someone had gone to get the editor in chief. We had worked together for the past six years on *Hot Style*. We weren't the kind of friends who shared sushi after work. Standing around a glass conference table, we ate fried rice and sweet-and-sour pork delivered late in the afternoon. We had a working relationship built on knowing what it took to get where we were. She was tough. The way I used to be. We had worked our way through the ranks together, stumbling into each other on magazine stints. She was six years older than I, married to a seasoned television anchor of a major network out of New York. When she was presented with the top gig, she took me with her to run the haute couture section. I owed her.

The morning after our phone conversation, she was at my side at the sink, watching me dry-heave. My face felt hot, although I wasn't red. White consumed me. Blank, like a piece of paper. I had had panic attacks after my mother killed herself. Not many, but two is enough to cling to a towel rack when you're in your own bathroom and can't leave. The doctor pre-scribed Lexapro, Xanax, and behavioral therapy. I carried one emergency Xanax wrapped in a Kleenex folded into a neat square the size of half a matchbox car. I zipped it into a tiny compartment of my wallet. Knowing it was in my purse made me feel safe. I refused to carry around an entire bottle of drugs. I told myself I was less dependent if I held on to one pill at a time.

WITH MY BOSS'S hand on the small of my back, I leaned over the sink.

"Maddy, I want you to take a leave of absence. You need to get out of here for a while. You can work as a freelancer on the larger stories. But you've got to make the deadlines. You've got no choice. Make your own hours, but get the job done. You're failing at this one. You've lost your edge. If we feed you some freelance work, you'll be under less pressure. You can come back, but . . ." She shook her head, lowered it, raised it, and looked around the tiled bathroom.

"Everyone is tiptoeing around you. I can't run a magazine like this. I'm sorry."

No one had ever told me I had failed.

I began to object, but she dropped her hand and inter-rupted.

"This is not a suggestion. It's the way it is. You need time to figure out where you're going. I'm not tossing you out. I'm say-ing maybe if you work less . . . Look, I can't say 'I get it,' be-cause I can't get it. Take the time."

I had never told her about the nights when I got home late from working on deadline, how I'd sneak down to Evelyn's to paint. "I'll be back in a sec," I'd whisper into Steve's ear as he dozed on the couch with the television staring at the top of his forehead. On those nights, Rosa, our nanny since Vinni was born, had already fed Vinni homemade tortillas with guacamole and beans. She had fixed her a bubble bath and put her to bed. Steve kissed Vinni's cheek, nestled into her pillow, when he arrived home.

The editor in chief hesitated, as if she wanted to say something or throw her arms around me, but instead she walked away without waiting for me to break from the sink. One of the interns, young and fair—a recent graduate from Pace University—handed me a wet paper towel. "Feeling better?" she asked.

"Terrific." I mumbled an additional "fuckin' peachy" with my head lowered toward the bottom of the sink. I straightened up and looked at the face in the mirror. Lines of black mascara ran down the tops of my cheekbones. My eyes were watery, my throat scratchy from the dry heaves. My hair hung in sweaty chunks touching my ears. Was I failing at everything?

I had no idea how to live anymore. How was I supposed to find another life and make it stick?

Ten minutes later, I walked past my coworkers' offices, where family photos sat secure on their desks. My stomach somersaulted as I scratched at my arms through my shirt. Screaming inside did nothing to soothe the pain. Why did everyone else seem so safe?

Three freelance assignments were waiting for me when I reached my office. I buried their deadlines inside my head and left the building. I could not fail at this, too.

I had some savings from a small inheritance my father left me when he died. When Steve and I married, I kept the money in my own account on advice from a friend of my father's—an

Italian stockbroker who spoke with an accent so thick you'd think he had just arrived on Ellis Island. The broker's wife had dropped dead in a grocery store in the soup-and-condiments aisle after having just left her doctor's office with the phone number of a pain management center in Parsippany, New Jersey. Although her recent onset of migraines had made her miserable, she needed chicken stock for a recipe she had read about in *Prevention* magazine. All this and more came from the broker as Steve sat there, nodding and rubbing his chin, until I gently took his hand from his face and held on to it.

Steve balked at the idea of my father's money staying with me, but the broker's undulating words were so hard to understand, it was easier to agree so we could leave his office and drive away with our windows down.

THE POLICE DEPARTMENT in Spring Haven was seventy-eighty miles from Manhattan. Each time I drove there, I got a tight feeling in the pit of my stomach. The station might as well have been on the other side of the moon. At first, the town had extended a huge circle of support, but each time I returned, I detected a pulling-back. An uneasiness followed me from corner to corner.

I drove down Main Street and parked in front of the Spring Haven Religious Gift Shop. Cream-colored Irish pottery by Belleek filled the display windows. The woman standing behind the glass case of beads and necklaces recognized me right away. She laid a silver Miraculous Medal, one of Mary, the mother of Baby Jesus, with arms spread open and palms facing outward, on the counter to untangle a tiny knot. I waited to speak as she folded the necklace into a white box outlined in a thin gold line.

I thought about the time Vinni and I had come in to the shop to look at a silver ring with thin woven circles that we had seen in the window. I recognized the design from one my mother had had in her jewelry box. It represented the Holy Trinity.

"What's that, Mommy?" Vinni had asked.

The saleswoman sensed my hesitation.

"Maybe I can help you," she offered. "The circles mean you'll always be loved," she said with confidence. Vinni looked up and said, "Can we buy it?"

As the woman polished the ring, Vinni stared at her and smiled.

"Why don't you wear a ring?" she asked the saleswoman.

The woman laughed, but it was obvious she was surprised at Vinni's remark. At first, her lips tightened, but then Vinni said, "You're pretty" and the lines around the woman's mouth relaxed. She looked at me and said, "You're lucky to have her—children are blessings, aren't they?"

When we left the store, I carried the empty white box in my purse and Vinni wore the ring. She had it on the day she disappeared.

I hadn't been in the shop in several months. Two other women were browsing, picking up Waterford crystal vases and turning them upside down to check the high price tags on the bottom.

"You may remember me. I'm—"

"Yes, of course. How are you? Spring's in the air, I think."

The other women looked up at the sound of the door opening. A young girl, about ten years old, raced in, out of breath, and asked her mother for money to buy a cone at the ice cream shop next door. I stood frozen until the chill in the room drew a fine line of ice chips on the floor separating the others from me. If I crossed the line, I would make things messy—stir up the chips.

"I just wondered if you've heard anything more about my daughter. She's been missing since last summer—"

"Detective John D'Orfini is handling this, right?" the saleswoman interrupted.

"No . . . I mean, yes, along with the FBI."

It was the same every time I visited Spring Haven and asked questions. I reminded people of what they didn't want to know. My existence made them aware of evil lurking on the beach. I offered them nothing. No hope. No goodness. No possibilities.

I left the gift shop and headed toward my car, parked across the street in front of Lucy's Sweet Shop. The rear of the Mustang on the driver's side sagged to the left by the curb. As I got closer, I saw the collapsed tire.

"What the . . .?" I said quietly. I tugged at my knit tee and stretched it beyond my waist, only to have it ride up above my hipbones. I kept tugging as I walked around the car with my stomach clenched in uneasiness. Two women wheeling toddlers in matching red strollers passed without a glance. Three boys on bikes rode one behind the other on the sidewalk. On another day, it could have been a Norman Rockwell painting. But this wasn't an image on canvas. This was real.

The man from AAA told me the tire had been slashed.

"Are you sure?" I asked, as he reached into the trunk hatch for my spare.

"I'm afraid so. Funny, though—I don't see this kind of thing around here."

Where was everyone when the goon was slashing, sending me a message to leave the town alone? John D'Orfini had the answer. The town was in church at St. Catherine's, at the funeral mass for Father Delbarton, who had been the pastor for over thirty-two years.

"A perfect time to slash a tire, I guess?" I asked John D'Orfini.

You might think I would have been calling the detective by his first name by now, but whenever I thought of him or saw him, his full name was what slid into my brain or fell from my mouth. Saying his first name aloud without attaching it to his last was like wearing one shoe.

"What better time to commit a crime when everyone you know is praying for the soul of a priest?" he said with a smile.

Would Vinni have been scared if we had walked out of a store together only to find our car damaged? Would she have held my hand? Worried that she was in danger?

No. No. No.

Vinni was never scared.

She wasn't that girl.

She held my hand when she wanted to get closer. That's all it was.

ى

I SHOULD HAVE cared who slashed my tire, but I didn't. What haunted me was *why*. Why would someone come after me like this? A note tucked under my windshield wiper, threatening me to stop stirring up a bad memory, would have sufficed. The town's tolerance was waning, not because—and I can say this now—they were indifferent, but because they seemed to be ashamed of a bad thing happening where they lived. I might as well have been dressed in black from head to toe each time I stepped foot over the town line. No one in Spring Haven wanted to be reminded that a little girl had disappeared from the beach where other kids built sandcastles.

TEN

JOHN D'ORFINI TRAVELED TO THE CITY ONE SATURDAY afternoon in December.

"I'll take the train from Spring Haven. I'm not a city driver. Take me around with you on your walks."

"I walk everywhere, you know. I don't stop at the light. I just switch direction."

"That's fine. Just take me with you."

I walked all over the city. I told myself I had to keep moving to avoid drowning inside my emotions. I walked from TriBeCa, where the empty hole from 9/11 reigned over the dead, and across Broadway into the edge of Greenwich Village. I walked to the Museum of Modern Art, where I took the escalator to the sixth-floor photography exhibit to stare at the faces hung on the wall. I sipped tea in the sculpture garden at the Metropolitan Museum of Art on Fifth Avenue, and afterward I walked to St. Patrick's Cathedral to pray. As large as it was, the cathedral had become a haven. I purchased a pair of rosary beads in the gift shop and created a ritual in which, each night, I kissed the cross and folded the beads and laid them in a loop under my pillow. Sometimes I held the rosary between my palms and fell asleep, only to find it knotted in a loose ball near my feet in the morning.

The Cathedral provided a safe place for me to be alone, unlike my apartment, where Vinni's life hung suspended each time I turned the key.

ఎ

I STOPPED IN at St. Patrick's Cathedral on the day I was to meet John D'Orfini. This time, I sat on the side, to the left of the middle aisle. If praying is just words, scrambled and fragmented, then I was a master at it. The light from outside shone through the stained-glass windows and rested on my lower left arm. I walked up the side aisle and stopped at the statue of Elizabeth Sexton Seton. The artist had carved a stone child with her arms wrapped around the woman's hips. Her head was nestled inside the folded stone fabric. The candles shone brightly in the shadows of the cathedral. For a few seconds—that's all it was—I pretended nothing could hurt me in this sacred place. I reached inside my purse to pull out a few singles to buy a prayer. Instead of holding two $1 bills, I had a $100 bill and a single. My first response was to slip the large bill back into my wallet, but something made me stop. The idea of buying a slew of prayers at one time struck me. I dropped the $100 into the tiny collection box in the center of the votive candles. I calculated that this amount of money could buy me a world of praying time.

Here it is, God. Make something happen.

I met John D'Orfini outside Penn Station at Thirty-Second Street and Seventh Avenue. As I approached the corner, I saw his face turned in the opposite direction. I recognized the bulk of his neck. His full head of hair amused me. It was shaved close at the back of his neck, and the top had a wild curse about it. His shoulders were wide enough for someone like me to lean into. I was glad he had moved away from the crowd of people lined up at the taxi line. Smart, I thought, especially for an out-of-town cop.

We headed north and crosstown toward Fifth Avenue. As John D'Orfini strolled, I told him to pick up the pace.

"You're too slow. I can't walk like that."

"Like what?"

"Like a tourist."

"Well, I guess I am, aren't I?"

I hadn't warmed to John D'Orfini since I had broken down in the car on the highway. We never talked about it. He continued to call me Maddy. It didn't matter until later on, when I liked the way he said it.

He asked questions about gridlock and crime. I answered in sentences without adjectives, but mostly we walked in silence.

John D'Orfini broke through the noise of the street. "I thought walkers had fancy sneakers or special outdoor shoes. What are you doing walking in boots?"

I shrugged away my answer. I don't think he wanted one anyway. For the first time, I noticed how out of place he seemed in the city. He belonged where there was a body of water, a fishing pole, and a sauté pan.

For sixteen months, I'd been traveling down to Spring Haven. I wondered why John D'Orfini wanted to see me here in New York. The year before, the FBI had come to check out the living arrangements that Vinni and I shared. The head guy on the team asked me how long I had been living in the city. When I said, "Seven years," he nodded. I read into it that he liked the place Vinni and I called home.

John D'Orfini and I stopped for a coffee and a chocolate at La Maison du Chocolat on Madison Avenue.

"What's your favorite candy?" he asked.

"Coconut or dark chocolate truffles."

He bought one of each and picked out a chocolate-covered peanut turtle for himself. Together, we carried our candies on small napkins and sat down in the cherrywood café three steps up from the main selling floor.

"Why did you really come?" I asked.

"There's something I want to tell you." The coconut stopped going down as I chewed the same tiny strips slowly and carefully. With difficulty, I swallowed without taking my eyes off John D'Orfini.

"It's Vinni, isn't it?" I waited a full ten seconds and then said, "You know something." I put my coffee cup down. People around me slowed. The waiter handed the check to the couple next to us in what seemed like a painstakingly long sweep of the hand. The weight of the air around me hung heavy.

"We found a connection to Hilda in Brooklyn." He spoke slowly, saying each word so I could hear its fullness. "Rudy was supposed to be part of it. His death was a shock, but it didn't stop the plan."

"What plan?"

The light in the café dimmed.

Blue slipped through the window.

My hand touched his wrist, and, to my surprise, I kept it there too long.

"Hilda and Rudy lived in Spring Haven, but no one really knew them. From what we know, you and Vinni were the only ones they had to their home that summer. They kept to themselves."

I remembered the look that had passed between Hilda and Rudy when Vinni and I had eaten dinner with them that summer. Had they been planning something as we sat there?

"That's not a crime," I said.

"Right, but taking Vinni is." John D'Orfini picked up his coffee but didn't drink any. "They had friends in Brooklyn," he said.

"So why did they live in Spring Haven?"

"Rudy had retired from teaching at Columbia University. Maybe they liked the ocean and the beach. We don't know.

There's a tight German community in Brooklyn. They protect their own."

I stood up and said, "I have to use the restroom."

A ray of hope flew inside me, and I wanted to sit with it alone. If Hilda was being protected, I believed Vinni was safe. I washed my hands and threw the drying towel into the wastebasket behind the swinging door and walked back to the table. I picked up my jacket. John D'Orfini stood at the cash register. "Let's walk some more," he said when I came up beside him.

"Is this all you have?" I found it hard to believe that he couldn't have told me this over the phone. "What's the 'connection' you're talking about? I want names. Who are these people?" I tossed questions at him like a kid throwing darts at one of those boardwalk games where you know you have a slim-to-zero chance at winning.

"These things take time." We headed north toward Central Park, walking at a faster pace than before. We stayed on Madison Avenue.

"It's not enough. I want more." A hundred dollars was a large sum for unanswered prayers. The quiet voice I had used in the café fell away. I picked up speed until I was almost running. John D'Orfini kept up with me. He must have known what was coming, but he said nothing, so I jumped ahead.

"Things are taking too long. This isn't enough. I don't give a shit if I have to do it on my own." I breathed in the air faster and faster. People passed by me in a blur.

"Maddy, don't get more involved. Let us do our job." He cleared his throat and brought his hands up to his mouth. Fingers curled around an imaginary microphone by his lips.

I stopped short between Sixty-First and Sixty-Second Streets and turned to face him. For a moment, I didn't speak. Tears filled my eyes.

"I *am* involved. I'm Vinni's mother." The words came from

a place so deep and strong, I hardly recognized my own voice. "Go home," I said. "Go back to your little town with your safe little desk and your safe little nothing life." He took a step closer, but I moved away from him, yelling, "Go home!" as I turned and ran.

My heavy boots hit my ankles with every stride, making my skin raw and red.

"Wait a minute." John D'Orfini grabbed my elbow from behind and slowed me.

I screamed in his face. "You want me to be *uninvolved*. This is what you want?" People stepped around us on the sidewalk as I shouted.

Is this really why the detective had traveled all the way to the city from Spring Haven? To tell me to back off? Twice, he had mentioned how he'd run into Katherine Mulvey, who owned the religious gift shop in Spring Haven, and how she always asked about the investigation. Maybe he had come to the city to search my face for clues as he told me about the Brooklyn connection. Maybe he felt sorry for me and his pity was what made me see him differently. Whatever it was, he gave me a slight opening and I let loose.

"What aren't you telling me?" I beat the words on his chest with my fists. John D'Orfini grabbed my arms. "You're hurting me." Even as I said it, I knew it wasn't true.

"I don't want to hurt you. I want to help."

Maybe it was the gentle tone of his voice, but something inside me broke.

❧

AS I CLIMBED the stairs to my apartment, I sank into thinking how the world could get along just fine without me. I continued up the stairs but stopped when I heard an odd sound. I slipped behind the bend of the wall. I stayed still. I watched and listened. Dusk shadowed the hallway from the window high near the ceiling. Particles of dust danced in the lit space. Had it flown up from where Evelyn swept the mat outside her apartment door?

I heard her cry as she swept. Back and forth, harder and harder, as if she intended to rip the heart out of the dust hidden deep inside the mat's brushed weave, Evelyn swung the broom. I scraped my foot along the edge of the step to make a noise.

Evelyn looked up from the floor. "Maddy dear, you look like part of the wall. What are you doing down there?"

"I'm sorry, I didn't mean to startle you," I said, as I stepped closer and noticed the wet on her cheeks.

"It's nothing."

Isn't that what everyone says? It's nothing.

"Can you come in for a spell?" Evelyn asked, rubbing her fingers back and forth under her nose. Then she fanned them out across both cheeks to rub away the wet.

The light in the hallway to her apartment dimmed in the afternoon. "Don't you find it dark in here?" I asked, as I followed her into her apartment.

"Makes us appreciate the light all the more," she said, without turning around.

I walked over to the window. I had come inside to get away from what was outside, but I still yearned for what I could see below—ordinary people with ordinary lives. Was Evelyn sweeping to distract herself from something extraordinary? Was she beating the mat to tamp down something from bubbling up, only to push it further away to a deeper place? Often I found her sweeping or cleaning the top of the kitchen counter over and over, until it shone more brightly than it had the day before. When I asked her why she had five bottles of Windex stored in the cabinet underneath her sink, she simply said, "I like to make things shine."

"I saw John D'Orfini today," I said.

"I know. He called me when you ran away and left him at the park. He was worried about you."

John D'Orfini had talked to Evelyn many times over the past months. He knew I considered her more than a casual friend. In a way, she had become a mother replacement. My mother had died when I was a sophomore in college. She had slipped into her black Cadillac with the cream-colored seats in the closed garage and turned on the gas. The straps of her full-length slip had fallen off her shoulders when my dad found her slumped over the steering wheel.

When he called, I was finishing a container of Chinese vegetables on the bed in my dorm one block from Washington Square Park.

"You need to come home. Your mother died today," he said.

When I hung up, I called my best friend, Kay. She was on her way to class. Boston College. History of American Politics of the Twentieth Century. A precursor to her political career as assistant US attorney in Manhattan.

"Kay, it's my mother. She's . . ." I waited. Then I said it. "Dead."

A hush lay between us.

"Can you come home? Can you please?" I whispered.

Kay gasped. "Oh, God. Shit. I'm so sorry, Maddy."

The following summer, as we sat on the floor on the screened porch of her parents' house, I talked about the garage, the fumes, and my father's call. Kay listened.

"She was sick," Kay said. She held a Newport between her second and third fingers. "You know this, right?"

"Yeah." Then I rolled over and laid my head in her lap and

cried. Kay had seen me cry before—like the time in high school when I couldn't stop scratching my skin when my mother had washed my father's and my clothes together with the fiberglass curtains from the living room. There were other times—times that revolved around heartaches—from middle school through college. But then I met Steve and I wanted Kay to like him. "You're lucky. He seems like a good guy," she said after the first time we went out together in the West Village.

You'd think a friend like this would be a friend forever, but you would be wrong.

I never saw the signs.

I hadn't thought about why Steve worked late on four consecutive Friday nights into Saturday, showing up at noon, calling behind him, "I'm getting a shower." Working late was what he did. I thought I got it. I didn't know that Kay had found someone to sleep with whose socks I kicked out of my way each morning on my way to the bathroom.

୧

EIGHTEEN MONTHS HAD passed since Vinni's disappearance before I saw Kay. She had been following the case, and we had talked briefly twice. But as a friend who betrayed me twelve years after my mother died, Kay knew me better than anyone. That was why she had stayed away and waited for me to call and ask to meet. We hadn't seen each other in four years.

Kay was someone I had walked to school with since fourth grade and whom I had relied on when I couldn't figure out what had made my mother crazy. Her one-month affair with Steve ended years of shared cigarettes.

"I need to see you, too," she said before I hung up.

It was my idea to meet at St. Patrick's Cathedral.

"Maddy?"

I looked up and straight into my best friend's eyes. In four years, no one had taken Kay's place. She looked the same. What made Kay stand out was her posture. I never knew anyone who could sink into a soft-cushioned couch and not slouch. The first time I saw her in a courtroom, I noticed her shoulders. Tall and erect, Kay pulled her five-foot-seven-inch frame into the room, dropping her shoulder blades into perfect alignment. Her hips had the right amount of sexuality as she walked back and forth in front of a jury. Rifling through a mirage of thoughts, I let them go as quickly as they appeared. I clung to the only one that made sense.

I needed her.

I slid over in the pew and made room.

"I'm sorry, Maddy. I'm so sorry. . . . Please stop hating me. I want to help you. Let me. Please." Kay faced me and took both my hands in hers. She wore a thick sterling silver band on the index finger of her left hand. Her hair looked the same: black streaked with chestnut, cropped close like a cap. She was a forever kind of beauty. Her skin glowed in the dark of the cathedral. Her voice had always sounded like it came from deep in her throat. Seductive even when she was a teen, when boys looked down and fantasized.

Kay cried. I spoke first.

"You know, I wanted to see you cry. I did. But I don't want these tears to be for us. We don't have time. If these tears are for Vinni, I want them and I want you, too. But if they're for what happened between you and Steve, I swear I can't take it, Kay. I swear."

"Maddy, no . . . no . . . no. I don't want this."

Confusion pressed against my chest as I shot up to leave the pew. Kay grabbed my wrist with a cool hand and pulled me down.

"Listen to me. I know what I did is unconscionable."

During our brief phone calls, neither one of us had mentioned Steve.

Kay released her grip on my wrist. She curled her hand around mine. "I know I don't deserve your friendship. I don't even deserve to be sitting here talking to you. But I want to help you. I've been following the investigation."

Then she told me.

As assistant US attorney, she had been talking to John D'Orfini since Vinni had first disappeared. Her instincts told her she could follow the case better if she talked to John D'Orfini along with reading the documents the FBI provided. She told him we had been friends since we'd been children living in New Jersey.

"Let me help you," Kay pleaded. People in the pews around us began to notice. Her voice grew louder as she tightened her grip on my hands. My skin hurt. With a heart worn out from fear, I didn't have a choice. As tears fell, I nodded and leaned my body against Kay's. It seemed natural for her to lean against me. Together we created our own pieta.

$\backsim$

KAY LATER CONFESSED to me, after several glasses of pinot noir, that the month she had been with Steve had been the most confusing time of her life. After I heard this, I stored it away. We had been talking about the mayoral election, avoiding anything personal, until I couldn't take it and blurted out, "How did it happen?"

All she said was, "I don't know. Maybe I just wanted to feel something."

This was unusual for Kay to admit. Ever since I'd known

her, she had been the sure one. The one who never fell off her bike.

"Why Steve? Why did it have to be him?"

"I knew you didn't want him anymore," she said.

And she was right. Pure Kay.

ELEVEN

I HAD COME DOWNSTAIRS TO EVELYN'S APARTMENT TO learn more about the light-and-shadow technique she was working on. Not that I acknowledged why I had come. She had scribbled a note—"Something to study here. Let me know what you think"—and left it outside my door with a book about the Renaissance artists. As I flipped through the pages, I kept coming across the word *chiaroscuro* to describe how light and dark implied depth and volume. I stopped at the page discussing "black and pronounced shadows." Another emphasized the importance of the study of contrast—the value between light and dark—in composition. For a while, the book held my attention.

I knew Evelyn was trying to breathe life back into my existence. I believed she didn't give a damn whether the book made sense. Light and dark demanded stark choices. Sometimes she spent days upon days shading what she had already painted. I wondered if this was her way of adding possibilities to what caught the eye.

I DIDN'T LIKE John D'Orfini bothering Evelyn.

"He's worried about you, that's all. Besides, dear, that's his job," Evelyn said. "To ask questions."

He and the FBI had talked to her many times. If I had been more alive, I might have noticed the slight wrinkle deepen further between Evelyn's eyebrows when she spoke. I might have realized a sudden thickness had caught in her throat, and I might have caught how her third finger crossed over her fourth on her right hand, sliding it up and down as if she were stroking a child's cheek. Instead, how I responded had nothing to do with Evelyn or John D'Orfini. "Vinni loved the color blue. She used to tell me she would have a blue garden when she was older. 'Blue flowers,' she said. 'That's all I want.'"

I was hungry—and Evelyn *knew* it. Maybe that was why I kept dropping by and watching her. Sometimes she'd stop, step away from the easel, smile at me, and say one word. "There." How could I not smile back at her?

                        ℰ

I WANTED TO know more about Hilda's connection in Brooklyn, and John D'Orfini wasn't talking much. We spoke two days after our walk in New York. Both of us were polite. I made the call on Tuesday following a Saturday visit. John D'Orfini gave me one more piece of information. (He had two, but he kept one for himself.) On a slow drive by Hilda and Rudy's, he had seen a white van parked in front, with EXPRESS KLEANERS painted on both sides. A young man was unloading an armload of clothes bagged in plastic. It was a yearly sweep designed by the owners of the cleaners to deliver items forgotten by customers. John D'Orfini stopped the surprised driver, flashed his badge, and took the clothes back to the station. In Rudy's trouser back pocket—the one with the buttoned flap—was a receipt for an almond horn, one cherry-filled pastry, two coffees, and four strudels. The top of the receipt gave the name, address, and phone number of the bakery in Brooklyn.

"We're not sure who we're dealing with here. You've got to sit tight," said John D'Orfini.

"The name. I want the name of that bakery."

John D'Orfini let out a deep exhalation but then said, "Mueller's. A German couple named Hannah and George Mueller own it . . . on Ninth Street at Sixth Avenue." He hesitated. "Don't go alone. I'll take you myself. Maddy?"

I hung up after I heard what I needed. I could be there in less than thirty minutes on the subway.

ら

THE R TRAIN shook from side to side as I sat staring straight ahead. I studied the map above the door listing the stops, looking for Ninth Street. I hadn't been to Brooklyn in over four years, since I had attended a coworker's baby's christening in Brooklyn Heights. Park Slope was supposed to be different, although both boasted diversified neighborhoods with expensive brownstones and hard-to-find parking.

I got off at Ninth Street after asking a teen with a baby face sitting across from me, with three silver rings in his left nostril, if the stop was close to Sixth Avenue.

"Turn left at the top of the stairs," he said, in the voice of an altar boy.

I followed the directions and counted the blocks—two—from the subway station before I turned left down Sixth Avenue. The brownstones in the residential area were old but well kept. Handsome gas lamps stood in front of the brick homes, like guards keeping watch over the residents. I hustled past patches of grass, hanging ivy, and heavy wood doors.

I thought about Hilda. Had she brought Vinni here, less than a hundred miles from the quiet coastal shore town where I thought the world was perfect?

Mueller's Bakery had a small glass front with its name displayed in ivory-colored letters on a dark green awning. I pushed open the door and stepped out of the way of people leaving with bags filled with fresh scones and macaroon tea cookies. Clean ivory-colored walls set the backdrop for the wooden serving piece standing in the far left corner, open to customers to help themselves to coffee and herbal teas. Scents of almond and melted butter on baked apples hung in the air. How could a place that smelled this good be dangerous?

The light caught my attention as I looked at the muffins in the glass case. I had begun to notice slim strips of light in my life: on the sidewalk, in St. Patrick's Cathedral, and up and down the walls of tall buildings pointing toward heaven.

To the right of the front door were two pub tables. Café tables hugged the windows. Mini-crystal chandeliers lent an old-world sophistication. The dark wooden coffee bar stood against the wall with carved fleur-de-lis on the bottom cabinet doors.

Three little girls sat with their father around one of the café tables while I waited in line. The youngest claimed her dad's lap. As he held a chocolate-frosted doughnut in his hand, the little girl wrapped her fingers around his and bit into the Bavarian cream filling. Some of it spilled onto her dad's fingers, but he ignored it. The girls looked to be under nine years old. The tallest and, I assumed, the oldest was serious-looking, with a slight scowl held in place between her brows. The middle child—about six—fixed on her chocolate croissant as she tore the bread apart, making little dough figures with the fresh insides. The toddler, not quite two, was the princess of the three. She held her dad's attention, even while her sisters talked to him. I watched them all with an up-front ache while waiting in line. Two people, both women holding on to tiny hands, stood ahead of me.

Finally, it was my turn.

"Are you the owner?" I asked the older woman behind the glass case closest to the register.

"Yes, I'm Hannah," she said.

"I . . . I wonder," I stumbled. My eyes blinked more quickly. Should I keep my missing daughter to myself until I found out if the bakery had something to do with what had happened to Vinni?

"Can I help you?" Hannah asked again, sounding tired but courteous.

"Yes, please, may I have a scone for here?"

"Anything to drink?"

"Tea. Thank you."

Hannah reached into the case, her fleshy arm waving slightly in front of her. She grabbed a cellophane sheet and picked up a scone closest to the case's sliding door.

"Just came out of the oven twenty minutes ago. George's specialty, you know," she said, placing the scone on a small white ceramic dish and working the register without looking up at me.

My insides shook. I looked around, pretending to be casual.

"How long have you been here?" I asked.

"Fifty-two years ago, we came over from a small town in Germany. My George and I have been baking ever since."

"Hi, Hannah," a voice called, as the door opened. A young girl in her early twenties walked over to the coffee bar, picked up a large paper cup, and held it under the silver urn that read HAZELNUT COFFEE.

I took my scone and headed to the hot-water urn. I listened to the sounds around me, wondering if Vinni had heard the same ones, smelled the same smells, and bitten into a doughnut like the one the little girl feasted on while she sat on her dad's lap.

My cell phone rang, and John D'Orfini's name popped up on the screen. I thought about not answering.

"Don't worry. I'm sitting here quietly. I'm okay," I said.

"Why didn't you wait for me to go with you?"

"I told you. I'm okay. Really. It's all okay." I kept my voice low, talking into my lap at first, and then, gradually, as John D'Orfini spoke, I lifted my head. The three blond sisters had gone. Half of the chocolate doughnut remained on its plate.

"Did you speak with Hannah or George?" John D'Orfini asked.

"You know who they are. You know a lot more, don't you?" I asked.

"Call me when you leave the bakery. Please don't talk to anyone there. Don't ask questions yet. Promise me you won't do this. Not just yet. Promise me."

"I can't do that." I hung up. The line at the cash register had dwindled down to one lone, older man. Waiting would do nothing.

I walked toward Hannah. She looked up with a smile. Her face was old, full of lived-in wrinkles around her eyes. Her white hair hung back in a loose bun sitting off-center, to the right of her neck. Tiny wisps loosened from hours of a long workday flew around her face. Her waist was thick, to match her fingers. She wore a white-bibbed apron with her full name printed in the left corner by the strap.

Hannah Mueller.

"Excuse me, Hannah?" I wanted her attention, but she looked up casually, unaware that what was to come might change my life and hers. "My name is Maddy. I have a daughter who's missing."

Hannah stopped putting the macaroon cookies in the case and looked up at me. She rested the long baking sheet on the glass countertop. The wrinkles at the corners of her eyes hardened into deeper crevices.

I caught my breath.

"Have you seen her?" I asked. I held up a picture of Vinni. Already it was sixteen months old. Vinni was sitting with her knees tucked under her on the beach blanket at Spring Haven, wearing a yellow two-piece bathing suit. Her sun-streaked hair hung loose around her face.

Hannah walked from around the counter.

"Let's sit," she said.

The bakery was quiet, but a strip of light held steady in front of the glass cases.

I followed Hannah to a table in the far corner, closest to the kitchen. I put the picture of Vinni on the table, and she looked at it without picking it up.

"Your daughter is a beautiful child. You must love her very much."

"Have you seen her?" I repeated, as I leaned in across the table.

"No, I haven't. At least, not that I can remember. So many beautiful little girls come into this bakery. I don't think I can help you. I wish I could."

"The police think a woman named Hilda took my child."

Maybe I wanted it so badly that I thought I saw a hint of recognition in Hannah's eyes flicker in and out when I said Hilda's name.

"You are from Germany, right?" I asked, knowing the answer.

"Yes. This is true."

"And you have many friends from Germany who now live in the neighborhood." This wasn't a question, but Hannah nodded anyway.

"Yes. Yes. This is my home. It has been for over fifty years. But this is very sad for you. Yes? And you want me to tell you something that will help you find your Vinni."

My mind skipped. My ears closed and opened. Words I should have heard went missing. In the distance, a drumbeat.

"I've never seen your child. The police, they must be helping you . . . yes?" Her voice owned strong traces of Germany.

Hannah stayed calm as I lost words that had been pounding in my head for almost two years.

A man and a woman entered the bakery and stood quietly in front of the cookies. The man said something about how many pounds, and the woman looked over in my direction. Hannah's chair made a screeching noise as she moved away from the table and stood to face me.

"Please . . . I wish I knew something to help you, but, as you can see, I must work now. I am sorry—so sorry."

I had failed. John D'Orfini had warned me.

I stayed seated for a few more minutes, sipping the decaffeinated tea from the thick ceramic mug. The roasted liquid slid down my throat. Its heat reminded me I was alive. Other than that, I felt swept away by my own ineptness. I had thought all I needed was an opening—one innocent remark—and then I'd be okay. If John D'Orfini had been trying to teach me something, then maybe I had learned it. I couldn't just plow into a situation. Hell, was I really calling Vinni's disappearance a *situation*?

AS I WALKED away from the bakery with my head down, I bumped into a man standing about thirty yards away from Mueller's front door. "Whoa, leeettle lady," he said. "Slow down." He emphasized the first syllable of *leettle*, as if a thousand letter *e*'s were strung together. "Excuse me," I said, as I rushed past. He tipped his straw fedora, an odd accessory for a man wearing jeans and a black T-shirt with "Harley" scripted in green across the front. As I moved past him, the smell of an unfiltered cigarette reminded me of a guy I dated as an NYU freshman, who had a weird allegiance to thin brown cigarettes from Turkey. Their lasting aroma combined the smell of burnt toast with late-harvested corn husks. Not that I described it this way. My ex-boyfriend did.

I retraced my steps to the subway. Not more than an hour had passed. Oxygen shriveled up in my lungs as I walked into the dark subway station. The people on the train were different, but the same colors and smells permeated the atmosphere. Where could I put the hot vomit baking inside my stomach? I needed air. I wasn't getting enough in the belly of the city.

I could hear voices from behind me getting louder. I turned around in my seat and saw four men moving slowly down the aisle among the standing passengers holding on to the silver bars. They were singing a favorite song of mine, "Up on the Roof," a cappella. The four were a disjointed group of short, tall, and skinny men, dressed in what looked like rags from a Police Athletic Club clothes bin. They were probably in their fifties and older, but the wild thing about it was that they could sing. They could really sing.

The lead guy, the one with the mouthful of missing teeth, wore a black suede cowboy hat. In the gut of the city's belly, they harmonized high and low, switching off solo parts like they were playing Vegas center stage. As they moved closer to my seat, I steered my eyes away from them not to draw attention to myself. Seasoned subway riders know better than to make eye contact with strangers, especially those singing a cappella.

Just as the deep-voiced man hung onto the *ooouuuu* in *roof*, an explosion erupted in my head. I closed my eyes, fearing the loud howl might leak out into the aisle.

Jesus. Jesus. Jesus, I cried to myself. *Oh God. Jesus. What is wrong with me?* I rocked back and forth in my seat to the rhythm of the singing subway Motowners. My words fell in between theirs. Everything screeched to a halt in my head while I replayed the conversation with Hannah as we sat together at Mueller's. *Up on the roof*: the words provided a melodramatic background for my stunning realization. They shot up and down my spine, ripping me apart.

Hannah had called her Vinni. She had said Vinni's name without my telling her. I went over the conversation word by word, but I knew I was right. Hannah had recognized Vinni in the photo, and the flicker I had seen when I'd mentioned Hilda's name was real. She must have wondered why I didn't say anything. Why I didn't jump all over her. Why I left the bakery without dragging her out the door with me. John D'Orfini was right: I wasn't prepared for the hunt. I stayed on the train. Petrified.

TWELVE

HIS PRESENCE STARTLED ME. I HAD NO IDEA HOW LONG John D'Orfini had been standing by the console table to the left of the front door. I had just returned from a rainy walk downtown, past Union Square. The stone urns in front of the heavy doors drew me in every time I came home. In late spring, the landlord planted white narcissus. He faked the greens with plastic ivy, draping it over the edges. In summer, pink and white impatiens blossomed into voluminous domes.

"How long have you been here?" I asked, hoping John D'Orfini's voice would not match the conflicted look in his eyes.

"About forty-five minutes. Evelyn buzzed me in. I called her after you didn't answer your bell. She invited me upstairs, but I didn't want to intrude." He hesitated and looked away, like he was weighing his words before daring to say them out loud. "She cares a lot about you, Maddy."

"Come up." I cut him off midthought, brushed past him, and ran up the stairs.

He followed me in silence, except for the squeaky sound of his black Bostonian shoes. I unlocked the door to my apartment and pushed it wide open for John D'Orfini to walk in without hitting up against the coat rack to the right in the corner of the hallway. One of the best features of the apartment was the hallway. Vinni used to love sliding back and forth in her socks, pretending she was an acrobat on ice. Light fed through the three windows facing east in the living room. Without Vinni, her bedroom failed to reflect the northern light. Everything dimmed.

Besides the urns in front, what sold me on the apartment was that it was an elevator building and there were dark wood cabinets in the kitchen. I could fit a small table with three chairs in between the sink and the refrigerator.

Steve had wanted a doorman.

"Home means you eat in the kitchen, Steve," I said.

"Home means you have a doorman, babe," he shot back.

ᕋ

THE CREAM-COLORED walls throughout the apartment exuded silence. John D'Orfini stood at the edge of the kitchen.

"Can I get you something hot to drink?" I moved toward the stove and picked up the coffeepot, knowing that he never refused a cup of coffee.

"Sure," he said, and then added a "thanks" as a way of mending the anger he couldn't hide.

I opened the refrigerator and took out the ground coffee beans.

"Pretty empty refrigerator you've got there."

The almost full soyannaise jar stood isolated in the corner of the middle shelf. A package of newly opened gluten-free tortilla wraps—dry as shit—sat haplessly next to a pint of ruby-red strawberries. Dr. Goodman had encouraged me to eat the lush berry on days when I felt like I was walking in cement—when putting one foot in front of the other required herculean effort.

John D'Orfini took off his lined trench coat and laid it over the back of the kitchen chair. It was too big for his trim frame and looked like it belonged to another family. My apartment hadn't had a man's coat in it in over five years. The sleeves looked uncomfortable dangling off the chair, away from the buttons.

Finally, he spoke. "What happened at Mueller's? I need to know." The knot in my stomach tightened. His thick neck stood apart from years of working out in a paramilitary regimen.

"Nothing. I mean, well, yes. Something did happen." I turned around from the counter where I had plugged in the coffeemaker and faced John D'Orfini. The red light warned me that the water was getting hotter.

"Hannah has seen Vinni. I know it because she said her name—"

He cut me off.

"We—the FBI—have been watching Hannah and her husband, George, for a month now. I *planned* on telling you. You have a right to know, but I wanted to give you more information so you wouldn't jump to conclusions."

Is that what I've done? Jumped to a conclusion?

"So, my going to Mueller's was stupid? Is that what you're saying?" I stood up but dropped a bent knee on the chair, half balancing with my left arm on the chair's back.

"I'm saying be careful. I know you don't want me to tell you to back off, to stay away from the investigation, and I'm not going to do that. God knows, sometimes I've wanted to . . . to protect you. I just need you to listen to me when—"

"When you order me around like some child. When you tell me not to get *involved*. Okay, I get it. I do. But you can't keep information from me, because I'm going to find out. I went to Mueller's Bakery because I got sick of waiting. I don't know how to wait any longer."

I was tired and wet. I raised my hand for him not to speak. "Let me finish. Please," I said. If he had picked me up right then, I would have held on to him tight and stayed in his arms. All I wanted to do was rest.

But John D'Orfini did not pick me up.

I moved past him to the counter to the left of the sink, where I kept a pad and a mug filled with pens and pencils. I dropped my head into my hands. I could feel the tendons in the back of my neck stretch as I leaned lower into the cups of my palms.

"Give me a minute," I said.

John D'Orfini turned away and back again. "Where's the . . ."

"Bathroom's down the hall on the left," I said quietly.

I picked up a small, oval-shaped mirror tucked into the corner of the counter. It had been my mother's. The glass was centered among braided brass trim at least two inches thick. A long golden neck connected it to a pastel blue base with pink roses hand-painted by some obscure Frenchman whose name was signed across the bottom. My mother loved to pronounce it with an exaggerated French accent, rolling the *r*'s from deep inside her throat.

After she killed herself, all I wanted was the mirror. For years, it stayed in the bottom of a closet wherever I lived, but when I moved into the apartment with Steve, I put it in the kitchen, over the bread drawer. Vinni used to love to play with it. She'd pick it up and place it on the kitchen table at night when I was home in time to make dinner. With my back turned away from the table, I would hear her talk to her face. She told stories to the mirror, and I listened without her knowing it.

I wondered if my mother heard Vinni speak to the mirror.

Do people who kill themselves get a shot at heaven?

～

I SLICED A lemon and squeezed it into a mug of hot water. I heard the bathroom door open. When I looked up, I saw John

D'Orfini staring at a painting of mine of three women sitting at a café table in the middle of an urban street with cars pointed in every direction. "You've sure got a different way of seeing the world," he said, as he leaned back with his head resting comfortably against the wall.

He stood in the hallway as if he wanted me to come to him. An awkward silence floated between the two of us. "Are you still upset with me?" I asked, as I took slow steps in his direction, drying my hands on a dish towel. When I got close enough, I could smell the clean scent of his shirt.

"Tell me. Have I made things worse at Mueller's?" Tears— one at a time—fell down my cheeks and over my mouth.

I imagined that if I leaned in a bit more, the comfort of his chest would take my breath away. If he could, he would try to swallow my hurt. I was certain of it. My heart wanted to stay, but a sharp snap in my brain made me step back. We stood there, face to face, and said nothing. I broke the connection first.

John D'Orfini put his hands in his pockets like a boy. I wanted and I wanted, but I couldn't have what I wanted.

None of it.

"Tell me something about Vinni," he said. Silence passed between us. When I was ready, I started again.

"Vinni loved to play games."

"Describe one."

This was a different John D'Orfini.

"Look in the bread drawer," I said. I stood up, and John D'Orfini walked over and opened the drawer. "Where's the bread?" Laughing softly, he took out crayons of all sizes.

When I smiled back at him, I noticed the light from the one window shadowed the left side of his face. His eyes had softened. His cheeks flushed a bit at the top.

I explained.

"Vinni and I played a game where we made up names of new colored crayons: Apple Green, Dirty Beige, Yummy Lemon."

I told John D'Orfini how Vinni folded her lips one on top of the other when she was inside a thought. I told him how Vinni described the colors. "Baby's pink is clean, Mommy—like a baby, and shiny, too. But not too shiny—sort of just right. Perfect like a baby. You know, perfect like baby's feet."

The urgency in my voice replaced any leftover calm. "I have to keep watching everything for Vinni. I have to remember to tell her things I see when she comes back. She'll expect me to. She'll want to know what I saw when she wasn't with me."

John D'Orfini never took his eyes off me as I spoke. I studied the face behind the detective. "You're a good mother, Maddy. Don't forget it." He hesitated before he uttered, "Ever."

Something else was on his mind. As upset as he was that I had gone to Mueller's Bakery without him, I suspected there was another reason why he had hopped the train to the city and waited for me in the lobby of my building.

"You know Detective Geronimo?" John D'Orfini said. He poured himself a cup of coffee—his fifth of the day.

"Dennis?" Everyone called the full-bellied cop with the bad knees Geronimo. Although his last name had the uncommon distinction of being shared with the feared Apache leader of the nineteenth century, his first name rarely rolled off people's lips. *Dennis* couldn't top a name like Geronimo.

"What about him?" I asked.

"He's going to be in charge of the station for the next three months. I'll be away for some training." The blow came swiftly, like a medieval execution.

"No, no, no. Wait a second. You can't do this now," I groaned. "Geronimo? You want me to try to wake him up first when I talk to him?"

"Wait a minute. Dennis is a good guy. He's competent. He knows the file."

"How could he know the case as well as you?"

"It's just three months. And I'm not going to be far away. Quantico, Virginia, is just thirty-six miles outside of DC. I applied three years ago and was put on a wait list. An opening for a new outreach program in the community leadership development unit became available. It's a great opportunity."

"For you, maybe, Detective," I hurled back.

As much as I realized that John D'Orfini had traveled all the way to New York to tell me this in person, I hated the idea of his moving on like everyone else. Mother. Father. Steve. Who was next?

"Three months? Are you kidding? Are you telling me that Detective Geronimo is going to take over for you in Spring Haven for three whole months? I can't believe this."

"You've got a lot of people looking out for you. Kay is a top assistant US attorney—one of the best in the country."

No matter what you're told, to lose at something hurts. I had come to count on John D'Orfini's cool sense of calm and his gentle wit, even when those of us around him were frothing at the mouth like canines. He was the one I called when I needed a comforting voice.

"Geronimo will hand over the reins when I return from training," he said. "In the meantime, you can count on him while I'm gone. It might be hard to reach me."

THIRTEEN

STEVE CALLED ON A SNOWY AFTERNOON IN MARCH AND asked me to meet him the next day in the city. I had seen him the month before, when he had come to New York on business, and I knew he was flying into Manhattan a few weeks later. Although we talked almost every day in the beginning, by March of the second year, Steve had lost faith. It must have destroyed him, but I was too wrapped up in my own grief to notice any change other than that his hair, now speckled with gray, had grown over his custom-tailored shirt collar.

"You have to face what's happened, Maddy."

Steve looked ragged and tired, like an abandoned child.

"This is my life. Finding Vinni *is* my life," I said. I sat across from Steve in a new bistro that had opened in time for a Valentine's Day launch. Steve's formerly athletic body sagged as he leaned across the table. His jacket fell off his shoulders, leaving the seams riding at the tips of his biceps. His eyes—what had drawn me to him in the beginning—looked covered with a thin sheet of plastic, worn from hours fixed on the computer screen, trawling the Internet, responding to sightings of Vinni. We had been a good match when we both believed we could find answers to all our questions. But when faced with the biggest question of all, we failed to console each other.

I wanted the lunch to end and was about to ask for the check, when Steve brought up the topic of money. He knew I had taken a leave of absence from my job at the magazine and was freelancing.

Steve persisted. "When are you going back to work full-time?"

"I don't know." I caught the attention of the waiter and lifted my coffee cup. Our small table, tucked in the corner by the window, faced East Twelfth Street.

"I'm not giving up. Vinni is out there." The waiter returned with a hot pot of coffee. I stopped speaking. Steve sat back and looked away. When he turned to face me, he spoke in a hoarse whisper.

"She was mine, too."

"Was?"

"I know you think I didn't love her enough."

When Vinni was born, Steve had tried to keep things as they had been. Sunday brunches in the West Village with the *New York Times* in tow got complicated with a child in a stroller who cried and needed to be fed. When I'd snuggle her into my lap, away from the confines of a harness, he'd raise his gaze above the real estate section and say, "You spoil her."

"Steve," I interrupted, but he spoke on top of me.

"You love too big. There isn't room for the rest of us."

"Don't tell me that I don't love 'right.'" My voice rose higher.

"I'm not getting into this," Steve mumbled, as he moved his chair away from the table.

Both of us stopped speaking. Neither of us wanted to bring up old pain. Steve looked down. For a moment, I thought I might see him cry for the first time, but he stayed in that position until I reached over to touch his hand. He moved back with a jerk that was more like a shake, as if flicking off any remnant of feeling that we might once have shared. Then he spoke.

"*My* daughter's gone, too. All the police and the FBI know is that someone named Hilda possibly took her somewhere. That's it. That's all we've got." He cocked his head. "I'm a realist," he said.

"Shut up!" I couldn't bear the finality in his tone. I refused. "I will never—*never*—stop believing that Vinni is alive," I cried. Exhaustion made me want to curl up inside the sleeves of my coat.

"I hear her. She speaks to me at night when I put my head on the pillow. I dream of scooping her up in my arms."

I stopped myself. I went to the end of my thought, leaving out the middle of a recurring dream of faces and babies and distorted figures in milk bottles.

"She's okay because she knows I'm coming. I'm going to find her. She expects me to—"

Steve interrupted, "You're not the only one who wants her back."

I got up to leave the table.

"Sit down," he said firmly. I hesitated for a few seconds, but then I sat back down. Steve cleared his throat and did this nervous twitch with his lips.

"I've met someone," he said, as he looked away at the cold outside.

What should I have said? "Congratulations"? Or, "I'm happy for you"? Or ask him if he thought she faked an orgasm when his hand slowed down?

An involuntary sigh—something audible—came out of my mouth and chest.

"When? I mean . . . how did you meet her?"

"She's a journalist in San Francisco. After Vinni . . . well, she did a story."

"What kind of story?" I lowered my arms on the table and

sank my shoulders. Their roundness shrouded the cold omelet on my plate.

"It was a feature for the holidays. At first I wasn't sure I wanted to do it, but one day Gina just showed up at my office."

Gina, I thought. Short for Regina, as in Salve Regina, *Mater Misericordiae*. Prayer to the Virgin Mary, meaning, "Hail, holy queen, Mother of Mercy." We used to sing it every first Friday of the month when both the elementary and high schools attended Mass.

"Are you trying to tell me something?" I asked.

Steve cleared his throat, took a quick glance outside, as if the gray might have disappeared, and said, "I know the timing isn't perfect." Then he blurted, "We're getting married."

The omelet churned and rumbled inside. Not enough seconds to digest between verbal hits. The one thing I did not want to do was throw up.

"Now? When?"

"We haven't set a date. I just wanted you to know."

I started singing, *Salve Regina, Mater Misericordiae* in my head. I added drums, a cymbal, and a tambourine for background noise. Marriage meant the possibility of children. Did Steve think he could replace Vinni?

"I guess I'm supposed to be happy for you, aren't I?" I said, with a lopsided smile. I wondered why we couldn't both be happy at the same time. Was it even possible? I reached for my coat, hanging off my chair, and drew it closer around my shoulders. A cool breeze coming from somewhere stung my neck. Being alone wasn't something I thought about when I was growing up. I believed people took care of each other the way my father took care of my mother.

Salve Regina, Mater Misericordiae. I sang it in my head one more time.

FOURTEEN

I TURNED ON THE COMPUTER IN THE MIDDLE OF THE night when I couldn't sleep. Steve and I used to argue about the location of the desktop computer. "It shouldn't be in the bedroom," I said. "It's going to remind us both of work. Isn't a bedroom supposed to be about pleasure?"

When he left, I never got around to removing it. I avoided the website he had set up almost two years ago to help find Vinni.

Why did I avoid the website? Every sighting posted had been a false lead. All 287 of them. And that gets pretty damn sorry. Whatever possessed me to check the site could be summed up only as an invitation from the gods. One lone comment had come in earlier in the day. A female from the town of Canandaigua in the Finger Lakes in upstate New York wrote: "There's an older woman staying down the block with a young child. Both fit the description. Check out 73 Greens Lane. I live three doors down. I'm no snoop. Just a civilian doing her duty. Janice"

Steve had programmed the site so that it fell into a "read" column after he opened up the comment. So far, it hadn't been read. I looked at the computer screen.

At first, I dismissed it. Turned off the computer and sat in the dark. If I had smoked, I would have exhaled exotic circles. I would have done anything to drive my mind somewhere else other than Canandaigua. Instead, I turned the computer back on, printed the message, and pressed DELETE.

THE NEXT DAY, Kay called as I stood in the kitchen, drinking a glass of orange juice.

"I'm late. I can't talk," I said. I couldn't get Janice of Canandaigua out of my head.

Since the dinner at her home, Kay and I had gotten together a few more times. Each occasion was easier, each conversation reminiscent of the friendship we once shared. When she asked me to meet her in front of Bloomingdale's to help her select a cocktail dress for a political fund-raiser, I suspected she was trying to regain the comfort of being together that we had lost. I agreed, even though I knew she didn't need my approval on the silk sensation that I helped zip her into in the dressing room.

"I've got a feeling," Kay said, as she shimmied the dress down another half inch, "you've got something on your mind. Don't forget, we've been friends a long time. The tips of your ears are red, the way they always got in high school when you were hiding something." I reached my hand up to my ear where it folded like a knit hem. I felt the heat.

"You're right. I'm restless. I miss John D'Orfini handling the case."

I HAD SPENT two days in Spring Haven with Geronimo.

With John D'Orfini in Quantico, I knew I should have told Detective Geronimo about the e-mail I had deleted. I held back. Trusting wasn't easy. I was going to Canandaigua on a tip from someone named Janice about whom, although she said she was not a snoop, I had my doubts. Each time I took a step, I questioned how far I would go. Who surfs the Internet, looking for missing-person sites? Lonely people. Sick people. People who raise too many dogs in an apartment and wonder why it smells. Either Janice was one of these people, or she was someone who had stumbled upon the right site and would join me for Thanksgiving dinner for the rest of Vinni's and my life.

Geronimo surprised me. I had driven down to Spring Haven and dropped in on the detective while he was in the middle of his lunch. As soon as I saw the fried chicken in a red plastic basket with fries piled on the side, I apologized for the interruption.

"No problem, Ms. Stewart. I was just about to put the rest away for a snack later in the afternoon," Geronimo said, as he licked his fingers and then folded and wiped them inside a paper towel. "So, what brings you down here today?" His smile exposed a piece of chicken skin nestled between his bottom teeth. "It's too darn cold for a walk on the boardwalk," he said.

"All those sightings of Vinni on the website. What do you make of them? I mean, I know they've all been checked out, but I've never read a file on them or anything. I'd like to do that over the next few days."

"You mean you'd like to read the analysis of each of them? Is that what you're asking me? Because I want to help you out here, but I've got to warn you that a lot of these so-called tips are from crackpots." He leaned in across the desk and lowered his voice. "I know you'd rather be speaking to Detective D'Orfini." And then he did something that made me feel utterly foolish. He winked.

Did I giggle? Shit. I'm not sure. I hope not.

"I want to read the report of every one of those sightings," I said.

"You can't take any files out of the office, so let me see."

The skin on the back of my neck shivered. Geronimo started to cough deep and noisy from his chest.

"Are you all right?" I asked.

"Darn asthma. Acts up at the most inconvenient times."

Geronimo opened a desk drawer and reached in for an inhaler. Sweat broke out on his forehead.

"About those files?" I asked. I had read some of them in the beginning, but after the first 112 false sightings, I didn't have the stomach for them. Some people had odd ways of passing time, such as browsing a missing person's site and fantasizing about how to spend the reward money. That had been Steve's idea. "Money talks," he said. So he had put up $10,000 for anyone who could lead us to Vinni. That kind of money drew the most diverse circle of liars: postal clerks, retired nurses, kindergarten teachers, college students, male strippers, architects, gardeners, anthropologists, homemakers, pornographic filmmakers . . . the list went on and on. The only thing the "sighters" had in common was that they could tell a good lie. John D'Orfini had told me he could smell a lie a mile away, but the investigative team had to follow each lead to the end, even if they knew it was a waste of time. There was always that chance.

Janice was that chance.

Janice was in a different category.

Janice was not interested in the reward money.

And I was the only one who knew about her.

ع

DETECTIVE GERONIMO'S HABITUAL visit to the drawer with the inhaler coaxed me to say, "Detective, have you considered hiring a personal trainer or even a nutritionist for your asthma?"

"I can't say I have," he said. "I'm used to having a desk job with my trusty inhaler right close to me. Why're you asking?"

"Because you seem like a man who needs someone to look after him."

Without hesitation, Geronimo responded. "Not like your former husband, I suspect. Eh?"

"What?" *When did Steve enter the room?*

I shook my head in disbelief.

"It's just that Detective D'Orfini and I have always agreed about this one until your case. He's convinced it's all about the German couple, but I'm not so quick to join him in this assessment."

He paused, leaned back in his chair, and rested both hands on his oversize girth. He looked at me with a hard, cop-like stare reminiscent of actors playing police. He focused on me as if he thought Steve or I had been hiding Vinni all this time in a closet in the city.

But then Geronimo surprised me.

"My wife died two years ago this September," he said. "She was the sweetest woman who ever lived. We would have been married thirty-two years on Friday. There's not a day that goes by that I don't think of her. She was the reason I breathed."

What moved me was how Geronimo dropped his hands from his belly and folded them on his desk, as if he were a poet giving a reading, reaching out to his audience.

As quickly as I had imagined Steve in the room, he was gone.

"I don't know what you're going through, but I know it hurts when no one's there to love anymore," he said.

As I drove home that night, I planned my trip to Greens Lane in Canandaigua.

෴

THE STREET WAS nothing unusual, other than the fact that I was alone and hiding down the road from house number 73. I had circled the block six times, thinking that I shouldn't draw attention to myself, but who was going to notice me anyway? I ended up parking down the street from the house and sitting behind the wheel for close to three hours. The homes on the block were modest, with attached one-car garages. It was quiet. I had thought about knocking on Janice's door but worried about what to say. I had never responded to her, in case she was a nut. And "three doors down" could mean in either direction.

The shades were drawn throughout the house. I started the engine and moved my car across the street from number 73. I stared at the front door, willing Vinni to run out when she saw the car. I imagined leaping from behind the wheel and scooping her up. It got so real, my heart raced with excitement. I closed my eyes so the colors in my mind stayed bright.

A tapping on the window jolted me. When I looked up, I saw a police officer.

"Please step out of the car, ma'am," he said. Behind him, a woman in a brown coat and snow boots stood on the front steps of number 73. Her hair was cut short and blunt.

"What's the matter, Officer?" I asked, as I focused on the stranger on the steps. I began to shiver. My winter coat lay on the backseat.

"I need your license and registration."

Should I have blurted out the truth? Would you have? Or would you have raced up the steps past the stranger in house number 73 and screamed for your stolen child, running from room to room?

"I think I need to make a call, Officer. Detective Geronimo—"

"In Jersey?" He held my license and registration in his bare hand.

"Yes, in Spring Haven, New Jersey." By now, my teeth were chattering. Cold swallowed up the hope I had carried with me from the city. Despair sank in as I saw an unfamiliar child dressed in a red parka slip under the woman's arm. Strangers had never looked so sad to me, if only because they didn't match the picture in my mind. My chest swam inward and froze. I wondered if my eyes might see something different if I moved closer to the house. If their faces might change. If the child might be taller.

"What are you doing in this neighborhood?" the officer asked in a brisk tone. "Someone called in that you've been sitting here all afternoon."

"I've made a mistake, Officer. If I could just talk to Detective Geronimo in New Jersey, I know he could better explain why I've been sitting here."

On the ride back to Manhattan, Kay laid into me over the phone. Geronimo had called her after he had spoken to the officer in Canandaigua and assured him I would drive south immediately. He knew we were friends.

"What the hell, Maddy? I knew it! I knew you were up to something."

"It was a tip. I was following a lead from the website. I didn't do anything wrong."

"Wrong? It's not about right or wrong, hon. Don't go there. Don't pull the ethics card. You could ruin the investigation."

Maybe this is a test, I thought. *One I keep failing.*

FIFTEEN

Seeing the unfamiliar child in the red parka hollowed out my heart. I wished I could reinsert Vinni into the placenta and let her float. Whole days went by when I wished and wished and wished. I wished Vinni were standing next to me at the food market as we chose red tomatoes and sweet onions and tossed them in bags. I wished she were in the bedroom down the hall. I wished I could hear her laugh when I asked her why she plastered tiny star stickers on one cheek and not the other. I wished she appeared like a vision by my side on the wooden seat when I prayed at St. Patrick's Cathedral.

Steve used to say wishing was for wimps.

Two weeks later, I asked Evelyn why she had no children. She was painting. I was watching her shade the head of a boy. The question slipped out of my mouth as Evelyn feathered a line down the left side of the paper. She repeated the lines until almost—not quite—they created a wall. She looked up, put her pencil down, and gestured for me to sit with her over at the table by the side windows overlooking the street. Grayness washed everything into one enormous cloud.

"I need to darken that one," she said, looking over at the sketch. "Too much light."

I was surprised to hear Evelyn say this, as she rarely talked about a work in progress. I guessed she hadn't realized she was speaking out loud. Sometimes she did this, spoke without a trace of an introduction, as if the line between what she was thinking and what she was saying was nonexistent.

"Not having children was something I chose." Evelyn stopped at this brief explanation to take a sip of tea. She did not look at me straight away. Her hesitation made me rethink what I said next.

"Was this choice Dr. Goodman's also?"

"At first, no. He has two brothers and a sister. He grew up in a family of noise. Lots of grabbing for the biggest piece of whatever it was." There was a long pause, and Evelyn closed her eyes. Looking back, I realize I saw a pain glide across her face. I wondered if she had gone to sleep. I stared at the grayness outside, watched its opaqueness.

She picked up the conversation. "Stanley agreed with me. At first it was hard, because he had never thought of any other way of being married. But later, our lives took such different paths. We loved each other. Of course, you can see we still love each other. There have been others for both of us, but neither of us ever married again. Instead, we chose something else."

I persisted.

"And you have no regrets?" I asked.

She ignored the saucer and placed her teacup on top of the table. Then she closed her eyes once more. With right over left, she began a slow rub of the right thumb over the downward-facing palm. Her face looked old in the shadow of the outside gray.

"I could have had a child, Maddy. I told you, I made my choice a long time ago. I'm too old to think about regrets." Her voice cracked on the final word, as if straining for air. A lie floated around the lines above her upper lip. She brushed it away like a loose crumb from a piece of toast.

Evelyn's reputation as an artist was significant. But it had been a struggle to reclaim her footing in the art world after the loss of her friend Nina, an adored artist whose meteoric rise to fame was cut short by her early death.

"She was a dear friend when we were students at Cooper Union. I loved her, but we were young and foolish—she more foolish than I, perhaps. She took risks that killed her. I'm certain of it. All her work with synthetics: latex and fiberglass. In those days, there were no precautions. No one could have kept her from doing what she wanted anyway. I tried, but she'd lash out and turn away from me."

With each discovery into Evelyn's life, I questioned my own world—the one without my child. Who would love me? Now that Vinni was lost, I lived alone with my own words when I walked. I needed a blank canvas upon which to speak. Or scream. I needed to paint.

Evelyn understood.

Gradually, instead of watching her paint, I picked up a brush myself. When I painted, Vinni retreated into the middle of my mind. Space in the front opened for colors and shapes. When I heard myself saying, *This is good*, I felt uneasy. Guilt worked me over as I allowed the word *good* to sneak up on me and stay awhile.

Evelyn pushed me to go deeper.

"You remind me of her," she said.

"Who?"

"My artist friend who died from taking chances." Then she hesitated and said softly, "Her mother killed herself."

"Why are you telling me this?" I asked.

She shrugged and said, "I loved her."

Evelyn stood up, and for a moment I saw the younger version of her strong self. Her shoulders dropped into place inside her purple and lime–colored tunic. Her red skirt, asymmetrical but long enough to cover her ankles and drape onto the floor on the left side, looked surprisingly elegant. Evelyn pivoted and curtsied, moving her older woman's bulk in a graceful dance.

"Valentino says a woman should never show her ankles when wearing a long piece. What do you think?"

"I think Valentino knows what he's talking about," I said. Then we laughed until our cheeks needed a rest.

Before I realized what was happening, Evelyn reached for my hand and pulled me up to dance.

"We need to go to the market and buy some jewel-colored fruits," she said, as she twirled me under her arm. "Afterward, we must take a little walk. Yes?"

She had no intention of waiting for my answer.

"Good!"

My heart rate picked up, and I began to perspire. I moved away from the grasp of Evelyn's hand and danced alone. I lost myself in the motion. Each of us twirled around the room, making our own path, until Evelyn announced she was beginning to feel dizzy. "I need to sit a bit before we shop for the fruits," she said.

Of course Evelyn assumed I had agreed to go. How could I disappoint her? We had already picked a date to go together to the Morgan Library. Evelyn's idea.

SIXTEEN

THE BRISK APRIL AIR STUNNED US AS WE STEPPED OUT OF the taxi at the corner of Thirty-Sixth Street. Evelyn shivered inside her red wool coat. Spring's scent seemed far away, summer even further, with an out-of-season snowstorm predicted for the weekend. Evelyn's long skirt—royal blue trimmed in a thick border of magenta lace—skimmed her ankles as she picked up one side and twisted the fabric inside her hand. I had been to the Morgan Library twice. As I walked inside, I suspected Evelyn's tutelage would make this visit different.

Evelyn guided me to a single piece on a corner wall. She wrapped her arm around my waist and waited. I looked up and studied a woman bent and rounded in grief.

The Grieving Mother stared back at me.

"Let the piece speak to you." With a voice deliberate but kind, Evelyn pointed out the brilliance behind the black-and-white pencil sketch by the German artist Käthe Kollwitz. I had heard of her but had never studied her work. Kollwitz's work bespoke a pain I had had—until now—no words within my grasp to express.

"Käthe knew about loss. She lost her son and her grandson to war. Both named Peter. She swung between periods of depression when she painted. She took in the misery of others and put it onto the canvas. She gave them a voice even as she suffered bitterly herself. She refused to step outside her grief until she was done with it."

"Is anyone ever *done* with it?" I asked.

As we walked through the exhibit, Evelyn sighed deeply after I asked my question. Her face broke into creases. Lines grew longer outside the corners of her eyes. Fine grooves stemming from the edges of her nostrils down the inside of her cheeks dug deeper like highways to the mouth. Grief fed my doubt.

"Let's sit awhile," Evelyn said in a tired voice.

We had seen the light-filled courtyard café beyond the museum's entrance. Airy and bright, with glass walls and high ceilings, it was the kind of place where Vinni and I would have loved to sit and create stories to tell each other.

To tell. To tell. To tell. There will be so much to tell when we see each other.

As I studied the drawings, I felt alive.

Evelyn and I stopped at a piece titled *Nude from Back.*

"Look at her," Evelyn said. "See how the artist burrowed the woman's grief down inside the bones in her naked back?"

I never thought about how I looked from behind. How I walked those years without Vinni. How low my head hung. My shoulders caved. My round back rounded more. I carried grief around with me until I grew unseen fat that no one noticed. Only I felt its weight.

"You must paint, Maddy. You have a gift. Never mind the guilt."

"Guilt?"

"Of having more time."

A sting seared me from deep inside, where I reached for Vinni and held on tight. This was not what I wanted. Evelyn took my hand with hers across the table and covered it like bread, end to end. She curled her left fingers into a fist and softly hit the table. Once. Twice.

"I know you can't stop the grieving." Evelyn's dark eyes

burned like fired chestnuts. Her intensity deepened, and for a moment I withdrew. I leaned back in my chair, but my eyes fixed on Evelyn.

"What do you know about grieving?" I asked.

Her jaw relaxed into hung flesh. She closed her eyes. Words dropped from her lips, one slow hurt at a time.

"Stanley and I had a child. She died at five months. I had been painting all afternoon while she napped. I knew she had been quiet while I worked. Quiet for longer than the other afternoons, but I was painting . . . working. I didn't want to stop. When I went to check her in the crib, she had stopped breathing."

"Evelyn, I . . . I'm so sorry."

What do you say?

Before Evelyn stopped speaking, she said one last line that made me gasp.

"She had turned blue."

I moved my palm from underneath to top Evelyn's.

For a long time, we breathed in and out of the silence. We sat and sipped tea. Two years ago, I had met Evelyn, when she was seventy-six. I had not seen her true age until that afternoon. Old skin around her eyes creased more deeply. Folds under her neck looked fuller. I studied her hands as we held on to each other, dropping our clasp to sip our tea.

Had Evelyn lied when she'd said that she and Stanley had made a choice not to have children?

"But before, you told me you had made the choice not to have children."

"I know what I told you!"

Trust flitted in and out, but I did not grab hold. Didn't even consider wringing its neck. Evelyn looked away from me, caught inside a wave of pain. I could barely hear her when she spoke.

"The pregnancy was a surprise. And the child's death. Too

many surprises for a young doctor and a wife who wanted to paint."

"Did you separate shortly after the child . . .?"

"We tried to stay together, but I needed to conquer my guilt. It's strange, you know. Guilt. It grows."

I knew.

Finally, I said, "How long?"

The smell on my clothes of another winter's passing was too much to bear. I swallowed hard.

Evelyn looked at me and asked, "What do you mean?"

"How long until you could paint again?"

"I was young. And Stanley never blamed me. Only once did he walk into the bedroom, where I sat on the edge of the bed, and ask, 'Why didn't you stop painting and check on her?' Of course, that was the end."

"Of what?"

"I left Stanley even though I still loved him. I had no choice. The love had grown painful. I had to go. After the divorce, we slept together on the weekends, making love like young fools."

A slight lilt touched her voice when she said "young fools."

Tears slid down my cheek, but I needed to know the answer to my question. "How long before you painted again?" I repeated.

"It was so long ago. Two years. No, maybe three."

❧

AFTER THAT DAY in the library, I stayed away from Evelyn. Three weeks passed before I went downstairs and let myself into her apartment. From the hallway, I could see the northern light shining into her studio. I noticed more and more how she sat in the dark, and when I asked why she kept the shade pulled in her bedroom, her only reply was, "It suits me."

Discovering a dead baby in a crib could make you crave the dark, I thought.

Or keep you in the shadows.

I had a sudden urge to flee.

SEVENTEEN

KAY SWALLOWED A PIECE OF TUNA AND CROSSED HER
fork and knife like two sabers on top of her plate. Desperate
people learn to forgive. I had to forgive Kay because I needed
her. She looked around for the waiter to take her plate, but either he had gone home or, I imagined, he was shoveling down a
plate of picked-over paella in the kitchen. It was ten past ten.
The restaurant, Kay's choice, was out of my price range, but I
didn't care.

"Vinni was a blessing to you and Steve," Kay said, without
looking up to warn me where she was headed. She wiped her
mouth with her napkin, unaware of the verbal minefield she
had ignited.

"What exactly do you mean by 'blessing'?" I asked. I waited
a second to catch my breath. I wasn't looking for an answer.

Kay stared at me from across the table but made no attempt
to open her mouth. The muscles around her lips hardened.

"Do you have a nonblessing because you have no husband
and no children? Did God take his sword and refuse to tap your
right shoulder because he was low on blessings that day? And if
your God blessed me with Vinni, is he now hell-bent on bestow-
ing an unblessing? Tell me, Kay, why did God decide to 'un-
bless' me by removing my child from my life?"

More words filled my mouth and spilled over my lower lip. I
spit them at Kay and bit my lip in the meantime. Red stained
my fingers after I touched my mouth.

Kay never took her eyes off me. Her napkin fell to the floor. She pulled at the perfectly folded collar on her black knit turtleneck.

"Call it spiritual perversion. Yeah, I like that—I really do. I'm perverted because I'm unblessed. That's what this is, isn't it? That's what's happened to me. I'm unblessed," I said.

I screamed the word so the other diners could hear me: *unblessed. "Unfuckingblessed."*

I stood up and leaned my hands on the table, bending over the chicken on my plate. Thick and brown, it drowned in a butter sauce so rich, I tasted it later, in the middle of the night.

You'd think I would have stopped, but I kept on barreling forward, steamrolling over Kay and whatever sense of reason she thought I might have left.

"Wasn't my mother's suicide perverted enough?"

I had no intention of giving Kay the space to answer.

"Is this some half-assed way of teaching *me* a lesson? Is this what God is doing, Kay?"

Kay let out a quiet "Maddy . . ." But I gave her no room.

"Vinni gave me the kind of love I wanted. I don't want unblessings, and neither should you."

Silent diners looked over at us. They knew I was the loud one. The one with a spray of sweat over her upper lip.

"Stop it," Kay said. "Sit down."

I choked out one last line.

"Don't ever tell me Vinni was a blessing. Don't ever say that to me again. I swear, Kay, I'll fucking kill you."

Kay picked up her wineglass. She had one swallow of cabernet left. She began to bring the glass to her lips but stopped midair, looked me in the eye, and said, "A hell of an unblessing that would be for me, wouldn't it, Maddy? I'd say that'd be pretty damn perverted."

After a long pause, as the two of us stared back at each other, I smiled. First. Then I laughed out loud. Kay laughed after me. Soon, we doubled over our plates and howled. Tears streamed down our cheeks.

ℰ

KAY HAD INVITED both of us to meet at her office on Court Street. Steve flew in and stayed at the W Hotel at Union Square. He had been coming east less frequently, but for a meeting like this—the first with Kay and me together in the same room—he wanted to be there in person.

I told myself the affair had been a huge mistake.

I told myself I wasn't responsible.

I told myself I was tired of hearing shit from my inside voice.

All I had to do was show up and listen to what Kay knew about the investigation. Steve was already there when I arrived. Kay's navy suit, although conservative, had an elegant twist with the addition of a muted pink-and-deep-mauve silk scarf placed under the jacket's lapels and knotted loosely. The ends hung long below the third button. Her perfectly manicured nails reminded me of how mine used to look. When I gazed down at my fingers, I saw dried cuticles grown over small nail beds.

My mother's hands.

My black cuffed trousers hung so loose, I had to roll the waistband twice. I kept the cream wool jacket buttoned to hide the bulkiness. I breezed into Kay's office, nodded, and said a barely audible hi. This was the first time the three of us had been together in six years. I had thrown Steve out when he told me he had slept with Kay. He left without a hint of wasted energy. Falling out of love—for both of us—beat carrying around an oxygen tank.

"We made a mistake. It lasted only a month," he said, before he closed the door on his way out.

ॲ

THE PAPERWEIGHT SHIFTED as she pulled papers from a manila folder on top of a stack about to topple. "Let me tell you where things stand with the investigation. You probably have the same information, but I thought it would be good for us to review from the beginning."

Steve cleared his throat. The tip of his nose looked red from a cold he had caught on the plane from San Francisco.

The French cuffs of Kay's long-sleeved white shirt were held together by a pair of gold plated Herrerasaurus cuff links from the American Museum of Natural History. They had been a Christmas gift from Vinni.

"Maddy, what about the trip to Mueller's Bakery in Brooklyn? Anything more we should all know?" Kay asked.

I said, "No." The truth was that I had walked past the bakery three separate days since my first visit to Mueller's. I didn't tell anyone because there was nothing to say, other than that I sat at a table and ordered an apple turnover. I did not approach Hannah. I watched her. I watched and I watched, hoping to bore tiny holes into her chest. If she felt them at all, she never let on. Instead, she smiled when I walked in—the way she smiled at all the customers, including the man wearing a straw fedora and Harley tee. He sat inside, holding a hot cup of coffee in both hands. I had seen him before, on sunny days, when he sat at an outside table and drew on a tablet of unlined paper.

"Let me buy you a piece of chocolate cake," he said one day when I sat alone at the café table outside Mueller's. I agreed because I thought he might tell me something about the neighborhood. Before long, the sweetness of the cake wore me down.

"Have you ever seen this little girl?" I asked, as I pulled out the picture of Vinni in her yellow bathing suit from that summer day.

"No. Who is theeees?" His hat sat low over his eyebrows.

"This is my daughter. She was stolen from me two years ago."

The man's eyes went soft and sad. I detected compassion in his voice.

"I wish . . ." he began, and then cut short his thought. The pronunciation of his long *i* into a series of *eeeeeeeeeeeeeee*'s disappeared but then crept up again.

"Why eeeeeeeeees it that you look for her *alone*?"

"I'm not alone, really. The police . . . they, um . . . well, they're helping. It's just that it's been a long time that she's been missing." The man's half-open eyes irritated me.

"Why do you wear your hat so low?" I said.

The man slid his hat back over his head, exposing a mediocre forehead with the usual number of wrinkles. His brown eyes looked in at me.

"Is theeees better?" he said.

I excused myself to use the bathroom inside the bakery. Hannah looked up as I opened the door. I walked past the glass counters and down a dim hallway. Just as I was about to turn the handle on the bathroom door, a young girl, no more than sixteen, raced out and turned in the opposite direction of the street. "Excuse me," I said, "you're going the wrong way." The girl ignored me, as if she didn't hear. She lost herself in the dark at the end of the hallway. I heard a door open and close. Something made me follow her. I had taken only four or five steps, when the man in the straw fedora stepped out of the shadows. He surprised me. "You're headed in the wrong direction, he said, as he grabbed my arm. "Come, follow me."

"Ah. Yes. Thank you," I said. As soft as the man's voice was, his grip on me felt strong and protective, reassuring, like the familiar lines that ran across my father's forehead from side to side.

YEAR THREE

EIGHTEEN

AFTER JOHN D'ORFINI RETURNED FROM QUANTICO, HE
had an uneasiness about him. I sensed a distance on the phone
when he called to check in. His three months away had left me
feeling more alone, although my work on the canvas fed off my
misery. I knew I was painting a series because whenever I put
the brush down, I worried I might lose the continuity. When I
painted, it was as if I had found an unknown source of oxygen.
A sliver—not a crescent or a full moon, but a particle (I'm telling you this because I want you to know that it was so small as
to defy measurement)—of longing lodged in my chest. But, like
a shard of glass, it was there. Undeniably, it was there.

How long can you ignore a shard of glass?

My inside voice tried hushing the onslaught of questions.
When the detective asked if he could stop by on a Sunday, as he
was going to be in the city, I never questioned the reason. I confess to taking care in the shower, to shaving my legs, and to exfo-
liating my face with a lavender scrub. I brewed coffee for John
D'Orfini, although I had switched to drinking tea. Was I so
wrong to be ready?

When I opened the door, he stood with his hands in his
pockets. A placement that made me smile.

"Welcome back," I said. I think I took him by surprise until
he realized that I was talking about his return from DC. His face
was leaner, with an outdoor complexion of wind and sun. I had

a chicken roasting in the oven—the one thing I could roast with pride. I hadn't mentioned anything about an early dinner—it was only 4:45 p.m.—but as soon as John D'Orfini walked in, he smiled and said, "Chicken? I wasn't expecting anything. I hope you didn't go to much trouble."

I offered white wine, but he declined.

At first.

He asked me about my painting. I asked him about the outreach program he had studied in Quantico. Vinni sat quietly in the background. The chicken, long done, rested on top of the stove. By the time we got around to eating it later that night, it had marinated beautifully in its own juices.

Only a fool passes on a home-cooked chicken.

RIGHT BEFORE MY climax with the detective, I shut my eyes tight and prayed with my inside voice. *God, if this is wrong, then forgive me. If this makes me selfish, then send me to hell. And if you think I shouldn't enjoy sex this once with the detective, then send an out-of-control bus down Fourteenth Street to run right over me. But, God, if you're okay with John D'Orfini touching me, please send a sign, like . . . hell, I'm not going to tell you what kind of sign.*

Sex had gotten mixed up with loneliness. When John D'Orfini rolled off me, I noticed the scar on his buttocks. A small, dimpled line about an inch long crept along his left cheek.

"What's this?" I asked, as I tapped the spot.

"Nothing," John D'Orfini mumbled, as his inner door closed shut.

"Oh, nothing—right. I forgot. I'm not supposed to be the one asking questions. Isn't that right, Detective?" I let out one long sigh as my breasts spilled in front, splayed wide at the tip of my rib cage. I pulled up the sheet and folded my hands underneath my arms in a masculine standoff.

"This shouldn't have happened. It's my fault," the detective said, as he swung his legs over the side of the bed, showing an etched set of abdominal muscles. John D'Orfini stood up and headed toward the bathroom.

My inside voice went nuts.

"Where are you going?" I called out before he shut the door. With just enough time to wrap a towel around his waist, he leaned out through the doorway.

"I'm sorry. I should leave. It's late," he said, without looking at me.

What did I tell you about that shard of glass?

I pulled the sheet up more tightly around my neck. A few minutes later, I heard the front door close. Something had gone terribly wrong . . . again.

An hour passed, the bell rang, and John D'Orfini spoke into the intercom.

"Please take a walk with me. I'll wait downstairs."

I met him outside, sitting on the steps.

We walked in silence for three long city blocks until he said, "We crossed the line tonight. I owe you an apology." He kept both hands in his pockets even though it was a warmer-than-usual January. No sign of snow anywhere. No walking with our heads down to beat the wind.

"I'm an adult," I said. "What are you apologizing for?"

"For acting unprofessional. I don't want you to think that I've forgotten . . ."

"Forgotten? Forgotten what?" I stopped dead in the middle of the street. We had begun to cross Sixth Avenue in the direction of La Bandera, a Spanish restaurant down the block from Dance Theater Workshop, where Carmen de Lavallade was performing with other aging dancers who could still balance on one leg.

"*Who.* Don't you mean *who?*" John D'Orfini had me by the shoulders. "Don't make this harder than it is. We crossed the line tonight, and I'm trying to say I'm sorry. I don't want anything or anyone—including the two of us—to get in the middle of the investigation. And I want you to know—"

"Shh . . ." I placed my hand over his mouth and hushed up the good detective. Our eyes held each other still as lake water on a summer's eve. "You're okay, Detective D'Orfini. No one standing here in the middle of Sixth Avenue has 'forgotten' about my girl."

With my inside voice, I said, *Isn't that right, God?* Of course, John D'Orfini couldn't hear my inside voice. It dictated goodness when I needed a guide. My ranting at God cleared my head until the next time I lost my way. What was wild was that I was quicker at finding my way back than I used to be. Whatever I had learned in three years had something to do with fighting like a mother beast and refueling in the trenches to fight some more. One orgasmic roar was not going to deter me. And that's all it was—just one. Not a double or a triple or a disjointed unraveling but one smooth-sailing ride into a place sweet like a trip to heaven. That's all it was.

Dear, sweet John D'Orfini had no idea that I had my eye on Mueller's Bakery. He stepped back—which didn't surprise me—and I fell in line. If he felt it was the right thing to do—for him to withdraw and for me to follow like a well-rehearsed dance partner—I'd do it. What I didn't know at the time was just how far back that was, although I noticed how he kept his hands in his pockets. How he drew his elbows closer to his ribs, and how when he looked at me I wanted to lay my cheek against his, the way I had that night when I had roasted him a chicken and we had made love.

~

IN A SMALL town like Spring Haven, secrets passed with ease from mouth to mouth.

"People keep to themselves what they don't want anyone to know about," John D'Orfini said. "The rest hangs out pretty much in the open."

As time passed, I learned how he thought and worked and moved through one day to the next. His passion for getting the details right continued beyond securing his Eagle Scout badge on his seventeenth birthday. Hanging around Cryan's Deli for his morning coffee, as well as ordering a homemade blueberry muffin—a Thursday special—worked well for the detective. He was a man who lived inside his habits. If he were to learn why a child got stolen on his watch, he knew Cryan's was a good place to eavesdrop.

When Katherine Mulvey, the owner of the Spring Haven Religious Gift Shop, walked in one day, the left side of her neck twitched the way it had been twitching for the last twenty-two years, ever since she had lost her youngest child in a car accident, a senseless tragedy involving an out-of-towner speeding along Route 71 while ten-year-old Mary Mulvey rode her bike on her way to visit her best friend since Sister Anna's first-grade class. The stretch was only five hundred yards on the highway before she turned down the cul-de-sac, but it was enough to snuff the life out of her.

Over the years, Katherine's neck pulsed more viciously when she was upset. John D'Orfini had told me about the first time he had run into Katherine at Cryan's after Vinni went missing. The more he talked to her, the more her neck twitched in tiny, jerky stabs, as if trying to shoo away a mosquito. When she was questioned by the FBI, along with the other shopkeepers in Spring Haven, her only revelation was that Hilda had gone to the Religious Gift Shop from time to time to browse.

"At least twice," John D'Orfini said, "she crossed the street when she saw me walking in her direction. She ducked into the athletic store—the one with the tennis skirts in the window— even though she was scheduled for a hip replacement two days later and never played tennis a day in her life."

He had teased her about the trinity rings for sale on a casual drop-in to her shop, just as he had teased me about how I added a half cup of cream to my tea.

"Trinity rings? Guess God's pleased."

(For sure, Katherine must have opened her eyes wider.)

"They make people feel holy when they purchase them. Stirs up the idea of *hope*, too. Hope is pretty powerful stuff. Hard to hang on to hope. Virtue . . . well, that's even a tougher nut."

He was careful not to tread on any personal space, but he knew how to lower his voice into a confidential tone. He did this with me on the night we shared the chicken. Low and soft, he said my name until I wanted to hear him say it all night.

John D'Orfini knew timing was everything and although Geronimo had warned him about approaching Katherine on the anniversary of her little girl's senseless death, he showed up for the 8:00 a.m. memorial Mass at St. Anna's Church. He followed Katherine up to communion, ignoring the raised eyebrow of Father Pat when the detective extended his tongue for the blessed host.

"I'm sorry for the woman's loss, but she knows something," he said when he had called me while driving from the church to the local coffee shop, where he had convinced Katherine to allow him to buy her breakfast.

"What are you looking for?" I asked. I was washing paintbrushes used the night before—evidence of a tired artist who needed sleep.

"A revelation, but I'd settle for solid information," he said.

"Don't be hard on her. God, today of all days," I said.

"That's exactly why she might be more inclined to say something. Look, I know it's tough, but—"

"I know. You've got a *hunch*, Detective. I know." I had never spoken the word aloud before I met John D'Orfini. *Hunch*. I didn't even like the sound it made. Teeth clamped down, as if trapping the tail of a small animal.

Katherine's neck twitched as she and John D'Orfini sat in a booth by the window. He believed a good detective acted on facts, intuition, and a dose of gold dust. Timing was everything. This was his personal assessment, not something he had studied at the police academy.

ى

SOMETHING HAD BOUNCED across John D'Orfini's desk from the FBI. Young girls—ages eight to ten—were being snatched up from Orthodox Jewish communities. The FBI dubbed the investigation "The Virgins." It had been going on for years— young girls smuggled into Arabia for a band of princes whose taste for untouched skin traveled across the world.

John D'Orfini led the conversation with Katherine. "The Virgins" was a warm-up. Typical D'Orfini.

A mother and child had gone missing south of Spring Haven. Rumors of spousal abuse spread.

"The papers might have this one right," John D'Orfini said. "Why wouldn't a mother flee with her child if the father was a beast?"

"A beast?" Katherine said.

"Beast," John D'Orfini repeated, with a clarity that sent Katherine's neck a-twitchin' as she stood to leave.

Her rubber-soled Clark's skimmed the linoleum as she muttered *beast* to herself on the way out. She turned back to look at him. He nodded, but he tucked away her reaction to the word *beast*. He sensed she didn't like it one bit.

Later that day, I called John D'Orfini about the newspaper article. Lakeview was just three exits past Spring Haven on the parkway.

"What's this about a child and her mother gone missing?" I asked.

"I'm looking into it," the detective said. "I'm pretty sure there's no connection."

"Based on what?"

"The guy was beating on his wife and child."

᳗

I HAPPENED TO be in Spring Haven when the town turned out for the opening of a new shop, called Whimsicality. I stood across the street and watched the owner cut the ribbon positioned across the double-front glass window. Katherine Mulvey stood two spaces from the owner. From across the street, I watched the steady motion of her twitch identifying her as the woman whose young daughter had died in a bicycle accident.

I should paint this, I thought. *I should paint this piece of Americana stoked with madness.* Was John D'Orfini's scar on his buttocks the result from someone else's insanity? And Katherine Mulvey? Was she to blame for withholding information while carrying around grief stored inside a muscle in her neck, making the rest of us uncomfortable because she couldn't let it go?

NINETEEN

As I climbed the steps of the New York Public Library, I heard a tour guide outside explaining the architecture of the building to a group of out-of-towners. The guide told her group, "You can read between the lions," referring to the lions in the front of the library. Polite giggles brought a smile to the tour guide's face. I walked past them, turned off my phone, and opened my black tote bag for the security guard at the front door.

Despite all my walking throughout the city, the two sets of stairs winded me. I turned left at the top of the staircase and walked straight through to the Rose Reading Room. Once I sat down, I studied the cement wall at the back of the room. I had to make myself hard like the wall until I found Vinni. Nothing could get in my way. To compare my loss to the shade of evening was too soft. If *fucked* had a color, I would not be forced into pedaling backward into blue. This was my big worry—that I would start to pedal backward, unable to stop until I came to a cement wall. Then, of course, I would have no choice.

Bang!

I sat and stared and pretended to read a book on electricity I had pulled from a shelf by my chair. I have no theory about where ideas come from, but one banged into my head. I left in a hurry, and as I flew down the steps outside, I dialed Kay's office. Without waiting once her secretary connected me, I charged in. "Do you think I should go back to Germany?"

"Whoa . . . Where would you go? You've already been to Rodenbach, where Hilda grew up. You have nothing new. It's about facts, remember?"

"I believe I'm talking to an assistant US attorney now, right?"

"Indeed," Kay said. I imagined my friend's eyes looking off to the side of her office, landing on a stack of files piled high and staying there.

I still loved Kay. In the beginning, when Steve's name came up during a discussion of the investigation, we avoided eye contact. Grown women do this when one has slept with the other's husband. Oddly enough, or maybe because Kay knew me better than Steve, we both pushed the affair into the back of our brains. Vinni held steadfast in the front like the cement wall.

"Meet me at Gascogne's on Eighteenth Street after work, and we'll talk," Kay said.

"Eight?" I asked.

"No. I'm tired. Make it earlier. Six thirty."

I could walk there from my apartment in less than fifteen minutes.

Kay was already there when I arrived, sipping sauvignon blanc. "Mmm . . . this is just what I needed," she said. Before I ordered, she began a new conversation. "I think the serious detective has fallen for you."

I hadn't told Kay about that time we shared the home-cooked chicken in my apartment.

"Let it alone," I said. "I mean it."

"Do you ever think that maybe you deserve to live?" Kay said.

"Don't do this."

"I'll do it because I haven't said anything for almost a year." Kay pushed the sleeves of her midnight-navy top higher up her arms. A gold cuff graced her left wrist. "You've got to consider the idea that . . ." Kay looked away, but I knew where she was going. "People don't kidnap an older woman. But a woman with a young child and no ransom note . . ." She let the idea float.

"You're wrong. Everyone is wrong. I've told you. Hilda would not hurt Vinni. Hannah knows where they are. I feel it each time I see her in the bakery."

"Feelings lie." The slight movement in the hollow of Kay's left cheek signaled something else.

"What? Where's that coming from?"

Kay leaned forward. "I know you went to Mueller's last week. Don't think you can poke around without my finding out."

"Are you having me followed?"

"All I'm saying is that you've got to let our people do their work. They know what they're doing. You don't."

I took a deep breath but let it out fast and loud.

"I'm not stopping anything," I said. I gripped the edges of the table with both hands. Somewhere in the ceiling, a blast of warm air let loose from an overhead vent.

Kay and I stared at each other. We had years of history behind us. I wasn't sure what lay ahead, but I was certain I wouldn't stop going to Mueller's.

"Hannah's going to crack one day, and when she does, I'll be there to pick up the pieces," I said.

"When she cracks, you could be dead."

"How long can she hold out? Forever? Hannah will talk to me before she'll talk to the FBI."

"You're wrong. If Hannah knows where Hilda and Vinni are, then she's been smart enough to hold out for over two years. If she tells us something, she's going to want immunity."

Kay reached for my hand and drew her shoulders inward,

as if she were gearing up to drop a secret right in the middle of the dipping oil on the table.

"I don't want to talk about Hannah tonight, Maddy. I'm worried about the way you look."

"I'm fine. For God's sake, I'm telling you. It's just my hair. I know it's thinning. Okay, and my back hurts. Maybe it's old age. After all, we're months over forty," I said with a twisted smile. I thought of *Nude from Back*, by Käthe Kollwitz, and how her back hid grief inside its skeleton.

Kay signaled the waiter. "Okay, here it is: I booked you five days at a spa in Pennsylvania. Nothing fancy. Yoga, healthy food, and a few massages thrown in."

"I'm not going. I hope you can get your money back."

"I've spoken to Stanley to get his medical input, and he thinks you need to do this. He's even talked to the director of nutrition there and set up an appointment." Kay paused as she adjusted her bangle away from her wristbone.

"I guess I should tell you I spoke to Evelyn also. She thinks it's a good idea for you to go."

Kay had met Evelyn only a few times, but she had a habit of taking control. Even in seventh grade, when the eighth graders had a graduation dance, Kay orchestrated an invite for us to check coats. Her point was that we'd get to see what it was like from the inside, so we would know what to expect the following year.

"When?"

"The end of the week. I've arranged for a car to pick you up on Saturday morning. You have four days to pack."

Kay searched around for her handbag, an elegant aubergine satchel. The conversation was over. I was too tired to fight her.

ℒ

THE RIDE TO Pennsylvania took over two hours. At first, the driver started talking, but my silence shut him down.

"Good to get away, huh?"

"I guess." I dug out my oversize, wraparound black sunglasses from my nylon tote. The sun beat down on the highway. The sky had never looked so blue.

Kay had failed to mention that I would see a "dream therapist" at the spa.

The scent of jasmine greeted me as I opened the door to her office. The room was warm. The walls, painted a shade of yellow, whispered, *Come in*. The visit required less of me than I anticipated. The Dream Lady spoke in short sentences tumbling on top of one another.

"Do you dream? Describe one," she said, as she poked around her messy head of frizz with a pencil.

The truth is, I had one dream that replayed itself over and over, but I said nothing about it.

The Dream Lady loved her dream talk. "Dreams keep things alive," she said.

Anyone who had taken Psychology 101 in college would have understood where she was headed. What I feared was looking pitiful, as opposed to possessed. I didn't want the Dream Lady to see me as this pathetic mother who lost her child at the beach. The single parent living and working in New York City— in the fashion industry, no less. I didn't want some new age, *om*-breathing woman telling me what to do.

Where would dreaming take me?

The Dream Lady said it again. "It's important to dream."

I nodded and fell asleep that night and dreamed that one dream. *If you prefer not to hear it, I understand.* Dreams are supposed to mean something, but before now I'd refused to dwell on them.

In my dream, I return to the house where I grew up. I walk outside and look in through my parents' bedroom window. I hear myself say, "Where is she?" Then I see her. Vinni is older. She lies side by side, next to my mother, who is recognizable even in death. Vinni's eyes are wide open, and I see her chest move up and down. My mother's eyes are closed, her chest still.

A child—with my mother's violin-playing hands and Vinni's eyes—sits next to Vinni. In the dream, my child is now a young woman, old enough to have her own daughter lie beside her.

It is all so confusing, but I stay and watch them. The three of them. They talk, but I cannot hear them. I press my nose closer to the glass window. The temperature of the glass startles me, and I look down and see my feet covered in snow.

I tap on the window, and the child looks up, smiles, and waves back.

Vinni has her arm wrapped around the child's shoulder, the way a mother pulls her baby close in the dark. Why does she ignore me? Or is it that she doesn't see me?

The woman next to Vinni opens her eyes and looks out the window. She sees me standing outside, and I know she recognizes me. She waves for me to go, the way she used to when I was a child. She tells me to leave by the flick of her wrist.

"Be quiet, Maddy." That's what she used to say when I was older. "Be quiet."

I stare back at her, but she has turned her attention to my Vinni—the lost child-woman to whom I never got to whisper, "I love you" on her birthday when she was nine and ten. The child keeps smiling. She jumps off the bed, and I reach my hand through the glass window to touch her face. The glass melts away, turning the broken shards into lemons.

The child picks up a lemon and throws it directly at me. I catch it just before it hits my right cheekbone. I return the lemon like a sweet ball, and the child in my dream squeals as she leaps to her side to catch it. I laugh, but no one hears me. I laugh until tears come and the child cowers back onto the bed between her mother—my grown-up Vinni—and my dead-again mother.

"No, wait," I cry out. I try to stop her from leaving, but she slips away from my grasp.

2

KAY WAS RIGHT. I slept well. The hills of the Pennsylvania Dutch country tucked me into a cocoon where I found a balance of comfort and discomfort. The comfort came in the form of food—slabs of butter spread on bread. Discomfort was that oh-so-jazzy dream therapist with the softest of voices.

In my last session with her, she asked about my dream. I told her about the snow on my feet, Vinni as mother to her own child, the lemons and sweet balls. All the time I spoke, I wondered if the pencil resting inside her hair would slip out and fall to the floor. I was getting used to having two or more conversations happening in my head at the same time.

"In your dream, your daughter is grown, with her own child. Isn't that right?"

It seemed a day or two passed during the silence that followed. Finally, she said, "What's given you the most pleasure while you've been here?"

I answered, "The bread."

"Again?" She cupped her hand behind her ear, reminiscent of a child holding a conch shell to her ear to hear the ocean's roar.

"The bread," I repeated, "and the butter, too."

"And the indoor swimming pool? Did you take advantage of the guided relaxation exercises in the water?" she asked.

"I hate the smell of chlorine," I said. "I love bread and butter."

"So I guess the mealtimes have been satisfying for you, then?"

"No, just the bread and butter."

The Dream Lady sneezed and reached behind her for the floral tissue box on her desk. I rolled my eyes up to God, hoping he might send rain in through the roof and end the conversation.

"Is this something new?" she asked.

"You mean, is eating bread and butter a new thing for me?"

She nodded and hunched forward, the way a jockey does at the starting gate.

"I haven't had much of an appetite since . . ."

"Since you lost your daughter. Of course—the child in the dream."

The therapist adjusted a strap underneath her blouse, reached inside, and scratched at what—an imaginary gnat? She waited a second and settled back in her chair.

She didn't pursue the dream.

"Why do you think you latched on to eating bread and butter here?" she asked. We were far, far away from my dream now.

"Maybe because it was on the table."

"Salt and pepper were on the table also."

I leaned forward in my chair, letting my elbows rest on my thighs. "When I get home, I'm buying a loaf of pecan-and-raisin bread."

"Do you have butter at home?"

"Of course. Who doesn't have butter in their refrigerator?" I sat back and adjusted the two pillows against the small of my back. "My mother always kept the butter softening on the counter. It was disgusting. In summer, the butter sat and sweat."

I shot up. "It's time to go. My ride should be coming soon."

The Dream Lady stood and reached for my hand. Hers was cool. "I wish you the best. Take care of yourself," she said.

That's what everyone wished for—the *best*. The best peaches in the produce aisle, the best price on turnips, the best seat at Madison Square Garden, the best radiologist, the best egg cream, the best cashmere cardigan.

I started for the door, but suddenly I stopped and turned. "I know you've been trying to help me. I'm sorry if I've been . . . difficult."

It was true. I *was* sorry. On the drive home, I thought about how I responded when people asked me how I felt. It was always the same. "I'm doing as well as I can." Then, with a swift turn, I'd walk away.

People do not understand another's grief. They want to. But it is not possible. I learned this every day when someone would ask, "How are things?"

Things?

Time does not heal.

It stretches the pain so it lies flat like a sheet, but it does not heal.

TWENTY

TWO DAYS BEFORE MOTHER'S DAY IN MAY, I WENT TO Brooklyn. Vinni had been gone for thirty months. Mueller's Bakery was packed. Hannah's husband, George, stood slightly stooped. When he looked up and noticed me, he nodded and returned to the pastry cases, lining up raisin cookies and apple strudel triangles wedged against one another. He had one eye on the window to the outside. His tight lips locked secrets behind their natural crease. Hannah spoke to the customers for both of them, with an easy voice couched inside a lingering German accent.

Signs in the windows reminded customers to place their cake orders early. For two years, I had hoped that Hannah would break her silence. I ignored the facts presented by John D'Orfini and Kay—namely, that a child gone missing this long had almost no chance of being found alive. Steve called it a "realistic hypothesis."

Hannah had no children. Still, she must have had some hint of the hideousness I was certain she concealed. Could even a *hint* help her understand what it was like to wake each morning with the same ache? If so, how could she stay silent?

Hannah approached my table and laid a small slice of strudel in front of me. "You are a thin woman," she said. I shrugged my shoulders slightly, so as not to ignore her comment.

Evelyn told me all the time that I was too thin. I drank green tea with her but passed on the baklava she ordered from

Poseidon's Bakery on Ninth Avenue. Three generations of bakers had held on to their customers as the city rose up from the dead again and again. Evelyn was a loyal customer, dating back to her days as an art student, when she and her friends spent late nights mulling over the creative process as they chewed on apricot tarts.

To my surprise, Hannah slid into the seat across from me. George was at the register. The morning crowd had finally begun to thin.

"What will you do this weekend, miss?" Even though I was sure Hannah remembered my name, she avoided it. My long black skirt hung in an asymmetrical circle. A yellow cardigan shrug fit nicely over my cropped white T-shirt.

"This weekend is no different than the others," I said.

"This is not so good for you to think like this, is it?" Hannah asked.

Without hesitation, I said, "You know what is *good* for me, don't you, Hannah? You've known for a long time." I emphasized the word *good*, allowing it to stay long and deep on my rolled-up tongue.

I could almost hear John D'Orfini and Steve gasp in unison.

Hannah folded her hands on the table. Her heavy chest lifted and fell. Her eyes looked into mine, without a trace of what lay behind them.

"Have you tried George's cheese strudel?" she said. "It's a recipe passed down from his father who was a baker. George learned all his baking secrets from him. Since he was a boy . . ."

Hannah stopped. "He was a good boy, but later . . . it was not an easy time."

"What happened?"

Hannah covered my hand and looked away. It felt warm and old.

"I talk too much! I must help George!"

Hannah pushed her chair away from the table with care, as if she were questioning right and wrong. Her left cheek hollowed as she bit into it, and she shook her head as if to shake loose an answer. She stood up and brushed the lower half of her apron in an attempt to smooth out the wrinkles. Tears piled up in her eyes as she looked at me and parted her lips. She sighed with an open mouth, then turned and walked away.

As I left the bakery, I read the sign in the window of the wine bar across the street: ROOM FOR RENT. I walked quickly but misstepped over a puddle from the afternoon's storm and splashed a stream of rainwater onto my bare leg. I pushed open the door into a dimly lit bar built snug against the wall. Couches that appeared to be tossed had landed in the right spots. They zigzagged into intimate seatings where two, four, or eight people could drink in silence or engage in a loud discussion over the rise of subway suicides. It was Friday, which meant wine tasting started as early as 4:00 p.m. One couple sat on the couch, knees touching. The girl's skirt rose up her young thighs. Her male companion talked on his cell phone as his fingers drew small circles into her skin. I made a mental note: how easily his hand could slip inside her underpants.

"Hi, could I talk to someone about the room for rent?" I asked the bartender.

"I'm the *someone*. Interested?"

"Well, yeah. Could I see it now?" I scratched a bump from a bug bite on the right side of my neck. People think if you live in the city that the bugs can't find you.

"Sure. Let me get Sasha from the back to cover for me. Can I get you something?" The bartender had an easy way of moving from the bar to behind him, where wineglasses lined up on a mirrored shelf. I guessed he was a struggling actor in his early forties, with a string of episodic roles dating back to the first *CSI* series. His brown hair was curly, shoved behind his ears so the ends flipped.

"A glass of sauvignon blanc, I guess."

"You guess?" The bartender laughed. Some kind of chanting —Gregorian, I thought—an odd musical choice for a wine bar, filled the space. The lights were low enough to make you believe you might find love with a guy who ordered a Johnnie Walker Black Label.

I followed him upstairs.

The room had a small bathroom with a shower built into a sloping wall, suitable for a person no more than five feet tall. At five foot three, I imagined myself in a soft plié as I shampooed. The white walls were bare except for one left-behind painting of a woman with two arms ballooned like stuffed sausages. It took up most of the inside wall. I walked over to the one window that faced the front of Mueller's Bakery. A perfect view.

What am I doing here?

"There's a small fridge, but no cooking is allowed," the bartender said. "We rent month-to-month for $850, with a two-month security deposit."

"Can I stay here a minute and get the feel of the place? Alone?" I added.

"Sure. Just lock the door behind you and drop off the key at the bar. Uh . . ." He turned to leave but then stopped and said, "What do you think?" He kept both hands in his pockets, making noise with what I guessed were dimes and pennies hammering against quarters and nickels. In the back of my mind, I imagined the guy needed a large ceramic dish near the front door to his apartment where he could drop paper clips and receipts from the corner grocery store.

My voice, as true as a Tibetan singing bowl, said, "It's just what I'm looking for."

As I was about to move away from the window, I noticed the man wearing a Harley T-shirt and a straw fedora standing in the middle of the block. As I watched, he dropped his cigarette and stamped it out. He looked up and down the street before he walked away.

I stepped behind the curtain and waited. For what? After a few minutes—maybe three—I left the room and returned the key to the bartender. "When can I rent it?"

"Two months' security plus this month's rent prorated, and it's yours right away." The bartender reached across the bar to shake my hand. "I'm Ed. Welcome to Brooklyn."

I left the wineglass half-full at the bar.

As I rode the subway home to Twenty-Third Street, I debated whether I should tell anyone about my room. For a moment, I thought of sharing this with Kay, but she was too quick to respond. I didn't want her to shoot this down. Not now, when I had finally taken an action. Done something without asking anyone's permission.

Of course, I had doubts. I know how doubt tastes and moves. How it squats and burrows like a tapeworm, until it's so far inside, there's no getting rid of it.

If you must know, I had plenty of doubt, but I leaped over it as if I were stepping over mud.

All I knew was that I wanted to watch the front door of Mueller's Bakery. The next time I returned to the room, I had a gray camera bag slung over my shoulder with a brand-new lens tucked next to the black Rebel. Working as a fashion editor had inspired me to see things. I noticed details. I didn't miss what was in the corner of a picture. Others might. If a hair hung wrong over the model's cheekbone or the collar of a leather jacket didn't lie right around the neck, I vetoed the shot. My photographers were the best. I learned what to look for from them. When I watched from my window, I saw things—corner to corner, through the lens. Each time I traveled to my room in Brooklyn, I strolled the neighborhood. I photographed what was up and down the street, not knowing what I would stumble onto in the middle of one frightening night.

As the train rumbled underground, I called Kay at her office.

"I just left Mueller's Bakery. Hannah sat with me. I think I'm getting to her."

"What did she say?"

"It wasn't what she said."

I could hear Kay shuffling papers on her desk or shoving them into her designer tote.

"Body language doesn't carry weight in my business," she said.

"Sorry. I forgot that your business is different than my business," I said, with a coolness that made me cringe.

"What's that supposed to mean?"

Kay's lawyer voice grated on my nerves. I took a deep breath.

"Nothing. Let it go." Tension stitched up my throat. Kay didn't respond.

"Forget it," I said, and hung up. I was right. I couldn't share my room for rent with Kay.

The train pulled in to Twenty-Eighth Street, and I walked up the steps and out of the subway station. The bright sunshine reminded me summer was near. My original plan was to return to the house in Spring Haven for the month of August. I knew I didn't need the summer months to bring me back. I had been driving by Hilda and Rudy's house for over two years. But now I had a room in Brooklyn without an oven and a stall shower built for a woman with short legs.

What had I done?

*   ✑

I PULLED OFF the white hat I had bought in the bargain bin at Barbara Fineman's millinery in the East Village and hid in the open at the Rose Reading Room at the library on Forty-Second and Fifth. Row upon row of faces—long, bright, dark, and round—sat fixed to a book, paper, or computer screen. Men with beards and without, women in scarves and skirts, every one mixed in color, worked in silence.

I took a small sketchpad and soft pencil and drew the faces of those sitting around me. The man on the end had a brown suede coat draped over his shoulders. I wondered if he had a tattoo on his bicep—something spiritual, like "Hosanna in the Highest" or "Satan Loves Me." Three chairs down was a woman—young, her skin the color of mocha. She was probably not yet twenty-five. On her head, she wore a gray knit bandanna tied behind her ears. Her features were soft. My eyes looked up and down from my book in swift, dart-like motions. Back and forth, my pencil flew across the page, shadowing the unsuspecting woman's face, working on her mouth, catching the end of the bandanna poking from behind the left side of her neck. Without warning, the young woman stood up and left. I followed her with my eyes until she was out of sight. When I returned to the pad, I worked from memory, going as fast as I could, feeling the burn of getting something down before I lost it in my mind's eye.

After what had to have been longer than I realized, I looked up and, to my surprise, I thought I saw Evelyn, but no—an older woman wearing a purple shawl pulled up and around her shoulders stooped over a stack of thick books. Evelyn's shoulders wouldn't slope that way. She held herself proud, like a warrior who had battled enough in the past.

Once, when we had only just met and Vinni and I were visiting her in her studio, she said, "I've always believed people show up in our lives for a reason. Your moving upstairs with Vinni. Coincidence or fate?"

I flinched now as I thought about Hilda and Rudy watching Vinni and me on the beach three years ago. Why had *they* shown up in our lives? Was I supposed to believe that inviting us for dinner and distracting us with comfort food and gentle storytelling was part of some divine plan? Was my mother's suicide supposed to have helped prepare me for pain?

I ran my fingers over the spine of a book closed in front of me. I had grown into the skin of a worrier. The image of the man in the Harley T-shirt and the straw fedora standing around Mueller's sprinted across my mind. Something more to worry about, I thought. In and out. In and out. Just a neighborhood guy hanging out, right? Yeah, a *neighbor man*. I let it go the way I let go of wondering about the scar on John D'Orfini's buttocks. I packed up my purse, letting my pencil and sketchbook slide in without a sound.

It never lasted long, but going to the library made me feel less invisible. Rather than a woman with a missing daughter, I was a woman who sketched on a pad. Who popped Tic Tacs to squelch a stale mouth. Who bought a cup of tea topped with cream on the way home. The ordinariness of it had monstrous appeal.

Two to three times a week, I returned to my room across from Mueller's Bakery. I looked out the window, into the middle of the night, until I fell asleep with my head resting on my arm. Its weight made my hand go numb. Nothing happened. Of course, I don't know what I expected, other than a vision of Vinni running toward me. This went on until the end of May, when the nights got warmer. Right before Memorial Day, I headed out to Brooklyn with a backpack holding two pairs of underpants, two tees, and an extra bra. Toothpaste, face cleanser, and a bottle of Eucerin face-and-body lotion—the one with the pink cap—sat in the medicine cabinet above the sink in the bathroom. As I rode the subway, I thought about scrapping the whole idea of the room. I had made a mistake. I beat myself up for wasting money. The only saving thing about it was that I hadn't told anyone.

At least I wouldn't look like a fool.

Nobody knew where I was that last night before the long holiday weekend. Unless, of course, you counted Ed, the bartender. I had gotten used to floating through the bar to make my way upstairs with just a wave of my hand.

The northeast was experiencing an early heat wave. I opened all four windows. Only two had screens, but I needed the air. In the middle of the night, I got up, peed, and went and sat by the window. I should have gone straight to bed. If I had, I might have avoided stumbling into something that I knew nothing about. I must have fallen asleep with my head on my arm. At first, I thought it was the numbness from my lower arm that woke me, but when I opened my eyes, I saw a black limousine parked two buildings down from Mueller's. Had the car awakened me?

I moved behind the curtain of the window closer to the kitchen to get a better look. I wasn't prepared for what I saw. A tingling sensation traveled through me as I watched two girls get out of the vehicle. Their skinny legs told me that these were young bodies. At first, I held my breath as I stared across the street. The girls stood still on the concrete sidewalk, their faces covered by hanging locks of hair. A slim man dressed in suit and tie exited the limousine. They followed him to an alleyway where the limousine had stopped, and then all three disappeared from my sightline. I stayed at the window for what seemed like hours but in truth was only fifteen minutes, until I saw the slim man return alone to the limo and speed away. Somewhere down the alleyway, the two girls had disappeared.

This has nothing to do with my daughter, I thought, as the words danced round and round in my head.

Nothing.

You must go to bed and close your eyes. You must forget what you've seen.

But how could I?

I slipped on my sandals and quietly opened the door. I made my way downstairs, careful to avoid stepping in the middle of the last two steps at the end of the staircase, where I knew they creaked. I moved fast to the front door, and just as I was about to turn the doorknob, I heard Ed the bartender. "Hey," he said. "It's three in the morning." He set down a case of empty wine bottles and looked at me, dressed in a girlie nightie tucked inside a pair of jean shorts. Vinni had given me the nightie on the last Mother's Day we were together. Kay had taken her shopping.

"You okay?" Ed asked. He stood about twelve feet down the hall.

My hand gripped the doorknob more tightly. All I had to do was turn it and run outside and across the street to the alleyway to get a closer look at what I suspected was a bad thing.

"Uh, yeah," I said. I hesitated. Then I released my curled

hand on the doorknob. "I couldn't sleep. Too hot, I guess. I was thinking of going for a walk."

"Cool walking clothes," he said, and laughed. "How about you have a shot of whiskey, instead of walking around in the middle of the night?"

"Yeah, you're right," I said too quickly.

I ran back upstairs and closed the door behind me. I don't know what would have happened if Ed hadn't stopped me. Maybe I would have avoided all those nights ahead, watching from the window to see if I'd catch a glimpse of more girls disappearing down the alley. Maybe I would have slept and not wondered if Hannah and George knew what was happening two buildings down from their bakery.

Vinni was going on eleven years old now. She would be taller and look older than her age. Would she be wearing her hair long and hanging over one eye?

All I knew was that I had plenty of doubts I couldn't share. Not with Evelyn or Kay or even John D'Orfini. The man was a walking doubt factor forced upon him by facts. He could make you stop believing in vanilla ice cream if you gave him enough time. And Kay? We had gotten closer, almost to where we were years ago, before she made a mistake and slept with Steve. But she was a loyal assistant US attorney and I couldn't forget that. She had taken an oath. Sworn on a bible to uphold the law. I hadn't sworn to anything, so if I chose not to share information with the law—things I had seen from my window in Brooklyn—I told myself it was okay. And Evelyn? She played a key role in keeping me alive. At least this was one thing I had no doubt about. This is exactly why I chose not to involve her. Evelyn knew about art and painting. She stood in a separate place, far to the side of John D'Orfini and Kay.

I made a choice.

I kept quiet.

I mixed up colors on the canvas. I painted more to whittle my way out from the wound. Three years is a long time to believe in what others don't. Not that anyone said they believed Vinni had disappeared forever. They didn't have to.

Evelyn used to say, "'Art begins in the wound.' I read this somewhere once. It's true, you know. If you paint from the wound, you'll forget what day it is and the only thing that will stay with you is the *shade* of your last stroke. Not its name."

TWENTY-ONE

EVELYN KEPT THE WINDOWS TO HER STUDIO WIDE OPEN. The early-morning June light provided natural warmth. When I arrived one Saturday, she was already working at the easel. Without looking up, she said, "I want you to do something for me."

My first thought was how I might have to cancel my plan to go to my room in Brooklyn. Two weeks had passed, but I couldn't stop thinking about the girls disappearing down the alleyway by Mueller's Bakery.

"Of course. What is it?" Evelyn's requests usually revolved around escorting her to the Metropolitan Museum or the Opera House at Lincoln Center. She was a frequent matineegoer and for years, before her hips stiffened, had attended productions alone.

"What are we seeing?"

Evelyn's white cotton skirt, threaded with silver, shimmered in the sunlight. Although it was warm outside, she wore an oversize white shirt that hung near to her knees. Each sleeve was rolled up neatly below the elbow.

"Go change into something white. Top and bottom. Meet me down in the lobby in an hour."

My own wardrobe had begun to resemble Evelyn's. Long skirts—the kind I used to wear when I was an art student at NYU—had replaced half my selection of tailored trousers. I grabbed a multitiered lace skirt and snug white tee bought at a boutique on Amsterdam Avenue owned by a woman who imported clothes from Asia. The skirt was from Thailand. I walked into Vinni's room and twirled around with my hands on either side of the skirt. On the dresser was a hair comb decorated with white baby roses. I picked it up and tried to fasten it into my hair. It was too thin and too short to grab hold of the comb. I returned to my bedroom and chose a long silk scarf and wrapped it around my head, African princess–style. The scarf was white with cream-colored roses wound and rewound among green vines. As I played with the ends of the scarf, I ended up with knotted blooms on the left side of my head.

Three years is a long time to be blue. I looked pretty in white.

WHEN I ARRIVED in the lobby, Evelyn stood with her back to the stairs as she spoke to Stanley. Perhaps, I thought, he had come for a surprise visit. But no, he was dressed in white pants and a long-sleeved white collared shirt. On his head sat one of those natural white straw fedoras with a black grosgrain ribbon fastened around the inner edge of the brim. The three of us looked like we were on our way to an afternoon tea fest on the island of Barbados.

"There you are, dear. Stanley's going with us." Evelyn had changed her top to one with billowy sleeves bordered with off-white French latticed lace. Narrow strands of matching colored ribbon pulled the sleeves into a ruching effect above the wrists.

"Where are we going?" I asked.

"Maddy, good to see you," Stanley said. "It's beautiful outside. I took the liberty of having a car drive us." He waited for both Evelyn and me to settle on opposite sides of the long seats facing each other. Stanley sat alongside Evelyn. She looked excited. Flushed, almost.

From Chelsea, the driver took us to Twenty-Ninth Street, over to Ninth Avenue, and up to the entrance to New Jersey via the Lincoln Tunnel.

"Where are we going? What's the secret?" I asked, as I adjusted the silk bloom over my ear.

"It's not a secret," Evelyn said. "It had to be the right time to take you here." Then she looked out the window and said, "I wanted you to be ready, and now you are."

She hesitated, as if thinking about something, before she added, "Love your turban, dear."

Stanley smiled and nodded. He raised his eyebrows as if he were anticipating a ride in an amusement park. His eyes twinkled. This was a man who after all these years was still in love with his former wife. Anyone could see it. The way he looked at her with a distant gaze, aware that if he got too close, even this might disappear.

As we traveled south on the Garden State Parkway, I feared Evelyn was taking me to Spring Haven without warning. But two hours later, we exited the highway to a sign that read WEL-COME TO DAMSON.

We drove by home after home set back on long, manicured lawns. Many stood behind scrolling gates like those from a Medici painting. I rolled down the car window and breathed in the salty smell of the ocean. The driver slowed the car in front of a huge estate behind a pair of gates across from the pounding waves. As they opened, I saw men and women dressed in white, walking up a long hill. I looked at Evelyn and smiled. I had no idea what occasion this was, but I knew I was happy to be there. Evelyn had said, "Just a party, dear. Just a party with music."

Even if it lasted for only a minute or two or three. Maybe Evelyn was right. I was ready.

For what? A slip into joy. Dare I allow such a thought? I reached up and touched the silken bloom around my ear. For a moment, I liked who I was. Someone dressed in a flowing skirt. Someone who painted during the day.

Stanley walked arm in arm with Evelyn, aware of her slower steps. At times like this, he reminded me of my father: holding back from quickening his pace, avoiding any subject destined to bring up pain, and simply following the path ahead of him without questioning it. I walked behind them, admiring the multicolored gardens in the distance, to the right of the hill. One section displayed hundreds of dozens of purple-and-white irises in full bloom.

I heard music coming from over the hill. As we reached the top, I saw a huge white tent set with row upon row of white chairs arranged in a semicircle. Outside the tent, an eight-piece string ensemble played. I thought of my mother and her violin-playing days and wondered if she would have fared better had she become a violinist, instead of marrying my father.

Would it have been better for the three of us if two of us had been invisible?

༄

EVELYN NODDED IN recognition to many of the people inside the tent. A gentle buzzing sound of quiet conversation—not somber but anticipatory—filled the air. People embraced. Dozens of music stands stood in front of black chairs, waiting for a full orchestra to appear. Musicians warmed up their instruments, providing a welcome, unscripted score. A breeze touched my cheeks.

Without introduction, the concert began. I sat back in my chair and realized how little I had spoken since we had left the apartment. I slipped off my white sandals and let my feet rest on the moist grass underneath. A June breeze cooled my bare toes. A mixture of honeysuckle and lavender was in the air. I planned to walk around the grounds before we headed home. I checked the program. Beethoven's Ninth Symphony. A fitting opening to the summer. At times, the music reminded me of a wail—a long cry with dissonant screechings.

In the middle of the concert, Evelyn tilted her head to the left and looked over to me. She shifted her gaze to the side of the tent, where a small slit of light appeared between the seam of the fabric where it looked like it had been stretched too tight. This gap was not the only light. The white clothes, the tent without walls—the music's embrace. Light surrounded me on all sides.

As the concert moved to the end—the "Ode to Joy" chorus singers stood. Women in sleeveless gowns of pale gold and citron green with sequined bodices opened their mouths and sang notes rounder and wilder than I had ever heard. "Joy . . . joy . . . joy" rang in my ears. Stanley held Evelyn's hand, and Evelyn reached for mine. The air smelled sweeter than in the city. I dared to feel the twinge of feet-dragging happiness. Was this the intricacies of the heart? Or was I slipping into that delusional state from shades of loss?

"Joy . . . joy . . . joy." The chorus spread the word across the audience as swiftly as the speed of light. It stuck in my head and rang out amid the darker phrases that Steve and Kay, and even John D'Orfini, dared speak. I knew they were trying to help me accept the real possibility that Vinni was gone forever. Dead, even. But that's just it. It was their theory. Not mine.

"I'm going to walk around a bit," I said. "It's so beautiful."

Music sweetened the air as I meandered alone on the grounds of the lush estate.

Stanley took Evelyn for lemonade and macaroons offered in another tent. As I walked, I discovered sculptures in surprise places behind lilac hydrangea bushes as large as trees. Life-size figures of men and women picnicking along a dirt road sat frozen in stone. In the distance, I saw an older man sitting on a bench outside a large, fenced-in pool. He appeared not to notice me as I grew closer. Finally, he looked up and I stopped. Hannah's husband, George, was the man on the bench. His white slacks and short-sleeved white shirt made him nearly unrecognizable. Gone were his baker's apron and preoccupied expression. In the bakery, he moved from kitchen to display case. But here, his face had a present serenity that stunned me.

"I know you," he said in a low voice. He uncrossed his legs, and I saw the worn soles of both shoes. "Come and sit."

"Did you enjoy the concert?" he asked.

"Yes, everything is beautiful here." I said. George nodded and looked around, but then he turned to face me. "My Hannah is a fine woman. Leave her be. Hannah is my wife, and I must protect her above everything and everyone else."

"Protect her from what?" I asked. The sun beat down on my head without mercy. Thin streams of sweat slid along the sides of my rib cage.

George slipped more deeply into his European accent. For the first time, I noticed it was slightly different than Hannah's.

"Protect her from what?" I repeated.

From betrayal? The words stuck in my throat. He stood and bowed his head, signaling our meeting had ended. I wasn't ready to let him go.

"I have a child out there who needs me. You and Hannah helped your friend Hilda take her and leave the country, didn't you? A German woman. Don't you understand that you and Hannah could both go to prison for the rest of your life!"

George's face retrieved the preoccupied look I had seen at the bakery. I knew I had confirmed the truth. His shoulders tightened. His eyes narrowed into slits of compassion. He stood and turned to me as if he wanted to tell me something.

"Secrets—they bind us," he said.

"Whose secrets?"

"Have you never given your word, child? Made a promise to someone you loved?"

"What kind of promise?"

George shook his head. His eyes focused on the dirt beneath his feet. He walked away on the same road that had carried me earlier into an ocean of unexplainable happiness. I sat on the bench, aware of the wreckage of the day thrust upon me by George's words.

I hadn't been sitting for more than five minutes when in the distance I saw a man running toward me. I recognized him as a greeter who handed us a program as we entered the large tent. I stood up and walked quickly in his direction, opposite from where George had left me at the bench.

"I'm afraid your friend has fainted," he said

Evelyn had been taken to the main house on the estate, where the public was not allowed. The young man with a lithe physique led me into a sumptuous drawing room. Golds reflected off one another. Heavy drapes cinched at their waists, created a shimmer throughout the room. Chandeliers—three, I think—danced in place. I was sweaty and out of breath after racing up the mammoth outdoor staircase to reach Evelyn. Stanley, who had happened to be standing by Evelyn when she reached for a lemonade and fell to the ground, was bent over her.

"What's wrong?" I said. I brushed past a few onlookers, who

at first attempted to stop me from getting too close. I knelt down by Evelyn's side. She was lying on a rolled-arm chaise covered in gold damask. The buttons of her white top were open. I could see a woman's slip covering teardropped breasts like loose grapes. I was sure Evelyn's embarrassed expression had nothing to do with the open blouse but rather with the uninvited attention.

Evelyn sipped water through a straw. A woman dressed in a flowing, floor-length, white shawl stood by Stanley.

"Is someone watching for the ambulance?" she asked in a controlled voice.

I moved in closer to hear Stanley say, "It's taken care of, Tuba. Thank you."

"Good," the woman answered, without looking at me as she addressed Evelyn's former husband. "Let her stay and rest here until the ambulance comes. Don't move her."

Was that a slight smile I saw behind Stanley's face?

"Stanley, my hip?" Evelyn asked in a drawn voice.

He had been gently probing around both her hips, as if looking for a protruding bone. "You're not saying *ouch*," he said. "Always a good sign."

Evelyn caught my eye and sighed. "It's nice to have a doctor in the family, isn't it?" she said.

"You're lucky you didn't hit your head when you fainted," Stanley said.

I looked beyond the top of Evelyn's head, and for the first time I noticed a collection of hanging black-and-white lithographs. I recognized the work. Two sets of paired images hung side by side. I looked into Evelyn's eyes and read into them what I was thinking. A silent message passed between us. She knew I belonged here.

"Stop fussing, everyone. Stanley, I'm fine," said Evelyn. A pink color blushed her cheeks.

I moved toward the art on the wall. My heart leaped into my throat. All the art was by the German artist Käthe Kollwitz. By now, her subject matter spoke to me whenever I studied her work. Once again, a master hand had plucked me from my turmoil and positioned me where I could hope. Or had the master hand been Evelyn?

Earlier in the day, Evelyn had pointed out Tuba Schwimmer, the elegant woman in the flowing shawl who was the owner of the estate. Tuba walked over to where I stood as my back was to Evelyn.

"Maddy?" The owner spoke in a delicate voice. Her silver hair was swept into a classic chignon at the nape of her neck.

I turned, surprised she knew my name.

"I'm Tuba Schwimmer. Evelyn has told me about your loss."

Something curdled inside my stomach as I corrected this regal-looking woman. "The loss is temporary. Living wouldn't make sense if I believed otherwise." I felt awkward speaking to this elegant stranger, but I was three years beyond the rules of etiquette. "You have guests here who know where my daughter is. I don't know why they're involved in this, but they're hiding a terrible secret."

"Who are these guests?" Tuba hugged her shawl closer to her chest.

"Hannah and George—"

"Ah," Tuba interrupted. "The German bakers. I met them years ago. We were standing in line at the Botanic Garden in Brooklyn."

She moved closer. "I invite them to come each summer to hear the music and sit in my gardens."

"But what do you know about them?"

"Know?" Tuba looked puzzled. "I know they love Mozart

and the fragrance of a rose! My dear, sometimes grief clouds the mind."

Tuba gently touched my shoulders and spoke. "Put your pain next to Kollwitz's. Paint and you shall see that your work hangs in the house for others to study."

"How do you know I'm an artist?" I asked. To say the words left a lump in my throat.

"Evelyn is quite taken with your work. She's asked me to help you, and so I will. I help many artists."

"Did you help Evelyn?"

Tuba's shawl shifted off one shoulder, leaving it bare and bony. She focused on the painting on the wall as she seemed to contemplate her answer. "In the beginning, it was Evelyn who helped me, but that was a long time ago. I only returned the favor."

It was Stanley who filled me in later on how chance had sat Tuba next to Evelyn on a plane ride from Munich to New York. Two women. All those miles in the sky. By the time they reached New York, confidences had been exchanged. Tuba's husband was wheelchair bound because of a stroke that had also taken away his speech. It had given her a sense of freedom she hadn't felt since she was a young woman.

Evelyn's paintings were on the cusp of gaining international attention.

They promised to stay in touch.

TWENTY-TWO

EVELYN'S CONDITION WASN'T SERIOUS, BUT IF SHE FOR-
got to take her heart medication, she ran the risk of ending up
in a heap. Stanley rode in the ambulance with Evelyn as Tuba
arranged for her driver to bring me to the hospital. Once the
doctors in the ER were satisfied that Evelyn could leave, we
were on our way up the Parkway. Evelyn dozed next to Stanley,
resting her head on his shoulder.

When we arrived home, it was too late to call John D'Orfini. We had spent half the night in the emergency room. Three
years ago, I had stepped inside the same hospital where Rudy
had been taken, without any idea of the pain to follow, and had
asked, "Where's my daughter?" This night had catapulted me
back to the beginning of the nightmare.

Stanley took over at Evelyn's apartment. "I'll stay here tonight, Maddy. You go on up and sleep in your own place. I'll call
you in the morning to let you know how she's doing."

The dim light from the sconces in the corridor of the
apartment building threw shadows of fleur-de-lis on the walls,
although their shapes reminded me of curled legs cut off at the
knees. Their soft light dulled the green of the hallway carpet. A
hint of garlic from someone's evening meal floated down the
staircase as I walked up the flight to my apartment.

IN THE MORNING, I let myself in to Evelyn's with the key she had given me three years earlier. I found her reading the *New York Times Magazine* by the window in the tea corner.

"How are you feeling?" I asked, as I kissed her on the cheek and sat down on the floor next to the tea chair.

"I'm fine. Perfectly fine. I shouldn't have gone to the emergency room yesterday. That's what exhausted me."

Stanley walked out of the bedroom, dressed in his usual city attire: dark trousers with a button-down dress shirt. I wondered if he woke up looking this crisp every day. After a while, Evelyn withdrew for a nap. Stanley and I ate the muffins I had brought earlier.

"Thank you for taking such good care of Evelyn. You know how she likes her independence but I worry about her. Anyway, she loves you like a daughter."

His kind words filled me.

The good doctor waited a few beats and then asked, "How are you?" He drank his coffee from a white cup on a saucer with a baby-rose design. He was not a tea drinker like Evelyn.

"I met someone yesterday who knows where Vinni is." I scooted over to the edge of my seat and folded my hands on my lap like a child at the knee of a storyteller. Amid everyone's concern over Evelyn, I hadn't told a soul about my conversation with George.

"Who?" Stanley tilted his head to the side, as if he could hear better with one ear.

"The baker from Mueller's in Brooklyn. He and his wife, Hannah, helped Hilda steal Vinni. I'm sure of it." Saying it aloud scared me.

"I'm not a detective. I'm a doctor." He crossed his legs, and

I saw a tiny bit of skin exposed where his black socks withdrew from the end of his navy trousers.

"Yesterday, I saw George at the concert. He told me to leave Hannah alone. Why would he say that if he didn't have something to hide? Why?"

"I don't know. But as your doctor, I'm concerned about your health."

I interrupted because I couldn't stop myself. I took a deep breath.

"I've rented a room in Brooklyn across from Mueller's Bakery. I saw something. I think it might be connected to Vinni. But . . ."

"But?"

I stopped myself. If I were to tell Stanley about the girls disappearing down the alleyway, wasn't there the chance he'd go to John D'Orfini? Even if he thought he was helping me, I couldn't take the risk. I had come close to confessing it all to Kay one night when she was talking about the amount of files piled on her desk. Maybe by not telling what I had seen across the street—what I suspected—I believed I was playing a part in my girl's life. Not directly. But somewhere, the mothers of the girls who disappeared down the alleyway had to be asking themselves the same question. *Where's my daughter?*

"I can't abandon the idea of finding Vinni alive. I know she's out there somewhere, even if no one else does."

Dr. Stanley Goodman was the one who listened to my heart and took my blood pressure. He had no office staff. He did everything himself: copied insurance cards, scheduled appointments, and wrote prescriptions. He reminded me of my mother's doctor, a friend of my father's who came to the house and whispered something in his ear before my mother was carried out of the house on a stretcher. "Short term," my father said.

"I want you to take care of yourself. I'm insisting. Broken hearts take a long time to heal," Stanley said.

My own silence startled me. Stanley broke it up with his fatherly advice.

"Keep painting. Eat. If you don't do these things, you'll starve to death." He lowered his voice. "If Vinni is out there, you must take care of yourself while you're waiting for her to return."

TWENTY-THREE

SOMETIMES I AWOKE WITH AN URGENCY TO DRIVE TO
Spring Haven. I needed to feel the sand between my toes to take
me back to the last day I had shared with Vinni. When I sat in
the sand and closed my eyes, the taste of salt in the air found its
way onto my tongue. I imagined a woman with a mouth shaped
into a small circle screaming over me. I covered my ears, but the
screaming woman's cry pierced the air. As loud as she was, no
one came running to save me from the noise. No one pushed the
woman back into the ocean.

I called John D'Orfini on Monday and told him I was coming
down for the weekend and would arrive later Friday afternoon.
After I hung up, I booked room 2 at a Spring Haven bed-and-
breakfast called the Elizabethan. It faced the ocean and had two
large windows, a small private bathroom, one dresser, and a reading light over the left side of the bed.

As I drove down the highway with the other weekenders, I
thought of Detective D'Orfini. I hungered for talk about the
investigation. *Letting go* of the pain was not something I wanted
to do. The pain embedded inside the bone told me I was alive. I
sucked on it like a newborn greedy for her mother's tit.

The last time we had spoken, he had talked about wanting
to try a new recipe for tilapia baked in a coconut crust. I think
this was his way of trying to *settle* me—to talk about something
other than the lack of anything to report—as he *had* to know
that I didn't give a shit about tilapia.

THE BATHROOM TO the right of the police station's front door had pale green walls that reminded me of a hospital. Tiny floor tiles in the same shade square-danced when I stared at them through my open thighs from my squat on the toilet. The room was clean but cold.

I knew I had sat too long when my right leg went numb.

I flushed.

I knew the roar of the ocean could be maddening.

When I was near John D'Orfini, I felt something odd. I can't even name it. All I'll admit to is that when I was in his company, even at the police station in Spring Haven, curled up in the chair across from his desk, I thought, *So this is what it feels like to have someone's attention.*

John D'Orfini liked to cook.

"Good food nourishes. I learned this from my mother." He hesitated, and then, as if the words skipped out between his lips, he said, "I learned nothing from my father." What does someone reply to this? Instead, we both went silent until I felt the line's weight in the room. I don't think it bothered him. He let the words hang over our heads like a sagging clothesline. I ducked as I spoke.

"Nothing?"

John D'Orfini nodded. "My dad played guitar in a backup band. Guess he never grew up, even when my mother stopped following him from city to city. Eventually, she became a social studies teacher in the middle school in town. She could read a map and guess the mileage between that city and this one just by looking. My dad would go on tour and we'd expect him home, only to get a postcard in the mail from someplace in Brazil saying, 'Tour ended. Staying longer to rest up. Miss my boys.'

By the time my brother was seventeen and I was fifteen, it was just the three of us. He simply stopped coming home. When we read about him performing somewhere in the United States, we'd check a map to see how close he was to New Jersey. He died on the road. Heart attack."

John D'Orfini hesitated, as if he questioned the wisdom in second chances. "My mother taught me how to braise a pot roast and iron a crease into a pair of khakis." He laughed and shook his head.

ع

I SEE VINNI better when I close my eyes.

"Mommy, you'll come find me, won't you?" she said when she was little and wanted to play hide-and-seek in the apartment.

"Go hide. I'll close my eyes and count to twenty."

I was still counting.

John D'Orfini's stomach growled this deep-in-the-pit-of-the-stomach sound. "You're hungry."

"I can cook us something," he said

My inside voice whispered: *Pull over that bus veering off Fourteenth Street, God, and send me roses.*

"Come home with me," he said, with one hand—only one—slipped into his pants pocket.

I picked up my purse, he turned out the office lights, and we walked out of the Spring Haven police station. All but one night cop had already left for the day.

Today was the second time I had been to his home. The first time was in the beginning, when I ranted. Spring Haven is a small town. Finding an address is not difficult. I screamed at him from the street, and he brought me inside until I settled down. There it was again.

John D'Orfini's home was a single man's home. Neat, with leather. The location was farther inland, away from the ocean's noise, but the tiny backyard butted up against the bay. A small, round table with a faded navy umbrella in the middle and two patio chairs bore the erosion from salted air. The firm seat cushions were damp. A woman would have brought them inside each night.

There was a sweet smell—a combination of sage and lemon—that was unusual for a man living alone. When I told him this, he said, "Like furniture polish?" and he laughed.

The streetlights fell on small plots of grass near the curb. John D'Orfini had a narrow side yard that caught the light from the street. He had strung tiny white Christmas lights over and under the railing across his back deck and left them up all year. Between the miniature lightbulbs and the streetlamp, the bay in the back of his house shone a glossy topcoat.

He had a new pair of shoes. I had made a comment about his wingtips earlier—at least a year ago.

"New?" I said, and pointed toward his brown-blood Italian loafers. "Nice."

"Would you like a glass of wine?" he asked.

I held up my eco-friendly water bottle and shook my head. "Maybe later," I said.

I slipped off my shoes and settled into a corner on his brown leather love seat. He sat close to me. His dark eyes deepened. "A new piece of evidence was discovered in Brooklyn yesterday."

I unraveled my legs and sat up. Three years had taught me something: say nothing and wait.

"Hilda's car showed up in Brooklyn in a private residential garage. The owner of the garage died, and the executor of the estate—a guy from Queens—his nephew, opened the garage and knew it wasn't his uncle's. The guy didn't own a car. He was declared legally blind twelve years ago. Diabetes. The nephew told his buddy, a cop from Brooklyn, and they ran a check on the Jersey license plate. The make and model . . ."

John D'Orfini looked away, as if he didn't want to tell me any more. I helped him out.

"Matched Hilda and Rudy's, didn't it?"

He nodded. "The cop called the Division of Motor Vehicles for the Spring Haven phone number listed for Hilda and Rudy, but, of course, it had been disconnected. That's when I got the call at the station."

Hilda had slipped under the radar. The three-year-old theory was that she had taken the Garden State Parkway to the Outerbridge Crossing into Brooklyn. Someone had helped her dispose of the car. If the uncle hadn't died when he did, the car could have gone undetected for years. From Brooklyn, Hilda and Vinni had vanished. Hilda had followed precisely the plan she and Rudy had devised. Although Rudy's death had shocked her, it had not derailed her. Hilda wanted Vinni. And so she took her and left Rudy on the beach.

Why would a wife leave her husband's body on the threshold of death?

To take a child, that's why. Or was it to get one more chance at living the way she had dreamed?

"Geh. Geh. Geh."

Why had Rudy told Hilda to go?

"We assume the car's been in the garage for three years. The battery was dead."

"How far away is the garage from Mueller's Bakery?" I asked.

"I know where you're going with this. The FBI went to Mueller's this morning. I talked to the investigator."

"And?"

"And nothing. According to their story, Hilda and Rudy were customers. That's all. We have nothing to tie them in . . . except your—"

I slammed my hand on the leather space between us. "Hunch? I swear to Jesus, don't you dare tell me this. Not after all this time." I stood up and walked over to the screen door. The light on the bay dimmed in a mocking response to my stare. Without turning toward John D'Orfini, I spoke in a rush.

"I saw George in Damson at a concert. Call it serendipity. Call it fate. Call it whatever you want. But he asked me to stay away from Hannah. He said he would 'protect' her. Those were his exact words. Why would he say this? Why? Because, god-dammit, Hannah and George helped Hilda get away. My God, you know this is true, and yet no one seems to be able to do any-thing about it."

I thought for a second and then asked, "Does Steve know?"

"Not yet. I wanted to tell you first, since I knew you were coming down for the weekend. I waited because . . ." He did this little number with his shoulders that was between a shrug and a nod.

I could have crumpled, but I didn't. Hilda's car had been found in Brooklyn in a private residence, waiting for someone to die to be discovered.

"I took a trip up to the police station to talk to the cop who discovered the car. The young lieutenant suggested that I visit the funeral home where the nephew had arranged for his uncle's wake to 'check the guest book.'"

"And?"

"Hannah and George had signed in at the bottom of the second page. The uncle was a customer for over sixteen years. Every Thursday he came in for one loaf of brown bread with pumpkin seeds."

I pulled my knees up to my chest and hugged them.

"One more thing . . ."

I waited. My stomach lurched. Was this the end?

"They found a hair on the seat that matches one from your daughter's hairbrush."

He did not touch me or try to move closer.

When a victim is in shock, give them space. Wasn't that printed in a handbook somewhere?

I balled one hand into a fist and wrapped the other around it like a blanket. Turning my fist round and round, I went crazy with unrelated thoughts. I wanted to be alone by the water, but I didn't know if I could stand.

"Why don't you sit outside?" said John D'Orfini.

Streaming, always streaming. This was my mind curse.

Who takes a child? Over and over.

Who. Takes. A. Child.

I pushed myself up from the couch and walked outside, where the moon's light shimmied on the water. Sobs sprang up through my throat, but I pressed them back, not wanting to let go. John D'Orfini followed me. I lowered my head, but he took his hand and lifted my chin until I looked into his eyes. I suspected he knew something about the dark, but he was more adept talking about a rich cherry-sauce reduction.

"Do you like duck?" he whispered.

Without waiting for my answer, he began a slow, tender dissertation on how a good chef prepared duck. He studied my face as he spoke, caressing me with his sound, holding my gaze, rubbing his finger along my cheek, searching to see if he could keep me *settled*. Each word rose and fell as if he were reciting a sonnet. Tears ran down my cheeks. He didn't sing the lyrics. He spoke them.

"I'm going to grill two duck breasts . . . Don't worry about the fat. . . . Most people don't know how to get rid of the fat in duck . . . but you need the fat to give it taste."

John D'Orfini went inside and came back out with a plate piled with slices of uncooked eggplant and zucchini and two drenched-in-orange-marinade duck breasts. I looked up at the stars in the black sky, and I roared, "*Where are you, Vinni? Where the hell are you?*"

John D'Orfini continued basting the vegetables with olive oil and then laid them out on the grill as if he were putting an infant to bed.

TWENTY-FOUR

AFTER EVELYN FAINTED AT THE CONCERT, I WATCHED HER like a doting mother. She seemed less energetic, and although she resumed painting in preparation for her upcoming show in the late fall, I sensed a brooding soul had invaded the studio.

"I'm a little tired these days. That's all. Remember, I'll be eighty in another year." Her internal light had dimmed. I had read a study about aging and its effects on memory. What surprised me was that whereas short-term memory receded in the brain, long-term memory often gained clarity. The article emphasized how hidden turmoil or past traumas often revisited with unforgiving strength.

Evelyn's work turned dark. Her devotion to the primary colors faded to a newfound use of charcoal. Black dust crept under her fingernails and stayed. At night, I washed her hands as she closed her eyes. At first, she pulled back.

"Go upstairs and get your rest," she'd say.

"It won't take me long," I said in a soft voice, as I filled a basin with warm water and a packet of lavender powder. "Soak your hands, Evelyn." And that's how it began. Hands first. Then feet. She took in the nurturing like a baby sucking its own toes. Soon I was giving her baths, sponging her back, squeezing steamy water over her head, massaging her rounded shoulders, creased from years of standing at the easel. As Evelyn's body weakened, mine inched its way toward strength. At times, as I shampooed her hair in the tub, she closed her eyes and hummed. I wondered whether the wet on her cheeks was tears, rather than water from the sponge.

Once, she cried out about the baby she lost. "How I would love to have gotten to know her. How have I lived all these years without that baby child? Oh God, I don't know how I've done it."

When I brought up the subject the next day, she acted surprised.

"Why are we talking about this? That was so long ago. What makes you ask me this now?"

"Nothing," I said.

෧

I LEFT THE bathroom door open for Bach's *Impassionato* to float in from the studio. I lit candles of different shapes and scents—jasmine, gardenia, lavender, calendula, sage, and cherry rose—and placed them throughout the bathroom, careful to avoid the white towels piled on an antique table graced with pear-shaped legs in the corner. Evelyn collected soaps and lotions from every part of the world. I read some of the ingredients aloud to her as she soaked: coffee beans with dandelions, grapefruit seeds with honey, and sea salt with lemon. I became adept at choosing a complimentary soap with a soothing lotion to rub into Evelyn's feet.

She had the most energy right before lunch. She slept for an hour, but when she awakened, she seemed more tired than she had been before she closed her eyes.

"I received a call this morning from the director of the gallery. She wants to come by to see the pieces I'll be showing," she said.

Evelyn's show was scheduled for the end of October. This was mid-September. I had spent the month of August in a rental in Spring Haven. I sweated out the record highs in a house with one air-conditioning unit in the kitchen. A slight but noticeable breeze drew the lonely down to the boardwalk at 1:00 a.m. I was one of them. When I walked from one end to the other—an hour's worth of steps—I secretly hoped I'd see John D'Orfini walking toward me from the other end of the boardwalk. I wanted him to tell me something. But there was nothing new. Sometimes, in the afternoon, we met for a drink. Nothing alcoholic. Twice we had dinner together, but I drove my own car to the restaurant and met him there. Neither of us wanted gossip.

Once that month, I had to fly out to Iowa for three days to work on a fashion shoot for *Hot Style* magazine. They continued to feed me projects, keeping me in the family. Three young sensations—fifteen-year-olds discovered for their wholesome looks in farm country outside Iowa City—were turning the runways upside down. Designers wanted the tall, pale girls to model their creations on the farms where they grew up.

I watched as they smoked in between shoots.

Vinni wasn't that much younger. I wondered how tall she had grown by now.

~

"SOMEONE FROM THE *New York Times* is coming to interview me. I want you to be here when she visits," said Evelyn.

I turned around in surprise. "This is exciting, don't you think?" I asked.

She smiled, but that was all. Evelyn's last solo show had been seven years earlier, but now that news of her exhibit was creating a buzz, invitations to speak had started rolling in.

"I've been invited to lecture at the Ninety-Second Street Y in a series this fall," she told me one afternoon when I stopped by with a sample of fabrics she had asked me to pick up for her, all in varying shades of purple.

Often, I traveled with Evelyn uptown and listened and watched as she stepped up to the podium and spoke about her work. Her long, tiered skirts with elegant shawls distracted the audience from her slower steps. On the evenings of the lectures, I arrived at her studio two hours earlier and helped her get ready.

"Pick something for me to wear tonight. You're the fashion guru."

A month before her art show, she slipped and fell on the Persian rug in her bedroom on the same day she was scheduled to be the featured speaker at the Y. It was in the late afternoon, but within moments she had a solution. "You go. Speak for me. You can do it. You know what I was going to talk about. The charcoal paintings—the new series for the show."

I was stunned.

"Evelyn, I can't."

"Of course you can, dear!"

Stanley went in the ambulance with Evelyn. I traveled uptown in a cab. Sweat ran down my ribs. What would I say? I had been painting side by side with Evelyn for the past year. I had attended her salons. I had listened to her impromptu coaxings in my own work to pay attention to the light in order to traverse the dark.

I wouldn't tell them, "This is a lady I bathe several times a week, who hums in the tub. She has a tight-fisted muscle in a state of perpetual contraction above the left corner of her right shoulder blade. Throughout the day, she drinks a fusion of black and green tea poured into elegant cups purchased in places like

Provence, Lucca, Mendocino, and Quogue. We paint together, and it is very, very good, even though dying used to seem like the only way out after my daughter vanished from the beach."

I wouldn't say any of this.

I practiced out loud in the cab. The beginning was easy.

"Evelyn Daly is unable to be with us tonight. She is the most underrated artist of our time. Her place in the art world should be firmly established by now, yet it's not. What is wrong with us that we need to wait until the artist can barely hear our words before we give her recognition?"

I ended up repeating the phrase *What is wrong with us?* several times during my lecture. I answered my own questions. A fleeting sense of bravery overcame me as I spoke.

~

WITH A NEWLY replaced hip, Evelyn was deep into a difficult rehab, and I knew she was in pain. I tried to keep her focused on the exhibit. At the end, Evelyn planned on showing eighty paintings. Five of these were the new charcoals I had been working on for months.

I had finished the large piece that needed eyes. Inside one eye, I drew a sword, a kitchen knife, and scissors inserted into a baby's abdomen laid out on a white plate. In the other eye, I drew a sandy beach with a girl toddler wrapped and entangled within her own hair like seaweed. I painted a child's half face a choking blue. When I turned around, Evelyn was staring at the painting, nodding and smiling.

"Keep going. Don't stop," she said.

Evelyn hobbled throughout the studio over the next three weeks as I painted four more in a series I called "Charcoal Blue." The canvas gave me a place to be free. I felt out of breath, as if I had been racing for years to catch up. I felt . . . exuberant! Excited to be alive.

How dare I have felt this way? My skin tingled. Guilt hovered around the edges.

"Yes, my love. You've done it. You've come back," Evelyn said.

Later, I overheard a phone conversation she had with the exhibit's director. "I want to add five more pieces to the show. They're not mine, but I want them hung."

ر

JOHN D'ORFINI HAD a habit of arriving late for non-police-related events. When I arrived with Evelyn an hour early, he was standing outside the Warehouse, a gallery in the former Meatpacking district, now turned cutting-edge in the world of art. Originally scheduled for a gallery in Greenwich Village, the show had attracted such huge anticipation, the venue had to be moved. Evelyn's friend Nina, who died during their years at Cooper Union, had a sister, Helen, who had risen in the art world as caretaker of her sister's estate. She had been interviewed for an article in the *New York Times*. Her support drew dozens more followers. Helen wielded a strong arm in the art world. Caretaking for her sister's estate had taught her the importance of good relations with the art critics in Manhattan. She did not shy from the powers of skillful marketing and chose her words with a keen ear.

"The underappreciated artist Evelyn Daly was close to Nina. Of course, I'm looking forward to going to her show. Nina would want me to be there." The director of the exhibit hired an assistant to deal with the influx of calls from artists around the world.

JOHN D'ORFINI HELPED us move Evelyn into a wheelchair. We had had many discussions about the chair over the past week.

"I will not—do you all hear me?—will *not* attend this opening in a wheelchair."

I covered the seat in an elegant purple silk to match the long skirt she wore. It looked like a throne with yardage flowing over the back like a train.

Kay arrived, dressed in slim trousers and over-the-knee black leather boots. I might have been jealous of how good she looked, except for the wall. Evelyn had demanded that I have one short wall dedicated to my "Charcoal Blue" series. I wore a long lilac skirt bustled in the back with thirty-six antique fabric-covered buttons. I had found the blouse in a consignment shop a year before—lilac and green like young grass, cropped in the front, with a flowing back shaped in a V before the bustle. The matching jacket was cropped at the waistline.

"You look good," John D'Orfini said when he saw me.

"Do I?" I asked.

"Yes." He hesitated, as if deciding what horse to bet on, then added, "Radiant."

Although we spoke on the phone, we hadn't seen each other since the evening he'd told me about the discovery of Hilda's car—when he had cooked duck.

Once, I had caught my own reflection in the mirror in Evelyn's bathroom and noticed my hair seemed thicker. Short. At least it didn't look sick. The steam from Evelyn's baths cleansed my skin. As I knelt on the floor and hovered over Evelyn from behind to massage her worn muscles, the steam rose up and fed me.

Radiant was too strong a word. Wasn't it used to describe an inner glow? Hardly a way to describe a woman like me. A childless woman who longed for the womb. Of course, John D'Orfini saw things in people that others missed.

"It's my job to notice," he said.

⁓

WITHIN ONE HOUR of the opening reception, over four hundred people had arrived. More were expected as crowds lined up outside. Excitement crackled in every corner of the vast space. Evelyn had never shown the series she had been working on at the time her baby stopped breathing. Until now. As people walked by, a hush felled them into silence. Sixteen paintings began with the baby as an amoeba in Evelyn's womb, followed by birth and then death. In one piece, a toe—perfectly balanced—sat on top of the pointed side of an upturned elbow. Another held five empty glass milk bottles with fully formed babies—one each—floating in water in the fetal position.

Evelyn called the series "Life."

The opening was a huge success. The *New York Times* referred to me as Evelyn's student and discovery—"someone new to the art world but worth paying attention to."

Near the end of the reception, I saw an elegant-looking woman with silver hair pulled into a chignon walk through the door. At first I couldn't place her, but then, as I watched her weave her way through the crowd toward Evelyn, I remembered. She was Evelyn's friend Tuba, the art patron and owner of the estate in New Jersey. Now she was here and she would see what I was capable of. As I made my way across the room to speak to her, I stopped as my gaze left her and settled on the rounder female behind her.

John D'Orfini followed my steps. He had seen Hannah a few seconds before I did.

"Let's go outside for some air," he said.

"No, I don't want to go outside."

"Come with me." His voice had an edge that matched the feel of his hand on my arm as he steered me toward the door.

The fresh air snapped me back into autumn and real life— far away from *radiance*. The cool night propelled me as I broke away from John D'Orfini. Hannah was directly in front of Tuba in the archway of the door.

Right before I lunged for her, Hannah's head jerked back in surprise, someone grabbed my arm midair.

A mother beast doesn't let go. Must I explain to you that I could no longer control myself? That practicing control wears down the soul? That something inside me snapped at the mere sight of Hannah—this woman who I knew hid something vile?

I wrestled the tips of my fingers toward Hannah's neck. My desire to squeeze out what she knew about Vinni came to an abrupt halt as John D'Orfini lifted me off the ground and carried me away from the crowd. I turned and screamed, "Talk to me or I'll kill you!"

Language wounds but never kills. I had no desire to kill Hannah. All I wanted was for her to speak to me. To tell me what she knew.

Hannah put her hand in front of her mouth. Her round shoulders rounded more, as if she wanted to disappear. *Yes, go hide,* I thought. But then she lifted her head and shot me a look that I will never forget.

She was scared.

Kay linked her arm in mine and steered me down the street, away from the gallery. In a voice low and stern, she instructed me, as she had for years, "Stay away from that woman, and, for God's sake, stay away from the bakery. You could jeopardize everything we've been investigating."

She, John D'Orfini, and I went for a drink around the corner. John D'Orfini sat between us. Kay was already plotting the scenario for the judge. I knew Hannah wouldn't do anything. She had too much to hide.

"What were you thinking?" Kay asked, as she raised her arm for the waiter. "You were out of control."

"Who invited that woman? That's what I want to know," I said.

Kay began, "Look, Evelyn's exhibit has been advertised all over—"

"She's following me. What I do. What I paint." My mouth felt dry from the combination of cool air in the gallery and the chill outside. "She's watching."

"What Hannah Mueller does is one thing, but how *you* react is another," Kay said.

"Oh, shit, please. You know as well as I do why Hannah came to the gallery."

"Why? To see if you've gone crazy yet? Well, now she knows, doesn't she? I want you steering clear of trouble. And that means restraining yourself from attacking bakers."

"Maybe we should all stop worrying so much about the law. What good has it done us?" I said. I looked over at John D'Orfini in time to see him raise his glass in a silent toast.

TWENTY-FIVE

JOHN D'ORFINI LISTED BULLETS ONE THROUGH FIVE ABOUT why I had to control myself.

"Number one: the law requires following protocol. Number two: *trained personnel* means just that—*trained*. Number three: a kidnapping is a dangerous crime, and you are not trained. Number four: the deduction is that Hilda took Vinni, but there is no unequivocal proof that a third party was not involved. Number five: even the threat of pulling out a criminal's eyes doesn't mean you can coerce a witness to talk if she can live with the guilt of remaining silent."

"I've got it," I said.

"I'm not sure you do. Assuming Hilda took Vinni, we're still in the dark about why."

"I've got it. Now walk me home." The exhibit already seemed a distant memory.

"Walk?"

"Yes. Walk."

It was well after midnight. I knew Stanley had taken Evelyn home.

"Don't worry, Detective, I'll protect you. It's my city."

As we turned the corner, I caught sight of a black limousine parked in front of the gallery. Headlights shone onto the cobblestone street. Late-night passersby ignored the truck parked behind it.

"What's going on down there?" I said.

John D'Orfini slowed to a stop. "Wait here," he said.

"No way. I'm going with you."

He pulled me into a doorway as we watched four men lift painting after painting into the truck. I gasped out loud when I saw the curator of the exhibit, Helen Henning, step outside. She pulled at the white silk jacket around her shoulders. A hand extended from the window of the limousine, and she reached in to shake it. Moments later, the limousine pulled away, with the truck close behind it. Helen stood at the curb, hands crossed at her chest. She was smiling. The white of the jacket glistened against the night.

John D'Orfini grabbed my hand, and we ran toward the gallery. "Just let me do the talking. I mean it. Be still." I was out of breath when we reached Helen, who looked startled when she saw us.

"What was that all about?" John D'Orfini asked her. "Please step inside."

Helen and I followed him.

In the light of the gallery, I could see she was almost giddy. "Why do you look like a schoolgirl?" I asked. I had already forgotten about being quiet.

"You'll be smiling, too, Maddy, when I tell you," Helen said in a triumphant voice.

She continued to speak, but I heard nothing from that point on. The wall where my paintings had hung was bare. John D'Orfini charged several steps ahead of me.

"Where are Maddy's paintings?" he asked.

"That's what I've been trying to tell you. They sold!" said Helen.

"All of them?" I squeaked. "Who bought them? No one mentioned anything to me during the reception."

"He wasn't at the reception. My assistant and I were talking on the phone after we had locked up for the night. A man knocked, and from outside the closed door, he said he wanted to make a large purchase. I hung up right away. He told us that he was the attorney for a client who knew about your opening, Maddy, and his client wanted to purchase your work immediately and remove it from the exhibit. Of course, we explained that this was not standard protocol, but he was adamant that we'd lose the sale if we didn't comply with the client's request. He gave me a check from his firm's trust account for twenty-five thousand dollars for your five paintings. Congratulations!"

Helen reached into her pocket and pulled out the check to show me.

"He didn't by chance mention the name of his client, did he?" John D'Orfini asked.

Helen shook her head but said, "You should be very proud of yourself, Maddy!"

"I'll need a copy of this check," John D'Orfini said.

"Detective, you don't think that this has anything to do with . . . with Maddy's *circumstance*, do you?" asked the curator. She looked at me with a troubling glance.

John D'Orfini shot me a warning. *Be still.* Of course, he had no idea how *still* I truly was, as the black limousine reminded me of the one I had seen near Mueller's from my room across the street.

Helen put her arm around my shoulder. "Dear, whatever you're going through right now, you must congratulate yourself on making such a sale on the opening night. And besides, the gentleman in the limousine was quite polite. He even wished me a good night."

"Did you get a look at him?" John D'Orfini asked.

"In the dark?" Helen countered. "I heard his voice as he

extended his hand. He had some kind of accent—Lithuanian, maybe. I never saw his face."

"The lawyer left his card," Helen said, as she handed it over to John D'Orfini. DONALD HOWARD, ESQUIRE.

‿

WE REACHED THE steps of my building.

"You should be in a support group with other grieving parents," John D'Orfini said. He liked to do this—switch highways—as though we were driving along in separate cars.

"I'm not grieving. I'm fighting. Why aren't you talking to me about Donald Howard?"

"I will when I know something."

I was exhausted, worn from the excitement of the exhibit, from the mess with Hannah, and now from the idea that a mysterious collector had bought my paintings.

"Come up," I said. It had been three months since we had been together.

John D'Orfini reached out and touched my arms. I sensed the warmth of his hands through the sleeves of my jacket.

"Do you want me to?" He spoke with such gentleness, I thought my heart would break.

Vinni had been taken almost four years ago. Up until that night, I hadn't known what could dull the pain. I had unleashed a passion that began with my fingers on Hannah's throat. John D'Orfini's hands continued the story, gently smoothing out cries from inside the cage that housed my ribs. I believed that nothing, not even John D'Orfini, could reach me—it was to be a physical thing. That's all. Afterward, right when he came inside me, it changed. The physical crossed over, and although I had guarded it, I managed to squeak out, "Don't stop." He must have heard me, because he gave me more until I cried. He wiped my face with gentle strokes. I came again. I thought of the woman at the coffee shop who blessed herself before she took the first spoonful of her yogurt. Even if I could unwrap my arms from around his back, I couldn't make the sign of the cross. He was still inside me. Like a man who had found a home. John D'Orfini rested his head on my shoulder. The sound of his breathing, even and sweet, rocked me into a deep sleep. The next morning, when I awoke, there was a note on the kitchen table.

Hope you don't mind. I made a cup of joe. I'll get back to you on D. Howard.
Thanks. John

꙳

"MEN ARE LIKE that," Evelyn said, when I had to tell someone about the note and I wasn't ready to talk about it with Kay. "It's not what they say; it's never about that, dear. Nothing would have been built. Starting with Rome."

We laughed until our cheeks hurt.

"There's one more thing. Someone bought my paintings last night." I waited a second and then said, "All of them."

Evelyn's eyes widened. She repeated, "All of them?"

I nodded. "Someone by the name of Donald Howard—an attorney—came in after the gallery had closed. Helen was just settling things for the evening. He bought the paintings, as directed by a client of his, for twenty-five thousand dollars. Of course, I know Helen takes a commission, but it happened so unexpectedly . . . I've got a strange feeling in my gut."

"Let it go," Evelyn said. "Take the money and let it go."

I didn't understand how Evelyn could dismiss something so fast. She'd been doing this lately. Listening. Reacting. Then moving on, as if her mind couldn't stay for long in one place.

Of course I was thrilled that my paintings had sold. Someone willing to pay a handsome price wanted my work and wanted it quickly. Although I tried returning to the topic of my first paintings being sold, Evelyn never engaged. I didn't know why she was unwilling to discuss it, other than perhaps because Helen Henning represented a painful time from Evelyn's past.

As I cared for Evelyn, I noticed a pattern. She'd simply wave her hand when she didn't want to talk further, or else she'd say, "I have larger things to think about." I guessed it was a way of keeping her priorities in order. She had disciplined herself from an early age to work without distractions.

Vinni was an exception. Ever since we had met Evelyn on the stairwell, she had made time for Vinni. She set up a small table and chair off to the side, away from the stacks of her work, and encouraged Vinni to draw a picture in her mind. "What do you see right now?" she'd ask.

With confidence, Vinni would say, "The blue blanket on my bed" or, "Mommy's face!"

⁐

EVELYN'S ART SHOW had been a huge success. Although she had loved the opening, she was exhausted, and the following week I often found her asleep on the chaise in the studio at the end of the day. The northern light lowered to a slit and cast a shade of gray. No signs of blue anywhere.

YEAR FOUR

TWENTY-SIX

IT WAS EARLY MORNING. I RECOGNIZED STANLEY'S VOICE on the phone. "I'm downstairs at Evelyn's. I need to come up right away."

He sounded as if he were almost whispering.

"Okay." I hung up the phone on the night table. Steve had suggested two years earlier that I forgo the landline, but I couldn't bag up my old life. I hung on to the landline in case Vinni tried to call.

A soft knock stirred me more awake. I walked to the door and opened it.

Stanley's eyes told me before he spoke a word.

"She's gone," he whispered.

Evelyn was dead.

MOTHER GONE. FATHER gone. Now Evelyn gone. Vinni, too—not dead, like the rest, but gone. I began to shake. I leaned against the door outside the apartment. I slid down the wall, skin to paint. I pulled my knees up and dropped my head on my arms and cried. I wondered why Evelyn hadn't called me when she fell ill. She had known it would take Stanley at least twenty minutes to reach her apartment.

"Oh, Maddy dear," Stanley said, as he reached for me. The

New York Times rested outside on the welcome mat. Sounds choked up through my throat. My belly contracted. Stanley hugged me to his chest. He waited for me to lift my head.

"What happened?" I asked.

"Evelyn called me last night around midnight. As soon as I heard her voice, I knew something wasn't right. She couldn't find the words. She spoke as if she were pushing them out one by one. I asked her if she was okay, but all she said was, 'I feel faint.' I wanted to send an ambulance and meet her at the hospital, but she wouldn't listen. Over and over, she kept repeating the same words. 'I'm sorry . . . I'm sorry.'"

"Sorry? About what?"

Stanley choked on his own tears. "The baby . . . she . . . we lost. I tried to hush her. She never forgave herself. Even at the end, it consumed her."

"You need to sit," I said.

"I raced over to the apartment, but I was too late. When I opened the door, I saw her on the floor—at the end of the hallway."

I let out a deep breath.

How could Evelyn be gone? Four years ago, she had swooped in and saved me.

∿

IN JUNE, EVELYN'S friend Tuba arranged for a boat to take the three of us—Stanley, Tuba, and me—out on the ocean to scatter Evelyn's ashes. Tuba read from Sanskrit as the ashes swept farther out to sea.

> *Look to this day!*
> *For it is life, the very life of life,*

In its brief course
Lie all the verities and realities of your existence:
The bliss of growth;

The splendor of beauty;
For yesterday is but a dream,
And tomorrow is only a vision:
But today, well lived, makes every yesterday
A dream of happiness,
And every tomorrow a vision of hope;
Look well, therefore, to this day.

After the spreading of the ashes, Tuba invited us to lunch at her home. Stanley mumbled something I couldn't hear in response to Tuba's asking, "Stanley, you'll stay and rest overnight, I hope. Yes? You always enjoyed the gardens when you visited with Evelyn."

"I . . . I . . ." Stanley looked confused. Tuba was a close friend of Evelyn's, but Stanley held a position on the periphery of their circle.

"Of course, Maddy, you must stay as well," Tuba said. "Let me show you the blue garden." She touched Stanley's arm gently. "What do you say? Will you stay?"

My heart skipped a beat. The idea of a blue garden belonged to Vinni. She had shared it with me, but it was *her* vision.

Stanley looked at me as if he didn't know what to say. He had just scattered his former wife's ashes. His white hair was blown to the side from the ocean's breeze, and he kept clearing his throat, complaining about a constant drip that had started two weeks ago. He removed his light jacket, revealing a rumpled long-sleeved shirt. A lonely old man had replaced his usual meticulous-looking self.

TUBA WASTED NO time sharing her thoughts as we sat on the patio. She directed her focus to me, even twisting in her chair so I could see the directness of her intent. "Maddy, it's your turn to continue where Evelyn left off."

What was she trying to tell me?

"Evelyn loved you the way she would her own child. When she was alive, I promised her I'd help you show your work. I intend to keep that promise. No question. But I want you to consider a mother-love exhibit."

"I'm not sure I understand."

"You're not the only mother in pain," Tuba said.

"Are you asking me to paint other mothers who have lost their children?"

Tuba leaned in, bending slightly from her slim hips. "I'm asking you to look beyond yourself. Then paint what you want. You're the artist," she said. She did not coat her voice with kindness, but neither did she ice over it. She spoke plainly.

Evelyn had lived the kind of life she wanted. I wasn't sure if this was a bad thing until I thought about her dying alone on the floor of her home. I didn't want to die like that. My mother died alone when she shut the garage door and started the engine. My father died alone at home in the chair where he read the newspaper. His bony knees poked out between the edges of his Bermuda shorts and his knee-high socks. When they found him, spit and vomit had run down his chin onto the front of his shirt.

Tuba's words stunned me into silence. I needed time to be alone. I would be selfish with my pain. Dredge it up to feed me. Although we had finished lunch, no one moved. A plate of sugar cookies sat untouched in the center of the table.

"In the early years, Evelyn spent much time here," Tuba said.

"The early years?"

Stanley spoke up. "After the baby died, Evelyn needed a place to rest. She found it here." Discomfort settled on his face, but then he said, "This place gave her a refuge—something I never found a way to do." His voice turned hoarse. "Evelyn loved many people. I was just one of them."

The beauty of the surroundings softened the gentle storm behind Stanley's words. I looked at him, sitting across the table. A silver spoon balanced on the edge of a crystal sugar bowl. Tuba moved her chair away from the fold of the tablecloth resting on her lap. I stood up and faced the garden to the west of the dining room. Shades of blue covered the ground. I walked down the wide stone staircase behind her. Stanley extended his hand, and I took it.

"Lovely, isn't it?" he said.

"Vinni wanted a blue garden when she grew up. She loved the color blue. We used to walk past a flower stand on the way to school, and she'd stop and point to all the blue flowers she wanted in her garden: hydrangea, iris, bluebells, cornflower blues."

"A child is a blessing," Tuba said, without turning around to see my face.

This time, I let the words ride over me.

As the path narrowed, Stanley fell back.

Blue was everywhere. I made a mental note to bring Vinni here when she returned. I knew she would love it. Tuba stopped and turned around, waving her hands gracefully in the air. Her face glowed.

"Wasn't it Monet who said, 'More than anything I must have flowers, always, always'? Yes, I think it was." She laughed lightly to herself. I drifted as she spoke, floating to a place where

I heard Vinni's voice. *I'm here, Mommy. Come find me.* I sat down on an iron bench placed on a patch of perfectly manicured grass. All around me towered blue spires of delphinium with petals like schoolgirl petticoats. A circled pattern of narcissi claimed the far edge to the right of the lower tier. Heads of blue hydrangea bushes filled in the back like the mezzanine in a theater. Tiny buds of forget-me-nots bloomed inside carefree clusters of violet.

A conversation beat in my head. *Mommy, I'm taller now. I'm singing. Come find me.*

How I missed my girl!

❧

TUBA ARRANGED FOR her driver to take Stanley and me home. I looked out the window at the cars speeding by and thought about Evelyn. If only she had been here, I would have gone to her and asked, "How much longer must I wait?" But a dead person's advice doesn't travel.

It wasn't more than three weeks after we scattered Evelyn's ashes in the ocean that Stanley offered me the opportunity to buy Evelyn's apartment. It was Kay who encouraged me to buy it.

"Think of it as continuing who you've become," she said.

"And that is?"

"Someone new."

❧

THE FOLLOWING SUNDAY morning, Kay asked me to go running with her. I agreed because I had already turned her down twice. Being friends since we were ten was too long to ignore, but most of all, we missed each other's company.

In the middle of a pit stop, with both our heads lowered, arms resting on our knees as we sat on a park bench, Kay blurted out something that had obviously been on her mind for years. "I never understood why you changed when you married Steve. Your Saturday painting class . . . you gave it up because of him, didn't you?"

She already knew the answer.

"And Evelyn? She brought it all back. She helped you see what you could do. But now she's gone, so it's up to *you*, dammit, to keep on painting. Buy her place and make it yours. You've got a gift. You've always been the one who had the talent."

Kay's mother died of a heart attack in her sleep when Kay was twenty-seven years old. Her father rolled over one morning and noticed his wife had stopped breathing. A year later, he died the same way. Kay withstood it all without missing more than two days' work when her mother died and one and a half days for her father's wake and funeral. He died on a Saturday, leaving behind a spotless ranch house with a newly paved patio off the kitchen. He had laid the stones himself the previous summer.

People in pairs or alone ran by us to a silent beat, un-aware—or were they?—that life was so fucking unfair.

Kay took my hand inside both of hers. "I want you to be happy," she said.

"I know you do," I whispered.

My mother was nothing like Kay's. My mother died alone when she shut the garage door and started the engine.

᮫

I'VE TOLD YOU twice now.

TWENTY-SEVEN

JOHN D'ORFINI COULDN'T LET GO OF SOMETHING THE nephew said about his uncle, the man who owned the garage where they found Hilda's car. On the second interview at the station house in Brooklyn, the nephew—whom John D'Orfini described to me as "not the brightest bulb"—called his uncle "the fixer."

"The what?" I asked.

"The fixer. The community fixer. According to the nephew, his uncle helped people fix their problems."

"What kinds of problems?" I asked.

"Money, immigration, family disputes. Anything that a bankroll and a strong arm could fix. I think the uncle was sort of like the godfather of the neighborhood. Russian immigrants who spoke little English moved into the neighborhood. Dear old Uncle stepped in, and I don't think his involvement was limited to language. I've talked to a few neighbors on his block, and they speak of the guy like he was a saint. At his wake, hundreds and hundreds stood outside in line, waiting to pay their respects."

I found out more later. Uncle, although legally blind, presented an immaculate appearance. People remembered him as meticulous. Whether he dropped in at Mueller's Bakery or had an appointment at the dentist, he wore a suit and tie and a monogrammed shirt with French cuffs. His dark sunglasses sparkled, without a trace of dust on either lens. Polished Italian leather shoes in black, brown, and burgundy coordinated with his custom-tailored suits.

჻

JOHN D'ORFINI CALLED me on Thursday.

"I was thinking you might want to come to the Brooklyn police station tomorrow," he said. "Let the nephew see you. You can't ask him questions. Let me do the talking. Do you believe you can do that? Just sit and be quiet?"

"Probably not, but I'll try," I said. I visualized John D'Orfini in his office with his phone attached to his ear, his face about to brighten from one side to the other until it spread over his forehead.

"I'll be there," I said.

჻

EVERYTHING ABOUT THE interrogation room was cold. "Tell me about your relationship with your uncle." This was John D'Orfini, obsessed with solving the crime committed on his watch.

"I told the other cop here last week. I didn't see him much. He was kind of a busy guy. I mean, he couldn't see good or nothing, but he still got dressed like a dude every morning."

"I thought you didn't see him much."

"Who's telling the story here, man?"

While the nephew spoke, he scratched at his chin, where a cluster of red pimples looked ready to burst pus. John D'Orfini slammed the table and made me jump, spilling the water down the front of my turtleneck. He reached across the table toward the nephew, who was as surprised as I was by the noise.

206 | JULIE MALONEY

"Whaddaya want to go and do that for? Look, Uncle and me didn't talk much. That's all I'm saying."

"That's not all you're saying, unless you want to have more to cleanup than that sick pus on your chin."

I felt a hint of compassion for this twenty-six-year-old, acne-ridden slouch who was counting on the money he hoped his uncle had left him so he could open a sub shop. "Cash, ya know. And I like the smell of red onions on my fingers."

He rubbed his hands on the sides of his pants, as if they were wet. Rolling them over and over. Then he asked, "Can I smoke? Makes me remember things."

To my astonishment, John D'Orfini reached into his pocket, took out a pack of Parliaments, and slid them across the table to the nephew. Since when was he a smoker? Or was this part of the guise when Country Cop came to the city and played with the NYPD?

"What do you know about the car in your uncle's garage?"

"Nothing. Honest, man. Nothing. Shit, I was surprised to see it there. That's why I called my buddy at the station. I mean, I wanted the thing outta there so's I could sell the place. I didn't want no lady's car."

"How did you know it was a lady's car?" John D'Orfini picked up the pack of cigarettes and placed it back inside his pocket.

"It was powder blue, man."

John D'Orfini didn't buy that Uncle was a saint, but he ended the conversation with the nephew on a sweet note.

"Confuse them. Always confuse the suspect," he'd say.

"Well, thanks for coming down to the station. Sorry for your loss."

I raised my eyebrows into a question reeking of profanity.

"One more thing. I want you to look at Ms. Stewart and tell

her you know nothing about her missing daughter. I want you to tell her how sorry you are that she hasn't seen her little girl in almost four years."

"You want me to say all that?"

John D'Orfini nodded. I stood up and walked to John D'Orfini's side of the table.

The nephew took an exaggerated drag on his cigarette and exhaled circles in full moons. I stepped out of the way of the smoke.

"I'm real sorry to hear this, ma'am. Real sorry."

He gave the abbreviated version.

John D'Orfini opened the door, and the nephew walked out, wiping his chin with the back of his hand.

☙

WHEN THE NEPHEW was no longer in sight, I said, "I don't know about this guy and his uncle. *The fixer?* I mean, come on."

"If Hilda's car was found in Uncle's garage, then I guarantee you Uncle had something to do with it getting there."

"You're beginning to sound like a character in a movie," I said.

He looked at me hard so I couldn't turn away. "You need a break."

This was what I loved about him.

"Let's stop for a cup of tea," he said.

☙

WE TOOK A booth in a corner in the back of a coffee place that boasted twenty-seven coffees guaranteed to reboot your metabolism. As John D'Orfini walked up to the counter, I looked out the window, wondering how I became a childless mother. Grief washed over me like a wave. It came without warning—so strong it stopped me no matter where I was. If I was driving in the car, I missed signs. If I was walking down Fifth Avenue on my way to the library, I missed sight of the lions outside until I found myself at Union Square, twenty-eight blocks from my destination. If I was brushing my teeth at night, grief stabbed me in the gut until I hunched over the sink, barely able to spit. Grief struck me down, but acknowledging the statistics wasn't an option. And yet there were times—times that I would never speak aloud—that made me want to put my head down and exhale a final breath.

Hadn't Kay told me she wanted me to be happy?

What was I doing renting a room across from a bakery in Brooklyn?

Watching young girls being shuttled down an alleyway in the middle of the night, wondering each time if I might see Vinni. Praying I wouldn't. Was it all a weird coincidence that I had stumbled upon something bad two buildings down from Mueller's Bakery?

JOHN D'ORFINI LOOKED at me from across the coffee shop. Both our mouths turned up—not into the shape of a smile, but rather into an acknowledgment of caring.

Forgetting the pain in the daylight was impossible. Months ago, when John D'Orfini had walked me home and stayed the night, it had been under the shield of darkness. Some nights when I couldn't sleep, I slipped my hand under the sheets and stroked myself. I thought about John D'Orfini and released the way a woman is meant to—with or without a partner.

"Where are you?" John D'Orfini commented on my faraway look as he stood at the booth with two steaming Styrofoam cups in his hand. I wondered how his expression might change if I responded by saying, *Under the sheets.*

He placed my tea down and slid across from me. The warmth from the cup felt good inside my hands. I reached for two packets of sugar and stirred them in my sweet detective's cup. His eyes softened. I pushed his cup closer. He took a sip.

"What are you hiding?"

For a second, I worried he knew about my room across from Mueller's, but then I realized that he was talking about something more intangible. A feeling? A runaway thought?

"I want to turn back the clock and do it all again. I want to begin at the beginning with Vinni, from when she was a baby. I want to try harder. I want to keep her safe. That night at the end of the summer when Hilda and Rudy invited Vinni and me to dinner . . . I remember how Hilda focused on Vinni when she talked. I thought she found her engaging, the way everyone did. Vinni had a way about her beyond her young years. She spoke in complete thoughts. I mean, my God, she was just eight years old! But I forgot! I honestly forgot that she was so young, because she *got* things. She fit into new places and situations so easily. She wasn't afraid."

I stopped and briefly touched the fingertips of my detective. His hands wrapped around his cup as he lifted it to his mouth. I looked into his kind eyes.

"I failed her."

We were in a public place in Brooklyn, not far from the police department where he had just twisted and turned the nephew into an unsuspecting mess. Touching wasn't allowed in the daylight.

John D'Orfini knew how to wait.

↵

I KNOW I'VE mentioned this before (turn back the pages), but you need to understand that knowing how to wait requires patience, and patience is a virtue of which I believed I had none.

↵

"WE'RE LEARNING MORE. I know it's slow going."

He lowered his voice and leaned in across the table, but with his hands nowhere close enough for me to touch. I wanted him to be inside me. I separated one part of my heart from the other. It would have been easier to tell him everything, but I resisted because I believed Hannah and George knew where my girl was.

"If we can find out more on Uncle, we can find out how the heck Hilda's car ended up in a private garage in Brooklyn."

"I wasn't prepared for any of this," I said. "I had a daughter. I worked and painted a little. I divorced Steve because we stopped loving each other. I used to drink coffee with a twist of lemon rind. I was ordinary and I was okay with it."

John D'Orfini circled me back. This was a stay-the-course kind of guy.

"There's nothing *ordinary* about your paintings," he said.

This was the first time he spoke of my work this way. I felt the heat on my face.

"There's a reason Hilda's car showed up here. I want to find out why."

"Let's go to Mueller's Bakery and ask George," I said.

"First, I have to pick up a file. I'll meet you at Penn Station tomorrow, in the morning, and together we'll head out to Brooklyn."

He said it as if we were going to another state—Ohio, or even farther west: one of the Dakotas.

෫

THE NEXT MORNING, John D'Orfini handed me the file. It was Saturday. "I thought you might want to read this," he said.

"What is it?"

"Just read it so you know who we're dealing with."

Over the years, Hannah had been careful—selective—cautious around the neighborhood "fixer." She baked with her head down.

But when it came to others who needed help, she was a kind of broker. She overheard conversations by making herself invisible when necessary, lost inside cookie crème filling and a pastry cutter. When a woman beaten blue around her right eye sat silent with her shoulders turned inward, husband at her side, Hannah talked to Uncle in a quiet voice. Two weeks later, no one questioned the husband's disappearance. When an eighteen-year-old about to graduate from high school was expected to turn down a full scholarship to Yeshiva University to go to work and help support his three younger sisters and one brother, Hannah spoke to Uncle. The following September, the boy attended his first college class. Four years later, Uncle was at his graduation ceremony. For the right price, Uncle could get you out of the country with a "paper package," including passport, credit cards, and a new Social Security number.

"Twenty thousand dollars can buy a new life." John D'Orfini said. "A 'package' on the street is as easy to get as a new washing machine." He pointed to the file open on my lap. The subway rumbled underground, making enough noise to hide our conversation. "There's pages of deals here that were made at

Mueller's Bakery," he said. "It seemed Hannah ran a kind of social services department without the paperwork. She brought the stories to Uncle. She described what the people needed, and Uncle made their problems go away. No questions asked. I suspected the fixer did more than help the needy."

"Was Hannah afraid of him?" I asked. D'Orfini shrugged.

"I'm pretty sure Hannah did the talking, but George was never out of sight when she did the brokering. Uncle got rid of people he thought were a problem. As far as we know, Hannah and George made sure not to create problems for the guy. I think they knew how to play it right. They understood that things could go a whole lot smoother with a delicate touch—like the way they turn out those iced pastries. It's what I call finesse."

"That's an interesting way of putting it."

"Hannah and George have finesse. In my business, finesse requires a strong set of closed lips. I think Uncle knew they could keep their mouths shut. Hell, look at them. What have they told us? Nothing. This takes practice. Most people don't know when to be quiet."

"Mmm," I said.

～

WHEN WE ARRIVED at Mueller's, George was behind the counter, replenishing a half-empty baking sheet of miniature fruit tarts. He must have suspected why we had come: one more set of questions, one more denial. The FBI had already paid a visit to Mueller's Bakery, but Hannah and George had revealed nothing.

They continued to bake, skilled at keeping their heads down.

George called for Hannah to come out front. The two high

school girls who worked on the weekends behind the counter ignored us.

"Hannah!" George called, just as Hannah swung through the door from the kitchen. He nodded toward me first, but Hannah acknowledged John D'Orfini and then me with a closed smile.

"Ah . . . I know what you will like." She scooped up two almond biscotti dipped in chocolate on one end. Hannah was a server—the type of woman who knew what people needed before they asked.

ℳ

"How well did you know this customer of yours named Kosinski? You know he died recently." John D'Orfini hammered. Hannah spoke ahead of her husband.

"Mr. Uncle came in for his bread every Thursday."

"Did you ever ask him for a favor?"

"What kind of favor?" George asked, ignoring Hannah's eyes.

"Any kind." After four years of listening to John D'Orfini's style of "ask, listen, write it down," I knew the less he said, the more he thought. He liked to refer to his investigative method as "planning where to put it." "I'm planning what to say to catch the bastard who's lying to my face."

John D'Orfini lowered his voice. He spoke slowly, careful not to frighten Hannah and George away, although his words were sharp. "Kidnapping is a federal offense," he said. "I don't like one bit that whoever stole Lavinia Stewart thought he—or she—could come into *my* town and take a child." He stared at the bakers. He hesitated, letting the silence build. His eyes darkened. "Both of you better understand that any questionable relationship you may have had with the deceased—Mr. Kosinski—could lead to serious punishment."

A light perspiration built around John D'Orfini's temples.

"Kosinski was a bad man. We've been watching him for some time now."

He stopped again and turned away. He was a master at increasing tension. He looked back at Hannah and George and said, "We suspect that he's involved in a prostitution ring. He may be responsible for the kidnapping of this woman's eight-year-old girl."

What was he saying?

George winced. Which horror made him react? The idea of child prostitution or the kidnapping? He and Hannah carefully avoided the other's face. *Give nothing away.* I could see it. I could imagine the conversation. . . .

We are bakers. We bake with our heads down. We buy our flour and sugar and butter from the man who pulls his truck around to the back each week. We do not ask his name. We do what we are told. We pay three percent of our profits to the man in the truck. We tuck the money inside a paper bag with one fresh-baked turnover.

John D'Orfini chipped away at their blank faces.

"Do you recognize the seriousness of what I'm telling you? You could go to jail for life." He picked up his coffee and waited before continuing. He knew just how far to tilt his head, fold his arms across his chest, and whisper, as if in a horse's ear. "I wouldn't want to see that happen to such fine bakers."

He dipped the chocolate end of his biscotti into his coffee and took a quick bite. He kept his eyes on George, who hadn't left Hannah's side. If George was the weaker of the two, then John D'Orfini wanted to be the one who broke him.

"Ah . . . yah. Mr. D'Orfini. Yah," George said, while Hannah folded her hands tightly, her knuckles white from the baking flour. Her lips closed.

John D'Orfini stopped speaking. His tongue swooshed

around the inside of his cheeks, cleaning up loose crumbs. He knew I had flinched at the sound of the word *prostitution*. It started a ringing sound in my head, until it bloomed into a bang from temple to temple across my forehead.

THE AIR IN the subway hung hot and heavy over our heads as we rode back into Manhattan. John D'Orfini spoke in a voice so quiet I had to lean in, nearly putting my head on his shoulder.

"Uncle was in the mob. The Russian mob. That we know for sure. The FBI has a file on him that's a mile long." He spoke looking straight ahead.

"He was involved in a prostitution ring seven years ago, but he served no time. His hotshot lawyer played up his medical disability. His blind status got him off when the jury couldn't prove beyond a reasonable doubt."

I held my face as still as could be. I gave nothing away. "What did he do for a living?" I asked. This was my chance to tell John D'Orfini about my room in Brooklyn, but I let it slip by without even reaching for it. It was too soon. I didn't know enough. Or was I afraid of what he might find out?

The train rumbled underground. John D'Orfini waited as we rode out into the daylight. "He owned a tiny shop around the corner. Fixed clocks and timepieces all day before he went blind from diabetes."

"Clocks? A repair shop paid for his custom suits and dress shirts?"

"Don't forget the timepieces," John D'Orfini said.

John D'Orfini didn't pursue the subject of prostitution. I remained quiet as we continued the ride into Manhattan. I went over how he had threatened Hannah and George. Only once had he raised his voice, but even then they had sat there stone-like, drinking coffee.

I broke my silence as we exited the subway at Thirty-Third Street and Sixth Avenue.

I took my time as I spoke. "I know you wanted me to see Hannah and George today so I wouldn't feel left out or ignored. And I know it's been four years." I hesitated. "I just want to say thanks."

I floated above the anguish. Evelyn's death had shown me that things didn't stay the same. Vinni was four years older. Twelve. If my mother had been here, she would have said that twelve-year-olds don't believe in hope. That hope doesn't bring happiness even if we were to sing the line in a song. But my mother was dead and Vinni was not.

ON THE CORNER of Twenty-Third Street, John D'Orfini stopped and faced me. We stared at each other until I said, "What?"

Finally, he said, "I should go."

He jumped into a cab and headed for Penn Station.

I suspected he didn't want me to ask about the prostitution ring. Was he dismissing me or holding back something he knew would make me scream? He didn't know that I had been watching the bakery from my room across the street.

Hadn't he said, "There's nothing ordinary about your paintings"?

Couldn't he see that my paintings screamed in the dark?

I had stumbled upon the girls—young and skinny—as they disappeared down the alleyway two buildings away from Mueller's. As they lost their way into the dark, they seemed less real than Vinni. Less real than her voice in my head. Of course, I knew my mother believed the voices in her head were real, too. I knew voices could get so loud that you couldn't hear a thing.

I waited for his cab to turn, and then I walked down the stairs into the subway to catch the train back to my room in Brooklyn.

∾

AT 2:00 A.M., I was certain most of Brooklyn was asleep. I watched from my room across the street as the rain splatted against the window like angry darts. My focus fastened on the black limousine parked near Mueller's Bakery. Now was not a good time to relieve myself, so I squeezed my pee in tight. I waited by the window for what seemed like forever, hoping to see the limo's door open. The pee pushed harder on my bladder. My heart pounded through my chest as the idea to bang on the driver's window lodged in my brain with a fierce voice. I had to move. Maybe it was the possibility of warm urine running down the insides of my legs. I threw the keys in my jeans pocket and left the room.

The leftover bar smell of fried calamari stank up the hallway. When I opened the outside door, I saw the limo's parking lights shining on the street. I heard the hum of the engine.

Just as I ran across the street, thunder and lightning ripped apart the sky. The limousine sped away. There were no girls in sight. Maybe they had run like hell down the alleyway to get out of the rain. Or the driver had seen me and decided against dropping them off. I sat down in the street and peed all over myself, letting the rain wash me from head to toe. All my strength left as I watched the red taillights from the racing limo fade.

I dropped my head on my knees and howled. I thought the roar of the rain had stifled the sound of my tears, but someone had been watching and listening. A pair of strong arms pulled me up from behind and draped a blanket over my shoulders. "Child," the man whispered in my ear, "if you continue this, you'll be no use to her when she comes home."

I saw the back of his head. I recognized the shape of his body, the inward curve of his shoulders, the slow way he walked in the rain. I watched him turn before he opened the door to Mueller's Bakery. I reached for my keys, but my pocket was empty.

"George!" I yelled across the street. "Wait!" I cried. But he was gone.

The rain whipped across my face. It hit my shoulders like stones. Although it was unusually warm for a night in January, I smelled the isolation of winter. The street was empty, and I was locked outside my studio apartment. I had nothing. No phone. No money.

No child.

Sometimes Ed the bartender slept in the room behind the bar. I banged on the door, but no one came. I banged again. A voice rose from behind me. I jumped and lost my grip on the blanket wrapped around my shoulders.

"I theeeeenk I can help you. Theeeees must be yours." He opened his wet palm to show me a shiny set of keys.

A stream of rain fell from the brim of the man's straw fedora, pulled low over his eyes. Before I could say thank you, I wondered where he came from and how two different men had seen me huddled in the street in the middle of the night.

Who else was watching?

TWENTY-EIGHT

STANLEY SUGGESTED I TAKE MY TIME BEFORE I MADE A decision about buying Evelyn's apartment. "Imagine yourself in the space alone," he said. Plenty of artists opted for aloneness to do their work, but who among them had lost a daughter to a kidnapper? "Sleep there a few nights, if you like," he said. "I want you to be sure the apartment suits you."

Tuba had phoned one afternoon and inquired about the space. "Stanley told me he's offered you the apartment before anyone else. Buy it, dear. Buy it and get on with it all." I imagined this was what Tuba was doing. Ever since I had met her, she had impressed me with her crispness, although others might have described her as "cool." Her flowing garments disguised whatever story she had hidden. She moved with a sense of airiness, as if stopping too long might freeze her in place.

Steve weighed in with an opinion after Tuba's.

"It's up to you. If you want to sell your place and move into Evelyn's, it's yours to sell. Just be sure it's what you want."

I was surprised to hear Steve urge me to do *what I want*.

When I wanted my mother to die because she was crazy, I didn't really mean it. Four years ago, I wouldn't have considered moving into another apartment, in case Vinni came looking for me. But she was older now. She would find me if she were close.

❧

I AGREED TO Stanley's price—so reasonable, the apartment felt more like a gift. With it came Evelyn's studio and the timely promise of an art show. Tuba had already invited me to lunch to discuss the promotion of my work. If I moved in February, I'd have time to concentrate on the exhibit, scheduled for an invitation-only reception held before the first concert of the summer series.

One year after Evelyn died.

❧

MY MOVE-IN DATE was set for February 15. Weeks before, I helped Stanley go through Evelyn's closets. Together, we agreed on what to keep, archive, and destroy. We had given away a few pieces of furniture and moved things around, except for the large velvet couch in front of which Evelyn had fallen the night she died. I already had several paintings of my own in varying stages taking up space in the studio. Evelyn had a hand in all of them. I felt her distant presence guide me as I headed into unfamiliar territory. When Stanley first asked about my buying Evelyn's apartment, I wasn't sure. I didn't know if I was trading one empty space for another. But Evelyn's words about the light—"It's always about the light, dear"—urged me to do it.

❧

"I'M GLAD YOU decided to live here," Stanley said.

I smiled and hugged him. I opened a window a few inches from the bottom to freshen the air.

"Makes it easier in some way. Knowing Evelyn's gone but *you're* here makes it a natural transition from one artist to the next. It's as if she's passing on to you a blank canvas. I know she'd be pleased."

I lifted a white box from the bottom drawer of Evelyn's dresser. With no indication of what it was, I opened the lid. Inside sat a perfectly preserved baby's lace bonnet, booties, and organdy dress. A cry stuck in my throat.

"Stanley," I called. With a few books in hand, he returned to the bedroom and stood there in silence when I held out the box.

"What?" I asked. Before I could think further of what words to choose, Stanley took the box and left the room. Later, when we were done for the day, I saw he had placed the box in a shopping bag, along with several framed photos of times he and Evelyn had spent together. The latest was a photo I had taken of the two of them when Stanley had accompanied Evelyn to the costume ball at the Metropolitan Museum of Art. Stanley had insisted on holding Evelyn's elbow, steadying her as they walked down the hallway stairs to a taxi.

ر

KAY THREW HER own birthday dinner so she could pick the place. John D'Orfini had called earlier in the day, when the city was waiting for snow, and asked, "Do I need to wear a jacket and tie?"

"Be comfortable. You'll be fine," I said.

I knew Kay suspected something was brewing between John D'Orfini and me. After all, this was Kay. I checked the mirror to see if the tips of my ears were red. But, once again, he and I had distanced ourselves like dancers moving to random choreography based on chance. Roll the dice and see what numbered pairs show up.

Kay was feeling no pain. Dressed in a short, winter-white wool dress and a twenty-three-inch triple strand of cream-tone pearls, she looked like a successful New York bachelorette who had no idea how to poach an egg. John D'Orfini walked through the door to the restaurant dressed casually in dark pants, shirt, and no tie. His sport jacket looked like a steady afterthought. As reliable as soap and water.

Before our entrée came, Kay brought up the subject of my upcoming move-in date. "Are you excited?" I hesitated and rein-forced both posts on the amethyst earrings Evelyn had be-queathed to me.

The couple who were moving into my apartment had agreed to keep my name next to theirs on the buzzer, in case Vinni returned. They had no children of their own, but they spoke with great affection of a huge Andy Warhol serigraph of Santa Claus that, they explained, hung all year over the fire-place in their country house in Rhinebeck.

The day I moved in was a record-breaking temperature low. Not since 1979 had New York City experienced such a freezing February. It was easier to move downstairs than I had expected. As Evelyn's paintings disappeared from her studio, mine grew into life. In Evelyn's space, I had two people to talk to who were not there in body: Vinni and Evelyn. I knew Evelyn would have wanted me to make the apartment my home and not to worry about the color of the hallway and the two bedrooms—all of which I had painted a color called Brighton Blue.

"A European-drawing-room kind of color," the clerk at the paint store told me. "Works well with white trim. We can do a glossy trim and paint the ceilings and closet doors with the same finish. Looks real sharp."

I repainted the studio in the same soft white Evelyn had used. In the bathroom, I asked the painters what they'd suggest to go with the Brighton Blue hallway.

"Baby's Feet is nice," one of the painters said.

I reeled back. That was the shade of the stone in Vinni's collection: Baby's Feet.

"Baby's Feet is a new color: cream with a blush tone. We can paint the trim the white gloss to match the rest of the place."

"Yes, I'd like that." I didn't need to see a sample. I knew Baby's Feet would be the right color.

I left the apartment on the day the painters came to work on the bathroom. I needed to get out of the way. I was often distracted by the memory of George's finding me in the street in the middle of the night during the January storm. More and more, I noticed how he stayed hidden from the customers at the bakery. I wondered if Hannah knew what he had said to me when he'd lifted me up from the rain. *You'll be no use to her when she comes home.*

Once, I caught him looking at me through the window on the door to the kitchen, where he baked. Hannah turned when she saw me staring behind her at the counter, but George had stepped out of view.

ى

I SHOPPED FOR a green tree for my new bedroom, where French doors opened to a tiny balcony fit for a slim woman with no hips. Strange how Evelyn had ignored this spot. Previous coats of white paint had painted the doors shut. After she died, I discovered their possibility and hired a painter to scrape away layers of years.

TWENTY-NINE

I TURNED DOWN FIFTH AVENUE AND WALKED UNTIL I came to Au Bon Pain, where classical music played all day till closing. With green tea and a muffin in hand, I took a seat. People came here to eat quickly and move on to where they needed to go. Messes of already-read newspapers sat on empty tables and chairs close together. People didn't relax here for long. They skimmed headlines and turned pages fast. They stopped, took a breath, and kept going. Maybe it was fear. Stay too long, and something could happen. It was that pulse of the city—undying—that fed coffee shops like this one. It kept the wheel turning.

As I sat and read the "Week in Review" section from the previous Sunday's *New York Times*, I looked up and saw a family enter the coffee shop. A young girl of around ten or eleven, with blond braids fixed like Heidi's from the children's book, walked in with her mother and father and another adult woman. They spoke German.

The woman who appeared to be the mother said something to the child, who was fixed on her digital camera, obviously browsing through the pictures she had taken. I assumed she was on holiday, as she looked particularly pleased with herself while she clicked through the photos—smiling, pointing to the screen, and showing her not-too-interested father. The mother gestured for the child to come with her to look at the pastries in the glass bins. In a flash, the child rose and joined her. The father returned to reading a map provided by a New York City tour-bus company. He kept flipping the brochure up and down, looking at mapped streets in the city. The girl pointed to a chocolate-frosted donut and giggled. The mother and the other adult woman walked to the back of the coffee shop, toward the restroom, and left the girl alone by the pastry bin.

Something overtook me. Desire. Longing. Maybe even temporary insanity. I smiled across the room, hoping the child would look in my direction. Her skin was white. Her face bespoke threads and threads of twined innocence. Her blond braids were perfectly parted down the middle. I wanted to touch her. Be gentle with her. Lay my hand on the top of her head.

I spun my own fantasy.

I could take her. Walk out of the café and make her mine.

Was this what had happened to Hilda? Had she and Rudy fantasized over Vinni as they sat on the beach? Had she whispered into Rudy's ear?

This is the child I want for my own. Give me one year.

I studied the girl. We could be mother and child. Madonna minus the good.

I could snatch her. Flee the country. Soothe her when she called for another mother. Brush her unbraided hair at night before I tucked her in bed. When she was older, I could explain how I had lost my own daughter.

Can good people do bad things?

The door to the street was open. We could be outside in three, maybe four steps.

The mother's voice interrupted my thinking.

"Angelika," she said. She took the child to where the father sat at the table. She said something to him. He shrugged and went back to his map. But first he leaned over and kissed the child on her cheek.

I left the café. Terrified by my own darkness. I began to run, fleeing from my fantasy. As I slowed to a fast walk one block from the library, I felt a strong hand on my arm. A voice from behind spoke into the back of my head.

"Don't turn around. Keep walking."

"What do you want?" I said. Intuitively, I began to turn, but the hand from behind dug deep into my skin and stopped me.

"Walk toward the black limousine parked in front of the library."

People moved around us, not noticing. My head froze in position. I saw a black limousine just ahead at the curb. When I was about three feet away, the door opened and the man's voice steered me toward it.

"Do not try anything to draw attention to yourself. Step into the car carefully."

With a quick turn of my head, I grabbed a look at the man who spoke behind me. He wore sunglasses and a Giants wool ski cap pulled low over his ears. Without seeing his hair or his eyes, I had no way to identify him. As I lifted my foot, someone grabbed my arm and pulled me into the vehicle. I stumbled and fell onto the floor as I heard the car door slam shut. The last thing I saw was a darkened glass window separating me from the driver. Immediately, a blindfold was slipped over my head, my hands tied behind my back. My shoulders retracted into a painful ache.

"What the hell is this?" I screamed. Someone dug his fingers into my armpits, lifted my shoulders, and pushed me onto a seat. The back of my head tapped against the windows. My body swayed out of control without my arms to steady me.

The limousine pulled away. As I twisted in my seat, a strong arm stopped me.

"Stay still."

The blindfold sat above my mouth so I could breathe, although fear made me breathless.

The man spoke each word with precise articulation. Was he Russian? Yugoslavian? I couldn't be sure.

"You sniff like a hungry dog. You get in the way of my business, and this I cannot tolerate. My perfect plan cannot be undone by one woman. I am a careful man. I have learned from the best how to work and be quiet. I have had to prove myself, and now that I have, I will not have you . . . sniffing. I am not a stupid man!"

He made a sound in his throat like he was clearing a passage obstructed by thick phlegm.

"What business?"

Keep him talking.

"You have a daughter named Vinni who has been missing for four years." At this, the man stopped speaking and sighed.

A rush of blood jammed my head.

"We have been watching you."

Is this how George found me in the middle of the night?

"We hoped you would stop asking questions. It would have made sense. After four years, the police tell you that your child is . . . who knows? Dead, perhaps? This is sad, yes?"

"No one's told me that my daughter is dead. No one!"

"What do the police know? Stupid twits. I am a quiet businessman. Your country is a good place for business. But the noise you're making disturbs me."

I felt his breath. I smelled peppermint from his mouth. He was that close.

"Step away from the window across from the bakery. Do you understand?"

My shoulders began to ache from their pinned position. My heart raced.

"Otherwise you will not see your daughter again."

"Where is she?" I scooted close to the edge of my seat. I suspected the car had gone over the George Washington Bridge. Cool air breezed in through an open window. I believed we were on our way out of the city.

"She's safe. Happy. Grown."

I sickened to think what I had lost. "Why should I believe you?"

"You have no choice, do you?"

Everything around me heated up as the sunlight spilled onto my right side. I tried twisting in my seat, but each time I moved, a firm hand pushed at me. Strong. Nonnegotiable.

"Why would you choose not to believe me? Don't be stupid!" The man's voice filled with disgust.

"When is my daughter coming home?"

"Hilda is not so good now. It is only a matter of time," the man said.

"Hilda! This is certain?" My head turned toward the voice to my right.

"This is certain. Believe this. Do not get too close. Stop sniffing. You are getting too close to what is none of your business. If you want to see your child again, you must wait."

"What do you mean, 'wait'? I can't wait anymore. I want my daughter."

The sun from the window burned my thighs.

"Hilda just wanted to borrow your child for a while. It was a simple plan."

I couldn't believe what I was hearing. "What are you talking about? You don't *borrow* a child!"

"You went to dinner at Hilda and Rudy's."

I whispered an excuse through my tears. Crushed. Broken. My heart was all of this and more. "That was a long time ago.

Almost five years," I said. I thought for a second. "How do you know about this? Who are you?"

He continued. "When you went to dinner, they wanted to see your daughter closer. They saw she was the perfect choice. The perfect one to borrow. Not forever, you see. They never intended it to be this long. Time is funny thing. Yes? It moves when we stand still. You will see your child."

"When?"

"When Hilda's time comes. Soon."

"But Hilda has kidnapped my child!"

"No, no, this is not a kidnapping. I told you. Hilda borrowed your child. Understand this. You were so busy. The American way. Yes? Work while your child grows up. Yes? Hilda could see: writing, painting. And the child? Hilda could see."

Tears slid down my cheeks. I tasted the salt from a few strays circling their way into my mouth. Hilda's words from four years ago stung me again.

Your work, then, it keeps you away from your child?

Had Hilda thought she could do better than I at being Vinni's mother? Did she think I could tolerate the pain of losing a child? My box of pastels (my plein-air box). How many times had I actually used the pastels? Once, twice? On most days, they stayed buried in the bottom of the beach bag. Had Hilda heard Vinni ask me, "When will you be finished, Mama?" when I had taken out the box at the beach? Once? Twice? Had she used the words against me to satisfy her own yearning?

~

WE RODE FOR at least an hour outside the city. I asked questions but was ignored. "Who are you?" I repeated over and over.

He commented on the air. "It's good to smell clean air." Finally, the man said to the driver, "Head back."

"Where are we going?" I asked.

"Back to where we picked you up."

"When do I see Vinni?"

"I don't know."

I started to beg. "Please, tell me." I could feel my body breaking down. "Please," I whimpered.

"You must stop with the questions. This little car ride is a warning. I will not be patient with you the next time. You have this one chance to listen. Tell anyone, and we are done with you. Step out of line, and you will never see your daughter again."

The man moved close to my face. "Never!" he said.

"Four years is a long time," I said.

"She did not think it would be this long."

"People don't take someone else's child!" I screamed from behind the blindfold.

"You see how loud you Americans are! You must be quiet. Hush, woman—you tire me."

This wasn't the nephew with the acne. I would have recognized his roughed-up voice.

"How do I know Vinni is still alive?"

"You'll believe me because that's all you have. If you tell the police about this, you'll never see your girl again. That's a promise."

In that instant, I believed him.

He hesitated and then said the preposterous. "Kick off your shoes."

"What?"

"Lift your leg up onto the seat."

I moved my leg, my knee bent onto the seat. A hand wrapped around my foot underneath my toes.

While we had been driving and talking, terror had kept a slight distance, but now it pounced inside my chest. A shadow passed in front of my blindfold; I figured out later it must have been his arm coming down, setting the hand just so, moving it swiftly, with the confidence of an expert.

Pain stunned me. My foot went cold, then hot. I wasn't sure what had happened. The pain nearly made me pass out. I stopped breathing. I tried to catch it. My breath. My breath. Where had it gone? I couldn't catch it. Shock pulsed through my throat. The car swerved. The man yelled, "Watch it, you fool!" to the driver. I heard something drop onto the seat next to me. "Now look what you've done. My jacket—disgusting." Again to the driver: "Tiny tools work the best."

I needed air.

"This is a little package, Ms. Stewart. So I leave you with something. A reminder. That's all. No police. No more sniffing. Bad, bad things happen to stupid people who interfere with my business. I tell you this to warn you."

A pause.

"Pull over," the man said.

We returned to the corner of the library where we had started two hours ago.

"Put your shoes on. I'm going to untie your hands and place something inside them. If you want to see your girl, you'll wait for the call. You'll ask no more questions. Mind you, take no chances. If you don't, next time I slice you in half. Do what you are told. Stay away from the window in the middle of the night. Agh. There is mess on my trousers. You see how you trouble me."

Holding on to my shoulders with a rough grip, the man threw a book into my lap. I heard the door open, and someone leaned in, removed the blindfold from over my head, reached in, and pulled me out of the car. I squinted up into a pair of dark sunglasses and the same wool Giants hat. The man jumped into the car, and it sped away.

∽

I STRUGGLED TO catch my balance.

I looked down, and in my hands was *James and the Giant Peach*—the book Vinni had been reading on the beach four years earlier.

Shaking uncontrollably, I hobbled a few steps up to the first cement landing of the library. On sunny days like today, people sat scattered on the front and side terraces. I moved closest to Forty-First Street, away from the crowded area on the opposite corner, and sat down to examine my foot. I held Vinni's book close to my chest and pressed my lips together hard to silence the chattering.

I slipped off my left shoe. At first, all I saw was blood. It took me a few seconds to realize I had a toe missing. My pinky toe. I grabbed tissues from my purse and wrapped them around the top of my foot.

I fingered the pages of the book. I turned each one, expecting to smell Vinni. Something slipped out and fell onto the stone steps. A photo of an older Vinni stared up at me. A picture of a preteen with lighter hair, thinner cheeks, and a longer face stunned me. My daughter stood holding the reins of a horse in the middle of a field surrounded by snowcapped mountains in the far distance. She was smiling. Not like a little girl anymore but rather like someone older beyond her years.

I smoothed my hand over her face and brought the picture up to my heart. My head dropped back. My mouth shaped a silent howl. Corners of my heart broke. I ignored the throbbing of my foot. I was so close to having my child back, but I couldn't tell anyone.

THIRTY

"WHAT HAPPENED, MADDY?" ASKED STANLEY.

"I bumped into a pretty nasty metal casing on one of the legs on my easel." My head spun. Thoughts like *Where was I?* and *What just happened?* flipped on their sides. I eased myself into the nearest club chair.

Stanley removed the red-soaked mess of tissues attached to my foot. "Dear God, your toe is gone!"

"I flushed the bloody mess down the toilet," I said. "I wasn't thinking."

Stanley stared at me the way he had when I had first visited the doctor's office with Evelyn four years earlier. "Maddy?"

"What?" I refused to look at him straight-on. Instead, I lowered my head and bent over my knees as I fondled the leather at the tips of my toes. "My shoes are ruined," I said.

"We should go straight to Presbyterian Hospital," Stanley said. "I was just about to close the office anyway. You're not going to hobble up there alone."

"No, no, no. I'm sorry. I should have gone straight to the emergency room."

"I'm glad you came to see me. The first thing I've got to do is disinfect this thing."

Stanley studied my face. "You look like you've seen a ghost. Is everything okay?"

Everything was not okay. The voice of the man in the limousine played in my head.

"I get woozy at the sight of my own blood. That's all."

"Well, you can get 'woozy' as long as I'm here with you."

I hesitated. I needed someone to whom I could tell the truth. I turned away as I fought back tears. When I looked up, the good doctor said, "Is there anything you'd like to tell me?"

I shook my head, but our mutual silence sealed an unspoken agreement. I had something to tell that I could not . . . and Stanley knew.

It was too bad Evelyn had gone first. They belonged to-gether. Stanley looked older since Evelyn's death. His back hunched more, and his eyes lost focus as he spoke. Sometimes I had the feeling they drifted out to sea, where Evelyn's ashes floated at the bottom of the ocean.

Stanley broke the tension. "Have you eaten today?"

I thought back to the morning and my desire to steal the blond child in the coffee shop. "I'm good. I just did something stupid."

Stanley cauterized the open skin with a local anesthetic. I jumped from the exposed bone and raw flesh. I held my eyelids closed, forcing the last two hours behind my chest bone.

"How long do you think before . . ."

"Before you're not limping?"

"Yeah."

"You'll be limping for a few weeks. Walking a little funny after that. Right now, you need stitches. We'll clean you up first. You've got some exposed bone that's got to be covered. The best scenario for an amputation like this to heal, my dear girl, is probably two to three months. Of course, some residual healing will take maybe an additional four months. You'll be walking pretty close to normally sooner than you think. What I do sug-gest is that you get rid of that damn easel, for God's sake!"

In the ER, a tired-looking resident with a twenty-four-hour shadow stitched my toe and then hooked me up to an IV streaming a heavy dose of Ancef. I don't know what he said, but Stanley warded off any suspicions from the doctors. After all, the slice was clean—too clean.

I played the role of absentminded artist—someone so engrossed in the ethereal, she walked into furniture. I left the hospital with a prescription for Keflex, another antibiotic. I persuaded Stanley that I was fine to taxi home alone. When I returned to Evelyn's apartment—mine now—I put the book in a drawer by my bed. I touched the opening pages and closed my eyes. The secret bound me tight, but at the same time I felt free. I limped over to the closet, where I had stored a painting Evelyn had created of an imagined older Vinni. I lifted it out of the corner and unrolled it onto the top of the bed.

Vinni stared up at me.

ے

I TOLD NO one about the ride in the black car. My foot was a constant reminder that worse things could happen if I opened my mouth.

Fear. Excitement. Torment. They turned and twisted me until I spun, unsure which way to step forward. Nothing was for certain. If I told John D'Orfini or Kay about being whisked away in a black limousine in the middle of the afternoon in front of the library, they'd say I was lucky to be alive. I did feel lucky, but not because of what I was sure would be their conclusion. And Steve? I couldn't tell Steve. He had been working more and more in Sydney, flying back and forth, having a life that relied on distance. When he did call, we were polite—like strangers deferring over the same armrest on an airplane.

The truth? I didn't want to tell him.

As long as no one knew about my conversation in the car, I could keep it safe. I worried that Steve would insist we alert the FBI. I simply could not take that chance with my daughter's life.

Yes, yes, I know what you're thinking: foolish woman!

But a mother beast relies on instinct.

❧

AFTER THE LIMOUSINE ride, I stayed up night after night, unpacking and removing boxes from the spare bedroom. The Baby's Feet paint color in the bathroom was perfect. I hadn't thought about the second bedroom, although I knew it was Vinni's. It made sense to get it ready.

I had the door closed when Kay visited one evening. As we sipped a $12 bottle of prosecco, I kicked off a pair of flats and Kay saw the bandage on my foot.

"What's that all about?"

"Nothing. I hit the metal casing on the easel last week. That's all. A couple of stitches . . ." I shrugged away the topic.

"Since when have you been clumsy?" Kay asked. She kept fiddling with one thin strand of hair fallen over her right eyebrow.

"Old age, I guess."

"You're a little jumpy tonight. Are you feeling okay?"

I tilted my head back and drained the rest of my glass.

"I'm okay. Tired, maybe."

"When was the last time you saw John?" D'Orfini's first name rolled off Kay's tongue more easily than it did off mine.

"Two weeks. He was away on some seminar for four days last week. He's convinced . . ."

Kay walked over to my chair and sat down on the floor. She

picked up my foot and began unwrapping the thin bandage. I hadn't told her I had one less toe.

"What are you doing?"

"Uncovering some shit, I think. Or else I'm going to kiss it and make it better, okay?" Kay laughed the way she did when she felt she "had" you. But we were far away from being school-age kids, and I wasn't going to let her see more than I could tell.

No police.

"What the . . .? Where the hell is your little toe?" she asked. Her eyes searched me out. "Maddy, I mean it. What happened?" Kay sat on the floor, examining me with the kind of intensity she had used to build her reputation as a show-no-mercy assistant US attorney.

I tried to laugh it off. "I had a studio accident, that's all."

"You'd tell me if something was going on, right?" Kay looked for the words I couldn't say. Her eyes searched mine.

"There's nothing going on. I've been running around like a nut. I've got the art show and deadlines, and I've got to make a decision about the story *More* wants to run on the anniversary of Vinni's five-year disappearance."

"Don't do the story," Kay said.

"Why not?"

"Because you believe she's coming back, right?"

"Yeah, and?"

"And I don't," Kay snapped.

I closed my eyes. I didn't want to argue tonight.

Kay rewrapped my foot slowly with the fresh-since-the-morning bandage. Tension flitted around the room, not knowing where to land. I wanted to tell Kay that Vinni was alive. I wanted to dance and cry. I wanted to scream out, *Vinni's coming home*, but fear kept me quiet. Fear kept me farther from Muel-ler's Bakery, but not so far away that I couldn't watch from the window across the street. I stayed behind the curtain like a spy following secret instructions. The only difference was that I kept still when I saw the black limousine pull up in the middle of the night. I walked by the bakery and looked in through the glass front of the store. I stopped asking questions, but I didn't stop watching.

I painted.

As I worked, I thought of the paintings of the mother and child by Käthe Kollwitz in the Morgan Library. The big hands, the bent back, the woeful eyes penciled into their sockets. I drew on Käthe's despair, and it fed me. Boldness found its way onto the canvas as I added six more paintings after the number sixteen. I titled each piece by number, just as I had with the work I had exhibited in Evelyn's show. I continued to paint whole scenes imprisoned inside large triangles for the eyes.

Memory of the man in the limousine telling me to wait hid in every cell of my being. Nothing eased with the passing of time. Keeping everything to myself—not telling—took its toll and stole my nights. When I closed my eyes, my mind raced. John D'Orfini lay next to me in bed. I made up a story with a cast of known characters: Kay stood at the foot of the bed. "There's no room for all of us," Steve said, knees bent into his chest, as he looked down from a shelf on the wall. Evelyn sat in one of her purple chairs with Vinni's book in her lap. George and Hannah licked each other's fingers, wetting their lips in satisfaction. The acne-faced nephew was there, eating a slippery submarine sandwich stacked with salami and red onions.

On nights like these, I woke up sweating—fearful that everyone knew about the conversation in the black car.

STEVE CALLED ME from the club room at the airport. I could tell he had had too many glasses of pinot. Twice before, he had called me from the airport half loaded out of his mind, but that had been within the first year Vinni had gone missing. Similar conversations took place from his home in San Francisco on Saturdays when Gina was out selling real estate.

"Why hasn't she tried to call me?" His speech was sloppy. Exaggerated.

Years earlier, I had asked myself the same question, but without an answer, I had let it go. What choice did I have?

"Vinni was smart. She knew better. Why didn't she try to call *me*?" He kept referring to himself as if *I* didn't have a phone or a home or a hand to hold things.

"You've had too much to drink. That's all this is," I said. Years of unsaid things had piled up until alcohol-induced words started spewing from his mouth.

"That's right. Play the compassionate mother. You're soooo good at this. You're so damn good at this. You're worried if Vinni called me, then you'd look bad. And you couldn't stand that."

"Steve, this is stupid. Sleep it off on the plane."

"You wouldn't tell me if she called, though, would you? You'd keep it to yourself. You and your Detective D'Orfini. You'd both keep it to yourselves."

Steve said John D'Orfini's name out loud as if it were the name of a pasta special. Enunciating the vowels of each syllable. Raising his pitch on the last *i*.

"What about Gina?"

"I love *you*, Maddy. I love Vinni. I love the three of us. When I return from Sydney in two weeks, I want to come home."

Steve sobbed. I knew he was drunk. Out of his mind.

He threw his own words back and forth like the volley in a Ping-Pong game. I held my breath. I kept quiet about the black car. I didn't know who he'd be once he sobered. The idea of our being a family again saddened me. It wouldn't happen. Steve's shadow flew in and out, but that's all it was—a shadow. He hadn't talked to Vinni for two months before she disappeared.

"Dad's busy, I guess, huh? He must get pretty tired flying back and forth to Australia." She looked up from stacking four boxes of rice crackers in the bottom kitchen cabinet. "Do you think he misses us?"

I had been packaging food for the freezer with my back to Vinni. I turned and said, "I'm sure Dad thinks of you all the time, honey."

She shrugged.

I didn't know if this was true unless he was intoxicated, but I believed my daughter needed to hear it.

෴

VINNI WAS TWELVE now.

I imagined her hair worn long. She'd want to move it away from her face. But then, didn't preteens like to cover their faces? Shy away from adults like they were an intrusion? She'd be tall, like Steve. Even at eight years old, she was the tallest of her school friends. Skinny. But that was when she was a child. I tried not to think about what I had missed. I concentrated on what we would do when she came home. When I couldn't see her clearly enough, I swallowed more Xanax. I closed my eyes.

My financial situation continued to deteriorate. A turn in the stock market plummeted my investment returns from my meager inheritance from my father. My freelancing career swung back and forth. My editor from *Hot Style* magazine fed me deadlines. Maybe she was testing me to see how I was coping. Sometimes I woke up in the middle of the night with my heart pounding, worried that I'd have to sell Evelyn's apartment or let go of my room in Brooklyn. I wasn't ready to do either. Just the previous month, the editor in chief and I had met for lunch and she had invited me to step back into my old role of fashion editor. I had asked for another three months. I had been extending time as if it were free. While sipping white wine, she had nodded and said, "Of course." In the meantime, I stuck to a low budget, scrambling white-shelled eggs for dinner and calling it a meal.

∾

ON A FRIDAY in July, I stopped off at my room across from Mueller's to add a few more photos to the wall. Photo upon photo told a story out of sequence of the black limousine with the same license plate. I captured pictures of young girls with their faces hidden by falling hair. I had shot after shot of their turning down the alleyway and then nothing. No return.

More photos popped up of the neighbor man in the straw fedora standing in the corner edge of the photograph. He was always around, whether it was three o'clock in the afternoon or four in the morning. Up until now, I hadn't gone down the alleyway myself. I had stopped sniffing.

I was afraid that Hannah or George might see me. Especially George.

I was afraid I might ruin everything and Vinni would lose her chance to come home. I convinced myself that the girls who disappeared down the alleyway had nothing to do with me or what was mine. I watched to be sure. All I wanted was my own child returned.

My life had stopped and stumbled into a different direction until the man in the black limousine had told me Vinni would come home. Afterward, it kept its own time clock. Each day, I awoke wondering if today I'd find Vinni sitting outside on the steps.

THIRTY-ONE

I WAS AFRAID KAY SUSPECTED SOMETHING.

On a Thursday evening two weeks before the art show, she arrived at my apartment unannounced. The door to Vinni's room was open. Dusk in August lit the walls a gauzy shade of silver. The buzzer startled me. I jumped and dropped the photo of Vinni standing by the horse. *Look at my girl*, I thought.

I pressed the intercom and heard Kay's voice. "I've got the prosecco. Get out two glasses."

When I opened the door, Kay stood there with a chilled bottle and a hunk of Corbier and crackers from Murray's Cheese Shop in the Village.

"What are you doing here this time of day? Shouldn't you be working?" I said.

Kay dropped her briefcase in the foyer and slipped off her nude stilettos. "We need to talk, Maddy."

Her tone startled me into thinking that she had discovered my secret.

"I spent the day yesterday with D'Orfini at the police station in Brooklyn. Apparently, dead Mr. Kosinski—*Mr. Uncle*—left a protégé. A cousin from Uzbekistan with the same last name has slipped into his position in the community rather gracefully."

"What position?"

"As the 'fixer.' We know he's been to Mueller's Bakery, talking to Hannah. We put a tail on him."

My heart stopped. I waited for the question about the man in the black limousine. Was the man the fixer's cousin? Instead, Kay spread cheese on two crackers and handed me one as she looked down at my foot.

"How's the wound?"

"Fine. I'm lucky, I guess. It was a clean slice." I winced at my own choice of words.

Kay got up and, with a glass of prosecco in hand, wandered down the hall and saw the door open to Vinni's bedroom. Without asking, she walked in and I followed her. Her back was to me when she spoke. I couldn't see her face, but, more important, she couldn't see mine.

I had hung new curtains earlier in the week. I shouldn't have spent the money, but I had. Pale blue fabric against the baby-blue walls created a monochromatic look. What stood out was Evelyn's writing table. I had moved it from the hallway to Vinni's bedroom.

"Why did you do all this?" Kay said.

"Do what?"

"Make this room for Vinni. Everything looks like she's coming home for Labor Day weekend."

Kay turned around and faced me.

"Is she? Is Vinni coming home?"

I wet my lips before I spoke, to give myself more time.

"You know I believe Vinni's alive, Kay. Nothing's changed. One day, she'll sleep in this bed." I spoke slowly, careful not to pause as if I were reconsidering how much to divulge.

I moved over to the bed, and Kay sat down next to me.

"What else do you want to tell me?" she said.

"What do you mean?"

We stared at each other as if we were in a contest of who might give in and speak first. I didn't flinch. Kay broke the silence. "D'Orfini did some investigating on his own time at the FBI storage yard where they took custody of the blue car. He found a gas receipt crumpled into the size of a spitball underneath the driver's seat. The receipt was from a gas station in Montreal."

"Canada?"

"Yes. Someone could have driven Hilda and Vinni into Canada, dropped them off, and turned around and driven Hilda's car to Kosinski's garage in Brooklyn. A private garage is a perfect place to dispose of a car you don't want found. Of course, then Kosinski went ahead and died and the nephew found the car, hoping for gold."

Kay couldn't resist an opportunity for sarcasm.

"Is this what John D'Orfini thinks?"

"Your detective is leaning on the fixer's cousin as we speak. He's back in Brooklyn today. He just finished with the guy a little while ago. He told me to call after I got here to see if he could meet us in the city for a dinner meeting."

It would be insane to tell Kay that Vinni was alive. Should I have whipped out the photo to show Kay and risked seeing my daughter again? I didn't believe Vinni was in Canada with Hilda. The background in the photo showed houses with orange tile rooftops. People go home when they're in trouble. Hilda took Vinni not to Rodenbach, but to someplace else in Germany where she knew she could hide.

ು

KAY AND I met John D'Orfini at Gascoyne's. The humidity forced his hair to curl more. His face had an extra layer of subway sweat from the steamy night. We were already seated when he walked in. Assuming we'd all order fish, Kay asked for a bottle of sauvignon blanc. The waiter poured John D'Orfini a glass. He gave it a sniff, nodded, and took a sip.

"Well?" Kay said. D'Orfini ignored her.

"Thanks for meeting me, Maddy. I know this is a surprise, but we may have something."

Thanks? I thought. *Thanks? Where did this man come from?*

Kay took over. "I've already told Maddy about the fixer's cousin. By the way, he's also named Kosinki. Not to confuse you," Kay said, as she looked at me from across the table. The dim lights made all of us look younger. Less hurt.

"I assume the nephew also claims to know nothing about the receipt found in the car?" Kay asked.

"Right. He's useless," John D'Orfini said, looking up from the menu. "French, huh? What should I order?" This was a modest Jersey foodie.

"Coq au vin," I said.

"I told the nephew that kidnapping was a federal offense. That it was simple. He tells us what he knows about his dead uncle and how that receipt got into Hilda's car, and we keep a world of misery away from him. There's no question he knows something about what Uncle was involved in—the older Kosinski had to be grooming his cousin to succeed him. All the nephew told us is that the cousin visited five or six times over the years but had difficulty leaving his country for good. The community now trusts him to be the new fixer, replacing his deceased cousin."

"It's the Canadian connection that's got me. Why would Hilda go to Canada? What's there? Or who?" Kay asked.

"That's the interesting part. The one thing Kosinski said . . ." John D'Orfini dropped his voice and added an imagined Russian accent. "Nobody from Brooklyn goes to Canada unless they want to hop a plane. I think he thought he was being funny, but he might have given something away."

"I know what you're thinking," said Kay.

"I don't," I said.

"What if someone drove Hilda and Vinni just over the border so they could catch a plane out of the country?" John D'Orfini asked. "If she'd been drugged, Vinni could have slept the whole way to Canada. The right dose could get her through the gate, too tired to talk but able to walk without Hilda carrying her. She'd be a sleepy kid. That's all."

I flinched when I heard this. It all seemed real enough to make a movie, but this wasn't a cinematic adventure. This was the story of my stolen daughter.

The young waiter placed the coq au vin in front of John D'Orfini and two identical entrees of lamb with pumpkin purée in front of Kay and me.

"*Bon appétit*," he said.

How am I going to pay for this?

John D'Orfini looked about to say something in response, as if he thought it was required. I touched his arm and said, "Is there an airport near the border?"

He turned to Kay. "I need your help with the answer to that. Can your office do some checking with the border patrol? Find out what kind of records they keep? It's got to be more secure since 9/11. Lots more paperwork. There might be records of cars crossing. Maybe surveillance cameras."

"Even if there are, it's almost five years ago," Kay said.

"I know, but can you put someone from your office on it?"

Kay nodded. Nothing was official. Both were helping me on their own time. Especially John D'Orfini. He had traveled to Brooklyn on his day off. At least he was having a good dinner.

"Nice chicken dish. I'd like the recipe for this," he said.

I watched his hands move with the grace of a skilled culinary artist. Deboning the breasts onto his plate. Working the dark meat from the legs and thighs, stewed in a wine sauce. Slicing the cipollini onions.

"You're awfully quiet, Maddy," John D'Orfini said. "I thought you'd be . . . I don't know . . . pumping me, like you usually do."

I had taken a single Xanax from my wallet and popped it into my mouth when I had gone to the restroom before the entrées were served.

I did have one question.

"Is the new Mr. Kosinski working at the clock-and-timepiece shop his cousin owned? Did he take over the business?" I asked.

"That he did, and more." John D'Orfini smiled, as if he had just swallowed a joke.

"What?" I asked.

"He restores antique dolls. That's his specialty. The guy couldn't stop talking about it. Seems people from all over are bringing him broken dolls to restore. The community is happy to see the shop reopened. The man calls himself a 'dollologist.' He changed the name of his cousin's place to the Doll and Clock Shop."

"Where is it?" I asked.

"Two blocks north of Mueller's Bakery."

Kay and I passed on the selection of soufflés for dessert. John D'Orfini chose chocolate, and for the next twenty-five minutes, he and Kay talked about Hilda's blue car and the two Mr. Kosinskis—one living and one dead—while we waited for his dessert.

I wanted the night to end so I could visit the Doll and Clock Shop in the morning. I wondered what the new Kosinski's voice sounded like.

Kay left before the soufflé was served. It was late. The restaurant had emptied.

John D'Orfini scooted the rich, dark dessert in front of me so I could taste. We were in a quiet corner, alone, except for a single man seated at a table for two. After a last bite of the heavenly chocolate, John D'Orfini said, "Let's go home."

He ignored my attempt to reach for my purse and paid the bill.

I took a quick look outside as we left the restaurant. We did not hold hands as we walked back to my place. Both of us had silently agreed a long time ago to hide our relationship from the public eye. Although we were more careful about it in Spring Haven, we still followed an understanding on the streets of New York City. When I closed the door to my apartment, John D'Orfini reached for me and slipped his hands, warmed from his pockets, inside my coat, finding their way underneath my sweater. His breath inside my ear, slow and deep, matched my reaching for him as I warmed myself against the insides of his legs. It was about the heat—I had been cold for too long. With Steve, when he had come inside me, I had daydreamed about cycling up a long mountain until I could reach the top and jump. With the detective, I wanted to linger so I could taste all of him. When he stepped back, I took his hand and led him into the bedroom.

Before he fell asleep, all he said was, "Great soufflé. That's an art. Baking a great soufflé takes real culinary skill." I leaned my head on his shoulder and *mmm*-ed in agreement. In the middle of the night, I slipped out of bed and walked into the studio. I searched through the bin of misplaced junk I had been collecting from my walks—screws, pennies, nails, buttons, key chains, hardware of any kind—and began gluing them to the canvas.

THIRTY-TWO

TUBA'S DRIVER PICKED ME UP IN THE CITY AND DROVE me to her estate in Damson. She had arranged for my work to be hung earlier in the week but wanted me to approve it. We had had lengthy discussions by phone, followed by e-mails confirming the placement of the paintings. "Welcome. We're ready for you, dear. It's going to be a wonderful weekend," she said when she floated out of the house, wearing a floor-length sea-green tunic. As she took my arm, she said, "I've invited some special guests to your artist's reception. Two curators from the Käthe Kollwitz Museum in Cologne. I will be pleased to make the introductions tomorrow." Her eyes lit up with genuine excitement.

Stunned, I felt inadequate and alone.

The evening before my show, Tuba's personal chef served a sumptuous dinner on the patio, with seared tuna as the appetizer. To my pleasant surprise, Stanley walked in just as we were about to sit. Tuba lifted a crystal flute and made the toast: "To Maddy and her art."

Stanley gave an enthusiastic "Here, here!"

I took a sip of the pink champagne.

"To Vinni!" I said, and raised my glass. My eyes glistened and filled.

Silence hung over the table for a few beats, until Tuba said softly, "Yes, of course—to Vinni!" She rearranged the wide sleeve of her tunic so it fell longer over the back side of her shoulder.

The next day, I awoke early to walk on the beach. After a

few steps, I had a sudden urge to go faster. I started running, but the sound of my name interrupted me.

"Maddy! Maddy!" Kay jogged from behind and caught up with me. Tuba had invited her to come and enjoy the day. Kay had mentioned it, but she wasn't sure she'd be able to arrive early. At the last minute, Tuba had arranged a car service. They had met only once, through me, but Tuba never missed an opportunity to lay the foundation for a favor.

"When did you arrive?" I said.

"Just now, but when did you start running? I thought you were a walker."

"I am. Something came over me and I couldn't stop."

"Are you okay?"

"I'm nervous about my work—all these people." I slowed down. Running was still difficult with my left foot.

Kay fell in step with me.

"I peeked at what's been hung in the gallery. It's magnificent," she said. Then she took me by the shoulders. "*You're* magnificent. Try to give yourself time off from . . . thinking too much. You know what I mean."

We walked back to the estate, arms wrapped around each other's waists like schoolgirls.

෨

JOHN D'ORFINI FOUND me in the gallery.

"Congratulations, Maddy. I'm impressed."

"Thanks for coming," I said, as if stones were soaking in my mouth.

"Of course. I wouldn't miss this. You knew I would come, right?"

"You never called." I bit my tongue.

"Uh . . ." He stopped and looked away, addressing the air around him. "Aren't artists supposed to focus on their art before a show?"

This was John D'Orfini's way of deflecting accusation with a touch of humor. I had known he'd come. It was his voice that I missed. I began to sweat. The silk fabric of my fitted white jacket was unforgiving in warm weather.

Tuba distracted me from John D'Orfini's attention.

"They're here," she said, as she guided me with her arm slipped into mine. "The curators from the Kollwitz Museum in Cologne. They want to meet you."

"Yes, of course." I believed it to be a simple introduction.

Two men stood in front of my painting *Number Eleven*. I had begun it on the last day of December when Vinni had been missing for three years. Babies with mouths open wide showed pink, watery gums. By the time I finished the piece—months later— dozens and dozens of baby heads poked in and among the clouds. The howling mouths startled people as they walked by, stopped, and stared.

Along one wall hung the series *Number One* through *Number Five*. In two pieces, I painted a single, oversize eye in the shape of a triangle. A cyclops container. The points of the triangle dripped onto the canvas like a teardrop brushed in black charcoal. Inside the eye lay another eye, distorted and compressed. In the cyclops version, scenes of horror included miniature versions of fragmented fingers, tiny feet, an elbow bent into a sharp rectangle, and a pair of lips.

Number Six through *Number Ten* moved away from the face. Once, on a walk to Harlem in the heat of July, I came upon a group of half-dressed children, no older than six, running in and out of gushing water sprung from a fire hydrant. Their laughter howled into steamy streets.

I thought about the difference between a howl of pain and one of pleasure. I tried to capture this in the next five paintings—a series of headless torsos. Where was the thinking child? The vital child? The whole child? Where was *my* child? I knew I disturbed the viewer with expanded ribs of a baby caught inside an internal cage. I scripted one word repeated on the outer edges of this series—"Hosanna"—culled from a hymnbook my father kept in a bookcase in the living room.

Number Twelve and *Number Thirteen* shifted to the lower legs and feet of a child. Crippled and bowed, the legs swelled around the kneecaps. Paintings titled *Number Fourteen* through *Number Eighteen* concentrated on a baby's plump body drawn curled inside the mother's womb.

I noticed one woman sobbing quietly with her hand over her mouth as she stood in front of *Number Eleven*. When she saw me looking in her direction, she nodded, acknowledging me as the artist. I had told Tuba that I didn't want any introduction. I wanted to mingle with the group in the gallery. Some recognized me from the photo on the poster outside the entrance. People walked by and shook my hand. Some lightly touched my elbow.

"Congratulations, Ms. Stewart!" said one of the men from Cologne.

"Thank you."

"We look forward to seeing you in Cologne at the festival."

Tuba smiled and said, "I haven't talked to her yet about the festival, but I'm sure it will work out."

I looked at Tuba. "Festival?" I was a freelancer in Manhattan who had lost a child. I had an achy foot and a crush on a detective from Jersey. To go to Germany to exhibit in an international art show was beyond my comprehension.

"*Number Eleven* for sure, but we'll leave the others up to our lovely hostess," said the second curator. He bowed slightly toward Tuba, and she blinked in silent agreement.

"I'll be happy to take care of things on this end," she said.

The men smiled at me and said, "*Gut. Gut.*"

I wondered what Tuba had planned. Was I traveling to Germany with her?

"Excuse me for a moment, Maddy." I was unsure whether I should follow and ask her what she was talking about, or wait. Instead, I lifted a flute of pink champagne from a waiter's serving tray and took a sip. The chilled rosé satisfied me. I removed my jacket and slipped it over the back of a chair. As I adjusted the sleeves, I felt someone standing behind me. I turned and looked into the eyes of a tired, pale-faced woman.

I pulled back. "You startled me." I had not expected to see the baker, although I knew Tuba had invited hundreds to enjoy the show.

Hannah's face looked about to crumble. She reached for my hand, and I let her hold on to me, but I did not return the grasp. "What is it?" I asked, frightened that she might tell me something I did not want to hear.

"Your work. The paintings of the babies with their mouths open. The wailing."

"*Number Eleven,*" I said.

Hannah pushed.

"Secrets . . . they make us do things," she pleaded.

In the quietest of voices, I asked, "What things?"

Hannah laid her other hand on mine. "You will paint different babies soon. Happy babies," she said in a low voice. She touched my arm just above the wrist.

I looked into Hannah's tired eyes. She leaned in and whispered into my ear as her cheek touched mine. "Soon, you will receive a call and life will be good again. You will paint happy babies. You wait."

My response was to hug her, throw myself into her arms, but all I did was grab her shoulders. "Wait?" I said. "How much longer?"

Hannah placed her hands over mine. Her lips trembled. "Not long. Of this, you can be sure." Then she moved back into the crowd.

I stood alone in the middle of the room. Kay caught my eye from a cozy corner where she was engaged in a conversation with two men, each tall and available-looking. I watched as she maneuvered her way toward me.

"You look like you've seen a ghost," Kay said, as she brushed a few thin hairs behind my ear. "What's the matter?"

I shook my head.

"Come on. I saw Hannah talking to you. What did she say?"

"It was nothing."

John D'Orfini had disappeared. It would have been nice to have him at my side.

Kay leaned in and said, "You're lying."

I rolled my response around in my head, weighing my options.

"I love you, Kay. I've always loved you."

Kay looked shocked. "Well, I love you, too, but that's not going to let you off the hook. What did Hannah tell you?"

"She told me to wait."

"Wait for what?"

"For Vinni to come home."

THE SIGN ON the shop window said CLOSED, but lights were on and the outer door was wide open. A locked screen door was the only clue the shop was closed to the public until the following week.

I rang the buzzer and knocked. I could see and hear people talking inside, a few feet away from the storefront. I had no intention of leaving until I heard the dollologist speak. I had known I'd recognize the gruff voice of the man in the black limousine. My foot had healed faster than I'd expected, but my heart thumped wildly when I thought of his promise that Vinni would be mine if I waited.

"We're closed." I recognized the brash voice of the fixer's nephew. I wished John D'Orfini were here. He was late, just as I had known he would be. His plan was to meet me in Brooklyn at the shop.

"You want to *drive* in to Brooklyn?" I'd asked.

"Why not?" he said.

"Think about the traffic and the parking."

"I'm good with it. I'll meet you there at ten thirty."

჻

JOHN D'ORFINI THOUGHT I wanted to go to the Doll and Clock Repair Shop to ask the fixer's cousin what he knew about Hilda and Vinni. If he was with me, I had to be guarded. If Kosinski turned out to be the man in the black limousine, I'd want to either lose John D'Orfini or hide behind his shield.

"I know you," said a voice behind the screen door. "Can't you read the sign?"

"I'm doing a fashion story and wanted to talk to the owner of the shop."

I knew the sleazy nephew would tap into the word *fashion*,

thinking if I mentioned him in the story, he might have his fifteen minutes of fame and get invited to the Oscars or enjoy a private tour of Madame Tussauds wax museum. I pushed harder to get him to open the door. I imagined John D'Orfini was stuck in traffic at the bridge while sipping coffee from a paper cup.

"This won't take long. I only need fifteen minutes." The nephew shifted his weight from one foot to the other, wanting me to believe that my interruption was an over-the-top inconvenience.

Little shit, I thought.

I wasn't going to leave until I heard the owner speak. I hadn't thought what I would do if his voice matched the sound lodged in my head from the man in the limo.

The nephew unlocked the door, but Kosinski must have heard him, because a chilling voice called out to him, "What are you doing? What are you doing? Stupid boy, I told you I'm working. No people this week."

The voice—even in the distance—was the same.

Why didn't John D'Orfini come in to the city last night and stay with me?

I stepped inside to face the man behind the agitated voice. When he saw me, he stopped his rush toward the door. I stared at him. Shock spread across his face, but he quickly recovered, as he exchanged one mask for another.

"Miss, you can see we are closed this week." There it was—the way he said *miss*. The dance began like an intricate waltz, sidestepping, dipping, almost bowing to the other as if we were partners.

I had my own mask ready to wear. "I . . . I'm doing a story on antique themes in fashion, and I heard you worked with antique dolls."

Kosinski glanced down at my foot and back at me. My foot throbbed as a reminder not to step on glass. Did I detect a slight smile from the man with the peppermint breath? A smug turn in his posture?

"What can I tell you? I repair clocks and dolls. You say you're doing a story on fashion? What can I tell you?" He stroked the skin above his lip with his thumb and forefinger, fanning a nonexistent mustache. He walked over to a large glass cabinet where costumed dolls—many dressed in period Russian garb—smiled through their reflection. The shop's clocks—at least fifty of them—chimed in unison.

"I'm working on a very expensive doll for someone from the Russian embassy."

"Just ten minutes. That's all I need."

"Then sit." Kosinski pointed to a chair covered in gold brocade. It seemed out of place in a repair shop where I expected more dust and dirt than light.

"I like my customers to enter a calm place when they come to my shop," he said.

Was it with a sense of bemusement that he said this?

His nephew had disappeared into the back of the store, slipping behind a brown curtain.

"You closed the shop because of this important doll?" I asked.

"No, no. Three men whose mother is dying of cancer brought in several of their mother's dolls. The mother hasn't long to live, and so they come to me . . . to repair the dolls. It is their mother's final wish that the dolls be restored. They'll be back the end of the week. I don't want the sons to disappoint their mother."

"How kind of you," I said. My voice dripped with irony.

"The mother is dying, as I told you. A mother deserves a

last wish, don't you think, miss? I don't think you've told me your name. I've never seen you in my shop."

"Maddy. Maddy Stewart." I waited, but he revealed no sign of recognition, other than the sound of his voice, which proved he was the man in the black limousine.

"I have a child who was stolen from me four years ago." I stopped as the dull ache in my foot reminded me to slow down. I had found what I'd come for: the man who owned the Doll and Clock Shop was the man who knew where Vinni was. He had sliced off my toe and warned me to stop asking questions. He had given me a photo of what Vinni looked like now, almost five years later from the moment she was kidnapped.

"Ahhh. Miss, I am sorry to hear this." Kosinski tapped his fingers on the table. Hitting them like quarter notes. "But you've come about the dolls. Yes? And I must get to my work . . . so, what you want to know about my 'patients'?" He was a doll doctor—another kind of fixer, like his cousin. But this Kosinski had a link to Hilda, or at least to someone in the German community who knew where Hilda had taken Vinni. And he had told me I would see Vinni again.

I did the dance.

I pretended to be interested in the dolls in the glass cabinet.

"May I see one up close?" I asked.

Kosinski raised his eyebrows, perhaps surprised I hadn't run out the door. Instead, he reached for a key in his pocket and walked over to unlock the cabinet. "You've come alone?" he asked, without turning to face me, dipping into a sidestep as graceful as a ballroom dancer. Sliding into a much darker conversation.

"I always . . ."

He didn't wait for me to finish. When he turned, he had yet another mask over his face. He was smiling.

"I like to keep my children locked up safe," he said. "Some become like family. People bring me their dolls, knowing I will take care of them as if they were my children. Their owners attach themselves . . . I'm not sure how to say it in English . . . they wrap their arms onto the past and squeeze tight." Kosinski shook his head side to side, as if he were weighing the cost of the past. He did it again when I left and stopped outside the shop to stare back at him through the storefront glass.

THIRTY-THREE

I STUDIED THE RETURN ADDRESS THE WAY MY FATHER used to—with both hands on either side of the number 10 envelope—eyes reading and rereading the numbers and letters until I froze from recognition. Donald Howard. He had shown up at Evelyn's art exhibit at the end of the evening and snapped up my five paintings.

Howard, Block & Bach
Attorneys at Law
512 Lexington Avenue
New York, New York 10007

An uneasy feeling washed me from head to toe as I tore open the envelope, careful not to destroy the corners.

Dear Ms. Stewart,

On behalf of a client who insists upon anonymity, I am pleased to enclose herewith your original Note and Mortgage, dated April 22, 2012, given to the First National Bank and Trust Company of New York on the purchase of the property located at 219 West Twenty-Third Street, New York, New York. The indebtedness has been satisfied in full, the Note has been marked "Paid in Full," and the mortgage has been duly canceled of record.

As of Friday last, there were no recorded liens against this property. Payment of quarterly real estate taxes and municipal utilities remains your continuing responsibility.

You may wish to consult with your own tax advisor as to the implications of this matter. I am precluded from advising you in that regard.

With best wishes, I am
Very truly yours,
Donald Howard
Attorney at Law

What if Donald Howard wouldn't reveal what I wanted to know?

I tore into myself but then exhaled. What-ifs are for writers, not mothers of missing children. I dialed the number on Mr. Howard's letterhead. A friendly automated voice picked up and connected me after I pressed number 2, as directed by the menu.

Donald Howard told me the same thing three times: "I'm sorry, Ms. Stewart, I can't disclose who paid the note. Client confidentiality. As much as I'd like to help you, I can't. The same applies to the purchase of your paintings. I've already told this to the detective."

Around 5:00 p.m., I found myself standing outside the building that housed the law offices of Howard, Block & Bach. I needed to talk to him. I had printed out a picture of Donald Howard from his website and folded it into a square in my pocket. The next night, I sat in a booth in the window across the street in Andrew's Coffee Shop. Grease from a day's worth of cooking on the open grill filled the air. I returned for two more nights before I eyed Donald Howard leaving his building. I followed him for one block before I caught up to him. What had started out as a fine mist in the morning was now a rainstorm with a cold wind howling across my face.

ℒ

"MR. HOWARD?" HE walked tall and fast, with a chin squared and strong enough to slice toast. Tiny tufts of white peeked from inside his ears. His jowls had already begun the journey downward. I guessed he was in his late fifties.

"I'm Madeline Stewart. You sent me a letter about an anonymous person paying off my mortgage. My daughter was stolen from me over four years ago, and I think . . . I believe there's some connection." Mr. Howard stopped under an awning near the door to a wine shop. As I talked, I followed him into the store. He didn't speak right away, so I started in again before he interrupted.

"Mr. Howard, I'm the artist from the gallery downtown. My little girl has been missing."

"I know who you are, Ms. Stewart. As I told you over the phone, I'm sorry for your loss." Like the inside of a Hallmark card.

Loss meant death. *Sorry for your loss.* As in, *The person you loved is dead and gone and there's nothing you can do about it, so take the condolences. Go settle on the beach somewhere and string beads.*

"As I explained earlier, I cannot divulge the identity of my client. Try to understand. Now, if you'll excuse me, I'm late."

Don Howard reached into his wallet and pulled out a black American Express card. This was a man who did well. He drank the finest wines, paid for by an international clientele. Earlier, I had checked his profile on his company's website. He was a senior partner, as well as a visiting professor at Columbia Law

School. He spoke five foreign languages: Italian, Portuguese, Spanish, French, and German.

He walked away as my heart's beating bore through my blouse. Faster. Faster. I felt like I could reach in and pull the bloody vessel from behind my bra, lay it in the palm of my hand, and show Don Howard the devastation. "This is a wild heart that beats broken," I'd say. Instead I walked home, hands shoved into my coat pockets. Someone had taken extraordinary measures to help me. Someone who knew I was having financial problems. Someone compassionate.

Or was it someone remorseful, motivated by guilt?

TUBA HAD BOOKED two tickets for Cologne for December 10. She had stayed much longer in New Jersey, even hiring more help to care for her wheelchair-bound, silent husband. Her decision to postpone her return to Germany in September after the final concert of the series on her estate surprised me. It revolved around the festival and her desire for us to fly there together. Her plan was to stay on afterward and travel to Munich for the Christmas holiday.

"Will you be alone?" I had asked.

"Not quite," was all she had answered.

The festival included works by seven emerging artists from around the world. The theme was "beauty, pain, and loss." It would be at the Käthe Kollwitz Museum. The opening was on Saturday night, with a panel of seven artists speaking on process the following afternoon. There would be translators for those of us who did not speak German. All I knew at the time was that a hand had led me to the art patron Tuba Schwimmer—Evelyn's hand. I continued to trust that Germany was where I belonged.

At first, I had refused to go to Cologne.

"I'm not ready for something like this," I told John D'Orfini and Kay after my showing at the estate.

"You should go," Kay said. "You wouldn't be invited unless the curators liked what they saw. It's too great an opportunity."

"I'll be gone for at least a few weeks," I said.

"Why is that a problem? Is it *Hot Style*? Do they need you to cover a story?" Kay asked.

"No, no, that's not it. I don't like the idea of the only home Vinni knew in the city left empty."

What if Kosinski brings Vinni back and I'm not here?

"Maddy," Kay said.

"No, I mean it. It's a big decision for me to make."

"Don't turn your back on this chance," Kay said.

"I told you. I don't know if I'm ready."

❧

A WEEK LATER, I met John D'Orfini on the steps of the New York Public Library. The weather was getting cooler, and I wanted to get in a few more outdoor lunches at Bryant Park. John D'Orfini had picked up sandwiches, along with two bottles of sparkling water and two chocolate truffles from Lilly O'Brien's chocolatier across from the park. I alternated between putting on my red leather gloves and taking them off because of the bite in the air. The tip of my nose felt cold.

"Let's go somewhere indoors and have a hot drink," I said.

"Sure." He took my paper bag with the half-eaten sandwich and tossed it with his flattened bag into the trash can.

"Aioli makes everything taste European," he said.

"It does?"

"Sure. It's the subtlety of spice and cream," he said. "When am I going to get you to enjoy food more?" He laughed and then added, "When do you leave for Germany?"

"December tenth," I said.

I limped a little as we stood up to walk across the street. The cold air affected my foot. I had been warned arthritis might flare up in the joint. John D'Orfini looked at my foot but said nothing as my regular pace picked up after a few steps. It was a small price to pay for silence.

"Okay?"

"I'm good," I said. "It's cold, that's all."

I wanted to slip my arm through his, but I held back. The park was full of people with stories. I thought how it could be with a man at the kitchen table at night—someone whose naked back I could place my cheek upon as he slept next to me on a matching pillow. Life was returning as long as I believed Vinni was still alive.

I had three freelance jobs to wrap up before Tuba and I flew together to Germany. *Hot Style* magazine wanted stories on two new designers who without caution used real fur, advocating a strong distaste for faux anything. My deadline for filing the stories was December 8—two days before I was set to leave from Newark Airport. Tuba was to meet me there, and together we would make the trip to her homeland. And to Hilda and Rudy's.

❧

"LET'S STOP IN and light a candle," I said. The doors to St. Patrick's Cathedral opened to a steady stream of visitors. A wedding ceremony was about to end. John D'Orfini and I stood with the crowd at the back, gawking at the bride and groom in the distance on the altar. The cardinal of New York was giving his final blessing to the newly married couple. His red robes were the only way I knew the man leading the ceremony was higher than a priest.

I whispered in John D'Orfini's ear. "I heard from that attorney, Donald Howard."

"What did he want?" he said, as he kept his eyes on the bride at the front of the altar.

"He has a client who paid off my mortgage. He won't tell me who it is."

The bride and groom turned to face the guests sitting on both sides of the massive church. Women dressed in shiny necklaces and high heels carried envelope clutches. Men in suits—some in tuxedoes—walked as if stuffed into Ziploc bags. The bride wore a strapless off-white gown fitted three-quarters of the way down her slender body. Like a trumpet, it flared out into a long train trailing yards and yards of silk and lace behind her as she headed down the aisle.

D'Orfini said nothing.

"Did you hear what I said?" I asked.

"I heard you. I'm watching the groom, that's all."

I turned my attention to the front of the cathedral.

My mother's voice novenaed her way in. *Don't believe common men can bless us, Madeline. It's nonsense. If you want to feel blessed, sit in your backyard and listen to the birds.*

John D'Orfini nudged my arm. "Where are you?" he said, "Other than a million miles away."

The bride had her husband's hand in hers as she raced—no, just about ran—down the aisle. I wanted to shout out to her, *Take your time. Don't rush through this, because you can't walk these steps again.*

"Too fast," I whispered to John D'Orfini.

"What?" he said.

"The bride. She's walking too fast. God, she's going to regret this."

"Why?"

The cardinal said something to the newly married man and woman. Words of advice? Another blessing?

What good would it do them now to have one more blessing?

They had already sealed the deal. Vowed for better or for worse.

"She's not smiling," I said.

"Neither is he," John D'Orfini said, as he removed his leather gloves and stuffed them into the pockets of his jacket.

"She just about pulled him down that aisle." We headed over to the other side of the cathedral, where the Christmas manger would be set up a week before Thanksgiving.

"He let her."

"How could he stop her?"

John D'Orfini smiled. "You don't really know that much about men, do you?" It was his smile that made me want to throw my arms around him and say, *Come with me to Germany*.

"I'm not sure I know much about anything these days." I stopped and turned to him on the street. "What about Donald Howard?"

"He's right. He doesn't have to tell you who his client is."

"But he has to tell *you*, Detective, doesn't he?"

"No." John D'Orfini tilted his head. "I fear a bull coming into the arena."

"Not a bull, a mother beast."

We walked in silence past shoppers carrying bags filled with gifts. How many of them needed what they couldn't afford? I wondered.

Detective D'Orfini broke the silence. "I think it's good that you're going to Cologne."

"You do?"

"Yes. You're talented. Evelyn saw something in you. All of us saw it at your show in September."

Although my hands were cold from the frosty air, John D'Orfini's words warmed me. This was the detective's ploy, so natural and used so often that he wasn't aware he had one.

"I know you spoke to the dollologist," he said.

Ah—the ploy!

I kept silent.

"Why didn't you tell me?" He stopped at the corner, waiting for me to explain.

"You were late that day. Remember? You got caught in traffic, and we ended up going to MOMA to watch a performance artist upstairs. I told you that the shop's sign read CLOSED. I was there for less than fifteen minutes."

"Obviously, somehow you walked in there, closed or not." He took my hand but spoke with his face looking straight ahead. "Why didn't you trust me to know you spoke to Kosinski?"

My foot throbbed out of the blue. "Let's get a hot chocolate. I need to elevate my leg."

"You're changing the subject," John D'Orfini said, looking around like a scout for an ornithological expedition.

"We didn't say much. I asked him about the period clothes on his dolls. That's all."

John D'Orfini brought his gaze to mine. He held my hand more tightly, and I shivered. We stopped at a coffee shop and found a seat too close to the door. A shot of cold air blew inside. I stretched my leg out under the table. Quietly, he lifted it and rested it against his knee. I picked up my cup and blew on the surface to cool the steaming foam.

"I mean it. We didn't say much," I repeated.

"I still don't understand why you had to go. Why couldn't you wait? Why do you always have to charge in?"

I hesitated before I spoke. I was close—so close—to telling him that Kosinski was the man in the black limousine. That he promised me I would see Vinni if I waited and stopped asking questions. That I was terrified it was all a lie. A ploy to shut me up and keep me from watching across the street at the alleyway that swallowed up young girls.

"Waiting is all I've been doing," I said, breathing air in between the words. My eyes filled, but I continued. "The babies in the paintings—they're all mine. They're screaming in my head, looking for their limbs to be returned. To be whole. Sometimes I wake in the middle of the night and I see a crowd in the bedroom—all children begging me to paint them. Give them wholeness. Call it hallucination if you like. But I see them all waiting for me to do something. I thought painting them would make them go away, but last night I woke again and they were all there. Only this time, one child moved forward and sat on the edge of the bed. The closer I moved to the child, the more she looked like Vinni. The room was dark. I could hardly see, but the moon slipped a sliver of light onto the side of the child's face. It was so real. When I woke up, I was thirsty, as if I had talked aloud to the children in the room all night."

John D'Orfini's face changed as I spoke. It softened into the man I slept with, who made me groan in the dark.

"You're right. I didn't tell you everything, but I'm telling you now."

"I can't help you the way I want if you don't trust me," John D'Orfini said.

"It's not about trust."

"It's *always* about trust."

"Not this time. This time it's about Vinni."

THIRTY-FOUR

THE WEATHER FORECASTERS PREDICTED A WICKED SNOW-
storm. If they were right, there was a good chance the subways
might shut down and I'd have to postpone going to Brooklyn.
My obsession to find out what was at the end of the alleyway by
Mueller's showed in the pictures I shot from my position at the
window. Day by day, they bloomed into something I could
barely contain.

Where did the girls disappear to?

Once upon a time, I had had a good life. Now it was gone.
If I tried to figure things out, I knew I'd go mad. Maybe that
was what happened to my mother when she tried explaining
why people who carried groceries in brown bags ignored possibilities.

I COULDN'T LOSE the images of the girls vanishing down the
alleyway. I struggled with a clawing in my chest, as if I were
being singled out to save them. I doubted my original decision
to wait in silence. I imagined a made-up misery where I hid behind the drawn curtain with closed eyes and missed sighting
Vinni from my window across from Mueller's. Vinni was older
now. Appealing. Her young body—almost thirteen. Younger for
sure, but not by much, than the girls I saw from my window.

და

I TOOK AN earlier train to Brooklyn. Ed the bartender had gotten used to my blowing in and out the door, stopping to pick up an order of calamari.

"I'll have Sasha bring it up when it's ready," he said. "We're running behind tonight. I don't want you to have to stand around here, much as I think you're cute as hell."

I gave him a wave, nodded, and flew up the back stairs. It was around 6:00 p.m. The snow was falling hard. I was glad to be in my room, settling in for a long night. The light upstairs from Mueller's Bakery told me Hannah and George were still awake. Their rooms went dark at 8:30 p.m.—bakers' hours— only to brighten at 4:00 a.m.

The wall over my sleeper couch had slowly transformed into a command headquarters. At least, that was what I thought John D'Orfini would call it. Pictures of the black limousine, the young girls exiting the vehicle, Neighbor Man, and grainy close-ups of the alleyway, so close to Mueller's, hung tacked on the wall.

Neighbor Man was often in the photos. He was either off to the side, two buildings away from the bakery, or in the nearby alleyway, but he was there. Smoking. Looking away from the limousine, as if he had just been dropped from the sky.

A knock at the door told me that Sasha had my calamari with a small bowl of red gravy for dipping sauce. I opened the door a crack and grabbed the hot plate, careful to block the view of the wall behind the door. At least five inches of snow covered the streets, and it was still coming down. The winter wonderland–like atmosphere should have quieted me, but instead I felt an undeniable twitching in my legs.

In the middle of the night, on my watches in Brooklyn, I often sketched what I saw down the street from my perch by the window. The rooftops; the cobbled streets, rough and old; the spilled spots of light from the streetlamps. I lost myself inside the pencil work until the lights turned on downstairs at Mueller's Bakery at 4:00 a.m. Sometimes as I dozed, my head swung down with such a jolt, I awoke in a panic, wondering where I was.

With the first light, I put on my hooded coat and boots and left the room. The streetlights cast a warm glow on the untouched powder on the sidewalk. My breath created tiny white clouds in front of me as I walked. I could hear John D'Orfini's voice in my head, saying, *Don't get involved.*

My plan was just to take a look. Walk the same path as the disappearing girls. In my mind, this was not the same as getting involved. Going to the Doll and Clock Shop proved I could rein in my mother beast.

I crossed the street and began my walk down the narrow alleyway just past the bakery. My heartbeat quickened as the snow continued to fall. I shoved my freezing hands into my pockets and followed the snow-filled path farther into the alleyway. As I neared the end of the building, I walked past a window with a shade pulled down. I came to the end of the building that paralleled the street to Mueller's Bakery. I turned the corner, walked for about a hundred yards, and saw a sign on a patch of white lawn that read ST. STEFAN'S, THURSDAYS, 6:15 P.M. *LET CHRIST SAVE YOUR SOUL.* It looked like one of those pop-up religious halls where people go for a cup of soup in return for the chance for some zealot to spout oracles of faith into a handheld microphone.

There was nothing unusual in the alleyway. Just one window and one door and a makeshift holy hall at the end to help the strays. I turned back to retrace my steps to my room.

Vinni was someplace else—someplace where she rode a horse and the sky was big.

I dropped my head to brace myself from the snow hitting my face, but as I passed the window, I noticed that the shade had been pulled up about two inches from the bottom sill. I was sure it had been securely lowered when I had walked by not more than three or four minutes earlier. I stopped and looked up across to the building on my left. Nothing. I half expected to see a monster pop out from the brick wall. I stepped to my right and knelt down in the snow to look under the two-inch opening provided by the raised shade. I squinted my eyes to narrow my vision, bending my chest even lower. My hands gripped the window ledge as I widened my elbows to secure a better position to look inside the room.

That's when I saw the girl on the cot.

She locked into my eyes like a laser.

I steadied my hold on the sill with my frozen fingers. Her eyes pierced mine as the snow swirled around me. We held each other still for maybe ten seconds, until her eyes darted back and forth—to her left, to me, to her left, to me. I moved my knees, frozen from the snow, to get a better look into the room.

What was the girl trying to show me? And then I saw.

A giant of a man sat on a chair with his head flopped against his chest. An open bottle of vodka rested on its side on the floor. My eyes returned to the girl—the *child*—who was small enough that she didn't reach the end of the cot, or else she was huddled with her knees pulled up close for warmth.

I focused on her face—so hollow that her cheekbones protruded like half moons. A second cot—empty—was next to the girl's. A slit of light from the raised shade splashed a bright strip against the floor. I wondered if the room carried the smell of young girls' terror.

The snow kept coming. The neighborhood would wake soon. The bakers would ice cakes and whip custard for ordinary people who passed the alleyway on their way to work. They wouldn't see the girl who needed saving.

Didn't Vinni need saving also?

Could I save them both? One here and now. The other across the ocean.

What about the warning from Kosinski to stop sniffing? He had told me that I might not see my child again if I didn't stay out of his business. Was I taking a chance with consequences too large to handle? I hated this choice. I hated it so much that I dropped my head and let myself sink into the snow. As the cold swept me up, I had a vision of Vinni in the photo—the one where she was smiling, as she held the reins of the horse.

The girl on the cot was not smiling.

The girl on the cot needed saving.

If I abandoned this child, I could never call myself a mother. I could never ask for absolution. Somewhere, a childless mother knelt praying for her girl's return. Never, never, never could I face myself if I did not try to help this other mother's child. Yes, Vinni was my daughter, but that did not mean that this child was not mine to save as well. I knew she was one of the girls the black limousine dropped off. Their hair, always fallen in front of their faces—this child's hair hung the same. Only when she had moved did I see her bony face; however, her eyes stayed strong, never leaving mine. Another ten—no, maybe longer, twenty—seconds, we held each other without words or movement, until I shifted my gaze to see the man in the chair stand and stumble out the door. I scooted on my knees to the edge of the building and peeked out to see the man open his trousers and pee onto the clean snow. I was only about twenty feet away when I saw him weave and fall face-first into the snow where his urine spotted the clean powder. I waited, but he didn't move.

The snow kept coming, falling on the man's head, burying

him. He lay motionless. I stood up and ran toward the door with my eye on the drunk. My heart was pounding.

Please, God, let this have nothing to do with Vinni!

There was no time to make a deal with someone in the sky. When I opened the door, I found the girl standing, shivering in a loose sweater and tiny skirt. Her knees looked about to buckle as I reached for her and she collapsed into my arms. She spoke a few words, repeating the same ones over and over with a desperation, a pleading, in her voice, but in a language that I couldn't understand. I wrapped my arm around her waist. Her weight fell into the side of my body so hard that I wondered if I'd have to drag her down the alleyway. When I opened the door, I saw the man still flat on his face and I thanked God that he hadn't awakened. The girl took steps with me as we moved silently down the alleyway. I felt her ribs protruding like sticks. I kissed the top of her head, the way I would have if she had been my own.

The snow swirled in front of us with such ferocity, I prayed the girl would make it across the street.

A voice said my name, or had I imagined it inside the howl of the wind?

"Maddy, give her to me."

Neighbor Man swooped the child up in his arms and steered me across the street to my building. The snowstorm fought us every step, but I could feel his grip on my elbow. I unlocked the outer door and raced ahead up the stairs. The girl must have said something, because I heard the man say, "There's no need to be afraid."

I didn't stop to think who or what I was allowing into my room. It was about the child.

You must know this. And you must remember it. It was about the child.

Her whole body shook. Yes, the night was cold, but I believed it was fear that made her tremble.

How did the man in the hat know my name?

Neighbor Man gently placed the girl on my couch, underneath the gallery of pictures of other girls dropped off at the alleyway. The girl reached for my hand. I sat close to her, held on to it, and squeezed. I wanted her to know that she was safe. Her blue eyes belonged to a child lost at sea and on land. You could drown in them.

❧

"I'M AL DOBSON, FBI." Neighbor Man reached into his jacket and pulled out a badge. "I'm undercover for an investigation of a Russian prostitution ring. We started to zero in on this area of the city about six months ago. That's when I came onboard. We got close to moving in on it, but then something happened and the whole thing went cold."

"Cold?"

"Look at your photos. When was the last time you saw a drop-off? My guess is it was three weeks ago. Which means they're off schedule. It used to be every two weeks. Two girls at a time. No more. The girls were filtered out through St. Stefan's. They've got to be onto something."

"That's why I never saw them leave from this side of the alleyway," I said.

He nodded but returned to the photos that I had tacked up on the wall. I touched the girl's forehead with a gentle stroking back and forth. I wondered how long it had been since someone had extended a small kindness, or told her they loved her.

A quiet hung over the room. I lifted the girl's head to rest in my lap. I looked up. "How do you know me?" I asked the agent.

"I met John D'Orfini in Quantico."

My sweet detective.

"He knew I was working in Brooklyn, and one night he mentioned the case of a missing child and Mueller's Bakery. He said there was no proven connection but he had a hunch that hadn't panned out yet."

Neighbor Man removed his wet hat and stepped closer toward the wall where dozens of photos hung above the couch. "I had my own hunch that you were the mother of the missing child from Spring Haven. What made you walk down that alleyway tonight of all nights?"

I shook my head. "I don't know."

Was it love?

Without Vinni, where could I put my love? Without her face, where would I find her eyes?

The child began to cough. Veins in her thin neck pulled taut like elastic bands colored blue. Her head jerked hard against her chest. Her cough got louder, and she opened her eyes wide. I tried to pull her up to help her catch her breath, but she was too weak to sit. She fell across my lap and opened her mouth. Blood splatted onto the carpet.

I looked over at the agent, but he had turned away, speaking into his cell phone or a plate on his chest or whatever undercover agents did when they needed to call for help.

He spoke over his shoulder. "They'll come around the back and bring her to the hospital. The guy in the snow's been carted off on his way to the station."

"In the kitchen, please, there's a cloth by the sink," I said.

He ran it under cold water and handed it over. I wiped the girl's face. She turned her cheek to face me. We were so close, I leaned in and kissed her forehead. This was someone's missing child. For the smallest of moments, I wanted to be her mother, to soothe her the way her mother would. I hadn't soothed a child in such a long time. My heart beat wildly, broken to see this girl child in such pain, speaking a language that no one understood.

Al Dobson removed his straw fedora, now drenched in melted snowflakes.

The wall-to-wall gallery had been in progress for four months. I had enough photos on it to build a house of horrors. He kept looking at it, rubbing his hands together in an attempt to warm them—or was he stalling for time to find the right words? I didn't know if undercover agents did that kind of thing.

What did I know about any of this?

"We've been documenting the Russians for two years . . . and not just here. They're in Chicago and Miami also, which means so are we. This is big. Damn dangerous. We were about to close in on this hideaway in Brooklyn—there's two others—but they all got quiet at the same time. This girl's the break we were looking for."

"I guess you think I fucked up your investigation," I said. The girl's head lay still on my fleece pants. "Do you expect me to say I'm sorry?"

"No, ma'am. It's just that there's a guy named Kosinski we've been watching. Looks like his 'uncle' groomed him to take over his business."

"The Doll and Clock Shop," I said.

Dobson spoke with his eyes cast downward. He avoided eye contact unless he was undercover, as if it might tire him to pay such close attention without a disguise.

I noticed how his receding hairline exposed a slab of forehead.

"John's told me the story of your daughter. If it helps, I don't think she's involved in this ring. They concentrate on teens. Your child was too young for them when she disappeared.

Anyway, they're into something more lucrative. It's all about money. Your case seems isolated."

But Vinni's older now, I thought.

His words pierced me in the same wound I'd been nursing for almost five years.

"Do you think Hannah and George are involved in the prostitution ring?" I asked Dobson as he studied the photos.

"No. We can't find any connection other than they live two buildings down from the alleyway on the same street. Wait a minute." Al lifted his eyes and turned. "This picture. The one of this girl." He pointed to one I had photographed where I had a clear view of a face. The girl in the photo held her hair behind her ear. She couldn't have been more than fifteen. Her eyes looked sleepy, with heavy lids shutting down a third of the world.

"I know this face. We found her dead last month in an abandoned apartment building. She was soaked through her clothes. Strangulation. When we found her, she was nothing but skin and bones."

At least now the girl on my couch has a chance, doesn't she?

Neighbor Man stepped into the kitchen, a few feet away. I knew he was speaking into his phone, but his face was turned away from me. He hung up right before there were three taps on the door, a pause, two more taps, and a ring on his cell phone. Al put his phone in his pocket and opened the door. The girl stirred in her sleep as two men entered the room. With deliberate care, one of them picked up the girl in his arms. The other adjusted a blanket around her small frame.

"What will happen to her?" I asked anyone who might answer me.

Al Dobson spoke in a gentle voice. "You did something pretty brave tonight. We'll take care of her from here."

The girl opened her eyes before they carried her away.

Al picked up his hat to follow them. "I'll need all these pictures. I'll send one of my guys down."

The door closed, and I reached for my phone.

"John?" To say his name in the middle of the night made my mouth go dry.

"I'm already on my way. Dobson just called."

AN HOUR LATER, I jumped at a light knocking on my door. My fingers felt sticky from the girl's dried blood—a few droplets I had missed washing on the third and fourth fingers of my right hand.

"It's John," he said. I guess detectives know how to enter a locked building.

I opened the door, and he quickly stepped inside. He pressed me into his cold woolen coat. He took both his hands and cupped my face.

"You're okay?" he whispered.

I nodded and gently brushed off a nest of snowflakes resting on his head.

"You took a big chance tonight. Nobody expected you to be in that alleyway. Nobody knew how it would go down. Agents were watching."

Shocked. I pulled away.

"You mean they watched me walk down the alleyway and go to the front of St. Stefan's?"

"You could have been hurt or even killed. What got into you?"

John D'Orfini wanted an answer.

I thought about it for a moment, but it was all very clear.

"The child needed saving," I said. The horror of the night struck me as I slipped to the floor. I broke apart from the inside and wept.

If thoughts make us who we are, then I worried about what kind of woman I was. I thought of last month, when John D'Orfini told me his former wife had gotten in the car in the middle of the night and driven away, leaving a note on the kitchen table. "It's not working. So sorry. Just forget me."

"As if she was a bad novel I had been forced to read in high school and could put down after I got through the final page," he said as we lay naked, stomachs full of pasta whipped with butter and cream. "We were only married seven months. Not much of an investment."

I was not someone who left a note in the middle of the night and snuck away. I was a mother who longed to hold her daughter. I painted so I could find a way to breathe. So I could stay alive and breathe in my child when she returned.

John D'Orfini drew back from the photos on the wall. "What the hell?"

"I had to do something," I said.

"What aren't you telling me?" He stared straight through to the place where I hid things.

Was now the time to speak? To say, "Vinni's coming home but I don't know when"? Instead I said, "I can't."

"Can't what? Talk to me?"

I shook my head and walked over to the window, where the curtain hung puddled and dusty on the floor. I drew it back and peeked out the window from the side, the way I always did. Dawn was breaking. The outside glistened with snow crystals. The streets lay quiet. My lips remained closed.

Remember, I am not someone who leaves a note in the middle of the night.

John D'Orfini walked up behind me and slipped his arms around my waist. I leaned back into his neck—a perfect resting place.

"Sometimes it doesn't seem real that I'm living this life. Children missing. My own daughter gone for so long. Kosinski." I stepped away and moved around the room, avoiding the bloodstains from the girl. "I know you're shocked by the wall of photos, but I had to be sure that Vinni wasn't one of these girls."

I told John D'Orfini only part of it—the part about being sure.

"I'm shocked." He gestured wide with his arm. He pointed to the wall with his hand turned open. "If you'd been caught . . . If the guys running this ring . . ."

"But I wasn't caught." I concealed Kosinski's warning.

"You've stepped into something you know nothing about," he said.

I began, "Hannah and George—"

He interrupted. "The FBI's been watching them because of the alleyway, but Dobson doesn't think they have anything to do with it. They're simple bakers, Maddy. That's it."

I stopped moving. "That can't be it! George knows I'm at the window. He's been watching me!"

"You've gone too far," John D'Orfini said.

"I've got no more to say." I left him standing in the middle of the room while I went to the bathroom. When I came out, he was sipping water from a tall glass. He had poured one for me and set it on the counter by the sink. My room was small, but I felt as if we were miles away from each other. He reached for the glass and offered it to me. Seconds passed before he spoke. I took a long sip. He waited.

"Why do you think George has been watching you?" he finally said.

"I was locked out one night. He found me outside the apartment."

It was part of the answer. Just not the whole thing.

YEAR FIVE

THIRTY-FIVE

TUBA HAD MADE RESERVATIONS AT THE EXCELSIOR HOTEL Ernst in Cologne, directly across the street from the cathedral. The girl at the reception desk told us we could walk to the Käthe Kollwitz Museum. In the breakfast room, I sipped tea in an elegant china cup etched with a gold-leaf scroll. I could barely eat, from nerves and excitement.

Since that first year when Evelyn had taken me to see Stanley and he had served me strawberries in a bowl, I never failed to remember how he had urged me to nourish myself in the midst of my despair. I chose six large, ripe strawberries from the buffet table and spooned them into my bowl. A young woman in a black skirt and black long-sleeved blouse, who had been standing nearby to assist the diners, took my plate and cut the berries into perfect slices. She brought the bowl to my table and offered me sweet cream as a topping. Thick, rich, pure, it coated my tongue as the juices from the strawberries burst inside my mouth.

TUBA LOOKED AT her watch.

"Are you worried about our meeting with the curators?" I asked.

"Oh, no, my dear. That's not it." She hesitated and inhaled

a breath so deep, I could see her chest shiver inside her demure white blouse. Sleeves hanging like falling leaves.

"I received a message this morning to wait in the lobby for . . . visitors," Tuba said.

"People you know?" I asked.

She nodded slowly and proceeded to put on her gloves.

"My children." Her eyes opened as if a window had been raised.

"You've never mentioned children," I said.

"Two. Only two now. Of course, they're grown. Living their own lives. I haven't seen them in a very long time. I'm a bit nervous."

Suddenly, her tight chignon looked wrong for the soft face across from me that looked about to crumble. Her eyebrows moved inward as the wrinkled skin in between traveled downward. As her skin fell, I wondered if I should reach across the table to catch it. Tuba lowered her face as she drew her shawl around her shoulders. The longer end fell with a series of painted red roses perfectly placed below her left collarbone. When she looked up across the table, she smiled. The shadow shifted slightly.

"Would you mind going on without me this morning? I feel a need to rest." Tuba said.

THE COLD STUNG my face as I walked outside. I looped my scarf twice around my neck and tucked the ends inside my coat. My flat-heeled boots made barely a sound as I walked in between the morning crowd. The museum opened at 10:00 a.m. My instructions were to arrive at eleven o'clock. I looked forward to meeting the six other artists. From the distance, I saw two large banners flying lengthwise on either side of the building. One banner had the words *SCHÖNHEIT, SCHMERZ, UND VERLUST*. Opposite, on the other side of the door, in English: BEAUTY, PAIN, AND LOSS.

The museum was smaller than I imagined. Two of the curators I had met months earlier greeted us warmly inside the front door. A private breakfast meeting awaited us downstairs, off a corridor from the lower gallery. One artist was from Spain, two from England, one from Nigeria, and two from Germany. I was the only American. At first, I was intimidated. What place did I have in an international art show? Self-doubt plummeted me into silence.

One of the German curators I had met in September at Tuba's estate by the ocean approached me. He must have sensed my discomfort as I stood alone.

"Your *Number Eleven* has caused some excitement," he said in perfect English.

The paintings had arrived earlier and were in the process of being hung upstairs and downstairs. My work was hung in the "Pain" section of the exhibit.

"Really?" I asked.

"It's already hung downstairs. Would you like to see it?" The curator gestured for me to follow him. Walking behind him as we went downstairs, I noticed how his torso leaned slightly toward the side. *A crooked spine*, I thought.

The two German artists stood in front of *Number Eleven*.

"*Dies ist der künstler*, Madeline Stewart." The curator introduced me, even though we had met upstairs. Both nodded. The female, blond, in her fifties, looked back at the painting. The male appeared to be much younger. Early thirties.

"*Das Gut. Gut,*" he said.

I mumbled, "Thank you." I was not used to this. To any of

it. How had it all started? Without Tuba with me, I felt so alone. The way I had felt in the middle of my marriage to Steve. The way I felt when I sat at the bar at the Bryant Grill Café and ordered a glass of champagne. The way older women in New York did who wore thick gold bangles on their wrists and waited for someone to notice.

After the male artist had complimented me on *Number Eleven*, I excused myself and raced up the stairs to where the "Beauty" section of the exhibit was being hung in the upper gallery. The Nigerian artist, a woman whose age I couldn't tell and whose face had the most luminous skin I had ever seen, smiled in my direction. I looked at her work. Spare, uncomplicated profiles of African children covered the winding hallway upstairs. Each oversize painting told a story of one child at a time.

As we watched the paintings settle onto their places on the wall, the Nigerian woman and I walked together. She spoke of being away from her daughters and son for the first time. How surprised she was to miss them, even amid the excitement of the art exhibit. Her turban, washed in creams and charcoal grays, wound round and round her head into a huge bouquet of braided fabric. Her teeth glistened white against her blue-black skin. Her smile matched the broad ones painted onto the faces of some of the children. At the evening reception, Tuba immediately picked the Nigerian woman above the other artists for her sensitivity and technique.

"She knows beauty," she said.

What do I know? I wondered. A bitter taste coated the inside of my mouth.

I was most interested in the panel scheduled for the following afternoon. Tuba and her son and daughter took seats in the third row. She sat between them and held hands with each of them. A string of tables faced the raised, stadium-like seating wound into a wide semicircle. Each artist had a microphone set in front of her seat. The moderator of the discussion was the curator who had showed me *Number Eleven* when it was first hung. He had sought me out twice at the previous evening's reception to introduce me to other artists from Germany. One was a couple who had traveled in from Munich, and the other a single, elderly man with paint still clinging to his whiskered chin. He seemed oblivious to the purples and blues hanging like drips of shampoo from a long-ago head wash.

Members of the media attended and asked questions. Some spoke only German, but a translator interpreted. "Does it depress you to paint such angst on the canvas?" "How long have you been painting?" "Did your parents support your decision to paint?" And finally, the question I prayed no one would dare: "Do you think you've become a successful painter because of dealing with your daughter's disappearance . . . maybe even death?"

There it was—the question Hilda had asked me almost five years before. Twisting and turning.

Does my work keep me from my daughter? Have I failed so miserably? If so, did Hilda have the right to take her from me?

"Tell us, Ms. Stewart, what propelled you all these years to paint?"

What to say? What to say? How much truth dare I say aloud?

"I have always loved to paint." I cleared my throat to continue.

"Painting allows possibilities. The possibility of my daughter coming home. The possibility of a new life, better than the old one. The possibility of finding myself after being lost."

The person who had asked the question nodded as she scribbled into a small pad. I closed my lower lip over the top.

Shame shut me down. Words banged up against one another. *The possibility of a new life . . . I should have explained.*

The Nigerian artist addressed each question eagerly. Again, her smile broadened, as if coaxing me along to enjoy the discussion. As the afternoon light dimmed outside, I noticed a woman stand up and make her way to the aisle. The museum had hired a videographer and his crew to tape the panel. The bright lights made it almost impossible to see the faces in the audience. Just as the woman stood, the lights went off. I saw her turn at the top of the steps when she was leaving. In my head, a noise that only I could hear exploded. The blood in my veins froze. My heart expanded into a racing mess of blood and muscle inside my chest.

The woman was Hilda.

Her hair was the same. Loosely tied into a bun in the middle of her head. Her body was thinner than I remembered, but it still had that round shape that Vinni used to say was like an apple.

I stood up, and the Nigerian artist next to me whispered, "We are not finished." I ignored her and left my seat, running and shouting, "Wait, wait! In the back. Someone stop her. Please!"

I tripped over the chair where the Spanish artist sat and landed on my right arm. Pain shot up my elbow, but I scrambled to my feet and yelled, "Wait, wait! Please. Stop her!"

The camera lights blinded me as they started up again. Fighting the brightness, I tried to run up the aisle steps. I thought I saw Hilda turn once more in my direction before she was out the door. I raced after her, but she had faded into the bitter winter afternoon.

Holiday shoppers crowded the streets. A soft snowfall rested on the shoulders of winter coats.

Someone called my name, but I ignored the voice until he

was at my side. I recognized him as one of the ushers who had greeted the gallery guests when they arrived.

I was out of breath and my side hurt from racing down the street, looking everywhere for a gray-haired woman wearing a tan coat.

"Here," he said, as he removed his coat and placed it over my shoulders. "You're shaking."

I threw my arms inside the long sleeves of the coat and wrapped myself up in a desperate embrace. I had no idea where to go. I walked up one street and down another.

Two hours later, I was frozen and lost. Had I imagined that I saw Hilda? How could I prove this to anyone, least of all the local police? If this were Hilda, then she had slipped through my fingers, but why would she have taken the chance and come to the museum? True, there had been articles in the newspapers leading up to the exhibit that mentioned my name as a featured artist. Hilda must have read about me. She must have wanted to see me—but from a distance. What if I *had* been able to stop her? What might she have said, other than "I wanted your daughter, so I took her"?

Would she have pleaded for my forgiveness?

I shuddered. Vinni had to be close. I leaned against a stone building and rocked my head into the cement. I could barely feel my lips, numb from the bitter wind that strengthened as the afternoon faded. The snowfall picked up and cast a sheet of white across all of Cologne. I continued to walk, not knowing where I was going.

Up ahead, I saw a sign: *POLIZEI*. I pushed open the door to the station. I ignored the oversize coat bearing down on my weakened limbs. I walked up to a glass enclosure where a policeman stood with his head bowed over papers. The man looked up. *"Kann ich Ihnen helfen?"*

I ignored his German.

"I saw the woman who stole my daughter. She's here in Cologne." I did not flail my arms or scratch at my head.

The policeman spoke in halting English. "May I help you?"

I repeated my words. "I saw the person who stole my daughter. She is here in Cologne." A strange feeling, odd and ill-fitting, overcame me.

The man rubbed his chin as he studied my coat. I knew he was looking at the sleeves and how they hid my hands. He reached for a piece of paper and asked if I wanted to fill out a report. He placed the paper in front of me. I could not understand the German words.

"A report. You must fill out a report," he said.

"No, you see, my child was kidnapped in the United States by a woman I just saw here in the city."

The policeman nodded a few times, as if to dismiss me. Then he tapped the paper and slid it closer.

I took the paper and shoved it into the pocket of the long coat. I began to walk out, but then I turned, ran back, and screamed as close to the policeman as I could get. Spit flung into the air as I opened my mouth.

"Get me someone to talk to! Get me someone!" I grabbed the edges of the countertop and started rocking myself back and forth. All of a sudden, two men were at my side as I screamed over and over, "Get me someone!" The coat dragged behind me as they led me into a room.

"Madame, we would like to help you, but what is the crime?"

I didn't want to sit, but they demanded I be still. They peppered me with questions, coming fast in an unfamiliar tongue. Then in English. I described Hilda. It came down to this: I was a woman alone, wearing a man's coat, screaming about my child who had been kidnapped almost five years ago.

"The crime you speak of did not happen in Cologne. Perhaps if you would fill out this report, we can assist you."

"We are wasting time! My daughter is here in your city."

The policemen exchanged glances. My hair, wet from the falling snow, hung like frozen strings of yarn. They studied me as I wrapped my arms around myself. What proof did I have, other than a glimpse of a woman I thought to be Hilda? Someone placed a cup of water on the table in front of me.

In my heart, I believed I was close to finding Vinni, but the heart is a lonely seeker of the truth. Unreliable when too tired to be called upon to set things right.

I smelled my girl. I just couldn't see her. This was all I knew.

I caught my breath and spoke slowly, with determination. "My daughter is nearby. She is here."

I rocked my body back and forth, unable to stop the motion.

The one policeman's mouth turned up a bit at the corners. "Madame, five years is a long time ago."

He didn't have to remind me. I kept rocking.

"We need more information. Please begin with the report we have asked you to fill out."

By now, would you have had any voice left at all? Would you have stopped rocking? Rolled up the cuffs from your coat?

و

I WALKED FOR hours after I left the police station. My eyes darted back and forth up and down the street, searching for Hilda. Finally, I caught a cab back to the hotel and asked the driver to wait while I ran in for money to pay him. Tuba was sitting in the lobby. When she saw me, she rushed to my side.

"You're frozen, child. Let me get you something warm to drink," she said.

"The cab . . ."

"I'll take care of it," Tuba said. "Go put on something warm, and I'll meet you upstairs. Everything was going so well for you until they stopped filming and turned on the lights. What happened?"

"I saw the woman who took my daughter."

THIRTY-SIX

By the time I got through to John D'Orfini, it was 10:00 a.m. Spring Haven time. "Are you sure it was Hilda?" John D'Orfini asked through the phone. Then he added, "I should have gone with you to Cologne."

"I'm sure. I saw her!" Even as I shouted, I wondered at my own certainty. "The woman I saw wore her hair exactly like Hilda's. And she looked at me. She stood up and hesitated for a minute. I noticed her as the camera lights went off. Before that, I couldn't see faces in the audience."

"Maddy, this is a good thing. I mean it."

"Good? What are you talking about?" I couldn't comprehend where he was going. My voice trembled.

"If Hilda read about you as one of the artists in the show and made the decision to show up . . . well, that means something."

"What?"

"She needed to see you. Did Hilda know you used to paint when you were younger?"

"Yes, of course."

"So she reads about you. She goes to the panel where she knows you're going to be speaking. Right before the end, while she thinks the cameras are rolling and the lights are shining on you, she gets up, and"—John D'Orfini snapped his fingers— "lights out, and she's the only one standing. She's caught. She probably knew right away that you saw her."

"I know she did. She stopped and looked at me."

"This is good," John D'Orfini said.

John D'Orfini made point after point to calm me. Twice he told me he wished he were with me. "If Hilda is starting to show herself, this means something. Soon she'll make a mistake. Right now she thinks she's hidden away with Vinni. She thinks she's safe."

"I . . . I went to the police station, but I had to file a report. I didn't do it."

"Let me take care of this," said John D'Orfini.

I did not—I could not—tell John D'Orfini that my first thought was of Vinni. That the "borrowing" of my child had ended. Kosinski had told me if I stopped asking questions, Vinni would be returned. I left out that part when I called John D'Orfini. If I had told him, I know it would have changed his theory why Hilda had attended the discussion at the museum.

Did Hilda need to see me out of guilt or remorse? Or was it morbid curiosity? Had she planned on approaching me and changed her mind when I had spoken on the panel about *Number Eleven* and what had motivated me to paint the wailing babies?

"The heart has a way of changing shape when being trampled upon," I said, as I sat facing the auditorium. "This is what I've tried to paint—the stampeding like wolves amid muscles and bone across the broken landscape of suffering." I took a sip of water. The other panelists waited for me to continue. "My child was stolen from me five years ago. I haven't stopped believing that she's alive." A hush came over the audience.

"I paint because otherwise I might kill myself."

Silence—corner to corner—filled the room.

❧

TUBA AND I had breakfast together the next morning. She had postponed joining her two children at their family home on the island of Chiemsee, outside Prien. "It will be just the three of us," Tuba said, as she sipped coffee over a plate of two poached eggs in the hotel's dining room. Her white gloves matched the cup's elegance. She had dined with her two children the night before while I stayed in my hotel room. It was impossible for me to sleep as I thought about Vinni. She would turn thirteen in May.

"Are you sure the woman you saw was the woman you believe took your child?" Tuba asked. Everything about her had softened since she saw her children. Her chignon—pulled less taut—exposed a side wave brushed naturally away from her face.

John D'Orfini had asked me the same thing. At one point during our conversation the night before, I had screamed into the phone, "Do you believe me? I've got to know that you believe me, or else . . ."

"What?" His voice went tender. "You'll give up? I know that's not going to happen."

I extended my stay in Cologne for another week. Tuba insisted on being with me. Together, we returned to the police station I had stumbled on when I was wearing a man's coat with sleeves that hid my hands. My story was the same. So was their response. After two days, I told Tuba to go. "Be with your family. It's the holidays."

Reluctantly, she left the Excelsior Hotel with a promise to call me every evening.

Although the staff proved kind whenever we spoke, their faces changed from compassionate to polite. They'd nod their heads, cross their arms over their chests, and glance sideways.

Five years ago, my daughter was kidnapped. . . . A woman here in Cologne . . . she took her.

Not only the concierge but two of his assistants—the man

working days and the woman who worked nights—checked in on me. I hardly knew what to ask for.

It was a week before Christmas. The city was full of life. I felt more alone in the crowds than ever before. I should go home. But how could I leave? Over and over I replayed seeing Hilda in my head. If she was here, so was Vinni.

At the end of the week, the concierge at the hotel took pity on me. His brother-in-law was a police captain in another precinct. He offered to accompany me himself to the station. "Perhaps a personal introduction could bring you some kind of satisfaction," he said. The captain offered me a seat in his private office while the concierge read from an aging magazine outside his door. He wore a pair of rimless reading glasses. A man in his late forties, he had a roundness that softened his stiff way of moving, as if he were put together in fewer pieces than the rest of us. The captain spoke English well. There were no wild arm gestures or voices raised. Vinni had been kidnapped in another country, five years ago. What could be done *now*?

"I wish there was something we could do, madame," the captain said as he stood. He showed me a book of pictures of women who had been in trouble with the law. I doubted each turn of the page. The next day, he assigned a young police officer to drive me around the city. I sat in the front seat of the vehicle, feeling like a child. I stared out the window, scanning every moving person, but I saw no one resembling the woman I had seen at the Käthe Kollwitz Museum. Hilda had vanished.

ℰ

I CALLED KAY as soon as I arrived back home, and told her I was sure I had spotted Hilda in Cologne. John D'Orfini had filled her in, but her response was not as sweet as his.

"I'm listening," she said.

"But do you believe I saw her?" I said.

"I believe you *think* you saw her. Other than that, I don't know. After all, I wasn't there," Kay said. "Eyewitness identification is often unreliable."

I wanted to tell Kay I was sure that Vinni was alive. Hadn't Kosinski sliced off my toe in exchange for my silence? I wanted to show Kay the photo of Vinni that Kosinski had given me. But I couldn't. I was too afraid to take the chance of losing my girl.

The next day, I waited for John D'Orfini. His train was due to arrive at Penn Station at 7:00 p.m. "I'll cook," he said. "Buy something, and I'll whip it up when I get to your place."

That night, over dinner, I came close to telling John D'Orfini everything. Words piled up as I grew quiet.

"Are you tired? Jet lag? What's going on inside that head of yours?"

I *was* tired—tired of not telling him all the truth.

"Look. Maybe it wasn't a good idea for you to come all the way up here," I said. "I'm sorry. I really am, but I don't feel like talking much." I sensed the irritation in my voice. I pushed up the sleeves of my sweater, even though I felt chilled.

John D'Orfini nodded, took our plates over to the sink, and started the water. He had lived alone so long, he didn't believe in using a dishwasher unless there were dishes for at least four.

"Leave them," I said.

"You want me to go, don't you?" His dark eyes slipped into a distant place I recognized from before, where he protected himself by drawing upon his profession. His voice stiffened in line with his shoulders.

"You need some time. You're in shock from believing you saw Hilda. Understandable."

When he spoke in one-word sentences, my heart broke. But I had made a promise to myself in Germany. No matter how long I had to wait, I would do it. And I would do it without telling John D'Orfini or Kay. I had come this far in silence.

❧

ON THE TRAIN ride home, John D'Orfini called me on his cell phone. I had fallen asleep on the couch and woke in a fit believing I was still at the Excelsior Hotel in Cologne.

"Maddy?"

I had no idea what time it was.

"Are you home?"

He laughed. "Only if you count halfway to Asbury Park as almost home."

"What's the matter?" I felt guilty having asked him to leave the city after he had trekked all the way up here to see me.

"Uh . . . there's something we should talk about," he said.

I sat up and wiped the corners of my dry lips. My phone said 11:22 p.m. He had left my apartment about two hours earlier. "What do you mean?" I had asked him to leave because I needed the space. Why was he calling me?

"You want to know about things when they happen, right? Well, there's some things . . . that you should know."

I knew he wasn't going to say much more while riding on a public train bound for Monmouth and Ocean Counties.

"Should I come down tomorrow, or do you want to call me when you get home?"

"That's an easy answer. We didn't really see each other tonight."

"I'm sorry."

"It's okay. I'll see you tomorrow."

Even in my half-awake state, I could tell that John D'Orfini had something on his mind.

Ǝ

I OPENED THE door to the Spring Haven Religious Gift Shop and saw Katherine Mulvey unknotting a gold cross necklace at the counter.

"Feel free to browse," she said, without lifting her head. We have some beautiful single-rose vases perfect for last-minute Christmas shopping."

"Actually, I'm meeting someone here."

Katherine stopped and looked up with the knotted cross lying gently between her fingers. She studied me as I looked to the right of her shoulder at a selection of little girls' white veils inside a glass case. "You're that woman," she said. The twitching on the side of her neck pulled at the tip of her collarbone. "John D'Orfini's waiting for you in the back."

I followed Katherine past the statue section, where dozens of wooden and ceramic versions of St. Christopher, St. Francis of Assisi, Teresa of Avila, and, of course, St. Joseph and the Virgin Mary lined up like commuters at a bus stop. I reminded her I had a name.

"I'm Maddy Stewart," I said.

She slowed a bit and turned at the display of amethyst and crystal rosary beads.

"Yes, I know who you are." Her neck pulsed violently.

My detective stood up as soon as he saw me, and pulled out a chair. Katherine took a seat on the opposite side of the table. I looked at him as I questioned what I was doing here. He had texted me earlier and said to meet him at the shop.

"How's your family, Katherine?" John D'Orfini knew to ask

about her five children, all of whom had attended St. Rose's elementary and high school one town north of Spring Haven. "Will they all be coming home for Christmas?"

"Ann Marie and her brood can't make it this year. The rest will start coming in tomorrow, God willing and the weather holds up, which means no nor'easter until after New Year's."

That was just enough police foreplay for John D'Orfini.

Katherine ran her polished nails over the tops of several of the religious statues in an effort to dust away what she had missed.

"The other day, Katherine, I believe I might have heard you at Cryan's Deli mentioning a woman named Hilda? Could I have heard that right?"

I began to feel as if I was there for dramatic effect—a life-size figure of a woman propped up in a ladder-back chair.

"It'll be five years ago this coming August that a little girl was kidnapped from the beach here in Spring Haven." John D'Orfini gestured toward me. "You may remember meeting her mother."

What the hell?

"The leading suspect has always been a woman named Hilda, who lived here with her husband. She vanished the day her husband died. So did a child named Vinni, here on vacation with her mother. You remember this?"

All the while John D'Orfini spoke, Katherine took turns fussing with the odd arrangement of wooden martyrs lined up on the table. Turning them at odd angles as if introducing them to one another at a gala.

"I know we spoke to you at the time of the child's disap-pearance, but I'm thinking something here, and I know it's a long shot, but you wouldn't have been talking about this same woman named Hilda today at Cryan's, now, would you have?"

Katherine did a once-over on top of the most expensive statue of the Virgin Mary—all crystal—without moving from her chair. She cleared her throat and excused herself for a glass of water.

"What am I doing here?" I said in a low voice. "I'm uncomfortable."

John D'Orfini touched my hand with his. "Trust me," he said.

Katherine returned with two glasses of water and placed one on the table in front of John D'Orfini and one for me. "Thank you," I said.

Katherine stood holding on to the back of her chair. "I was speaking about the same Hilda." She looked at me. "The summer your child disappeared, this woman walked into the store and we started chatting. She had been in here a few times but never bought anything and only said 'hello' and 'goodbye,' no matter how long she stayed and browsed. One day, she noticed the trinity rings—the ones in the front case—and asked me how much they were. I told her the rings started at thirty-five dollars and ran up to one hundred fifteen. She asked me if she could see one up close—the thirty-five-dollar one."

Katherine let out a long sigh before she continued.

I could barely breathe.

"She told me she had a daughter who died. It was a long time ago. That's all she said."

I loosened the scarf knotted around my neck.

"Why didn't you tell us this earlier? Like, five years ago?" John D'Orfini asked.

"I mind my own business, John—you know that. Doesn't the eighth commandment remind us never to bear false witness?" Katherine hesitated, as if she knew the commandments had nothing to do with it. Especially the eighth. Then she added,

"And besides, the woman had a sadness about her. I felt sorry for her."

"Sorry enough to omit crucial information? Suppress evidence?" John D'Orfini said.

Katherine's voice shifted into high-high gear. The muscle in her neck danced. "I did no such thing, John. I answered all the questions addressed to me during the time of the investigation. I resent what you're implying here."

"I'm questioning why a nice lady like you holds back information from an ongoing police investigation."

"I'm no gossip, John D'Orfini. Ask your mother. Why I know things about every person in this town and no one's going to get them out of me. They'll go to the grave with me and up to Saint Peter and the gates of heaven."

"What else did Hilda tell you?"

"Think!" I said, in a voice coming from the pit of my stomach. Harsh. "What else did Hilda say to you?" By now, I was standing and so was John D'Orfini. The temperature in the room skyrocketed.

"The day she came in to the shop would have been her daughter's birthday. One thing I do remember is how sad she looked—like her heart had been ripped out. Something about her touched me. She was a sad, sad woman, John."

"And what about the *sad, sad* woman standing right here in your shop who lost her little girl the day Hilda disappeared? What about her? Have you thought about *her* these past five years?" John D'Orfini picked up a statue of a crystal Virgin Mary and rolled it back and forth in his hands before returning it to the shelf next to St. Joseph.

"I pray for all of them," Katherine said. "I'm deeply sorry for you," she said, looking at me through her tears.

John D'Orfini dropped his hands to the table. His body

filled the space as he stretched across it. "What's that commandment your children memorized when they were attending St. Rose's? Oh yeah . . . the eighth: thou shalt not lie."

"I've done no such thing, John. No one asked me if I had ever spoken to Hilda. I told the police she had come into the shop a few times, but it was only on that one day that she had a conversation with me. Her daughter's birthday—that's all she told me. I swear it."

"And she never showed you a picture of her daughter?"

"Never! I swear it!"

John D'Orfini reached into the inside pocket of his jacket, but then, as if struck by a bullet, he dropped his hand by his side. He looked around the store without focusing on anything. "Thanks for your time, Katherine," he said, as he headed toward the door. "If you remember any more about your conversation with Hilda Haydn, I want you to call me." He dropped his voice further into that authoritative spot in his belly. "You have a duty to call me, Katherine. St. Peter aside."

Right before he opened the shop's door into the late afternoon, he turned and said, "Merry Christmas."

Outside, a few stragglers carried shopping bags in both hands. A white Christmas was predicted for the northeast. "I'll meet you back at your place," I said. I tossed the words behind me and ran out the door.

Hilda had a child who died. Was this why she wanted mine?

I drove to the boardwalk. The ocean's roar was nothing like its sound in the summer. A biting wind swooped over me as I walked to the spot where I had last seen Vinni. What had Hilda and Rudy seen when they had watched Vinni play on the beach? A child the same age as theirs when they had lost her. Had their pain wormed its way out of a wound that never had a chance of healing?

By the time I arrived at John D'Orfini's house, I was frozen.

"My God! Where did you go? You've been gone for over an hour," he said.

I ignored his question even as he held me close to his warm body. I spoke out loud as I laid my head on his shoulder, away from his face so he couldn't see me.

"What was the purpose of having me at the shop with the two of you?" I said.

He shrugged. "A hunch, maybe."

A lie—even when well intentioned—disturbs the natural flow of things. Everything changes. I knew my sweet detective wanted to tell me something. It was why he called me from the train the day before. But if withholding information impregnates a lie, then we were both guilty. His silence, as well as mine, rested alongside the other. Many nights later, it came to me, when my head hit the pillow, that whatever was in John D'Orfini's pocket had prompted him to rethink what information he'd share with me.

&

IF I HAD known sooner, if my sweet detective and I had not exchanged kisses in the middle of the night, would he have told me about the picture of Hilda's girl in his pocket at Katherine Mulvey's shop . . . having floated on down and landed at his feet when he was rifling through the pages of book after book, looking for a clue at Hilda and Rudy's house, nine months after my own girl disappeared?

THIRTY-SEVEN

Kay had contacted the museum in Cologne to see if there had been a reserved list of those attending the panel discussion. Indeed there was, but no one named Hilda Haydn was on the list. The museum had sent Kay and John D'Orfini copies of the weekend's guests for both the reception and the afternoon panel discussion. The name Ada Weber was near the end of the list. A name as quiet and undisturbed as a blade of grass, it slipped unnoticed in alphabetical order.

When I returned from Cologne, I experienced a strange numbness in my feet, undiagnosed by the two doctors I visited at Stanley's insistence. John D'Orfini had decided to take the train to the Doll and Clock Shop in Brooklyn on a windy day in March. Even though I couldn't feel the bottoms of my feet, I wished I had been there.

Retelling always loses something, especially when you hear a story's end first.

"Kosinki's been arrested," Kay said. "They picked him up this morning. Al Dobson was with them."

When Kay called, I was sitting at home, wiggling my toes, trying for the life of me to regain some feeling in the bottoms of my feet. I could walk, but it was an odd sensation not to fully

feel the ground underneath me. Stanley said it was stress re-
lated.

"I just received notice at the office. John will be calling you
later, but I can tell you it's been a busy day in Brooklyn at the
Doll and Clock Shop," Kay said. "Our Mr. Kosinski won't be
visiting Mueller's for a long time."

My thoughts went to Hannah and George. What had
prompted the arrest now?

$\backsim$

THE DOORBELL RANG at exactly 6:32 p.m. I didn't wait to
hear who it was before I buzzed him in. I knew it was John
D'Orfini. He hadn't called, so I had expected him to come in
person.

I flung open the door and met him at the landing one floor
down. "Kay told me about Kosinski," I said. "What happened?"
I stepped lightly around my words. "I mean, why now?"

"That's Dobson's domain. He alerted me so I could have
another shot at him before things went down."

"What kind of shot?" I couldn't look at him when I said it.

"I had some questions about his work. When I showed up,
he did some explaining about a set of three bisque dolls. One
had a large crack running down its left cheek into the neck. It
was also missing most of a leg. Another had a piece gone from
the head, and broken fingers—half off—on both hands. The
third was on its way to almost full repair. I even watched Kosinski paint a fresh mouth and eyebrows and scale back the cheeks
to smooth their surface with plaster of paris."

"Where's this going?" I said. By now, we were standing a
few feet from the door to my apartment. "Why the details on
doll repair?"

"That's just it. That's who Kosinski is—a detail man." He pointed at my foot. "He did that, didn't he?"

He placed his hand under my chin and turned my face toward him.

"Don't make me do this," I said.

I could see he was thinking how far to push me. I was afraid if he touched my cheek he'd break me and break my silence.

He dropped his hand from my face.

He let me breathe, but not for long. The teakettle began to whistle. I had filled it before he rang the bell and had forgotten all about it. Steam blew through the top, as if announcing an urgent message.

"I've done a little investigating on the work of a dollologist. A friend of my mother's, a woman named Irene O'Hara, used to repair dolls out of her home in the Heights, about five miles in from the ocean. Irene is ninety-two, living peacefully in Spring Oaks Nursing Home on the highway across from Doolan's Funeral Parlor. Up until a few years ago, when her eyesight began to fail, she repaired dolls for people living as far north as Canada. One afternoon, I visited Irene and asked her a question."

"About what?"

"That," he said, with a hard glance at my foot.

"It was an accident." Even as I said it, I knew how weak I sounded. John D'Orfini continued as if he hadn't heard me.

"Everyone in Spring Haven knew how skilled Irene was with a needle and thread or a spade and weed whacker. Irene knew what tools did what, including for her dolls. At sixty-eight, she took classes on doll repair. Irene was sure that any good dollologist would have the right tool to slice off a person's toe nice and clean."

All this time, I thought John D'Orfini's silence meant he had forgotten about my "wound."

"Do you mind if I make myself a cup of coffee?" he said, jolting me out of the imaginary conversation I was having with my own fleet of failures.

I waved my hand for him to walk inside.

John D'Orfini went into the kitchen and turned on the faucet for the coffeepot. He raised his voice so I could hear him above the sound of the water. "Hannah was at the shop with Kosinski. She was there when I arrived. She pretended she'd dropped off a watch for repair."

"Pretended?" I called out, as I followed him to the kitchen.

"The way she moved—another detail—as if she knew her way around him, even though she kept her distance. And those damn clocks. She jumped a foot in the air when they chimed in unison. Kosinski, on the other hand, raved about her. 'You must stop by Mueller's Bakery before you head south to Jersey,' he said. 'Hannah and George are the best bakers in Brooklyn!'"

"What about . . . I mean, did you question him?"

"No. Not directly. I didn't ask him about Vinni. After Hannah left, I questioned him on how well he knew the bakers— particularly Hannah. We want to find out how far he'd go to help them or even protect them if they needed it. All he said was, 'The bakers are good people. Sensitive people.' He barely took his eyes away from working on one of those bisque dolls. The guy does delicate work. That's for sure."

⁂

JOHN D'ORFINI STAYED the night.

⁂

TWO WEEKS LATER, my feet miraculously came back to life and I accepted a four-part feature assignment for *Hot Style*. I needed the money. My next show was at the end of June. Tuba, who told me it was already creating a "buzz," coordinated things with Helen Henning, the curator of Evelyn's last exhibition. I had moved past wailing babies to babies inside the womb. The pain wasn't less, but I was trying to find a way to paint hope, latching on to the journey of the babies down the birth canal, the explosion of the crowning heads. Since I had helped the girl down the alleyway, something inside me had changed and I found myself waking up glad I had another day to live.

Kosinski was locked up. In the months that followed—before summer took over—I walked by the Doll and Clock Shop many times. The sign on the door said CLOSED. I'd stop and stare through the window at the painted faces of the dolls, waiting for their owners to claim them. Hannah and George were nearby, baking bread at Mueller's, but Al Dobson—Neighbor Man—was gone from the neighborhood. Now that Kosinski was in prison, I wondered if I should leave Brooklyn, but I held on to my room across from the bakery. I slept through the night, no longer watching for a black limousine to pull up to the curb across the street. In the city, I worked on paintings *Number Twenty-One* through *Number Twenty-Eight*. Shuffling back and forth between eight paintings was crazy, but I loved the frenzy of it. After a good day, I'd fall into bed exhausted.

Keep working, I thought. *Just keep working. That's how time passes.*

THIRTY-EIGHT

THE CALL CAME IN AT 8:12 A.M. I HAD RETURNED FROM a job in Los Angeles on the red-eye and had fallen into bed as the bodegas on Second Avenue were brewing their first pots of coffee.

"Hello?"

"I want to speak to Madeline Stewart. Please . . ."

"Who is this?" I asked, with my eyes closed. My mouth was dry from the six-hour plane ride.

"I want to speak to Madeline Stewart," the voice on the other end repeated.

I pulled myself up on one elbow.

"Is this Madeline Stewart?"

I opened my eyes and tried to unwind myself from the tangled sheets.

"Who is this?" I asked.

"My name is Meta Adler. I call you today from outside Füssen."

"Where?" I heard a woman's voice with a strong accent. Yugoslavian, or Czech, or . . . German.

"Germany. I have a message for you, Madeline Stewart. You are Madeline Stewart, ya?"

"Yes." I bolted up, letting the sheet fall around my waist. My naked breasts hung sleepily near the top of my ribs.

"You are to come and get your daughter and bring her home."

My body trembled. The words I had longed to hear now spoken.

"How . . . how . . . do you know I have a daughter?"

Answers are important only if the questions keep us awake.

"Your Sophie is here. Just outside Füssen."

"Sophie?" I barely whispered, "I have no daughter named Sophie."

"Ya, ya. I am sorry. Hilda told me her name was Vinni . . . before Sophie. I didn't know. I only know now. You come and take the child home. Hilda wants you to take the child home. So you come. You come to Neuschwanstein. Immediately. Go to the Luitpoldpark-Hotel in Füssen. Wait for the driver to take you here."

"Where? *Neusch* . . . Spell it." I wrote the word on the back of an unused prescription for Zoloft.

"Do not tell the police. It will do you no good. Hilda is in the hospital . . . very ill. She is dying. She slipped into a coma ten days ago. The doctors say it will be soon. She is sorry for your pain—but I will tell you all when you get here."

"I don't know who you are. How do I know Vinni is there with you?"

"I am Meta Adler, caretaker of the farm estate owned by Hilda Haydn these many years. I only just find this out. I have papers for you. So you come, yes? Soon, you will see Sophie and you will be happy."

"Tell me something about my child." And then she said it. She told me all I needed to know.

"Sophie . . . no, Vinni . . . has a blue garden. She told me she always wanted a garden with only blue flowers, and so my husband and I, we helped her plant a garden of blue flowers. This made her smile."

I heard Vinni in my head.

"When I grow up, I want a blue garden. Only blue flowers. You can come visit, and I'll show you all the kinds of blue."

"I will leave here tonight," I said.

"Gut. Gut."

When I hung up, I shook uncontrollably.

Tears fell down my cheeks. I didn't scream or wail like the babies in my paintings. I dressed and walked down the same city streets I had wandered for the past five years. I stopped and sat on the steps of the New York Public Library and pulled out the photo of Vinni that Mr. Kosinski had shoved into my hands five months earlier.

I traced my fingers over her body, smoothed her hair across her face, and imagined what it would be like to feel her skin. Kiss her sweet neck. Watch her sleep in her bed. Everything inside tightened into a chain of knots. My mouth clamped shut.

I knew whom I needed to see to open it.

~

AS I WALKED from the subway to Mueller's Bakery, I wondered if I should speak to both Hannah and George or just Hannah. When I arrived at the bakery, Hannah was emptying loaves of fresh bread onto the shelves behind the cash register.

"Hannah?" I said.

"Mmm . . . yes?" She spoke as she turned, and I saw she had been crying. The lines around her face folded into creases of flesh, old and worn.

"The phone call," I whispered. "The phone call came early this morning."

Hannah nodded.

"You know about the call?" I asked.

Hannah walked from around the counter. She wiped her

hands on her apron and then took my face in her hands. She kissed me on both cheeks and said one word.

"Go."

"And bring her back?" A slight question hung perilously at the end of my voice.

Hannah wrapped me in her arms. I heaved sobs onto her shoulder as she stroked the back of my head. Hannah kissed me again.

"Go," she said. "We are almost free. Both of us."

As I left the bakery, I looked in through the glass front windows and saw George with his arms around Hannah, rubbing her back in small circles.

AFTER META'S CALL, I'd bought two seats for Munich on United Airlines. I had to get myself to Füssen. The message had been clear: no police. Hilda was dying from a recurrence of ovarian cancer. She had slipped into a coma.

I called John D'Orfini on his cell phone.

"I need you to listen and not to question anything I'm about to tell you," I said.

"Are you okay?" he asked.

"Please just listen to me."

"I'm listening."

"I've made two plane reservations for Munich for tonight. I'm going to bring Vinni home, and I want you to come with me. Not as a police detective. As someone I want with me. I received a phone call—one I've been waiting for for five months. One I was told would come."

"From whom?"

"I can't tell you this."

"Go on."

"The plane leaves JFK at eight o'clock tonight. I'll leave your ticket at the United Airlines customer service counter." I hesitated before I said the next part, but I felt there was a chance that he wouldn't come, and I couldn't involve myself with a bureaucratic mess.

"And, John, if you can't come, for whatever reason, don't call me. I'll be waiting at the gate around 6:30 p.m., and if you're not there . . . well, I guess I'll know."

My tone hardened.

"Under no circumstances can you tell anyone about this call or about my flight to Germany. I mean Kay, too. It can't go this way. Do you understand? It's too late."

"I—"

"No. You must promise. There is no choice."

"I promise," he said.

I hung up, feeling the knots in my stomach tug more tightly. I walked over to the window and looked out at my beautiful city.

*

KAY HAD LEFT a message on my cell phone that morning. *How's dinner tonight? Or tomorrow.* I was in the middle of packing the only piece of luggage I would take: my carry-on. Vinni's photo was safe in my wallet. The book she had been reading on the day she disappeared was inside my black nylon tote. I texted Kay on the way to the airport. *Swamped. Teaching tonight. Need sleep. xxx.* I hoped she wouldn't try calling, because I didn't want her to suspect anything.

John D'Orfini hadn't called me back, and I was glad. I feared if we talked, he'd want to know more. At the airport, the minutes ticked past 5:00 p.m. My anxiety level rose to high. By six thirty, it was on overdrive. I hadn't eaten anything all day. Before I had left for the airport, I'd opened the door to Vinni's bedroom, painted blue.

"Mama's coming," I said aloud to no one.

Soon, I would smell Vinni's scent mixed with mine. I lay down on her bed and swept my hand over the quilt where Vinni would lie. I stroked the seams where the stitching made wave patterns of creams and blues. I hoped she would like her new room.

I stood up and smoothed the quilt on Vinni's bed. I rearranged a set of candles on the dresser, moving all five to the center to create a circle. After Meta's call, I had thought of running out and buying things for Vinni, but I didn't know what she liked.

I didn't know her.

Five years is a long time.

⁓

I CHECKED IN and snaked through the long security lines. I studied my cell phone.

Nothing.

He wasn't coming.

I sat on the plane next to an empty seat with forty minutes to departure. I closed my eyes. I breathed in and out like the tide at the beach. Slow. Rush. Slow. The plane was hot. Noise from the overhead storage bins ran by me as, one by one, they clicked shut.

Someone tapped my shoulder, and I looked up into the eyes of John D'Orfini.

"I believe this seat is mine," he said, as he smiled in that slow way intended for tides to switch course.

My heart leaped. "What happened? Where were you?" I said.

"Damn traffic. How do you New Yorkers get used to it?" He sat down and took my hand and squeezed it. "I'm here now."

I rested my head on his shoulder. Without hesitation, he placed his hand on my cheek. One touch. That was all I needed.

THIRTY-NINE

WE RENTED A CAR AT THE AIRPORT. ALL JOHN D'ORFINI knew was that we had to get to a place called Füssen. He had already mapped our drive from Munich onto Autobahn A7. I suspected he had a list of questions, but all he said was, "Try to sleep," as he sped down the highway, trying to keep up with the other drivers in their BMWs and Lamborghinis, enjoying the absence of a speed limit.

We checked in to the hotel late. It was thirty-six hours after Meta's call.

"We've been expecting you, Miss Stewart," the young clerk said, as he passed one key over the counter. "You have a corner room upstairs."

The room was large. Clean. A view to the sky over the writing desk.

I objected to getting anything to eat. "You go. I'm not hungry."

"You're coming with me. I'm not letting you out of my sight."

We walked outside and into town. It was a warm Friday night. John D'Orfini held my hand. Music and laughter drew us to the town square, where there was a beer festival. At least fifty long tables on both sides filled the square. Women dressed in long chemises and aprons, and men wearing the traditional Bavarian leiderhosen carried trays of huge steins of beer. A band was singing rock 'n' roll in English. We stood on the sidelines with dozens of other passersby out on the town on a hot evening. People drank and sang along with the musicians. Only the mood steadied the night—gay and boisterous—as John D'Orfini held my hand and kept me close.

As the music got louder, I withdrew, scared my heart might stop. With each beat, I grew more anxious, afraid everything might disappear before I could touch it. The unusual ninety-degree weather didn't help. The music clashed inside my head, moving membranes like fallen dominoes. Too much warm beer escalated the drinkers' sloppy speech. I eavesdropped on the drunkenness of the German night.

Sleep was impossible. At first, I sat up in bed and leaned against the pillow. I stared out through the black glass of the window. The breathing of my sweet detective provided an easy rhythm. I slipped my body farther under the light blanket. I felt the warmth from his body.

I dreamed John D'Orfini and I were walking in New York City. We walked south along Broadway. We moved one foot in front of the other. Lifting our feet in exaggerated steps at the knee. My left foot throbbed as I limped. Finally, we came to the sixteen-foot bronze sculpture at the foot of Wall Street—a seven-thousand-pound bull the artist had donated to the city as a symbol of strength, power, and hope after the stock market crash of 1987.

As I drifted off to sleep, John D'Orfini's steady breathing reminded me how much I needed him. Even so, I had doubled up on my Xanax dosage, from 0.25 milligrams to 0.5 milligrams. Hardly noticeable for most women, but I had the kind of system that allowed a drug—any drug—to knock me out. Xanax stirred my unconscious desires into a vivid slide show while I fell into a deep sleep and dreamed of the bull. Only this time, the bull floated in the ocean with a boy on its back. The boy trusted the bull. He held the bull by the horns, and I watched the two ride over the tops of the waves from my seat in the sand. The boy laid his cheek against the bull's neck. His small fingers held on to the horns as the bull's nostrils flared. His back legs treaded ferociously to keep the boy afloat. "Don't let go!" I screamed out to the boy.

I sank deeper into the mattress. I had lifted the boy from the bull, turned him on his back, and let him float. I yearned to be the one clutching the bull's horns, whispering into the bull's ear, "Pull me under." But the boy—what about the boy? Was he still floating? I couldn't go under. Not now. I struggled to reach the surface.

Wet seeped its way up my legs as I woke to John D'Orfini kissing my face.

"What time is it?" I asked.

"Early. The light is just coming in through the window."

I looked over to the window, where neither of us had remembered to pull down the shades. The sun broke over the orange-tiled rooftops. Beyond them, the Alps reached toward what could only be heaven. I wrapped my legs around John's back the way the bull had wrapped his legs around me as I had floated farther and farther into the depths of the ocean.

Sobs. Salty. Sacred.

Tears dampened his cheeks.

"Maddy, I think . . ." He stopped himself.

"What is it?" I asked.

I had seen that look when John D'Orfini had passed from lover to officer of the law.

"I think things are going to be okay," he said. His hands wiped at my tears. I released my legs alongside his thighs and rolled over to his side. I looked deep into his eyes. Silence.

"I need a coffee," John D'Orfini said. "I'll jump in the shower first and then go get you a tea." Naked, he headed toward the bathroom. Just as he was about to disappear, he stopped and turned to look at me. His strong body, smooth and satisfied, was poised near the door frame.

"What?" I said.

The early-morning light bounced strips of burnt orange against the walls.

"I love you," he said. "I love you, Madeline Stewart."

For a second, it looked as if he were waiting for me to say something. I couldn't tell him I loved him. Not yet. I needed to see Vinni first.

I sat up on my elbows in bed. The heat from the morning's sun slipped through the window and rested between my shoulder blades. "Let's get Vinni and take her home," I said.

FORTY

I WAITED OUTSIDE THE HOTEL.

"Come inside. It's too hot out there."

"I'm fine," I said. A message had been left for me at the desk: a driver would pick me up at 10:00 a.m. Meta said she would send her husband, Armen. She explained they were tenant farmers. Together, they eked out an existence caring for the largest property on the outskirts of Füssen. At first, they answered to Hilda's father, who owned the land. He had bought up parcel after parcel of nearby properties. Telling no one. Filing papers. Hiring caretakers. Amassing a real estate fortune unknown to his daughter, Hilda, until his death.

There had been two daughters, but the oldest by six years had run away at the age of twenty to marry a young Hungarian boy, son of a baker, whom her father disapproved of, causing him to shut her out of his will. Year after year, Hilda received checks from her father's estate lawyers as Meta and Armen continued to work the land. Armen supervised the farm. Meta cared for the house and the gardens. They established a reputation as an honest, hardworking couple. Childless, they embraced the soil, the trees, the wildflowers, and the farm animals with the love others spent on their children and grandchildren. They thought of the land as their own, and they loved it the way you would love what belongs to you.

From time to time, they rented out a small cottage on the far end of the property with two bedrooms and a piece of land in the back of the kitchen suitable for a garden. The Alps circled the property and stood in all their majesty in view from every window. The rental fee from the cottage gave Meta and Armen much-needed additional income. "When they arrived on our doorstep, it was like a blessing. A child on the property . . . what joy."

ᨴ

ARMEN WAS UNSURE about John D'Orfini, but I insisted. He spoke little English, but he understood my dramatic arm gestures and the firm shake of my head. I'm not sure he saw my lips tremble, but he shrugged his shoulders as John D'Orfini guided me into the car. We drove in silence as the mountains grew larger. Cream-colored cows—unusual to see—slept on acres of green.

Life nudged its way in front of hope. Blue slipped away.

I thought about what I should wear to see Vinni. She was thirteen now. Would she remember how I used to hang the white clothes in the closet? All together. When she was little, she would help me choose what to wear.

She will remember, won't she?

My long white skirt, tiered into layers, rippled down to my ankles. My sleeveless shirt with the scooped neck and small-petaled blossom sewn onto the right shoulder hung loose and long, with asymmetrical pointed ends frayed in chic unevenness. Would Vinni notice my flowing skirt? My hair was held behind my ears in a loose ponytail tied with a blue ribbon.

The sun shone bright. The few clouds shifted with springs on their feet. As we drove farther from the center of Füssen, into the surrounding landscape of mountains capped with cream, my heart opened and astounded me. Joy made an entrance. Pain crouched in the corners of the heart. Neither held on tight, but together they created something new. I experienced a wildness unknown but known, close to panting, as Armen drove us deeper into the Bavarian landscape. I could barely breathe.

John D'Orfini reached for my hand. Speech would have taken too much space. My throat dried up as the heat seeped in through the open car windows.

Armen gestured out the window. "The Forggensee," he said. The lake to our left calmed me a bit. Families had taken advantage of the early heat in late May. Children stood at the water's edge while their parents rested on their elbows on blankets grabbed from the tops of beds. As we drove, I felt an enormous kinship with the land. The vastness of it. The colors. The Alps, although higher than any mountains I had ever seen, soothed me, as if calling me to rest on their foreheads.

If this was where Vinni had lived for the past five years, could I deal with the pain? Did she recognize the beauty, or was she too torn to notice? My heart cracked open, and sobs spilled from my lips.

"Maddy? What is it?" John D'Orfini draped his arm around my shoulder. Armen looked in the rearview mirror.

"She's all right. If this is where Vinni's been . . . look at the mountains," I said. They were the same as the ones in the background of the photo I hid folded inside my wallet. The photo John D'Orfini knew nothing about.

"We are almost home," Armen said.

Home.

This had been Vinni's home for five years. I was sure of it. She had lived where quiet had a chorus. Had this been her blessing? As much as a child can replace one love with another? Is it possible?

My head hurt.

Where is the bad amid all this beauty?

I needed only to see Vinni alive and well. If this were so, I would cut the anchor from my neck.

But panic intruded.

What if she's forgotten me?

"Stop!" I screamed. "Stop the car!"

I grabbed the back of the passenger seat with both hands.

"Stop, please!"

Armen stopped the car, and I jumped out. I started running in the direction we had come from with my skirt flying behind me. I ran and ran, crying, "I'm sorry, baby, I'm sorry." I ran—not like an ordinary mother beast but like a caged mama turned free. Why did I think that being a painter might quiet my inside voice? I was scared. All those years of my father hushing me so I wouldn't disturb my mother. Was this what Hilda believed she had seen? My busyness hushing Vinni? Had I done everything so wrong?

God help me.

I ran and ran and no one stopped me.

"Gut. Gut." I said it in German. Wasn't this how Vinni spoke now?

I pumped my arms at my side like a wild woman, until my feet couldn't keep up with my head. I tripped and fell onto the ground. I felt John D'Orfini's arms around my waist.

"What if she doesn't want me?" I cried.

"She wants you," my detective said, as he pulled me close to his chest. "Don't," he said, but I placed my hand on his mouth. He took it and kissed the underside.

"How can you be sure?" I asked.

He lifted my chin and touched my lips with his.

Armen pulled the car up beside us. He got out and removed

his cap and held it in his hand at his side. He pointed down the road.

"There," Armen said with an urgency. "There is home. I take you home now. Ya?" He gestured with his hand to come.

My palms stung from sliding hard into the earth.

⁊

SPACE. SO MUCH space in front of my eyes. It dazzled me. We drove up to a large manor house, passing a brown fence on both sides. The road was covered in smooth white pebbles. More cows, like the ones we had passed on the way, rested in silence. I could see at least three small cottages dotted throughout the property. In the distance, the mountains. Always the mountains nosing close to the clouds.

Trees clustered near the horizon. I shaded my eyes as Armen stopped at the front door to the house that had been Vinni's home for five years. Blue ceramic pots overflowed with pink and red and lavender geraniums. Matching blue globes— three—were carefully situated on the manicured grass in front of the house. But what caught my attention was the cottage in the distance, to the left of the main house. I stepped out of the car and stared at the window boxes tumbling over with flowers from each of the three sets of windows. There were two on the second floor and one on the first.

"Meta is in the front room, waiting for you," Armen said. "I will take you." He stopped in front of me and turned slowly. "Sophie is in school," he said.

"And Hilda?" I asked. Armen looked away.

John D'Orfini gently placed his hand on the small of my back and guided me up the front steps behind Armen. We moved—all three of us—in what seemed to be slow motion.

"Armen?" Meta looked to her husband liked a frightened cat. Armen shrugged. I could see Meta was worried I was not alone, but John D'Orfini calmed her.

"I am a friend. Please, shall we sit?" His voice softened, and Meta's face relaxed. He knew it was important that nothing and no one move an inch to the wrong side of the room. He knew how to be careful.

"Yes, sit," Meta said. "But first I introduce myself. I am Meta Adler." Her hair was white and thin. Her faded brown eyes looked at me with kindness. She stood with a slight bend to her shoulders, caving inward to a flat chest. Although it was unbearably warm, she wore a long-sleeved cardigan. A white blouse tied in a droopy bow at the neck. Her tan skirt fell beneath her knees near her calves, and she wore sensible, black-laced shoes.

Meta confused me. I didn't know if I should scream at her, slap her, shake her upside down until her story spilled out, or thank her for making the telephone call. I decided instead to step aside and let her tell it all. One word at a time.

I had waited five years.

Meta lowered her head and began to cry before I had a chance to say anything. Armen stood at her side. I looked at John D'Orfini. Both of us remained quiet. We could hear a clock ticking in the hallway.

"Sophie is in school. She does not know you are coming. I . . . Armen and I thought . . ."

I had had enough. "Where is Hilda?" I asked. "Take me to her." I picked at the stinging skin on my palms.

"We decided not to tell the child you were coming. We wanted to wait to see that you come. We did not want to give her a shock."

"Where's Hilda?" I said in a thin, tight voice.

Meta's chin quivered. "Hilda died after I called you," she said. She played with a wrinkled tissue in her hand, squashing it over and over, as if it were large and pliable. She stayed sleeping after she asked me to call you in New York."

I would never know the answers Hilda might have given to my questions.

Why did you steal my girl? Why did you keep her for five years? Why? Why? Why? What misery drove you to take what you had no right to take?

Seconds stretched in the silence. John D'Orfini broke through it. "The child's name is Vinni. Lavinia Stewart," he said. "This is her mother, Madeline Stewart."

Meta wept as she reached for my hand across the navy chintz. I let her touch me, although I refused to clasp my fingers around hers. She looked away for a moment but then continued in a softer voice.

"Yes, yes. Hilda told me all this. Vinni is Sophie's real name. I know now, but I never knew before . . . before Hilda died. . . . All this time Soph . . . So sorry . . ."

"Vinni has been separated from her mother for five years," John D'Orfini said.

"Where is Vinni's school? I'll go and get her. We don't need to stay and talk if she's not here," I said.

"No. No. You mustn't frighten her. Sophie—I mean, Vinni—will be home soon. Please stay. I must tell you what Hilda wanted you to know. She died ashamed that she hurt you. She knew she did wrong. Not at first, but at the end. She was going in and out of consciousness. She wanted me to tell you. Yes? You want to know?"

John D'Orfini nodded and sat back in his chair. "We want to know," he said.

Meta stared at her hands in the lap of her skirt. She rubbed her fingers against each other, massaging them as she sighed deeply.

"She told me her name was Ada and that she was the guardian of her cousin's child, Sophie. For the first year they were here, Sophie was very quiet."

"Go on," I said, in a voice I could barely hear.

"They just showed up at your door one day?" John D'Orfini asked.

"Armen and I rent out the cottage. Everyone knows this. It had been empty for close to a year. I never asked how Ada found us."

"Is Hilda the owner of all this?" John D'Orfini hurled it as a question, but I wondered if he already had the answer.

Meta nodded and continued. "I will tell you what Ada told me before she slipped into the coma. She knew she was dying. Sophie—eh, Vinni—knew as well."

She looked away as if she couldn't bear to say more.

"Go on," I said. Vinni was in school in the village, ten minutes away. Armen had left to pick her up. He would stop by for her after dropping off bags of soybeans on the way.

"Ada—"

"Her name is Hilda," I interrupted.

"Ya. Hilda told me how Vinni had been asleep when they carried her to the plane. They flew from Canada to Germany. Hilda wanted to bring Vinni home."

"Why did she want my child?" I asked. I had to know the answer. As much as I wanted to see Vinni walk through the door, I needed to know why she had been kidnapped.

"Hilda's only child died at the age of eight, when she was thrown from a horse. Hilda watched her child die instantly. Her name was Kaethe. I knew the man who owned all this had had a granddaughter who died. We never met him. Armen and

I were hired through his lawyers. But this was many years ago."

"So Hilda inherited everything." John D'Orfini said. He surprised me with his interruptions. Affirming what he knew or what he suspected.

Meta nodded. "Ya . . . more sadness. Hilda told me she had caused her sister, Hannah, much pain."

I inhaled sharply.

Sisters?

The pain of a promise. That was how George phrased it when he asked me to stay away from Hannah.

"Hilda loved her sister. They had been separated for years. She confessed."

"Confessed?" I inched forward in my seat. My mind reeled. My shoulders tensed.

Meta looked down. "Not to what you are thinking—to something a long time ago. Hilda was a child of fourteen when she discovered Hannah and a boy named George together in the barn. Hilda was the horse lover. Hannah less so. She begged Hilda not to tell their father."

"Tell him what?" John D'Orfini asked.

"That they were planning to run away together that night. George's cousin was waiting for them at the end of the path in the woods at the edge of the Haydn farm. He drove them on to Heidelberg. Hilda told me she had to promise. Her father, she said, 'knew sternness like the skin on his thumb.' Hilda never forgot her sister's words.

'Don't tell Papa. Ever. I will send letters to you through George's cousin, but you can never tell Papa where I am. Promise me, baby sister.' Then she hugged Hilda tight. Hilda watched her run into the woods, holding George's hand.'"

Meta continued with her hands folded. Her head lowered.

"After Hannah ran off, Hilda's father turned bitter. He

wanted her to marry a German. He suspected the Hungarian boy had taken away his oldest daughter, but Hilda kept the secret so Hannah could have the life she wanted—a life with George."

John D'Orfini took my hand.

"And Hannah kept Hilda's secret so she could have the life *she* wanted . . . with Vinni," said my detective.

I looked at him. How much had he known and not told me? To spare me or to help me forgive?

Meta continued. "Hannah sent word to her sister through George's cousin that she and George had left for America. They settled in Brooklyn, New York."

I closed my eyes.

John D'Orfini reached for my hand and said, "There's something I must show you."

I waited.

He took out the picture of little Kaethe Haydn and laid it in front of me on the coffee table.

I put my hand over my mouth to suffocate my cries. The same chin, the eyes, the hair, the smile, stared back at me.

Meta nodded and touched the picture.

"Ah . . . poor Kaethe! So young!"

John D'Orfini placed his hand over mine. I slipped it away and reached for my purse. I knew where to find what I was looking for. I never left the house without it. I placed the picture of a smiling Vinni, slapped upon me in the limo, alongside Kaethe's picture.

"Where did you get this?" John D'Orfini asked, lurching forward in his seat.

I shook my head. It was too late to worry about that.

The three of us stared at the resemblance in silence. The slight dip in the chin, an almost perfect circle for the shape of the face, and the full lips, so unusual for a child—they were all there, looking up at us from the table.

Tears slipped down my cheeks. What had Hilda thought when she had looked at my girl on the beach and seen her own? How distraught had she been to take what was mine?

Meta continued.

"Hilda came to me six weeks before she died. She was dying of ovarian cancer after fighting it for twelve years. She had been in remission for five years, but then it returned with a vengeance. 'I am Hilda Haydn,' she said, and then, of course, I knew why she had come. I recognized the last name. She had come home."

"You haven't told me why Hilda wanted Vinni," I said. But I knew.

"Ya. Ya. It was only to be for a year, and then she would give the child back. She wanted to be a mother for a time, but then she grew to love the child and one year grew to two and then three and four . . ."

Meta lowered her head. "Hilda went crazy with grief over Kaethe's death. She told me how it drove her mad. When she knew she was dying, it became clear what she had done. Before, all she could see was how her grief had grown over the years until she could no longer bear it."

I wondered if Rudy had taken Hilda's conscience with him when he died. Left on her own, had Hilda forgotten or simply abandoned the plan to return Vinni after a year?

Hilda wanted to be a mother, but between us there was only one child.

"The night when Vinni and I went to Hilda and Rudy's house for dinner, she said something about how my work kept me from Vinni. I've often thought about why she would bring that up. Why she said that."

Meta lowered her gaze. "I know nothing. I know only what

Hilda told me . . . before the end. Ada—I mean Hilda—said I must call you. She made us promise. What to do? So much pain. Armen and I didn't know what to do. So we call you as Hilda said we must."

As Meta talked, I felt a strange kinship.

Dare I say it?

Hilda. How she must have suffered.

Insanity from grief had replaced reason. Without reason, the good in Hilda and Rudy hid but never fully disappeared.

"Vinni has a beautiful voice. She loves to sing. She loves the color blue, and she loves her blue garden. Hilda sang to her in German, and one day, after five months, I see them outside together and Hilda is helping the child plant a garden, but I see Hilda is tired, and so Armen and I, we offered to help."

"She always talked about having a blue garden," I said.

"Only blue," Meta said. "The garden brought her back to life. She started to speak to Armen and me. She told us . . ." Meta looked away and lifted her clenched fist to her mouth to stifle her tears.

"What did the child tell you?" John D'Orfini said.

Meta looked up at me. "Hilda told her you had died. It was later that she made a story to tell the child. She was afraid Sophie would hate her if she told her the truth."

John D'Orfini interrupted Meta. He took my hand and looked into my eyes.

"Vinni had no way of knowing anything other than what Hilda told her, but Hilda had to know that it was a matter of time before Vinni would start asking questions," he said.

I looked hard at John D'Orfini and walked over to the open window. A warm breeze rustled the clean curtains.

Will I risk my child's happiness if I take her back to New York, away from the beauty and the life she now knows?

"Do you want to see the garden?" Meta asked.

I nodded. I followed Meta down a long hallway, through the kitchen, and out the back door. We walked on the grass in silence. The mountains watched as we made our way toward the blue grown from the ground.

FORTY-ONE

I LOOKED BEHIND META TO JOHN D'ORFINI. HIS FACE had relaxed since we had entered the house. Armen had handed him a tray of glasses filled with iced tea and left the garden to return to the house for biscuits.

"We'll sit in the shade by the arbor, Miss . . . uh . . . Miss Stewart," Meta said.

"I thought Armen left for Vinni's school," I said.

How I hated being called miss. It reminded me of Mr. Kosinski.

"He brings us biscuits first, and then he goes."

What was I doing sitting in Vinni's garden without Vinni?

John D'Orfini was unusually quiet.

Meta's sun-spotted skin hung loose around her chin and neck. Armen brought us the biscuits. He tapped Meta on her hand and kissed her forehead before he left. To me, he said, "I bring the child to you. You must take her home."

Home.

When Armen said the word, my heart squeaked open like the sound of a rusty hinge swinging a porch door. I felt the heat on the top of my head weighing me down as my foot's ache spiraled all the way up my leg.

Home.

Meta spoke into the silence of the blue garden.

"The child sings like an angel. She is the star in the pageant."

"What is the pageant?" I asked.

"It is a tradition every year at Christmas. The child began to sing two years ago, after she had been . . ." Meta stared down at the brown spots on her hands. "Quiet."

"Did she ever speak of me?" I asked.

Meta smiled. "She told us how you sang together." But then Meta's expression turned inward. "You must be careful with the child. I see it in her eyes—the quiet so close again."

Hilda had replaced me. The idea of mothering a child like her lost Kaethe attached itself like a sore. When she saw Vinni on the beach, possibilities emerged and grew sweet.

"What do you mean by quiet?" I said.

"It is only a few days since she lost Hilda."

"She lost me five years ago."

Meta inhaled deeply.

The wind outside changed. It was as if it blew open my body and shifted my organs until nothing felt right. Meta suggested we go inside to wait. I hadn't seen the rest of the house. Vinni's bedroom. I needed to smell it.

"I'd like to see Vinni's room," I said.

"Ya. Ya."

We all stood as the cool wind appeared to die down. I knew I would return to the garden, but when I did, I wanted my child's hand in mine.

I let Meta take my hand, and together we walked up to the house in silence. When we reached the back door, the phone was ringing and Meta hurried inside to pick it up. I decided to walk through the house on my own. As I turned down a hallway, I stopped short.

Two of my paintings hung on the wall.

I stepped back and stared and then walked through a narrow hallway into a formal dining room. There were the other three pieces purchased by Donald Howard for his secret client. Hilda Haydn.

When Meta hung up, she looked for me and found me staring at the paintings. She spoke in a soft voice. "You are a talent, miss," she said. Five beats. Six beats. Silence passed between us.

"Armen will bring Sophie—Vinni—home later than expected. She is rehearsing for the school choir."

"Take me to her now," I said. "No more waiting. She must find out I'm alive." I felt large and rough as I stood in front of my paintings next to Meta.

"Vinni believes you are dead. Why shock her when she has already suffered so much loss? Please. Stay here. Wait."

"What if you're lying to me?"

"My God, no! You must believe that your child is coming home to you." Meta's face contorted into a wrinkled rush of sympathy, for me for having lost Vinni, but I wondered if it was also for herself and for fear that she might lose her place on the land after all these years.

"Hilda loved the girl. She was good to her."

"Hilda was insane. She had no right to take what wasn't hers," I said.

"Hilda left all of this," Meta said. She opened her arms wide. "All this property and much more is yours and the child's and, yes, Hilda's sister's as well.

"Mr. Haydn invested wisely. Armen and I hope to stay on as tenant farmers. We want nothing more than to help you. We did not know the truth. You must believe this. We knew nothing."

"All I want is my daughter."

"Ya. Ya. When we cannot undo the past, we make it right today. It will be right again. If you wait a little more. Let Armen bring Vinni home, so she does not get frightened. You cannot go there now. No!"

Meta's face turned red. Then white. She looked away from me.

"Once, Soph . . . Vinni did not come home directly from school. Hilda was frantic. This is a small village. Everyone takes care of the other. The child was in no danger, but Hilda paced up and down the front room until she walked in at dinnertime, explaining that she had stopped along the way to collect stones. Only then—only then—did I think something was not right. But what could we do? We have spent a simple life on this land. We own nothing. We worried we could lose everything if we asked questions."

I closed my eyes. Everything ran through my mind at once. Rudy's body on the beach, Evelyn's tea table, Mother's black Cadillac in the garage, Kay unwrapping my foot, the wailing babies in *Number Eleven*, and John D'Orfini standing in the hotel room in Füssen, telling me he loved me.

I needed to make the right choice.

I needed to be the mother my own couldn't be.

Go or stay.

My own mother had chosen to leave. Or perhaps her mind had twisted into too many voices, making it impossible to hear through the noise.

"Please take me to her room," I said. "I'll wait there." I was sure this was what I should do.

Stay and wait.

"*Gut.* Ya," Meta said, as she reverted to the comfort of her native German. Meta walked ahead, and I followed her.

I stepped over to the bed and pulled down the white quilt— an embroidered medallion of pinks and greens perfectly positioned in the center. I slipped under the sheets and rested my head on the pillow. Slowly and with care, I breathed in my girl's leftover breath from where she slept. I laid my cheek against the soft cotton where her cheek had been. I caressed the smooth lining of the quilt's silk border. I looked up at the painting on the ceiling—a circle of angels with fingertips touching—floated against a background of blue and white clouds. I pulled the sheets more tightly to my neck as I shivered inside the heat of the room.

The midday sun beat against the earth. I left the bed and opened the door to the tiny closet to the right of the window. Two pairs of denim overalls hung in front of an assortment of plaid shirts and jeans. Simple white collared shirts—at least six—cleaned and ironed, lined up one behind the other. Three pairs of leather boots filled the closet floor. I walked over to the dresser and opened the top drawer. I rifled through mismatched socks and a young girl's first bras. The middle drawer held a small journal with a brown leather cover. I opened it and read, "Happy Birthday, Sophie. Love, Ada."

How many times can a heart break?

But as I turned the pages, I read the words *Dear Mama* over and over again and a strange peace overcame me. A peace I had never experienced in the whole of my life. Vinni knew I would always be Mama. As the dates moved forward on the pages and Vinni wrote more deeply, she described what it was like to live on the farm.

Ada and Meta and Armen gave me a special gift today for Christmas. My own horse. I named her Chelsea. Ada worries when I ride, but Armen is teaching me how to be a good horsewoman.

I read page after page, until I heard a door open farther down the hallway. Sets of footsteps climbed closer into the house. A voice! I recognized the sound of Vinni's voice.

"Ich habe noch nicht in den Garten heute und der Himmel ist eigentlich auf Wolke später am Nachmittag."

"Speak English, child."

"Why, Meta?"

"So you don't forget. There is time to work in the garden. I know you're worried about the weeding. First, you come into the front room. Armen and I must talk to you."

"But, Meta, the garden . . . and Chelsea."

"Ya, ya, child. First you come with us and sit awhile."

I heard the sliding door of the front room open and close. Vinni's voice sounded older. Deeper. Impatient. The voice of a child who believes others will derail her from what she needs to do.

"Meta." I heard Vinni's voice in the distance. I held still. Unable to move. White clouds skated in front of the blue until all the blue disappeared. Voices speaking in German slipped through the walls. I heard a pocket door slide open. More quiet.

Then Meta's voice in English.

"Go, child. She waits for you."

As I heard her footsteps come closer to the bedroom, I froze out of fear. Fear that she would have to learn to love me all over again. I had been cheated of my daughter's life for five years. In the meantime, something had happened to my heart. It had stopped and started up again. What had happened to Vinni's? Would her heart explode from joy or slink into a distant murmur? I had no way of knowing as I sat in her room. Maybe I would be her blessing and she would be mine. And we would ride the back of the bull together. Clutching its horns. Riding the waves.

"Mama?" Vinni stood at the door. Her long hair fell over one eye. *Beauty* is too tame a word to describe her, *love* too simple a sound to say. Neither of us moved.

I was the mother. I knew it was up to me.

"Meta told me you have a blue garden," I said.

My voice trembled. Tears bound by five years of believing broke free and slid down my cheeks. Vinni leaned against the door frame, her face still dry.

Where are her tears?

I walked closer and cupped my hands around her face. I kissed her forehead. My lips rested against her skin. I smelled her, and then I broke and shook until I felt Vinni's arms wrap around me. They were strong but unfamiliar. She had grown up while we were apart. She was almost as tall as I.

She whispered, "Mama" from inside her throat, and I knew that she still loved me. She had not forgotten. I could feel her heart against mine, racing inside her chest. I smoothed her hair on the back of her head. A sound like I had never heard before came from my girl. Not a howl or a wail, but something else that kept her from letting go all at once.

"It's okay, baby," I said. "It's okay."

The note continued until finally her mouth split open and together we slid down to the floor as she let out a piercing cry.

"Ma . . . maaaaaaaa."

Over and over, she screamed for me.

"Ma . . . maaaaaaaa."

We rocked back and forth. She shook uncontrollably, trying to make her body smaller, curling up inside my arms.

My little girl was gone. In that moment, I knew we would never get back what we had lost. We had no choice but to lead each other to someplace new—someplace where love would never be blue.

"I love you, baby. Oh, God, how I love you." I whispered her name into her hair.

"Vinni. Vinni. Vinni." Over and over. At first, saying it stung my heart, but then it sweetened.

I leaned my head into hers to inhale her. To smell her. How would I make her mine again? I had no idea. It would take time.

"How did you find me?" Vinni said in a voice I could barely hear.

Tears slid over my lips into my mouth. "I never stopped believing," I said.

Vinni kissed the palm of my hand, turned it over, and kissed the outside. She gave me a slight smile, and I smoothed her hair back from her face as we stared at each other.

I kissed her cheeks. I kissed her neck. I kissed her hair. I couldn't get enough of my skin against hers.

"Would you like to show me the blue garden?" I asked.

Vinni uncurled from my lap. She took my hand and helped me up from the floor.

"The garden. I wanted the garden because . . ."

She stopped. Who knew the answer?

"The garden needs weeding."

"I can help," I said.

It would take time.

There are moments on most days when I feel a deep and sincere gratitude, when I sit at the open window and there is a blue sky or moving clouds.

—Käthe Kollwitz

ACKNOWLEDGMENTS

To begin, I must thank the countless listeners who took this journey with me. Many have heard my discoveries on the page during writing workshops I have led in my home or on writing retreats in Sea Girt, New Jersey, and on the island of Alonnisos in Greece and in St. Gauderic, France. Their kind attention confirmed my belief that something was working. I am grateful to those who refrained from asking why it was taking so long.

A heartfelt thanks to my dear friend and colleague, novelist Jacqueline Sheehan, whom I met on the island of Cumbrae in 1998 at a writer's retreat, for her steadfast support and encouragement. I am grateful to Chief David Stokoe from the Randolph Police Department in Randolph, New Jersey, for his guidance on police procedure, to John Crisci, retired New York DEA agent for his expertise, and to Thomas E. Maloney, Esq. for his legal mind. Thanks to Julie Gridinsky Friedman, friend and artist, for her generous insight into what it means to paint. Thanks to Michael and Kathleen Robbiani, gracious owners of a real live doll and clock shop, for giving me a private tour of their shop in Marlboro, New Jersey, and for answering my many questions. I am grateful to Dr. Michael O'Neil for his prompt responses to my medical questions. Thanks, also, to novelist, Jenny Milchman, for her generosity of spirit.

To the readers who read early and later drafts, know this: I needed you. My thanks to all: Jacqueline Mitchard, Mary Logue, Caroline Leavitt, Joyce Norman, Juanita Kirton, Marilyn Nusbaum, Ellen Kahaner, Elizabeth Caputo, Joanne Edelmann, Elizabeth Cipriano, Rosemary McGee, Susanna Rich, Mort

Rich, Vasiliki Katsarou, Kayla Jerz, Virginia Dillon, JoAnn Claps, Priscilla Orr, Janice Molinari, Lynne Rosenfeld, Susan Ganjamie and Nancy Pickard.

I am indebted to my dear friend and reader, novelist MaryAnn McFadden, for telling the truth during our regular breakfast critique sessions. How fortunate am I.

My gratitude goes deep to all the writers of WOMEN READING ALOUD throughout the USA and across the ocean who hold me up by being present.

Thank you to She Writes Press, led by the indomitable Brooke Warner, with Lauren Wise, Cait Levin, Annie Tucker, Julie Metz, and the entire team for their enthusiasm, kindness, and unflagging support.

Most of all, I owe big thanks to my glorious children—Jenna and David and Kayla—for loving me. And to Tom, their father and my husband, whom I met by chance and whose love fills me each day.

ABOUT THE AUTHOR

Photo Credit: Sue Kenney

JULIE MALONEY is a former dancer/choreographer and artistic director of her own modern dance company. She is a poet whose work has been published in many literary journals. Her book of poems, *Private Landscape*, was published in 2007. As founder/director of Women Reading Aloud, a non-profit organization dedicated to the support of women writers, she has been leading workshops and writing retreats in the US, Greece, and France since 2003. *A Matter of Chance* is her debut novel. She lives outside of New York City in Morris County, NJ.

SELECTED TITLES FROM SHE WRITES PRESS

She Writes Press is an independent publishing company
founded to serve women writers everywhere.
Visit us at www.shewritespress.com.

Shelter Us by Laura Diamond. $16.95, 978-1-63152-970-2.
Lawyer-turned-stay-at-home-mom Sarah Shaw is still struggling
to find a steady happiness after the death of her infant daughter
when she meets a young homeless mother and toddler she can't
get out of her mind—and becomes determined to rescue them.

The Tolling of Mercedes Bell by Jennifer Dwight. $18.95, 978-1-
63152-070-9. When she meets a magnetic lawyer at her work,
recently widowed Mercedes Bell unwittingly drinks a noxious
cocktail of grief, legal intrigue, desire, and deception—but when
she realizes that her life and her daughter's safety hang in the
balance, she is jolted into action.

The Rooms Are Filled by Jessica Null Vealitzek. $16.95, 978-1-
938314-58-2. The coming-of-age story of two outcasts—a nine-
year-old boy who just lost his father, and a closeted young
woman—brought together by circumstance.

Last Seen by J. L. Doucette. $16.95, 978-1-63152-202-4. When a
traumatized reporter goes missing in the Wyoming wilderness,
the therapist who knows her secrets is drawn into the investigation—and she comes face-to-face with terrifying answers regard-
ing her own difficult past.

True Stories at the Smoky View by Jill McCroskey Coupe. $16.95,
978-1-63152-051-8. The lives of a librarian and a ten-year-old
boy are changed forever when they become stranded by a bliz-
zard in a Tennessee motel and join forces in a very personal
search for justice.

Eden by Jeanne Blasberg. $16.95, 978-1-63152-188-1. As her
children and grandchildren assemble for Fourth of July weekend
at Eden, the Meister family's grand summer cottage on the
Rhode Island shore, Becca decides it's time to introduce the
daughter she gave up for adoption fifty years ago.